T0114629

Praise for the novels of Belinda Jones

"Fast-paced, enthusiastic, good-hearted . . . [A] wise and witty read about the secret desires deep within us." —*Marie Claire* (UK)

"There's something about Belinda Jones's writing that takes you away to whatever beautiful setting she's evoking and leaves you there right until you reach the last page." —*Daily Express* (UK)

"Great gags but undercut with genuinely moving emotion, this is a cut above most romantic comedies. A gem." —*Woman's Own* (UK)

"Definitely worth cramming in your suitcase." —*Cosmopolitan* (UK)

"You'll be laughing out loud from your sunbed." —*Wedding & Home* (UK)

"A glitterball romp." —*Glamour* (UK)

"Essential for that girls-only summer trip." —*Company* (UK)

"Deliciously entertaining." —*Heat* (UK)

"Fun, romantic, and set in various exotic locations, it's the perfect escapist read." —*Closer* (UK)

"Perfect." —*B Magazine* (UK)

"A sparkling read." —*OK!* (UK)

Dearest Reader,

What an utterly yummy experience it was writing this book for you—because of you I got to sample an abundance of sweet treats and call it work!

My first experience of The Wonder of Cake *was eagerly waiting for my mum to let me lick the mixture from the bowl as a kiddywink, so it seemed appropriate that I set out on the research trip with her. The only snag is that she really doesn't have a sweet tooth, so as I would be marveling at all the exquisite fondant-swirled delights on offer, she would be ordering a bowl of carrot soup. (Though I have to say, she did succumb to the Boston Cream Pie!)*

Of course, there's more to The Traveling Tea Shop *than cake! With four leading ladies, there is an abundance of emotions to explore, as well as the idyllic setting of New England. I knew it would be leafy and picturesque but I was amazed how different each state was, though it was the littlest—Rhode Island—that captured my heart. That said, I look forward to hearing where you would most like to have afternoon tea!*

In the meantime, cozy up with a cuppa and a cupcake—you are welcome to leave little smudges of frosting on the pages as you turn them!

Your author,
Belinda xx

The
Traveling
Tea Shop

BELINDA JONES

BERKLEY BOOKS, NEW YORK

THE BERKLEY PUBLISHING GROUP
Published by the Penguin Group
Penguin Group (USA) LLC
375 Hudson Street, New York, New York 10014

USA • Canada • UK • Ireland • Australia • New Zealand • India • South Africa • China

penguin.com

A Penguin Random House Company

Copyright © 2014 by Belinda Jones.
Penguin supports copyright. Copyright fuels creativity, encourages diverse voices,
promotes free speech, and creates a vibrant culture. Thank you for buying an authorized
edition of this book and for complying with copyright laws by not reproducing, scanning,
or distributing any part of it in any form without permission. You are supporting writers
and allowing Penguin to continue to publish books for every reader.

BERKLEY® is a registered trademark of Penguin Group (USA) LLC.
The "B" design is a trademark of Penguin Group (USA) LLC.

Library of Congress Cataloging-in-Publication Data

Jones, Belinda (Belinda C.)
[Travelling tea shop]
The traveling tea shop / Belinda Jones.—Berkley trade paperback edition.
pages cm
Previously published as The travelling tea shop. London : Hodder, 2014 and
Hodder & Stoughton Canada, 2013.
ISBN 978-0-425-27960-1 (paperback)
1. Tour guides (Persons)—Fiction.   2. Television personalities—Fiction.
3. New England—Fiction.   4. Domestic fiction. I. Title.
PR6110.O56T73 2015
823'.92—dc23
2014040139

PUBLISHING HISTORY
Hodder & Stoughton mass-market edition / May 2014
Berkley trade paperback edition / March 2015

Cover photos: *cutting board* © sprng23/Thinkstock; *Chocolate lower case type* © istarif/Thinkstock;
Chocolate upper case type © istarif/Thinkstock; *torte* © Mi. Ti./Shutterstock; *tea pot* © grafvision/
Shutterstock; *cupcakes* © Jane Rix/Shutterstock; *whoopie pies* © AnjelikaGr/Shutterstock;
bus © Dario Lo Presti/Shutterstock.
Cover design by Sarah Oberrender.

This is a work of fiction. Names, characters, places, and incidents either are the product
of the author's imagination or are used fictitiously, and any resemblance to actual persons,
living or dead, business establishments, events, or locales is entirely coincidental.

146122990

To Kate Gordon
(Every author should have such a fabulous champion—
who also happens to be an ace baker!)

ACKNOWLEDGMENTS

A bumper batch this year . . .

My first book was dedicated to James Breeds, and in a way they all are. Thank you for the most splendid week in NYC, my sweet-toothed soulmate.

Cream-swirled gratitude to this tasty bunch: Charlie Romano & David Garcelon at the Waldorf Astoria New York, Warren Brown of CakeLove, Paul Drumm at Kenyon's Grist Mill, Amanda Bryan at The Newport Sweet Shoppe, Kim Houdette at AD Makepeace, Scott Cunningham of ScottCakes, Tuoi Tran and John Murtha at the Omni Parker House Hotel and Robert Alger, Jennifer Vincent and Sam Messer at the Trapp Family Lodge.

A generous slice of appreciation to the travel experts: Andrea McHugh at Discover Newport, Andrea Carneiro at Newport Preservation Society, Tai Freligh of Visit New Hampshire, Charlene Williams of Nancy Marshall Communications and Kathy Scatamacchia at Discover New England. (And I highly recommend you do!) Thank you so much for guiding me to so many gems!

The hosts with the most: Nancy and Bill Bagwill at Cliffside

Inn, all at the Castle Hill Inn, Rauni Kew at Inn by the Sea, Mary Jo and Michael Salmon at the Hartstone Inn, Zorina and Larry Magor at the Omni Mount Washington Resort and Sam von Trapp at the Trapp Family Lodge.

Cupcakes galore to my U.S. publishers The Berkley Publishing Group, in particular the exuberantly wonderful Jackie Cantor and lovely publicity mastermind Courteny Landi.

My fabulous, inspiring new agent Madeleine Milburn and lovely assistant Cara.

My dreamy mother Pamela (always) and character-inspiring Charles. You two were always worthy of a romance novel! Dad Trefor and Suzanne for their weekly Skype sessions, Brother G for summer memories at Dartington and Sam Adam for the ultimate teatime treat at the Wolseley!

Special canine love to Bodie, who tagged along on the road trip to help me walk off the extra calories and relished every dropped crumb.

And finally, my husband Jonathan, who no doubt is still wondering how I could spend a year immersed in baking and still be utterly without skill in the kitchen.

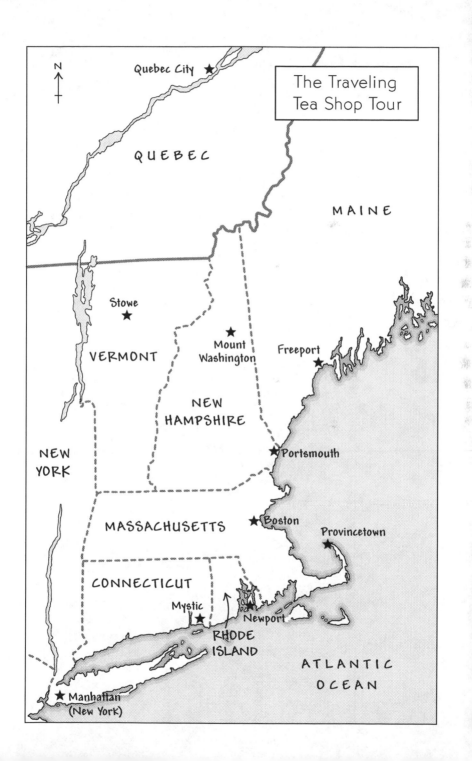

The Traveling
Tea Shop Tour

N

Quebec City ★

QUEBEC

MAINE

Stowe
★

VERMONT

Mount ★
Washington

Freeport
★

NEW
HAMPSHIRE

Portsmouth
★

NEW
YORK

MASSACHUSETTS

Boston
★

Provincetown
★

CONNECTICUT

Mystic
★

Newport
★

RHODE
ISLAND

ATLANTIC
OCEAN

Manhattan
★
(New York)

I never really understood the appeal of Prince Charming. Yes, he has that flippy hair and a fancy line in epaulets but for me it was always The Candy Man.

—Laurie Davis

Chapter 1

I look up at my clock. 1:30 P.M. My stomach flips like a pancake. Or should I say PamCake?

In just ninety minutes I am meeting England's most beloved baker, Pamela Lambert-Leigh. Can you believe it's nearly twenty years since Babycakes made her a household name? Those mini fairy cakes were so whisper-light that I used to think of them as dandelion clocks—one puff and you'd send a flurry of vanilla sponge crumbs out into the ether. Her daughter's cherubic face gave the packaging such an innocent, Shirley Temple vibe. Forget those sticky-sickly treats that made you groan and go cross-eyed, a Babycake was just a little kiss on your button nose, a butterfly in your tummy . . .

You could eat six and barely even feel sick.

I know because my mum once spelled out my name—LAURIE—one letter per cake on my birthday. I was rather miffed when she did the same three months later for my sister Jessica, especially since her name garnered an extra cake.

I was wondering about telling Pamela this story, possibly

leaving out the fact that my sister and I were teenagers by this point, but I don't want to come off as overly fan-ish. Besides, what if she made a casual inquiry about my nearest and dearest? My response would only make her uncomfortable—"Both women are gone now," I would say. "One to heaven and one to hell."

But no dwelling on that today. I mentally will the avalanche of emotion to retreat and hold off a while longer. I'll get to you soon enough; for now I need to keep things bright and peppy and focus on the interview . . .

Perhaps I'll just make a joke about having a sweet tooth: "The amount of sugar I consumed as a child, it's a miracle I have any teeth left at all!"

Hmmm. That sounds a bit off-putting.

What about, "We used to say that instead of blood running through my veins I had syrup, like a mini maple tree. With legs."

I tut myself. I'm not auditioning for a stand-up show.

I just want to prove to her that I'm Cake's Biggest Fan. Not some pretender who'll toy with the slim end of the wedge, leaving a great bookend of frosting on the plate.

Which reminds me, I'm sure I've got a childhood picture here of me taking a bite out of a cake that's twice the size of my head. I could snap it and have it neatly to hand on my phone.

I rifle through my desk drawer, I saw it just the other day . . .

I hesitate as I locate it. My hair in pigtails, white Peter Pan collar on my red dress. I must have been about seven. Gosh. Thirty-one years ago.

I didn't know about calories then.

I knew the truth about Father Christmas. I knew about divorce and that I couldn't bear to see my mother crying—it would just scrunch me up inside and make me want to cry too—but I didn't know any of those threatening phrases like:

"A moment on the lips, a lifetime on the hips."

Or "You can never be too rich, or too thin!"

Or, the most insidious of all, "Nothing tastes as good as skinny feels."

Whoever said that has clearly never been to Magnolia Bakery.

Drrrrrinnnng!

My phone ring startles me. But I smile when I see my best friend's name on the display. I wouldn't pick up for anyone else right now.

"Krista!" I squeak.

"I don't want to hold you up, just wanted to wish you good luck!"

"Oh thank you," I pip. "I don't know what to do with myself— this feels almost too good to be true!"

"There is no one better suited to this job than you, Laurie. It's like your greatest passions colliding!"

It really is. Cake and travel.

The travel aspect is my *actual* line of expertise. Before I met Krista, I was one of those all-but-extinct breeds: a travel agent. (RIP Lunn Poly, Marble Arch.) She's a former magazine journalist and together we launched a girlie travel-planning website called Va-Va-Vacation!, custom-designing itineraries and offering bonus features such as "What I Packed versus What I Actually Wore" and the popular "Man of the World" eye candy section.

We both firmly believe that life is too short and travel too expensive to waste a single coffee-stop in a strip-lit chain when you could be basking in a secret courtyard with a waiter who's going to slip you a complimentary macaroon. I'm even picky about which airports I schedule a stopover in, because a cool bar with an innovative menu and a docking station at every table beats the congealed orange chicken and plastic forks at Panda Express every time.

I remember Krista saying that if her magazine hadn't just cut their travel section in favor of running more weight-loss stories, she would have written a column with all our tried-and-tested tips. I said perhaps she should start her own blog. She said she'd love to create an online travel magazine and she knew a designer who could make it really eye-popping, but she couldn't figure out how to earn a living from it. Which is when we decided to combine our skills.

We've done some pretty fun themes to our custom itineraries over the years—dance-themed, family tree, a Starbucks-free coffee tour of Seattle; I even created an entire schedule from Ryan Gosling movie locations for one superfan. (And who can blame her fixation?)

I think one of the reasons the setup works so well is that we have clearly defined roles: I'm mostly in charge of logistics and wangling the discounts that give us a competitive edge. (I began with my personal travel contacts—"Go on, Yiorgos, give us an extra twenty percent off and we'll give you the best October occupancy the Elounda Blue has ever had!"—and still today we favor privately owned boutique properties over the big chains.) Danielle the designer holds down the fort in London, where Va-Va-Vacation! was founded, and she does all the beach resort reports (even rating the flirtiness of the local bartenders), whereas Krista, our main writer, travels all over—Tahiti, Costa Rica, Argentina . . . She's currently based in Quebec in Canada—she went there to research their epic Winter Carnival and in between ice-skating and snow-sculpting she fell madly in love with a husky-eyed dogsledder named Jacques. (The guy has a French accent, 112 canine children and can seemingly summon the Northern Lights at will, so she really didn't stand a chance.)

Around the same time, I got the opportunity to relocate from Maida Vale to Manhattan, and oddly that has worked out really well for our friendship since we are now only a ninety-minute flight apart, as opposed to eight-plus hours had either of us stayed in London.

Not that anything could have persuaded me to miss out on a chance to live in New York; I have been coming here every couple of months for years, on a mission to keep our Va-Va-Vacation! city guide current and comprehensive. I may not have Krista's pro writing skills, but I pride myself on knowing (and loving) the Big Apple pips, core and all.

Which is why Pamela Lambert-Leigh has come to me. Well, technically her agent set up the meeting. And I'm not the only "travel professional" she is meeting with today. I have rivals. Which is why I am so ultra-keen to prove that no one loves cake as much as me.

"So have you made your final selection for the Cheesecake Challenge?" Krista wants to know.

That's our big test—each of us has been charged with presenting Pamela with The Ultimate New York Cheesecake Experience. The winner will get the job. But we won't know exactly what that job entails unless we are the winner. All the more reason to be the best.

I've been really torn over my choice. Junior's gets the popular vote and has all the right credentials: founded in 1950, now with a hub in Times Square offering at least twenty flavors (including Sugar-Free Low Carb!) but the design is a bit orange lino diner and it would mean subjecting her to the tourist crush, so I'm not sure it would be a good fit.

I was fleetingly considering taking Pamela over to Brooklyn for a *Moonstruck* moment but the Cammareri Brothers bakery has since closed and its affiliate F. Monteleone (a bijoux box of old-school treats) has seating as limited as Pamela's time.

So that narrowed it down to two . . .

"Remember Veniero's Pasticceria in the East Village?" I prompt Krista. "The one where we took a snap under the vintage neon sign?"

"Est 1894! It's up on my board here!" she cheers, recalling the ceilings of pressed copper and stained glass. (Personally I was most struck by the never-ending parade of cannolis.)

I had it in my head to wow Pamela with both their traditional New York Cheesecake and the crumblier, less sweet, Sicilian version, which is made using ricotta and looks a bit like a soufflé nestled in a deep-dish pie-crust.

"Double whammy!" Krista enthuses. "And it's just twenty minutes' walk from your place."

"The only thing is . . ." I pause as I call up today's online news stories. "I saw this paparazzi shot of Pamela at the airport . . ."

I press send.

"Oh gosh!" Krista gasps as she opens the image at her end. "I don't know that I would have recognized her."

I had the same reaction. The Pamela we know and love from her *Teatime with Pamela* TV show has always had a delightfully mellow look to her, as if she has just emerged from a stroll in her English rose garden, complete with a freshly plucked flower wound into her soft, wavy blonde hair. In fact her whole product line—the cookbooks, the packaged cake ranges, the signature bakeware— makes you feel connected to a more wholesome time, when life was sweet and simple and you might find yourself spending the afternoon reading in an apple orchard, as opposed to sitting in a technology daze in some office cubicle. Though Pamela typically wears crumpled linens or palest, washed-out denim, she always has a lipstick that precisely matches the design on her pinafore and nails to match that, even though she'll soon be up to her cuticles in flour and pastry. But this snapshot gives the impression that she ran out of the house in the middle of the night and is still trying to figure out where the hell she is going in such a hurry.

"She looks totally frazzled."

"I know. And it's sweltering here today and you know how stingy most places are with their air-conditioning."

"God yes," Krista cringes. "Remember when we were at The Boat House and they didn't even have their ceiling fan on the fastest rotation?"

"I know, the passing waiters were generating more of a breeze."

"So what are you thinking?"

"Lady M."

"Lady M?" she queries.

"We haven't been. I only discovered it two weeks ago but everything about the place is cool and pristine and upmarket zen."

"Really?"

I nod into the phone. "Five minutes in there and I swear your hair starts to de-frizz. The walls are white, the tables, the chairs, the plates—everything is so clean!"

"Sounds like a lab!"

I chuckle. "You know, they actually call it a cake boutique!"

"How very swish!"

I click on the website just to check for the hundredth time that I have the correct address—41 East 78th, Upper East Side.

"You're not worried it'll be too posh?"

I know what Krista means, Pamela is more naturally sun-kissed than lacquered sheen.

"I was," I confess. "But then I tasted the cheesecake . . ."

"Ooooh. Say no more."

"Plus she's staying at the Mandarin Oriental," I add. "So it's just across the park."

"For her; you're all the way down in Little Italy! Shouldn't you be leaving?"

"I'm getting a cab in five minutes. No subway today. I've booked a table and I'm just going to sit there and be all serene and accommodating of her every whim."

I don't think I could be any better prepared. My laptop is primed with multiple open browsers and a list of Favorites linking to everything New York and cake-related. Yesterday I bought a small pink leather-bound notebook and a gold pen. I have a pack of hand-wipes should Pamela want to clean up without trekking to the bathroom, and two small tubes of Fresh's brown sugar hand cream—one to offer her a squeeze and one to give as a gift if she likes the scent as much as I do. I've printed out a pocket-size list of What's Hot in New York Today, should she perhaps have an hour or two free, and attached my business card: LAURIE DAVIS *Travel In Style*. I've even packed a second pair of shoes and a shirtdress in case I fall down a manhole or get knocked over by a bolting horse and carriage on the way.

I have to have every eventuality covered because, if they've come to me, my guess is that Pamela needs help planning a detailed itinerary—cramming as much into as few days as is physically and logistically possible, while still maintaining a seemingly effortless flow. And that's what I do best.

If she'll just give me the chance to prove myself.

"Trust me, this is your moment!" Krista encourages.

I take a breath. "I really hope so."

I don't know when I last wanted anything this much.

Actually I do.

I felt the same way about moving to Manhattan . . .

Chapter 2

Little-Laurie-Worry, my mum used to call me.

But not here. Not in New York City.

One inhalation of yellow cab fumes—mingling with pepperoni pizza, hot trash and Tom Ford's Café Rose—and I find myself in an Empire state of mind . . .

That's what I love most about Manhattan: *it brings out a sassy side to me.*

In the concrete jungle it's sink or swim: you can't be timid or tentative; you have to forge through, make your mark, enter the fray!

Last week I stepped off the curb and nearly got run over by some smoke-windowed Chrysler, and my instinctive reaction was to bang on the boot and cry, "Hey! Watch where you're going!"

I'd seen some cool urban chick do it once and now I'd joined the Pedestrians Fight-Back Club. I was on a high for the rest of the day.

Krista was horrified. She finds the whole place too in-yer-face. "Who knew walking down the street had become a contact sport?"

She's right, of course. It's crazy. But I love that feeling.

I remember the first time I came here, I returned to my hotel room after a day's sightseeing exhausted, feet throbbing, calves tweaking, head thumping, and I collapsed on the bed for a few minutes and then I thought: I want more! I want another fix! So I stepped back into the insanity, weaving my way through the crush on Fifth Avenue, standing amid all the tourists ogling Bergdorf Goodman and Harry Winston, raising their cameras to try and ensnare the jutting angles of skyscrapers. I felt simultaneously charged and exhausted all over again.

It was just what I needed.

Krista finds peace mushing huskies across plains of pure glistening white, but I need the chaos, the distraction of overstimulation. Back in London, I'd gone through a phase of reading way too many self-help books, gazing deeper and deeper into my navel . . . Sometimes I'd come to a complete halt in the street, questioning my next move—my motives, intentions and every possible consequence. Was it in the best interest of my Higher Self? In NYC you have to keep moving forward, stride with purpose. As you do so your attention is pulled every which way, away from yourself. And, for me at least, that is a source of great relief.

I know I'm not the only British person to feel this way. I see the faces of my fellow countrymen transform in this city. I see their amazement and fascination mingling with a surprising sense of belonging. The most unlikely places can feel like home here. There's this place, the Brooklyn Diner on West 57th, to be precise, and the first time I went there it was tipping down with rain, but they were playing Tony Bennett and had matching Tony Bennett French Toast (thick-cut cinnamon raisin and pecan), and so I sat there, drinking filter coffee from one of those squat cream-colored mugs that hold next to nothing but come with endless refills, observing the mostly older clientele and some bulky Sopranos-looking family, and I felt so *cozy* there. Maybe it's because you feel like you're in a movie half the time you're in New York. Maybe it's because things are happening all around you and, just by standing in the middle of it, you feel like something is happening *to* you. I don't know. And maybe the reasons don't matter. It just feels good.

"Taxi!" I step out into the street, instinctively rising up onto my tippy-toes as if I'm in Carrie-esque stilettos.

Appropriate that I should be heading to the Upper East Side!

Sliding across the collapsed, cracked black leather, I issue the address and then glance back at my redbrick building.

That's the only time I have a little wobble, when I put the key in the lock and I know it's just me and the apartment for the rest of the night. I still have the impulse to call my mum and tell her how my day went. I feel so hollow in that moment, so echoingly, despairingly alone. And then comes the rage, as I think of my sister.

"I don't want you here!" I say it out loud sometimes, trying to banish her from my head. But she's always lurking.

We stall at the lights beside one of the granite-thighed pedi-cabbers. Do you know they actually have credit card machines on board? They need to; they're actually more expensive than regular cabs now. I look beyond the cyclist's khaki shorts and focus on charting our route through Gramercy Park and the Flatiron dis-trict, checking off each cross street along the way—23rd becomes 34th and then 42nd, making us level with Times Square, just a few blocks from Rockefeller Center. I take a breath, unable to decide whether to quell my butterflies or embrace them. Talk about the American Dream! Just knowing that my cake-loving tummy is going to be seated across from Pamela Lambert-Leigh within the hour seems fantastical.

"Central Park!" the driver motions to his left.

I smile. That vast expanse of greenery always has an

appropriately "centering" effect on me. I wonder if Pamela has had the time to look out over the treetops from the Lobby Lounge at the Mandarin Oriental? Thirty-five floors up with panoramic windows, it's one of the best views in the city, utterly justifying the $7 price tag dangling from your tea bag.

Of course the park is pretty nice at ground level too. Even if half the New Yorkers fit the overachiever profile. Here the word "relax" becomes an active verb—running, cycling, rollerblading, skating, basketballing, boating, bowling, dog-jogging, tai-chi-ing . . .

I generally go there to sit down. Perhaps wiggle my toes in the grass, maybe blink up at the leaf-dappled sunlight. My regular spot is beside a bronze husky called Balto—ears pricked, chest proud, tail curled, he's a beauty. He was part of the relay team of sled dogs that battled the elements to bring life-saving vaccines to a remote Alaskan village, inaccessible by any other means. Now he stands immortalized on a rock in one of the more picturesque nooks of the park. Just being around him makes me feel connected to Krista, which is always reassuring. If tinged with some new emotions these days . . .

I wasn't expecting to feel the way I did when she moved in with Jacques. It's strange how something that makes you so happy—to see your best friend embarking on a wonderful new life with a good man—can also make you so sad. Prior to their romance we were in it together—the relationship bafflement fog. It was oddly comforting—if someone as lovely as Krista couldn't find love, then it proved it wasn't just my shortcomings keeping the right man at bay. We just weren't destined to get lucky in that way. Better we fill up our hearts with other pursuits. As far as I was concerned, Manhattan was all the man I needed! But now . . . Now she has gone and proved that true love does exist, the pressure is back on again.

Even from Krista. She has started having expectations for me whereas before there was just an acceptance that we had such awful taste in men we were best off out of it.

I remember the first day we met—at a mutual friend's wedding reception. I was under one of the dinner tables eating a second slice of the wedding cake, not wanting my enjoyment of the pink champagne icing to be tainted by my boyfriend's look of disapproval. (He had this conspiracy theory that I had hooked him with my feminine wiles, all with a dastardly plan to eat my way to enormity, purely to spite him and shame him in front of his friends. I wasn't even plump then. But just the sight of me eyeing the dessert trolley would give him the heebie-jeebies.)

Anyway, there I was, prom dress all fanned out on the carpet, feeling like I was five years old, having a lovely time shoulder-popping along to "Crazy in Love" when an arguing couple plonked themselves down beside me. Her foot was bleeding from being skewered by a stiletto on the dance floor, and his main gripe seemed to be that she should have been wearing high heels too.

"Why can't you just be like everyone else?"

And then he'd stormed off, telling her she could find her own damn Band-Aid.

That was the point at which I revealed myself and offered to make a little bandage using a torn napkin and a cocktail stick. She told me her big toe now looked like one of those pigs-in-blankets hors d'oeuvres, and her giggle gave me such hope, even when I learned she was married to this guy.

We talked for a while (mostly about that soul-destroying shift when your man switches from admiring to admonishing), but Krista said the moment she knew we were going to be bonded forever was when Andrew (her then husband) returned and I drove my steel-tipped vintage heel into *his* foot. Accidentally, of course. I just lost my balance as I was climbing out from under the table . . .

That seems like a lifetime ago now. By the next time I saw her, I was single. And I've been that way ever since. On purpose.

I was very clear by that point that I couldn't risk hooking up with another controlling calorie-counter (always my calories, not theirs!), because I honestly didn't feel like I had any more escape acts in me.

And my boyfriends have always been so easy to leave, on paper at least. They gave me so many reasons, but I always stayed way too long. Krista thinks it's because my working life is so geared to finding solutions, making the best of any situation, streamlining, honing—I have to try everything in my repertoire before I'll throw in the towel, and by then I've got myself into some kind of habitual behavior that has nothing to do with any genuine feeling toward the other person, but keeps me held there until they ditch me. Urgh! Even thinking about this raises my blood pressure. Switch that thought!

"Do you know there are nine thousand benches in Central Park and if you placed them end to end they would stretch for seven miles?"

The cab driver glances back at me, seemingly deliberating whether or not to let on that he speaks English.

"Oh! This is it—Lady M!" I scooch up in my seat and point ahead.

He peers with curiosity at the jarringly modern, glass-fronted white box tucked into the otherwise historic *grande dame* neighborhood.

"Cakes," he grumps.

"Yes," I cheer as I step onto the pavement.

I pause before I enter, looking around me and wondering what Pamela's impression will be.

A 1920s matriarch out walking her short-legged pooch would not be out of place. But then neither would the *Sex and the City* girls. If they were coming for tea they would all be in jewel-colored dresses and glinting metallic heels. I shift the dragging laptop bag on my shoulder, straighten my cotton frock and reach for the chrome door handle.

Instant cool. I love the frisk of air-conditioning on a sauna day.

"May I help you?" A gamine server with a black head-kerchief greets me.

"Hello, I'm Laurie—I called earlier?"

My heart is palpitating as I go through the arrangements.

With everything in order, I slide onto one of the molded plastic chairs and try to convince myself that this isn't a big deal. Even though it is.

I just pray I've made the right choice. This place definitely has a snoot factor. And I'd forgotten how bijou the tables are. I hope Pamela doesn't come with a lot of paperwork or anything that needs fanning out.

"Would you like anything while you are waiting?"

"No, no, thank you, I'm fine."

I could actually do with a glass of water but I don't want a half-drunk glass with a lipstick smudge ruining the pristine setting, so instead I focus on my posture and forming an open, welcoming expression. Every now and again my heart loops as a figure passes the window, but so far each person who has entered has been male. And Chinese. I look at my watch. Any minute now . . .

At 3 P.M. I expect a siren to go off and balloons and streamers to drop from the ceiling. But nothing happens. Life goes on as normal. Without Pamela.

A further five minutes pass.

Anticipation turns to anticlimax.

What if she doesn't show? What if she's having such a great time with one of the other itinerary experts she's decided she doesn't need to take any more meetings? I check my messages, no polite let-down from the agent. Just an invitation to try out the new ramen burger craze.

I'm starting to get fidgety. I could catch up on my Words with Friends games but I don't want to look like one of those people always zoned in on their phone, letting the world pass them by. Besides, there are far prettier things to gaze upon in here . . .

"I'm just going to have a little look," I tell the server as I approach the counter.

I feel a mix of serenity and awe as I contemplate their pristine cake selection. It's just so unique. Take the Gâteau aux Marrons—it looks as if a pan of spaghetti has been heaped atop the almond flour cake, when in fact the strands are lavish pipings of chestnut-infused cream, dusted with snow sugar.

Snow sugar!

I'm telling you, this place is in a league of its own. You never saw a glossier ganache finish. The only item I'm not sure about is the Green Tea Mousse Cake on account of its lurid chartreuse coloring. Then again—

"These are the ones I saw in Oprah magazine!" a voice bustles in beside me.

She's pointing to Lady M's Mille Crêpes—twenty paper-thin handmade crêpes layered with light pastry cream to form their signature cake. You can even keep "tiering up" until you create a wedding cake.

"Aren't they incredible?" A quieter, more reverent voice inquires. "Like the most delicate of petticoat layers."

I look up to smile in confirmation and find myself face-to-face with the legendary Pamela Lambert-Leigh.

Chapter 3

It's a strange thing, standing so close to a celebrity. There's an initial jolt of recognition and then a questioning as you review their multifaceted 3-D form—is it really them? You look away and then look back—if you didn't know better, they could almost pass for human . . .

Turns out those paparazzi shots weren't far off. Pamela's formerly radiant face is washed out, her nails polish-free and her casual back-of-a-cab dab of lipstick doesn't match anything that she's wearing, which is probably just as well since today's dominant hue is elephant gray.

"I have to apologize for the state of me," she begins. "My luggage didn't make it to New York and I haven't had time to shop for anything new."

"Oh how awful," I sympathize.

"Well, it's really such a fleeting visit, it's not the end of the world. I'm just aware that I bear more than a passing resemblance to a bag lady."

"Only without any bags!"

She laughs. "Yes—probably just as well they didn't make it!"

I smile fondly back at her. "Would you like to take a seat?"

She nods gratefully, expelling a long breath as she takes in her surroundings.

"This is quite the haven, isn't it?"

I nod. "I know it looks like they could offer you Botox or an acid peel in the back room—"

Pamela hoots and then covers her mouth. "Oh, excuse me!"

"Not at all!" I'm just happy to see her face brighten. "We can do as we please and pass it off as being English Eccentrics."

"Good point," she says, eyes straying back to the cake counter. That's my cue!

"So, I took the liberty of ordering . . ." I nod to the waitress, who promptly sets down two glossy white plates before us.

"There are two types of cheesecake here: the traditional Gâteau Fromage . . ." I let her take in the simple slice with its subtly burnished edging offering an almost sepia tone. "The thin base layer is crisp shortbread cookie crust and the cheesecake itself has a vanilla accent."

She nods.

"The second," I begin, trying to disguise any favoritism in my voice, "is the Gâteau Nuage—Cloud Cake."

"Oooh." She looks intrigued.

"They describe the base as cinnamon-kissed," I smile. "And then there's the airy whipped middle band of cheesecake and the top layer—"

"The *pièce de résistance*?" She raises a brow.

I nod. "Sweetened sour cream."

"I like how cool and silky that looks," she says, holding the plate up to her eye level. "You know, in comparison to the denser texture of the cheesecake."

My toes scrunch in expectation. I feel exactly the same way!

It actually puts me in mind of a layer of white gloss paint, but I don't say that out loud in case it throws off her palate.

"And if I may offer an alternative to tea?" I venture. "I rather like hot water with a slice of lemon and a tiny drip of honey."

"To counterbalance the creaminess."

"Exactly."

"Well then, that's what I shall have too."

The waitress arranges the shiny white cups and saucers—Limoges, *naturellement*!—with painstaking precision. Even the lemon slices look perfect—all zesty and juicy as opposed to predominantly pith.

I wait nervously for Pamela's verdict, not knowing if I should speak while she is in taster mode, presuming she needs to focus fully on the—

"Are you not having any?" She looks up at me.

"Oh. Well, I didn't want to crowd the table but I did order." I look to the waitress, preparing to give her the sign to bring over the second set of plates.

"Please," she interrupts me. "Share mine."

"Really?"

"You can imagine how much cheesecake I've had today, and I hardly need the extra pounds."

"Well, if you're sure?"

I don't say anything about her weight but she does seem a little curvier than I recalled. Not that it looks bad on her. She's one of those womanly women whose exact dimensions are irrelevant. Big boobs are the key. You look at them and the first word that springs to mind is *voluptuous*. And how can that be bad?

I take a bite of my beloved Gâteau Nuage, smearing the textures around my mouth to maximize the bliss. I could even do without the crumbly base; just give me a scoop of the filling and I'd eat it like ice cream. But what does *she* think?

"Sublime!" she pronounces.

My face brightens. "You like it?"

"Oh!" she fans herself. "So soft and smooth . . ."

"How does it compare to the others?" I dare to ask.

Her face changes as she leans in close. "One woman got me eating tofu cheesecake."

"I'm so sorry." My brow crumples.

"It's all right. I stayed on after she left and had the Amaretto."

"Ooh, I bet that was delicious!"

"It was." She takes a sip of hot lemon water. "One appointment we had to cancel because it turns out her suggestion was The Cheesecake Factory."

"Not an entirely illogical suggestion . . ."

"And I'm not opposed to a chain when they serve Pineapple Upside-Down Cheesecake, but the nearest location was Hackensack, New Jersey."

"Oh."

"Now where were the others?" she strums her chin and then smiles fondly. "I did like Veniero's."

"That was on my list!" I pip. "First runner-up."

"It's a classic. But guess what?"

I shake my head.

"The woman I met there didn't even touch her slice!"

I tut in disgust, assuring her that I'm very much of the no-crumb-left-behind persuasion.

"You'd think she would at least have asked for a box to take it away."

"She didn't?" I gasp.

"No!" She hoots. "Just got up and left!"

"That's not right."

Pamela sits back in her chair, taking another sweep of our surroundings. "Would you agree this Lady M has a somewhat French flair?"

Much as I'd like to claim the M is for Manhattan, I can't deny it.

"I just thought—it's so hot and everyone needs that moment in a New York day when you can just exhale and regain your composure."

"That's very considerate of you."

"Well, these factors matter—the weather, your mood that day, what you are hoping to achieve . . ." I leave my words hanging.

She smiles. "I suppose I should tell you a little more about this project of mine."

"Only if you like—"

"I do. I like you, I like this place. I think this will work very well." Did she just hire me?

"So. My agent, in her infinite wisdom, has decided that this is the year for me to break America."

"Gosh!" It hadn't even occurred to me that she wasn't known here since she's such an institution at home.

"It's certainly the right time for me to take a break from the UK, but she wants to move a lot faster than I had originally intended."

"Okay . . ."

"Basically she wants to get a cookbook out for Christmas."

"Christmas recipes?"

"Actually no. What it is . . ." She pauses, waiting for the family standing beside us to be seated before she continues. "Basically, the idea is that I travel around the U.S. trading traditional British cake recipes for American favorites, like New York Cheesecake, Boston Cream Pie—"

"You want to go to Boston?" I wasn't expecting this.

"I want to go everywhere that a great American cake originated."

"Oh wow."

"But!" she takes a breath. "That won't be possible in the time-frame so we went through the list and it seems that all the best recipes are concentrated here on the East Coast, because of course that's where the first settlers arrived."

"Well, not quite the first . . ." I venture.

"Funnily enough we were reading about a Native American tribe based at Plymouth Rock; they have this dish called Indian Pudding . . ."

"So there's a dessert element to this too?"

"I'm open to anything and everything you could possibly have at teatime."

"I love teatime," I sigh.

"Me too. That's why we're calling the book *The Traveling Tea Shop.*"

"That's so sweet!" I enthuse. And then a thought pops into my head. "What about Whoopie Pies? They're cakes really, are you including them?"

"Are they the ones from Maine?" She rifles through her bag in search of her notebook.

"I think so . . ."

"Yes," she confirms as she finds the corresponding page. "They actually helped us decide that we want to focus purely on New York and New England."

"So we're talking Connecticut, Rhode Island, Massachusetts." I begin mentally working my way along the coast.

"Maine, New Hampshire and Vermont." Pamela brings us inland. "And then back to New York."

The only state I've actually visited. Not that I'll be mentioning that.

"So are you including New York's other edible celeb?" I ask as I clean off the last creamy smear from my fork.

Pamela looks bemused. "And what would that be?"

"Red Velvet Cake."

"I thought that was from the South." She returns to her notes.

I shake my head. "Common misconception. In fact, if you

turned left out of here," I say, motioning to the door. "Take the first right onto Park Avenue . . ."

"Yes?"

"Then just keep going until you hit the Waldorf Astoria."

She looks amazed. "That's where Red Velvet Cake was created?"

I nod emphatically. "I know the executive pastry chef there—Charlie."

"Could you arrange an interview?"

"Of course."

"I'd like to stay there as well, when I come back."

"No problem!" I note down her request.

I think I've got it! I think this is my job. It's a lot bigger than I was expecting but that's okay. I can rise to the occasion—'scuse the baking pun.

"I'll ask my agent to e-mail you over the notes from our conversation, so you have a starting point for the itinerary."

"That would be really helpful," I concede. "So you're basically looking to try out a cake recipe that's native to each state we visit?"

"Yes, or at least celebrating an ingredient that is specific to the area. Like maple syrup and Vermont."

"Cranberries and Cape Cod?"

"Ooh, I could do with a Cape Cod cocktail about now."

Her whole body loosens up, suddenly looking in urgent need of being horizontal and fanned.

"Um, I've actually drawn up a list for you of bars that have a great atmosphere."

She sits up and takes my micro-guide to NYC but skips over my secret speakeasy suggestions.

"Ricky Martin is in *Evita*?"

"Oh. Well, I didn't know if you were the musicals type—"

"I am, I don't have time on this visit but . . . Have you seen him?"

"Actually, yes. He was good."

"Good enough or really good?"

"Really good. A proper leading man. His voice was flawless, his stage presence commanding," I take a breath. "I just wanted him to dance more—"

"Knowing what he's capable of?" She gets a glint in her eye.

"Exactly!" I grin. "He was wearing this white granddad shirt and braces the whole time. I just wanted him to do a *Dancing with the Stars* turn and whip off his baggy trousers—"

"And the glitterball comes down from the ceiling . . ."

"And he unleashes his Latin shimmy!"

We take a moment to picture the scene and then Pamela sighs, "He seems a good chap, you know, decent."

"He does," I agree.

Both of us look a little wistful.

For a second I think I might ask after Pamela's husband, but seeing as I only know him from the press pictures of him tasting her latest bakery goodie, I realize I would just come across as nosey.

"So." I clasp my hands together, ready to seal the deal. "Is there anything else I should know before I start planning?"

"Oh, there is one thing I forgot to mention!"

I blink expectantly.

"We'll be traveling in a double-decker bus."

I blink some more.

"You know, one of those classic red London busses."

"You want me to source a London bus here in New York?" I gulp.

"Oh no. It's already arranged. You don't have to worry about that. Just the route. And the hotels. And the cake shops. And the cafés. And the bakers. And the recipes. And the ingredients. And the history. And the general logistics."

"Yes, yes, that's fine. But, back to the bus. Where exactly is it?"

"Newport, Rhode Island."

I take out my laptop and go straight to Google Maps. Approximately four hours' drive. Mostly along the coast of Connecticut.

"So would you be happy to be in another kind of vehicle until we get there, or will you need it to be in New York itself?"

"Oh no. It's fine to collect it there. I'm sure it would be a liability here. Besides, it's not like we need it for continuity. No TV crew to please."

"Well, that certainly makes it easier. Though now you mention it, this would make a great TV series . . ."

"I know. I just didn't fancy being in front of the camera at the moment."

"Oh." I nod understanding.

"And it's not just my weight, it requires a lot of energy when you're filming. You've always got to be 'on.'"

"Yes."

"It's not the right time for me to do that kind of project." Her voice sounds a little tremulous.

"That's okay," I quickly assure her. "We'll focus on making this the best book it can be." I give her an encouraging smile. "I think it's going to be a wonderful trip."

"Really?" Her eyes search mine.

"Yes," I confirm, telling her what she most wants to hear. "A real tonic." I look down at my list. "So. We just need a driver. For the bus."

"Oh no, that's covered too."

"Really?"

"Yes. My mum's going to do it."

My jaw gapes. "Your mother?"

I do a quick calculation in my head. Her mother has to be in her seventies, maybe even eighties . . . Gearing up to drive a thousand or so miles of unfamiliar terrain. On the wrong side of the road.

"She's got new glasses and everything."

"Oh good," I quell a splutter.

Surely she must know this is madness? Should I speak up? She seems so blasé about it, like her mother is the obvious choice, the latest road-tester on *Top Gear*. I'm still trying to word my concern while Pamela is already on to the next:

"So we can share a room and then get one for you, obviously."

"Same location?" I check that she's not expecting me to be down the road in the local Motel 6.

"Of course. I'll need you on hand round the clock."

Why does that concern me more?

"Everything else, we'll e-mail to you—the budget, the contract, all the business side of things. If that's all right?"

I nod dumbly.

"Well." She looks at her watch. "I have to get going but it was lovely to meet you, Laurie!" she reaches to shake my hand. "And I'll see you in a little under two weeks."

"Excuse me?" I balk.

"Oh. We didn't even discuss dates, did we?" She gives a "silly me!" tinkle.

"No, we didn't get to that."

The mention of Christmas seemed reassuringly far off, but of course books typically have to go to press way in advance and it is already June.

"We're arriving on the fifteenth of this month," she taps my calendar. "Is that enough time for you to make all the arrangements?"

No.

"Yes, yes, of course."

No sooner is she out the door than I call Krista.

"I'm freaking out!"

Chapter 4

⟳⟳⟳

Realizing that high-pitched panic is neither appropriate nor welcome at Lady M, I cross over to Central Park and bring Krista up to speed while hurtling toward the turtle pond.

"Okay. Breathe," she counsels me. "You're a pro."

"You do realize that, in European terms, that's like researching six different countries in a matter of days?"

"Well, I can at least do two."

"What do you mean?" I frown.

"Why don't you let me sort Vermont and New Hampshire for you—they're just across the border from here. If I have to, I can drive there to check out the cake scene."

"Really?"

"I've got a map right in front of me. It can't be more than five hours."

"You'd do that?"

"You know I would, and I'd love it too."

"Oh Krista, you're an angel." I close my eyes and let the dizzying hysteria subside.

"Anything in particular I should know?" she asks, already raring to go. "Tastes? Preferences?"

"Well." I locate a bench and flick back through my notes. "She mentioned having something maple syrup–themed for Vermont."

"I know a thing or two about that."

"Of course!" I laugh happily, recalling that her fella Jacques switches to maple syrup tapping when the snow season ends.

"Oh my god!" Krista blurts. "I've just thought of somewhere I've been dying to go!"

"Where?"

"In Vermont—the Trapp Family Lodge."

"Sounds like something from *The Sound of Music.*"

"It is! After they escaped the Nazis, this is where they set up home."

"Right . . ." I frown. "Where's the cake connection?"

"Maria's Linzertorte. They make it there from her original recipe."

"It's supposed to be American recipes."

"Well, it's the American *dream*, isn't it? Come on!"

"I'll think about it. What about New Hampshire? I don't really know what that state is famous for—except for Mitt Romney." I pull a face.

Krista gives a little chuckle. "Did you hear about the bakery that makes the presidential cookies? They do a red border for Republican, blue for Democrat and then stencil on the face of the respective candidate in the middle."

"Really?"

"They've been doing it for the past seven elections and every time they correctly predict who will win based on the number of cookies sold—the percentages even match up!"

"And they're in New Hampshire?" This could be fun.

"Ohio."

"Oh."

"Hold on, Jacques just got in. *Chéri!*" She calls to him.

Their voices are muffled across the room. I look around me, wondering how loudly I've been talking and what on earth an eavesdropper would make of our conversation. One of the turtles does look particularly bemused. I'm becoming transfixed by his beaky-gummy mouth when Krista rejoins me.

"Well, this sounds promising—a year or two ago, Jacques went to a friend's wedding at the Mount Washington Resort. Can you check it out on your phone?"

"Wow," I say as the pictures come into view. "Talk about presidential! This place is stunning."

"Kind of like a mountain version of the Hotel del Coronado," Krista notes, comparing the grand white building and distinctive red roofing. "I'm betting they do a lovely afternoon tea there." I hear a rattling of keys. "Oh my god! They do three: The Victorian, The Royal and The Mad Hatter."

"Mad Hatter for sure," I cheer, picturing Pamela seated between the White Rabbit and the Red Queen.

"Wait. That's just for kids under ten: peanut butter and jelly sandwiches."

"Oh."

"You want The Royal, that's the one with the champagne. And it's served in the Princess Room. How divine!"

"You're brilliant!" I whoop. "I feel so much better already."

"I'm here for you, kiddo."

"Thank you," I sigh.

"Seriously, don't worry about a thing. It's going to be a piece of cake!"

I give a little snort. "Did I mention that we're traveling in a London bus, driven by her half-blind, aging mother?"

Silence.

"Krista?"

"You might want to double up on the travel insurance."

Chapter 5

And so begins an all-consuming blur of Googling, cross-referencing, route-planning, hotel-pricing, negotiating, scheduling and salivating. All those online images of cakes with their glistening richness and perfectly piped fondant swirls! There was one Ice Cream Sundae Cupcake that was drizzled with chocolate sauce, scattered with sprinkles and topped with a glacé cherry! I could barely keep from licking my laptop screen.

By day three I find my cupboards to be bare (I work from home), so I part with my pajamas and hole up in a back-room nook at Bread (my favorite local Little Italy café) and enjoy the convenience of having a steady stream of lattes and nibbles delivered to my table, literally from breakfast till close at midnight. (Highly recommend an apple-pie Martini to revive one's flagging fingertips around 7 P.M.) Every now and again I find something so cool I can barely keep from grabbing the waitress—"Look at this! We're going to the place where the doughnut hole was invented!"

At least Krista is always good for a squeal. I do my due diligence and check out her suggestions for New Hampshire and

Vermont and I have to say they can't be bettered! She's even going to meet up with us at the Trapp Family Lodge as it's the last destination on the itinerary.

"I have to be there to see Pamela's face when she checks out the view from the on-site bakery. The hills are alive, I'm telling you!"

I wanted to get the final seal of approval from the woman herself before I confirmed everything, but her agent told me that her plate was too full to trouble her with details. They trusted my judgment. Pamela's mother wanted to know the exact driving route but, other than that, I could do a big reveal when she gets to New York. So, as you can imagine, by the time I arrive at the airport to collect the Lambert-Leigh ladies, I am beside myself.

I have the itinerary all printed up in a special ribbon-tie folder with different-colored information sheets for each state including a cutely designed recipe card for each of the featured cakes. I've even bought a new camera so I can properly document the journey. This trip is going to be a dream! An absolute dream!

Just as soon as we get out of the hellhole that is JFK.

"Don't mind me!" I mutter as I get bashed for the umpteenth time, trying to hold my position at the Arrivals barrier. I've been elbowed, jostled, lunged across and had several signs held directly in front of my face. But I'm not budging. I patiently continue to fend off the fray and track every face as it rounds the corner.

I wonder what Pamela's mother will look like? I did try and Google her but there were very few family pictures available. Despite all her on-screen success, Pamela seems to be an otherwise private person. Perhaps that is why her marriage has lasted an impressive twenty-one years. I can't quite figure out what her husband does for a living. Or did. He's probably retired now but I'm guessing something suit-y at some point. There was one anniversary picture of them in Paris, taking a boat trip down the Seine, and I thought, I wonder what that's like, to have a smooth-flowing love life. One that glides ever onward through the years. Mine has been more of a series of leaky, slowly sinking rowing boats.

A while back, Krista asked me to name the defining quality of my ideal man. I said someone who would make me orange-scented brioche on a Sunday morning. And then I saw Pink on TV talking about the advice her dad gave her in terms of attracting an ideal partner—*whatever qualities you are searching for in someone else, be those things yourself*; be honest, be adventurous, be affectionate. Or, in my case, be a brioche baker. I was seriously looking into some classes when *The Traveling Tea Shop* offer came in. Talk about learning on the job! Oh that just being in the presence of Pamela Lambert-Leigh could cause me to attract someone lightly smudged with flour and smelling of orange zest—

"Laurie!"

I can't believe it! She's here! I snap out of my daydream and into pro mode as I hurry over to greet her, and the two uniformed men she has with her.

One is pushing a trolley heaped with luggage. The other has charge of a woman in a wheelchair. This surely cannot be her mother—she looks like a collapsed blancmange, held together with a velvet wrap. Her neck is concertina'd into her chest, her coiffure tips forward concealing her face, all bar her mouth, which is distinctly *glistening* at the left corner.

Surely not?

I force my brightest smile. "Welcome back!"

"Laurie, I'd like you to meet my mother Gracie."

I look down at her limp hands, one of which has just slid off her lap and is hanging dangerously close to the wheel.

"But now is not the time." Pamela looks rueful, securing her mother's straying hand under the voluminous wrap. "I'm afraid she overdid the sleeping pills on the flight."

"Oh, dear. Well, we'll get her straight to the hotel and into bed. I'm sure she'll be as right as rain in the morning."

"I do hope so."

I go to turn to lead the way to the limo but Pamela halts me.

"There's one more thing. I'm so sorry I didn't get a chance to forewarn you . . ."

"Forewarn?" This doesn't sound good.

"I didn't have a minute at Heathrow, we were running so late . . ."

"Yes?" I mentally put myself in the brace position.

"There's going to be four of us on the trip."

"Okay."

"My daughter will be joining us."

"Babycakes?" I can't help but gasp. Oh this is quite a coup!

"Well, she doesn't really like to be called that anymore."

"No, no of course, I'm sorry."

"Her name is Ravenna."

"Yes. Lovely. When will she be arriving?" I reach for my notepad.

Pamela looks behind her. "Any minute."

"She was on your flight?"

She nods. "I think she nipped into one of the shops."

I join her in scanning the flow of pedestrian traffic, looking for a blonde halo, expecting a pair of blue eyes to flash out to me like sapphires. The Babycakes of my mind would by now have grown into an Amanda Seyfried-like beauty. She'd be carrying a candy-pink vanity case and probably the phone number of the pilot, eager to take her on a date.

"So, Laurie . . ."

"Mmm?" I turn back to Pamela.

"Would you be able to arrange an extra room for Ravenna?"

"I'll certainly try. I know a few of the places were fully booked."

"Oh." Pamela's face falls. "Well. Perhaps a camp bed in with us?"

"Oh, don't be silly, she can have my room. I can always stay elsewhere."

"Or perhaps you wouldn't mind sharing? Only where necessary of course."

I'm torn. From my past experience I need every moment of privacy I can muster on these escorted trips. On the other hand, the story-potential of having Babycakes as a roomie . . . Already my mind races ahead—what if we were to bond so seamlessly she became like a baby sister to me? Her rosy smiles the perfect antidote to Jessica's druggy glaze. Perhaps my own mother has engineered this whole thing from her office in the clouds! I'm about to wink heavenward when the girl in question comes into view.

It's only the scowl of derision at her mother that gives her away.

Ravenna Lambert-Leigh, the face that launched a thousand vanilla sponge puffs, is wearing a dingy off-the-shoulder sweatshirt, drooping so low on one side that it's hanging off her elbow. The vest beneath is flatteningly unflattering. Her skin-tight jeans are indecently low-cut, revealing jutting hipbones, her boots thuggishly tough and straggling neon laces. What is going on with this family? She's not even properly blonde anymore.

I turn to Pamela, looking for some kind of explanation.

"I know," she shakes her head. "It shocks me every day too."

I look back at Traveler Number Four. Much as I wish I could put her on the next flight to Los Angeles and get Rachel Zoe to give her a makeover to fit with my ideal, I have to face the horrible reality.

Deep breath!

"Welcome to New York, Ravenna! I'm Laurie." I step forward, searching her face for some kind of proof that it's actually her in there, under the cat-flick eyeliner and Amy Winehouse bouffant.

Her look conveys one word, "So?"

"I'll be making sure everything on this trip runs smoothly, so if you have any special requests, just let me know."

Her eyebrow twitches in a way that makes me want to add, "No drugs."

I look back at Pamela. "Is that everyone?"

She concedes a smile. "I think that's enough, don't you?"

On the way to the limo, I snap a sneaky picture of Ravenna and send it to Krista with the message, "Can you imagine this face on a pack of Babycakes?"

She taps back in seconds. "Special Halloween edition?"

And then she adds, "You know, for all her don't-care street-kid styling, that handbag is a Mulberry?"

For some reason this irritates me all the more, though Krista makes me smile when she suggests this caption: *Rebel with a Purse.*

I'd love to break away and bring her up to date, but for now I need to direct the Skycaps and limo driver as they try to maneuver Gracie's dead weight into the backseat.

"Mind her head!"

I hear one of them muttering something about *Weekend at Bernie's.* I'm about to check that Gracie is still breathing when she starts to snore.

Well that's one less thing to worry about.

"All right! We're all set. The journey into town should take about forty minutes, if it's not too bumper-to-bumper, so I thought I'd take this opportunity to run through our itinerary."

Ravenna makes for the drinks cabinet.

I have to bleep out her reaction when she opens it.

"I switched the decanters for Red Velvet Cheesecake!" I explain, reaching for the plates, admiring the neat two-tone stripes of textured red and smooth cream. "I thought it was the perfect combination of New York's finest! Here you go . . ."

Ravenna turns away like a baby refusing its spoon of stewed carrot.

"She doesn't really eat," Pamela grimaces.

I wait for her to finish her sentence. *She doesn't really eat cakes.* Or, *She doesn't really eat anything with refined sugar.* Or *anything that tastes good.* But that's where she stops.

Ravenna is certainly skinny enough to verify this. As she reaches to adjust the air-conditioning above her head, she reveals a stomach that is positively concave.

"Oh. Well. All the more for the rest of us," I chirp.

"Actually, I'm not hungry," Pamela also declines.

I look over at Gracie. Her mouth *is* lolling open . . . But no. I guess we'll just keep them for later.

"So. The itinerary—"

Pamela holds up a weary hand. "Do you mind if we go through all that tomorrow?"

I gulp back my disappointment. "No, of course not. I'm sure you're all really tired after your journey."

I look down at the package. Perhaps I could just tell her about the *Downton Abbey* connection with Newport, Rhode Island? Just to lift her spirits? I look up at her, but already she's a million miles away, staring lifelessly out of the window. I sigh. It's a look I saw all too often on my own mother's face. Emotional and physical exhaustion. My eyes narrow at Ravenna. Outsize graffiti-print headphones denting her backcombed hair, picking at her blue nail polish, big ole boots up on the seats. I wouldn't be surprised if she's the prime cause.

And then I remember I offered to share a room with her.

Not wanting anyone to pick up on the desperation in my voice as I call around the list of hotels, I text my request to Krista.

"I'll literally take the broom cupboard. Or the spa massage table after hours. *Anything.*"

And then I sigh. This is so not what I had planned. I have selected the most elegant accommodations, the kinds of genteel, historic places that make you want to carry a lace fan and curtsey at the doorman. When I think of rolling up with this motley crew . . . I shake my head—it comes to something when I'm the best-dressed person in the room. And with all their money too.

The last I read, Pamela was worth an estimated £15 million. Surely you could buy a new daughter for that?

"Sorry kiddo," Krista taps back. "The first place I could get you in is Maine."

I scan the itinerary. That's over halfway into the trip.

"I've got you on the waiting list though."

"Thank you."

"At least tonight you get your own bed—just as soon as you've got them all tucked up at the Waldorf, right?"

I suppose I should count my blessings that everyone wants an early night, even if I did get Pamela front-row seats for *Evita*. Obviously she can't leave her mother unattended. And Ravenna wouldn't be caught dead viewing anything as cheesy as a musical. Even if there are some pretty edgy ones on Broadway these days.

I see them all checked in. (Fortunately I am able to add an adjoining room, which keeps everyone happy. Relatively speaking.) And then I prepare to head home.

"All right. Well I wish you a good sleep and I'll see you here in the lobby at nine A.M. for our Red Velvet Cake-making demonstration!"

I'm about to step into the revolving door when Ravenna comes scurrying down the carpeted steps toward me.

"You said you can get whatever we need?"

Here we go. "Within reason."

"I need a fake ID. For tonight."

I stare back at her. "Really?"

"It's totally ridiculous—this morning I was legal drinking age and I get here and suddenly it's off limits. I mean, I'm twenty years old."

Diplomacy, remember diplomacy. "I totally understand your frustration—"

"Great. You can just have it sent up to the room." She turns to leave.

"Ravenna." I lay a hand on her bony shoulder. "I'm sorry. That won't be possible."

"Why not?" She looks outraged.

"Because I like living here. And I don't want to get deported."

"So it's all about you? I thought you were supposed to be taking care of us."

"Without turning to a life of crime, yes."

"It's just one lousy ID!"

"That's all it would take."

"So you're saying no?"

"I'm saying no."

She steps closer, eyes flitting with desperation. "If I'm going to get through this trip, I'm going to need to drink."

"Well, I'm sure we can come to some arrangement in the hotel rooms, with your mother's approval of course, but as far as going out on the town goes . . ." I give a little shrug. "Not going to happen."

For a second she stares openmouthed at me. I don't think she's used to hearing "no" too often. That's fine. I'm more than happy to up the quota.

"All right," she says, pacing now like a prison inmate trying to figure out how to get even with her guard. "But just know that it's been noted."

"What has?"

"Your unwillingness to help me out."

"As has the unreasonableness of your request," I counter.

"Excuse me?"

"I'm watching you too, sister."

No doubt Ravenna now thinks I've been hanging "in da hood," but I guess it's more of a Freudian slip than anything. I know her type. All. Too. Well.

Chapter 6

ᬟᬟᬟ

It always amazes me, how different two siblings can be. Same parents, same upbringing, two polar-different attitudes to life.

I was the little workhorse—always wanting to be occupied in some productive capacity, always making lists and laying out little stepping stones to get from A to B. I would have made an excellent scout because I was Always Prepared.

Jess was a sleepier individual, more the type to wait for things to come to her. Somehow harmless daydreaming morphed into a sense of entitlement and she would become utterly indignant when she didn't get her way. "How could Mark Allen ask Claire out instead of me! I'd already picked out the dress I was going to wear on our first date!" This in turn became a sense of deprivation—everyone else had it easier than her; she was the one who had to struggle against a cruel world. Her misfortunes had nothing to do with the choices she made (or the lack of effort on her behalf); she was an innocent bystander, randomly cursed and often beginning her sentences, "It's all right for you . . . ."

Mum used to say that Dad leaving had affected her younger

daughter in a profound way. She thought that was the trigger for the sense of lack. But he left when we were nippers and elected never to see us again. I hardly think him sticking around would have been a bonus. As far as I was concerned we were extremely lucky to have a mother who was so devoted, so encouraging, such fun—how ungrateful would it be to focus on a disappeared dad? Shouldn't we be glad for the good things?

Instead Jess seemed hell-bent on finding a way to make us suffer as deeply as she supposedly was. She needed to bring us down to her level. At least, that's how I saw it.

Of course you can look at the drugs as a cry for help or a means of escape. And we certainly tried to put an empathetic spin on it when we first found out. Our initial instinct was to help her through this, to get her back on track. My mother and I even went to a "family skills for drug abuse prevention" workshop. But I must confess I struggled with their insistence that we had to let go of any judgment.

I wanted to thrust my hand up and say: if addiction is a disease, how do you first catch it? I mean, if you've never tried a single sodding drug in the first place, how could you become addicted? You couldn't. It wouldn't be possible. You are making a choice that first time. You are volunteering for the addiction. You know it's wrong and self-destructive but you do it anyway.

Alcoholics I understand better. Alcohol is everywhere. Alcohol is foisted on you at every turn in every walk of life. Even in church communion.

I don't mean to be deliberately controversial. This stuff just gets me *riled up*. I think more than anything it's the waste—the waste of life. Of your life. Of other people's. The toll it takes is so far-reaching. So insidious.

"Why did you do it?" I wanted to ask Jess, over and over and over. "Why did you even begin? You knew no good could come of it and you did it anyway. You wreaked havoc on all of us. And you don't even seem sorry."

I feel the emotions flare within me again. I mustn't let this overwhelm me. I mustn't let frustration take hold because when I do it throws off everything in my life. And I need the next few days to flow smoothly.

That being said, if Ravenna thinks I'm going to look the other way while she depletes and dishonors her mother, she's mistaken. I don't have my mother to defend anymore. I didn't do a good enough job of protecting her.

I heave a sigh.

It's one of those situations you replay in your mind, trying to force history down a different path, to a different outcome.

It should have been the other way round.

I can't get this thought out of my head—it should have been my sister the drug addict who died, not the mother who loved her too much to ever give up on her.

I'm mad at Ravenna for bringing up these feelings in me but, to be honest, it doesn't take much. I have no idea how to lay this to rest. I've become quite skilled at squishing down the tears and the raging sense of injustice out of necessity. But I can't seem to make peace with my mum being gone. How can I? There's no "everything happens for a reason" platitude that can make sense of this.

Once in a while, Jess will try to get in contact. But I'm not convinced her motive is remorse. I just think she's coming for me next and I need to stay away. Right now I cannot even contemplate being in her presence. Ever again.

Okay. Enough. I just have to block her out and focus on where I am now. She can't get me here. I'm safe, nestled amid the skyscrapers—she finds them intimidating and threatening. To me, they are like bodyguards.

Chapter 7

෴

Perhaps you've seen *Maid in Manhattan*—the movie where Jennifer Lopez plays a hotel chambermaid who borrows a socialite's Dolce & Gabbana ensemble and catches the eye of senatorial candidate Ralph Fiennes? Or *Scent of a Woman*? Or *Serendipity*?

If so, you know the Waldorf Astoria—its art deco frontage, the sleek silver-gray stone contrasting with the luxe gold lettering, the legendary Starlight Lounge with its retractable roof.

I barely gave the property a second glance yesterday, so today I got here half an hour early so I can drink in the understated swank and class. Before the Lambert-Leighs arrive and ruin it all.

I had prepared a little introductory talk—I wanted to tell them that the Waldorf Astoria was the first hotel to have room service, that this is where Marilyn Monroe stayed while filming *The Seven Year Itch* and that the Conrad Suite was the chosen venue for the engagement party of His Serene Highness Prince Rainier III and Grace Kelly. But, after the utter lack of interest at my itinerary talk in the limo, I've decided to ditch it and cut to the cake.

It's funny, in all the time I've known Charlie (and his lovely wife Rosaria), I've never before asked how Red Velvet Cake is made or what makes their version so legendary.

It would have been like seeing behind the curtain at Oz. That being said, I am really excited to see Pamela's Victoria Sponge materialize before my very eyes. I can't tell you how much I "heart" Victoria Sponge. We chose it as a match because of the red and cream pinstripe of the jam and cream filling and also because British royalty has favored the Waldorf Astoria (specifically Elizabeth II). I wonder if it will be the best I've ever tasted? I mean, the M&S triple layer version is hard to beat . . .

"All right, all right," I soothe my stomach as it yawps impatiently. "Not long now."

I check my watch against the ornate bronze clock centerpiece and smile. The rich mahogany wall panels, the black marble columns, the inlaid ceilings with their abundance of gold flourishes—the whole room feels like being inside a 1930s jewelry box.

I settle into one of the velvet-hug chairs and people-watch. Or rather, people-judge. I cannot for the life of me understand those folks who spend an arm and a leg to stay on Park Avenue and then put said arm in a T-shirt and said leg in a jean. And I'm not talking some chic little Helmut Lang scoop neck and J Brand denim but Walmart's finest. Look at this one family—bundling through, yanking and scrapping as they go. It's just so uncouth! *I know.* I sound like I'm eighty years old, despairing at the youth of today. But I do. I really do.

And then my face brightens—now that's more like it!

A woman has emerged from the lifts looking as if she's been performing a Noël Coward play between floors. I do love a dame who can wear a scarf with flair. I wonder if she's French? Or maybe she really is an actress? That dress is beautiful, silky with raised velvety patterns. I bet her lipstick casing is heavy gold and her compact mirror exquisitely engraved.

Oh gosh. She's caught me staring. And now she's heading straight for me.

"Laurie?"

"Yes?" I startle to my feet.

She extends her hand. "Gracie Lambert-Leigh."

I know my mouth is gaping but yours would too. The transformation is extreme.

"Judging by your response, I must have been quite a sight yesterday!"

"No, no, not at all!" I gulp, trying to regain my composure. "How are you feeling after, er, your lovely rest?"

"Rest? It was more like a coma. Still, I had to do something to get away from that awful girl."

My eyebrows rise. "You mean your granddaughter?"

"Oh don't!" she shudders. "The fact that we are genetically connected gives me chills."

I remain stunned.

"Of course, her mother is a co-conspirator. Or, what's the modern term for that, remind me . . ."

Dare I say what I'm thinking? "Enabler?" I venture.

"That's it. Here she comes now."

"Good morning Pamela!" I turn to smile at her, relieved to see that she's looking a little brighter than yesterday. (Her smock top has a soft lilac print and I really think you only reach for florals when you're feeling optimistic.)

"Ravenna not joining us?" I check.

"Oh no, she's still in her pajamas. She was up late with her boyfriend."

"She has a boyfriend here in New York?"

"No no, he's back in England. They were on Skype. Or Face-Time or something."

"Though who'd want to spend any time with his face . . ." Gracie shudders.

"Anyway," Pamela tuts her mother, "Ravenna is really more interested in going shopping, so she's going to give us a call when she's ready."

"Ready to milk the guilt money."

"Mother, please. Could we go one day without the sniping?"

Gracie thinks for a moment and then says, "I can't make any promises."

"Ah! Here's our host now!" I'm relieved to see my pal, the executive pastry chef, making his way over to us.

Charlie Romano is a brown-eyed, handsome man with a sweep of dark hair, sheeny olive skin and an Italian accent, which Gracie at least seems to appreciate. She takes his arm as he leads us away from the lobby, through a side door and down into the wonderland that is the Waldorf Astoria's kitchen.

Or should I say "kitchens"? The food preparation area spans an entire city block. It's almost like a culinary department store down here—avant-garde reception party nibbles prepared here, sixteen-dollar soups *du jour* over in the West Wing . . .

"You know the Waldorf Salad originated here?" Charlie chirps.

"The clue is in the name," Gracie tinkles.

"Also Thousand Island dressing."

"And the Manhattan cocktail!" I chime in.

"And Red Velvet Cake . . ." Pamela's eyes widen as Charlie opens the doors to the chilled baking department.

"It's so spacious," she coos as she enters. "And immaculate."

She's right. There's not a sprinkle or crumb out of place. Just acres of marble countertop and a fleet of stainless steel stacking trays on wheels.

Charlie has already set out all the ingredients, including, rather surprisingly, beetroot!

"We don't use any dyes or colorings," Charlie explains. "The beetroot gives the basic chocolate cake batter a red hue, plus beetroot is great for keeping the cake moist."

Pamela nods in agreement as she takes in the mascarpone cheese and double cream that will make up the filling, as well as the thick layer of "icing" that will cloak the entire cake. This is going to be delish!

"Have you ever tasted pure cocoa before, Laurie?" Charlie asks, directing my attention to a small glass bowl of what appear to be dusty dark chocolate buttons.

"I don't think so," I frown.

"In that case, the answer is no," Pamela laughs. "If you had, you'd remember."

"Try one," Charlie holds out the stash. "These pieces are ninety-nine percent pure chocolate."

How can that be bad? I pop one in my mouth.

Almost immediately my tongue is encased in bitterness. Oh my god!

They all laugh as my face contorts and I try to shift the powder-dense coating.

"Some water?" He offers me a glass.

"Yes please!" I wince, then watch as he empties the rest of the buttons into a metal bowl set over a saucepan of boiling water and gently melts them to a sheeny sludge.

"It tastes better combined with other ingredients."

From this point he starts juggling assorted bowls, mixers and baking tins. As he does so, I recall one (possibly apocryphal) story that tells of a woman, back in the 1940s when the Red Velvet Cake was first introduced, writing to the hotel requesting the chef's secret recipe. The hotel obliged by mailing her a copy, along with a bill for $350! She consulted her lawyer who said she was liable for the cost and so, by way of revenge, she distributed the recipe far and wide, to every friend and family member, which actually served in spreading the popularity of said cake.

"Excuse me a moment." As Charlie steps away to check on the oven, Pamela's phone rings.

"It's Ravenna." Her face falls. "She's ready to go shopping."

"Do you think she needs an escort?" I ask, a little bemused.

"Oh, would you? I'd be so grateful! I really don't think she should be left unattended at the moment."

Ah. I've just inadvertently talked myself out of an up-close-and-personal encounter with my favorite cake.

"Of course," I tell her, though my heart has just collapsed in the middle. "I'll go straight up. Just give me a call if you need anything in the meantime."

"One second." Pamela reaches into her handbag and pulls out her credit card, extending it to me. "Take this."

I hesitate. "I tell you what, why don't you keep hold of that for now. Ravenna can have a good look around, and then if she sees something she falls madly in love with, you can come along later and decide if it's something you'd like to buy for her."

"Oh I like this girl, Pamela." Gracie smirks delightedly.

"I-I . . ." Pamela flusters.

"You keep it," I guide her hand back to her purse. "Thanks again, Charlie!" I call over and give him a little wave before I head back upstairs, ready for anything Ravenna can throw at me.

Chapter 8

꩜

"Where's Mum?" is Ravenna's predictable opening gambit.

"She's working. I said I would take you." I rather enjoy her look of dismay. "So, where do you want to start? There's a Forever 21 over on Seventh."

She gives a little snort. "I want to go to Tiffany's."

"Of course. I should have guessed from the way you're dressed," I mutter under my breath.

Today Ravenna is sporting a micro-mini and a mesh top, though her hair is piled high on her head, just like Holly Golightly—if Cat had savaged her updo.

It's a ten-minute walk, but neither of us speaks along the way, preferring to let the silence between us be filled by horn honks, doorman whistles and wailing sirens.

"Here we are." I contemplate the imposing building with its aqua-accented window displays.

Last time I was here I was eating morning-after-the-night-before croissants with Krista. Not that we dared to go in. I never have. I certainly feel more than a little daunted now as I follow Ravenna.

She, on the other hand, is utterly blasé, scanning the sparkling glass cases, requesting certain items be presented to her, dismissing them and moving on.

I decide to wait by the door. Like backup security. I wouldn't put it past her, making a dash for it with some pink diamonds.

Eventually she beckons me over.

"I want this," she says, holding up an elongated sterling silver cuff bearing the inscription "T & Co 1837." I get that it would have a certain punkish Wonder Woman vibe on her wrist.

"Okay," I say.

"Well?" She holds out her hand. "Mum did give you her credit card, didn't she?"

"I told her to keep it."

"You did what?"

"I said she could catch up with us later, once you'd had a good look around."

"But I want to get it now."

"So pay for it yourself."

"I haven't got a thousand dollars to spend on a bracelet!" she splutters.

"Oh well. I guess you'd better start saving."

Ravenna rolls her eyes. "Next you'll be telling me to get a job."

"And that would be absurd because . . . ?"

"You know I'm at university? I could only work part-time. Do you have any idea how many hours I'd have to clock up to afford something like this? And what would be the logic in that, when I can just ask Mum and she'll buy it outright?"

In a horribly warped way, she has a point. What possible incentive does she have to work?

"So, where do you want to go next?" I ask her. "We only have an hour or so before we leave for Connecticut, so let's make it count."

"This schedule is pretty tight, isn't it?" she muses. "Not a lot of room for delays?"

"No room for delays." I try to sound authoritative.

"You know, I've just decided: I'm not coming on this trip. New England is just full of old people looking at leaves. I'm going to stay here in New York."

Oh god. As much as this is music to my ears, I know Pamela won't go for it.

"You know that's not possible," I begin.

"Why not? She doesn't want me there anyway."

"Your mother?" I'm about to beg to differ when she says: "No. The other one."

"Your grandmother?"

"She can't stand being around me."

"Well . . ." I stop myself from saying, "She does have a point."

"It's just going to be boring. Cake after cake after cake . . . What am I supposed to do?"

I shrug. "What every person your age does: tune out, text, listen to music, play games, go on Facebook. I mean, does it really matter where you are to do that?"

Her eyes narrow.

"Besides, you'd be doing your mother a huge favor."

"Huge is the word—have you seen the size of her? It's just so embarrassing! Who does she think she's fooling? Eat my delicious cakes and end up obese like me!"

"Stop!" I halt her. "I won't have you talking about her like that."

Ravenna scoffs at my objection. "You know, it's really none of your business what I say about my own mother."

"When you say those things in front of me," I counter, "you make it my business. It is not acceptable to my ears. Have you got that?"

She stares at me. And then she stares at the floor. Eventually her eyes return to mine.

"You know, you're right. It's the least I can do for her."

I can't believe it. "Really?"

She nods. "Forget what I said. I just want to pick up a little something at Diesel and then we can head back to the hotel. Is that okay?"

"Y-yes, that's fine. Let me just look up the directions."

"Okay, I'm going to nip to the loo."

Wow. That was a narrow escape. Maybe she's more reasonable than I thought? I was worried I'd gone too far, but something obviously got through to her. Thank goodness!

I tap at my phone. Perfect! Diesel is just three minutes' walk from here. We'd have time for a quick mani afterward, if she's game. Maybe I'll treat her to one of those rad new designs—I saw this dip-dye effect that I think she'd like. That's if she ever comes back.

I turn to the shop assistant. "Excuse me, where are the restrooms in here?"

"Up on the sixth floor."

Oh. That could explain it. She's probably got distracted, looking at more goodies. Until today I didn't realize Tiffany did so many non-jewelry items. There's even a tea set (tea pot, milk jug and sugar bowl) in angular sterling silver with rosewood handles and jade cabochon accents: $23,000 a pop. But that does include a matching tray.

I strum my fingers. I wonder how Pamela and Gracie are getting on. She did mention she wanted to try the Cronut craze (croissant-doughnut hybrid originating here in Manhattan), but the bakery is all the way down in SoHo. I'm not sure she'll have time. I look at my watch. I look at Tiffany's watches—the rose gold, the diamonds, the ticking hands . . .

Still no sign of Ravenna.

Perhaps it's best if I wait over by the door. I smile at the security guard.

"I'm just waiting for my friend."

"The one you came in with?"

"Short skirt, crazy mess of hair . . ." I squiggle my hands around my head.

"She left."

"What? When?"

"About ten minutes ago."

Oh god. Oh god, oh god. She just totally played me. What do I do now? Once again I find myself freaking out in an entirely inappropriate environment.

"Krista!" I wail as soon as I get outside. "I've lost Babycakes!"

I find myself instinctively heading for the Apple store, as if I might be able to harness their technology to create some kind of tracking system using her mobile phone number. Not that I have it. And not that I can ask Pamela for it, since that would give the game away.

"Okay, let's be logical about this," Krista calms me. "It's too early to file a Missing Persons report and there's no better place for a person to disappear than in New York City, so scouring the streets isn't going to work."

"So what should I do?"

"Have faith."

"Have faith?" I'm not convinced. "You think she'll have her little run-around and then see the error of her ways?"

"No, I just mean that without her mum's credit card, she won't have enough money to last a whole week in NYC. Very few people do."

"Oh." I bite my lip. Then I see some men leering at a woman in hot pants. "What if she turns to prostitution?"

"You've seen the state of her. Even punters have standards."

I sigh. "So what now?"

"Go back to the hotel and wait for her. Her things are still in the room, right? She'll have to go back for them."

"Actually, I asked everyone to check out before they left this morning, so we wouldn't have any holdups leaving at noon."

"Then her luggage will be in storage."

"Unless she went straight there from Tiffany's and nabbed it."

"Then you'd better get a move on!"

"All right! I'm on my way. And Krista?"

"Yes?"

"Thank you for always being there for me."

"My god, you've *always* been there for me. It's nice to be able to help you for a change."

I smile, put my phone away and then duck and dive through the crowds like an American footballer hurtling for the touchdown line.

Her bag is still here. That's something. I fall into the nearest seat, waiting for my heaving chest to settle.

Of course there's no need for her to come back to collect it before our departure deadline. She could easily wait us out. Check-in at her next accommodation wouldn't start until 3 P.M. Unless she's just planning on sleeping under some railway bridge, of course.

I get a swimmy-swampy feeling in my head. Could this trip be over before it's begun? Will the blame for its failure fall at my feet? I can't deny—I went too far, I let things get personal. My head falls into my hands.

"Laurie!"

"Gracie!" I jump up. "Where's Pamela?"

"Still with Charlie. They're working on some kind of

Velvet-Victoria hybrid." She pulls a face. "It was all getting a bit technical for me, fractions of ounces, I thought I'd come up for a cup of tea. Care to join me?"

"Er-um . . ."

Gracie studies me. "Is something the matter?"

"Well . . ." Dare I tell her?

"Ravenna ditched you once she realized you didn't have her mum's credit card?"

I blink back at her.

"I thought she probably would."

I sigh. "I should have just taken it."

"What did she try to get you to buy?"

"A thousand dollars' worth of bracelet from Tiffany's."

Gracie hoots. "Little minx. She was totally trying it on."

"Really? Because I might have slightly crossed the line in terms of what I said to her . . ."

Gracie smiles broadly. "Got a bit of Supernanny in you, haven't you?"

"I've got a big mouth on this topic."

"Me too. For all the good it does." She places a comforting arm around my shoulder. "Let's see if a cup of tea can make everything better . . ."

So this is the plan: we say nothing. And if anything needs to be said, I let Gracie do the talking.

Gracie is with Krista, in that she thinks Ravenna will turn up at the last minute.

An hour ago, this reassured me. But, as of now, there are just ten last minutes to go. And still no sign.

We've already loaded the car and lied to Pamela, telling her that Ravenna has just nipped to the hotel gift shop.

"I think I might go and chivvy her up." Pamela goes to turn back into the hotel.

"No, no!" I protest. "Allow me."

"Why don't you get comfortable in the car?" Gracie guides her to the Mercedes.

I take one last look up and down Park Avenue.

And that's when I see her. Directly across the street from us. *Watching us.*

I daren't blink for fear that she'll disappear. She looks so fragile, so small in this land of giants. I take a step in her direction just as a sightseeing bus passes between us, and then she's gone.

Nooo! My shoulders slump.

What did that mean? Was she just there to taunt me? Or see if we'd really call her bluff?

"Ms. Davis?" A male voice calls to me.

I turn back; it's the doorman.

"Mr. Romano has something for you."

Charlie is beckoning to me from the other side of the glass.

"I know you missed out on Pamela's Victoria Sponge, so I saved you a slice."

I gasp out loud, squishing him in a hug and then tearing into the box.

"You don't have to eat it now!" Charlie hoots.

"Yes I do," I muffle. "This might be my last chance to taste her cooking."

"But . . ." he frowns.

"Don't ask!" I hold up my hand. And then I close my eyes and, just for a moment, surrender to the cake—the moist-light sponge, the dairy creaminess of the filling blending with the strawberry stickiness . . .

"Good?" Charlie inquires softly.

"Ohhhhh!"

"I know!" he grins. "Please tell her that she's welcome back anytime!"

"That may be sooner than you think," I mutter as I dust off the blonde crumbs and head out to face her.

The time has come. I take a deep breath, dip into the backseat, only to find Ravenna occupying the front passenger slot.

"Wha—?"

"What's the holdup?" she asks before I can form a sentence. "I thought we had a schedule to keep to?"

Chapter 9

I don't know whether to kiss her or slap her. But I don't get the chance to do either because, no sooner am I buckled up than Gracie whiplashes us into traffic.

All too soon the yellow cab escorts and iconic buildings morph into a scene from a gritty, lowlife movie—grimy streets, clunky railway bridges and menacing characters, all bundled up even though it's a sunny day. I always used to turn my nose up at the London suburbs when I was heading home from Heathrow, but no more. They are a bucolic dream compared to this.

"Watch out!"

Vehicles weave, break and honk around us, as if they are in cahoots to keep us from staying our course. While I grip the hand-rest and resist the urge to close my eyes during the dicier moments, Gracie is astoundingly calm under pressure.

"Oh no you don't buddy, you can wait your turn." She denies a Mustang trying to barge into our lane.

I turn, openmouthed, to Pamela.

"How the hell does she do this?" She predicts my question.

"It's extraordinary. This is a total white-knuckle ride—my heart is in my mouth and she's as cool as a cucumber."

Pamela smiles. "She's spent the last fortnight memorizing every nuance of the journey. She's even planned which lane she's going to drive in."

"Are you serious?"

"She loves it!" Pamela takes a quick sip of water. "She took The Knowledge on her seventieth birthday, just to put a smile on her husband's face."

"Was he a taxi driver?"

"Bus actually."

"Ahhh, hence the connection in Newport?"

She nods, explaining how, about twelve years ago, her father helped a billionaire named Arby Poindexter to pick out the double-decker of his dreams.

"They actually became pals during his stay in London, and Arby was so impressed with Dad's knowledge and passion, he invited him and Mum out to stay with his family in Newport."

"So Gracie's been there before?"

Pamela nods. "And she can't wait to go back."

"All right!" Gracie announces. "It should smooth out from here."

She's quite right—suddenly the urban chaos streamlines into a green-bordered freeway. We can't see much of the places we're passing—Greenwich, Stamford, Norwalk—but I know we're in Connecticut now.

Most people know this state as a commuter belt, but it is also the home of PEZ candy's U.S. manufacturing facility and the first lollipop machine. As in the hard candy globes on a stick, rather than the British iced version.

"The idea started before the Civil War, when children used to have a bit of sugar candy stuck to the end of a pencil," I read from my notes.

"No concerns about lead poisoning back then," Pamela notes.

"Would anyone object to having the windows down, now we're away from the grime?" Gracie asks.

"Fine with me," I reply, quite enjoying the bluster. And then I ask Gracie if her husband taught her to drive. He did.

"And how did you two meet? If you don't mind me asking?"

"Not at all."

I settle in for story time.

"I was seventeen, still living at home but yearning for some independence. My parents were very formal—even breakfast was a fixed sit-down affair—and I took every opportunity I could to get out of the house, just so I could breathe. When I finally persuaded them to let me have a dog, I started to explore our grounds a little more and one day I saw this chap tramping across the bottom of our lawn. I tried to catch up with him but he was walking at quite a clip. I asked the gardener if he'd hired an assistant, but he said no. So who was he and where was he heading? I went back the next day to find out."

"By yourself?"

"With the dog."

"Oh. Okay."

"'Excuse me,' I said. 'Are you aware that this is private property?' He hesitated and then he said, 'I am.'

"'Where are you going?' I asked him.

"'To work,' he said. 'It saves me a good twenty minutes if I cut through here. Do you mind?'

"He had the most open face I had ever seen. Everyone I knew was either snooty or sly. He was just so straightforward. I looked at him some more and then I looked at this package in his hand—a little block covered in waxed paper.

"'What's that?' I asked.

"'My lunch,' he said.

"And it just seemed such a little lunch for such a big man. So I told him I would see him tomorrow."

I laugh. "Just like that?"

"I wasn't a very chatty child. I just spent a lot of time being silent around adults until I met Georgie. That was his name." She looks pleased even to say it.

"So what happened next?"

"Well, I decided I would make him a cake to go with his sandwich."

I look at Pamela. "Is this where all the baking began?"

She nods.

"I thought it should be the heaviest, most filling cake I could muster, so I made a fruit cake. Cut it into four, wrapped his wedge in a cloth napkin and sat in wait . . ." She smiles. "The next day he said it was the best cake he'd ever tasted and that everyone else at the bus depot was jealous. So I made another one and gave him the whole thing so he could share it."

"Gosh! I bet you were popular!"

She smiles. "I didn't meet the other chaps straightaway. For a couple of months it was just me and Georgie and our morning tea flasks under the oak tree. I wouldn't see him on the way home because the busses were running by then. But I was always thinking about him, always thinking about what I could make him next for lunch. Scotch eggs were his favorite."

"The way to a man's heart, eh?"

"Oh, he had such a lovely heart!" She swoons. "No rules. No caution. He didn't worry what anyone thought of him."

"Not even your parents?"

"Well, I didn't leave a lot of room for negotiation there. He gave me such confidence—when I presented him it was as my fiancé and that was that. And they grew to love him dearly. As did everyone who ever met him. It's a wonderful thing, when someone can make you laugh, all other concerns go out of the window."

I think how true this is. How disarming laughter can be. You can't be defensive and guarded while you are laughing. All you are is delighted.

"Did you ever get to drive his bus?"

"Oh yes. He taught me everything he knew. Sixty years we were together . . ."

She looks so proud.

It must be wonderful to be filled with admiration for your other half. I know Krista feels that way about Jacques. So that's two role models I have now.

"Have you ever been married, Laurie?" Gracie asks me.

"Oh no," I shudder. "No, no, no."

"Is that aversion toward the institution itself or—"

"Oh, I've nothing against marriage as a concept. It's just the thought of being married to anyone I've actually been in a relationship with."

"That diabolical?"

"Let's just say I've yet to find my Georgie." No need to gloom them with my romantic history. I turn to Pamela. "But you've done well too—how long is it with Brian, twenty years?"

"Mmm." Pamela turns to look out through the window.

Okay. We'll leave that there.

"What about you, Ravenna? How long have you been with . . ."

"Kevin." Gracie helps me out with her boyfriend's name.

Ravenna's eyes narrow. "It's Eon now, as well you know."

"Eon?" I raise a brow.

She juts her chin. "We've been together two years."

"God help us."

"What did you say?" Ravenna snaps at her grandmother.

"Are those giant headphones affecting your hearing? I said, 'God help us!'"

"How can you be so rude?" Ravenna gapes.

"Oh, when he speaks so fondly of us?"

"He'd never say any of that stuff to your face."

"How very discreet!"

"Um," I scoot forward in my seat, eager to change the subject. "We're just approaching New Haven if you would like to take a little break? It's not part of our official itinerary, but it is home to Yale University, and Louis' Lunch—the birthplace of the American hamburger—if anyone's peckish?"

"I'm happy to keep going," says Gracie, adjusting her grip on the steering wheel.

Ravenna gives a "don't care either way" shrug and Pamela doesn't even reply, she's so deep in her own thoughts.

"Okay, well we'll just keep on trucking." I slide back into my seat.

Gracie catches my eye in the rearview mirror. "You look disappointed?"

"Oh no, it's fine! I've just got a bit of a thing for university towns." I pull my cardigan around me. "Even though we're just getting into summer, they still make me think of argyle socks and scrunchy leaves and armfuls of books." I don't really mean to keep talking, but I do. "It seems so romantic to me—the idea of sitting at some creaky desk listening to a whiskery intellectual spouting mind-expanding wisdom—"

"I take it you've never actually been to university?"

"Ravenna!" Gracie scolds.

"It's okay," I respond. "I haven't. I got offered a travel rep job as soon as I left school and, at that point, the idea of getting paid to spend a year in Greece was rather more appealing than student loans and more exams. Not that I'm saying that was the smarter decision," I quickly add, conscious that Ravenna is still in uni mode.

Mercifully Gracie suggests some music: "My friend's grandson put together a CD for me . . ."

Ravenna rolls her eyes and lodges her headphones in place before she's even heard a note—Gracie could have opened with "Highway to Hell" for all she knows.

In actual fact it's the most laid-back, borderline melancholic selection from the 1940s—"One for My Baby (And One More for the Road)," "Sentimental Journey" and a rather ironic "Don't Get Around Much Anymore" . . .

By the time we get to our official first stop, both Pamela and Ravenna have nodded off.

"Now this is more like it," I whisper to Gracie, acknowledging the hand-carved, welcome-to-our-town sign (settled 1654), picture-perfect, pointy-spired white church and ye olde seaport with Captain Pugwash-style sailing vessels.

"Delightful," she agrees.

"Are we here?" Pamela croaks as we pull into a parking spot beside the wooden boardwalk.

"We are."

She reaches to jiggle Ravenna's shoulder.

"Don't wake her!" Gracie hisses.

"What do you mean? We can't leave her in the car!"

"It's fine—we'll crack the window."

"Oh Mum!" she tuts and gently touches her daughter's hair— guaranteed to render her wide-awake and riled.

"Where are we?" Ravenna asks—a simple enough question, though it sounds more like an accusation with her tone.

"Mystic," I announce.

She snorts. "What, as in *Mystic Pizza*?"

"Yes. Exactly."

She jolts upright and looks around her. "You're telling me the film was set here?"

"Set here, filmed here, inspired by here."

She releases herself from her seatbelt and steps out to survey the waterfront. We all follow.

"So Julia Roberts was actually here?" She seems to need a lot of convincing.

"Yes."

"Is there really a pizza place?"

"There is. In fact, we're a little early for our appointment, if anyone fancies a slice?"

Gracie and Pamela are keen, whereas Ravenna tries desperately to shrug off her eagerness.

Ah, the universal power of Julia Roberts.

We cross the Meccano-esque drawbridge to the main high street and find it crammed with tourist-friendly temptations like Mystic Sweet's fresh fudge and an array of nautical-themed knick-knacks. (I'm extremely drawn to a set of octopus, starfish and coral-print cushions but admit they wouldn't necessarily make sense in a Manhattan setting.)

"Mystic Pizza—A Slice of Heaven," Pamela reads the sign as we stop outside the pale-gray clapboard building at the top of the town. "It really is just like in the movie!"

"Apparently they renovated it to look more like the one in the film," I chuckle as we head inside.

Every inch of wall-space is filled with framed photos—either stills from the movie or freeze-framed sports stars. There's a friendly, family vibe and, best of all, the girl behind the counter is just about as lovely as Julia herself—a wild tumble of curls swept over the side, dancing eyes and huge, perfect-toothed grin. She serves us our triangles of thin crust Margherita with an impressive amount of *joie de vivre*. Looking between her and Ravenna, I see the great chasm between choosing to be sunny and sweet versus sullen and sulky. Apparently Gracie sees it too.

"Pretty girl," she notes. "Probably about your age, Ravenna?"

"You didn't get one for me?" she asks as we dig in to the juicy, drizzly tomato sauce and bronzed, bubbling cheese topping.

"Oh," I apologize as I dab my chin. "I didn't think you ate."

She gives an indignant pout. "I just need one as a prop for my picture."

"No problem!" I order Ravenna an individual box to go. "Would you like me to snap you outside by the sign?"

"I'll do it," she says, hurrying away with her stash.

"Another day, another selfie," Gracie mutters as she takes a sip of iced tea.

I smile. She's really a very savvy granny.

It's time for us to be heading on to our appointment at the other end of town. I feel as if I've pulled off quite a coup, setting up a cake-baking session with Warren Brown, host of the Food Network's *Sugar Rush* show and author of *United Cakes of America: Recipes Celebrating Every State* (including a rather intriguing Tomato Soup Cake from New Jersey, where Campbell's launched their condensed soup empire).

Today he's sharing his updated spin on Connecticut's Hartford Election Cake—Nutmeg Spice Cupcakes. (Connecticut is known as the Nutmeg State and its residents as Nutmeggers.) I know the results are going to be good because this is a man who says, "Baking is an act of love done to bring pleasure to the world." Isn't that gorgeous? Of course, I know better than to expect wild applause from Pamela. Not that she's not grateful, she's just so distracted . . .

Aware that we need to get a move on, Ravenna repeatedly lags behind. I can see this is stressing Pamela, so I suggest she and Gracie go on ahead, giving them the address of the host's bake shop across the bridge and reassuring them that they can't miss Warren's striking six-foot-three-inch form. For many years he was known for his slimline dreadlocks, but now his head is clean-shaven, all the better to see his bright smile.

Warren is actually based in Washington DC, but he's passing through Connecticut on his way home from a reunion at Brown University in Rhode Island. He graduated from there with a BA in history, went on to do a law degree with a master's in public health, and it was while he was working as a litigator for the inspector general that he found his true calling as a cake baker. He now owns three CakeLove bakeries and is moving into wholesale with an ingenious cake-in-a-jar product called Cake Bites.

Aren't people fascinating?

And annoying. Ravenna is now on the phone, slowing her all the more. At one point she even takes a few steps in the opposite direction.

"Come on!" I yell back to her. "We're going to miss the crossing."

I can see a tall ship approaching, and goodness only knows how long the process takes for the bridge to split, rear up and then rejoin itself.

At least Pamela and Gracie are safely across. I weigh my options—if I forget Ravenna, I can make it to where I need to be. On time. If I stay and play babysitter, I'll look unprofessional to the man I worked so hard to set up this meeting with.

"Ravenna!"

She turns away in annoyance, hand covering the phone. I begin marching toward her and then hear the sound of the barrier lowering across the street.

Will I never learn?

What is it that makes some of us choose to try and save the

contrary person while others accept that they need to be responsible for their own lives and don't even look back? Why am I still doing this when I really should know better?

"What's going on?" Ravenna finally appears by my side.

"They're letting a ship pass through."

"So now we just have to wait here?" she grumps.

"Because of you!" I want to scream, but what's the point?

It's like they say—if you want to develop more patience, spend more time with frustrating people.

Chapter 10

Pamela and Warren are getting on famously by the time we arrive. (Famously being an apt word, since they've both had their own TV shows.) Coincidentally his wife's name is Pamela and they both agree that patience is key when it comes to baking—taking your time every step of the way.

"The best parts of life are in the roads traveled to get to your destination."

(When I read this line on his website, I knew he had to be part of this project!)

He's equally thoughtful while ruminating on the joy-inducing nature of cakes: "I think it's all about memories—cake harks back to the earliest recall we have of gathering with others, celebrating with song, cheers, wishes and being in the spotlight. Everyone likes that a little and, even if you don't, it's still a special moment of every year that forces everyone to focus on themselves. I think that has something to do with the staying power of cake—especially when it's targeted as the unhealthy bogeyman in one's diet!"

As we watch him top the now-cooled cupcakes with old-fashioned buttercream frosting, I ask which recipe he liked best from his state-wide research for the *United Cakes of America*.

"Well, there are so many," he muses. "I enjoyed the avocado cupcake for California because it's so different."

"I'll say!" Gracie concurs.

"It's good; most won't give it a try. And the sweet potato cake for Louisiana is great—it reminds me of the holidays we spent with family from that part of the Deep South."

He then brings us neatly back to New England as he sets his finished batch of Nutmeg Spice Cupcakes before us.

"They smell so wonderful!" we chorus.

In between mouthfuls of flavorful sponge (and licking frosted fingertips), I show Pamela the 1796 recipe for the traditional Hartford Election Cake, which Warren notes "makes enough to feed an entire church." It also makes for amusing reading—the instructions may only comprise one paragraph, but they are curiously specific:

"Make a sponge of the milk and flour at four o'clock, at nine mix together . . ."

"Did you actually test it out?" I ask Warren.

"I did," he cringes. "Very bad. The entire pound of raisins made it way too heavy."

Gracie can't help but chuckle. "That's exactly what Georgie loved about my fruit cake. He said it sat like a brick in his stomach. In a good way."

And then she proceeds to show us just how weighty it is.

It's fun watching Gracie at work. She has so many similar mannerisms to Pamela. People used to say that about me and Mum. We both had very "descriptive" hands. And you couldn't tell our voices apart on the phone. I always liked hearing that. It's strange to me that Ravenna wants to distance herself from Pamela's identity in every possible way.

Ravenna's sitting outside now, watching a schooner prepare for its afternoon cruise.

Once we've bid Warren a grateful good-bye, promising to visit his DC shop next time we're dropping in to the White House, I head over to her.

"Are we going to the hotel now?" she sighs.

"Actually we're not staying the night in Connecticut," I disappoint her. "Rhode Island is just fifty miles away, so we thought it made sense to spend two nights in Newport, what with the bus to sort out and all."

"So we'll be there in about an hour?"

"Not quite," I grimace. "Today is unusual in that we have more than one cake appointment, the rest of the schedule isn't quite so jam-packed. Pardon the pun."

Ravenna holds my gaze. "Where *exactly* are we going next?"

Oh she's going to love this one.

"It's an old mill. Very rustic. We're going to learn how to make Johnny Cakes."

She raises a brow.

"Apparently it's some kind of fried gruel."

"Right," she nods as she gets to her feet. "This time you can leave me in the car." As she walks away she adds a muttered, "And don't bother cracking the window."

Chapter 11

⟿

It feels important to mention, as soon as possible, that the name Johnny Cakes may be the misheard (or slightly slurred) version of "journey cakes," as in an enduring snack you could pop in your sackcloth bag as you set off trekking.

They are not really cakes in the teatime sense, being neither sweet nor spongy. Mostly you find them on the breakfast menus at roadside diners.

"And the primary ingredient is white flint corn?" Pamela peers over my shoulder at my notes.

"Yes, it's one of the main food crops of the Native Indians— they were the originators of this recipe. Which also leads to theories about the name evolving from Shawnee Cake. You can hear the similarity if you say them one after the other."

"Shawnee Cake, Johnny Cake," she repeats. "Oh yes."

"The 'flint' aspect refers to the hard exterior of the kernels, and this particular strain is exclusive to the soils of Rhode Island," I continue, "which happens to be the smallest state in America."

"Bless."

When we arrive at Kenyon's Grist Mill in the little village of Usquepaugh, Ravenna keeps to her word by staying in the car. She can't see any reason to get out since there's just an excess of foliage and a few "ye olde" buildings beside a river.

Of course this doesn't stop her being a pain in the behind. Our charming host—Paul Drumm—is just explaining how the mill was founded in 1696, and showing us the giant granite millstone that grinds corn to flour (apparently stone ground is far superior to modern steel methods, both in terms of texture and preserving the nutrients) when Miley Cyrus's "Wrecking Ball" starts blaring out from the direction of the car.

"Excuse me for a moment." I elect to handle the situation, fighting the urge to take one of the blunt work tools along with me.

I rap on the window. "Headphones break?"

"What?" Ravenna yells over the music. "Can't hear!"

I reach to open the door and she quickly silences the stereo.

"What do you want?" I ask, crouching beside her in my best Supernanny pose.

"What do I want?"

"Well, you are attention-seeking, so here I am—you have my attention."

"I'm bored!" she huffs.

"So?"

"Well, what am I supposed to do for the next hour?"

"Eon not available for a chat now?"

"He's at a show." She lets her head loll back.

"You still have your music, your iPad—"

"Urgh!"

I take a breath. "Do you want to check out the gift shop?"

This is all it would take to perk me up as a child. I must confess I wasn't terribly enamored of nature myself back then. Jessica could amuse herself for hours making daisy chains, but not me. I was always more of the retail therapy persuasion, even if it was just picking out a funny little seaside ornament for my grandparents. I would study every little shell animal, determined to find the one whose eyes were stuck on straight with no wayward globules of glue. Even today, I feel the need to touch every item on the shelves.

"Stone Ground Johnny Cake," I read as I reach for a pack of Kenyon's White Corn Meal, admiring the vintage design—darkest navy background, red etching of the mill, white lettering. "This is what they'll be using to cook with."

To the left of the main building, Paul has set up an outdoor preparation table, just to add to the "simpler times" quality of the process. He seems a very nice man. People who love their work often are.

"So what is Mum trading here?" Ravenna shows a glimmer of curiosity as she follows my gaze.

"Scones," I reply. "We thought it should be something fairly robust; something you could throw in your travel bag that wouldn't fall to pieces along the way."

"Plain scones?"

"We're showing him the Devon cream variety."

"Ahh," Ravenna nods. "The added bonus of clogged arteries."

I pick up a packet of Poison Ivy Relief. It's a horrible thing to be prickled by that plant—major itching and irritation. I wonder if the cure would work on Ravenna?

"Don't get any ideas." She seems to read my mind.

"Did you ever help your mum in the kitchen?" I ask as we move on to the pancake section.

She gives me a look of suspicion. "Of course. When I was a child."

"But not lately?"

"Nope. I've got better things to do with my time now."

Ah, if only she could just remember what those better things are . . .

I wait by the till as she purchases a Scrabble tile bracelet. Bit of a departure from Tiffany's—little squares of wood branded with black letters. All very eco-chic. Then again, I don't know what word she is planning to spell out.

"Shall we go and see how they're getting on?" I ask as we step back into the leafy sunshine.

"You go. I'll wait in the car. With my headphones."

Well, at least she's learning some consideration.

Pamela's scones look a dream—all warm and buttery and golden. The clotted cream and strawberry jam I prearranged are sitting in china ramekins ready to be dolloped. My stomach yawps in delight. But I am not being offered one of those. (The bulk of the batch has already been assigned to a charitable institute in Newport that offers assistance to anyone affiliated with the sea—fishermen, sailors, former Navy personnel, etc. Arby's wife used to volunteer there with her church group and so Gracie thought a donation of freshly baked scones would be a nice touch.)

"Here, try a Johnny Cake." Gracie hands me a small plate featuring an insipid flattened circle the size of a Scotch pancake.

The white of the corn makes it look undercooked, rather too much like a splat of lard.

I take a forkful. Crispy on the outside with a gritty paste of an interior. I can't quite discern a flavor . . .

"Try it with a bit of butter."

I take another bite. Still nothing.

"Now with a drizzle of maple syrup. That's how most folks round here have them."

Better, though the dense, sandy texture does take some getting used to.

"Apparently they are best when there's leftover bacon grease on the hot plate," Pamela explains.

"I see."

"We're having a Johnny Cake Festival here in October with a whole host of varieties," Paul tells us. "Michael over at The Station House Restaurant is doing smoked salmon and crème fraîche."

Goodness! Could Johnny Cakes be the new crêpe? Of course to test this theory I would have to try one with a layer of Nutella, but sadly there's no time to experiment—my discreet phone alarm (set to the tune of "If I Knew You Were Comin' I'd Have Baked a Cake") is already nudging us on our way to Newport . . .

Chapter 12

∽∽∽

"Is it just me or did everything get that little bit more beautiful?"

We've been driving for about twenty minutes through perfectly idyllic countryside, but now I'm getting the sense that the scenery is shifting up a gear.

"Ah, this is just a little *amuse-bouche*," Gracie shimmers with anticipation. "First we cross the bridge to Jamestown . . ."

My chest swells with optimism as we elevate over the blue then enter an island of plush green foliage. We slow at the tollbooth ($2 per axle!), then I feel our collective hearts soar as we ascend the oh-so-elegant Newport suspension bridge, seemingly the gateway to heaven—at one point there is nothing ahead of us but a pale-mint arch and the sheerest blue sky.

Suddenly the ocean below us comes into view and I tumble in love at first sight.

Sapphire sparkling waters expand out as far as the eye can see. To our left the starched white kerchiefs of sailing boats glance across the water's surface, curving around the headland, to the right the pointy masts of moored boats cluster around a lush harbor. Ahead, slashing through the waves in an ostentatious fashion, are the sleek yachts of the nouveaux riche. Looking on with suitably regal disdain is none other than the *Queen Mary 2*. I can almost hear her throaty whistle and feel a silk scarf rippling around my neck.

"Isn't it glorious?" Gracie beams as we get a closer look at Newport's legendary wharf, complete with historic tall ships and low, long rumrunners.

"It truly is," I confirm.

As we transition from the bridge to land, we pass a giant lobster shack (you know you're in New England when . . .) and then a cemetery.

"Arby Poindexter, may he rest in peace." Gracie crosses herself as we pass.

"How long has he been gone?" I ask.

"Just a year or two. Such a shame. But his son has been most helpful with all the bus arrangements. He thinks they should be done with the final modifications by tomorrow."

"What kind of modifications have they been working on?"

"You'll see," she twinkles.

I look to Pamela, who merely shrugs. "God knows what she's been up to this time."

Ravenna, meanwhile, mirrors the stoicism of the *Queen Mary 2*, appearing utterly unmoved. I wonder what it does to your insides being so disconnected from life? I mean, if you're holding in all the wonder, the curiosity, the enjoyment—where does it go? Perhaps she's saving it up for the next *Hunger Games* movie.

"This is America's Cup Avenue," Gracie announces as we meet with a blaze of white sterns.

"I see everyone is dressed accordingly!"

Breton stripes seem to be a kind of uniform here. I have to confess it's one of my favorite looks: so fresh and sporty, so Brigitte Bardot.

"Red, white and blue looks good on everyone," Pamela opines.

And you just can't have enough anchor and knotted rope motifs when you're this close to the water.

"Look at that T-shirt logo," Pamela points ahead. "HOLY SHIP!"

Even Ravenna gives a little snuffle at this one.

"You better watch your blasphemy now," Gracie cautions as we pull into a spot outside a large redbrick building. "This is the Seamen's Church Institute."

"Ready to come aboard, Pamela?"

"Oh no, you go in," she shrinks back. "We're just dropping off the scones, aren't we?"

"Okay," I contain my sigh. "I'll just be a minute."

Lugging the teatime donation, I follow the sign welcoming "Mariners & Visitors" and head up the entrance steps, expecting to find assorted sea-ravaged characters grouped at plastic trestle tables. Instead I discover a wood-paneled lobby worthy of Captain Cook. Directly ahead of me is a marble fireplace with a shapely antique grate, above which hangs a lovely old map of Narragansett Bay in warm oranges, yellows and aquas, lit by a brass chandelier. Now that's a cozy respite after being tossed around the high seas.

"Hello!" I call into the kitchen. "Anyone home?"

Nothing.

I set down my wares on the counter and then curiosity gets the better of me and I find myself tiptoeing up the stairs for a snoop. The first room I enter is the library, entirely stocked with maritime-themed tomes—*Courage at Sea*, *Bligh*, *Unsinkable*. I'm just reaching for *Voyages to Paradise* when I hear a voice coming from the next room. Perhaps it's my contact, Deedra?

"Knock knock!"

I creak open the door and find myself interrupting some kind of prayer group.

"Oh! I'm so sorry!" I say backing out and directly into a woman with a white-blonde bob.

"May I help you?"

"Yes, yes, sorry! I'm Laurie Davis, I was just dropping off the scones for the sailors. And you. And anyone really. They're downstairs . . ." I trail off.

She smiles. "Come show me."

Her eyes light up as I lift the lid. "They're really best served warmed and then you cut them down the middle and spread a thick layer of clotted cream and then strawberry jam. There's a tub of each in the cooler here."

"These will be very much appreciated," she nods. "A nice change from soup! Are you in town for long?"

"Two nights."

"Well, if Miss Pamela does any more baking . . ."

"As a matter of fact, we have another session tomorrow. I'm sure we could bring over a few extra items, say around three P.M.?"

"Oh that's so kind! Thank you! We'll alert our local groups, have a proper English tea."

"Wonderful!"

I step out feeling like we're doing a very good deed. Or should that be good Deedra?

"All set?" Gracie is keen to continue in tour mode as she steers us away from the waterfront and up through the center of town. "Now this is really something. I'm going to take you down Bellevue Avenue." She sighs as we enter a dreamy, sun-dappled utopia.

"Gorgeous trees," I murmur, taking in the majesty of the giant oaks, horse chestnuts and voluminously draping weeping beeches.

"These are the Newport skyscrapers," Gracie quips. "And this was *the* summer address for the super-rich of the Gilded Age."

And when she says "super-rich," she's not kidding. Imagine Britain's finest stately homes set one after another, just a block apart.

"This is incredible!" I coo. "I had no idea there were so many mansions here."

Of course, some are fancier than the others—one minute you're looking at an immaculate white colonial clapboard with glossy black shutters and the brightest green lawn, the next a grand Italian palazzo, then a spooky-looking Gothic creation looms into view.

"Look to your left," Gracie advises. "You'll see Rosecliff."

"Looks familiar," Pamela squints at the pretty, snow-white building with its elegant central loggia/ballroom and burbling fountain, positively crying out for a wedding.

"That's where they filmed the original Gatsby movie, with Robert Redford. Talk about a golden boy! People used to say Georgie looked like him. I think it was the hair—thick as a rug. More like a dog's coat, really."

"Do people actually live in these places?"

"For the most part. A number are open to the public. They're even letting us into a couple, aren't they Laurie?"

Before I can reply, Pamela jumps forward in her seat. "Oh, look at this one! Mum, can you stop a minute? There's nobody behind us."

I watch Pamela gawp at the former summer "cottage" of William and Alva Vanderbilt.

"That's Marble House," I tell her. "It's modeled on the Petit Trianon in Versailles, though of course there's nothing *petit* about it—that's 500,000 cubic feet of Italy's finest right there."

"Wow."

Gracie highlights the colossal Corinthian columns of the front portico and admires the circular driveway, brimming with confetti-petalled hydrangeas.

"Do you like *Downton Abbey*?" I turn to Ravenna.

"S'okay."

I'll take that as a yes. "This is where the inspiration for Cora's character came from—the Dollar Princesses. Consuelo Vanderbilt was one—sent to marry an English duke, trading her family's fortune for a title. But I'll tell you all about that tomorrow."

Finally I get to announce one of the biggest coups of the trip: "Pamela—this is where you'll be baking tomorrow."

"What?"

"They're letting us use the mansion kitchens for the afternoon—a little trip back to 1892."

"You're kidding?" She gawps. "Gosh, I'm glad I packed my whites! So what's the recipe?"

"Well, for a Marble House I thought a Marble Cake!"

"Oh, I love it!" she clasps her hands together. "I can't wait."

We're nearing the bend at the end of the avenue, when Gracie takes a second pause and asks, "Ravenna, what can you see through those gates?"

She turns huffily but is sufficiently surprised to exclaim, "Camels!"

"Live ones?" I say, leaning across Pamela and spying no less than three, all the more surreal for having an ocean backdrop—mirage upon mirage.

"These are topiary but there used to be a couple of live ones roaming the grounds."

"Whose house is this?"

"Doris Duke, the tobacco heiress. The camels were part of a trade when she bought a private jet from Adnan Khashoggi."

My brow scrunches. "That name rings a bell . . ."

"Saudi businessman and arms dealer?" Gracie nudges my memory. "Dodi Fayed is his nephew."

"Gosh! So this history is a little more recent?"

Gracie nods. "She only died about twenty years ago. The house is just as she left it. There's an exhibition there I know you'd like—it showcases her world travels, along with her Louis Vuitton steamer trunk and all her passport photos throughout the years, blown up to poster-size."

"Gosh, I don't know how I'd feel about that," I cringe. Mine are definitely less jet set, more mug shot.

"She was quite a woman," Gracie whistles as we move on. "Both Lauren Bacall and Susan Sarandon have played her in movies, which I think gives you a small insight into her bold persona."

We take a couple more curves, then the vista opens out as we merge into Ocean Drive with its present-day properties.

When you're so busy with your life, focusing on making it to your next payday, you forget just how fantastically rich some people are. The house ahead of us has at least eight chimneys and what appears to be a private golf course for a front lawn. Well, why not, eh?

"How many bedrooms do you think these places have?" Pamela queries. "Ten? Twenty?"

"I don't think I know enough people to fill a Newport holiday home."

"Trust me, when you've got this kind of money, you find yourself with an awful lot of friends."

"Well, I suppose it's no good having all this if you don't share it. I mean, what are you going to do? Sleep in a different bedroom every couple of weeks just to ring the changes? You'd want to fill it or it would seem a bit echoey and lonely." I muse for a minute. "Do you think they invite people to stay in the same way that we might suggest meeting someone for coffee? You encounter some fun new people and say, 'Come for the weekend!'"

"That's what happened with Georgie and Arby. He was in

England for a limited time, he wanted to chat more about the London busses, he was grateful for Georgie's help with his purchase and he didn't think twice about having us in his home."

"What was it like?" I gurgle.

"A cross between a fairy-tale castle and the Ritz," she decides. "On the second night they held a party to introduce everyone to their 'new friends from England.' We were quite the toast of the town!" She peers ahead. "His house is coming up next, though of course there are different owners now."

We catch a glimpse through a stone archway of a Bavarian-themed fantasy—all twisting towers, curved balconies and decorative crenellations.

"They had this beautiful pool, right on the edge of the sea; you felt as if you could swim out to forever. Which reminds me, you know The Breakers—"

"Breakers?" Ravenna pipes up.

"It's not a hip-hop dance crew, dear, it's Newport's ritziest mansion."

"Oh."

"They have this bath hewn from a single piece of marble, and it has four taps—two were for hot and cold running *sea*water!"

"Speaking of which," Ravenna bristles. "Where exactly is the sea? Or do you have to own a mansion to get to see it?"

"Patience." Gracie hushes her.

Two more sweeping bends in the road and there it is—flowing out like some socialite's slinky-silky gown in the most exquisite shade of midnight blue.

Chapter 13

❧

I've driven coastal routes before, but none so close and so *level* with the water. Here there's no barrier between tide and tarmac, just a grassy verge dotted with benches and strutting seagulls. At one point a wave rears up onto the rocks and sprays our windscreen.

"Now this is where I want a picture of me driving the bus," Gracie announces as she applies the wipers. "I'm going to send it out with this year's Christmas card!"

Pamela reaches for her mum's shoulder and gives it a squeeze. "I recognize it now—this is where you took that picture with Dad, isn't it?"

She nods and points to a wall of rocks snaking out to sea. "If you three stood there and all took pictures as I passed by, I'm sure one would be just perfect."

"We'll be like paparazzi!" I laugh.

"God how embarrassing!" Ravenna mutters.

"Concerned what all the elderly leaf tourists will think of you?" I raise a brow.

Pamela intercepts any comeback from Ravenna by pointing ahead to a row of little beach houses set upon their own stretch of sand.

"Can you imagine?"

"You don't have to," I tell her.

"What do you mean?"

"That's where we're staying. Isn't that right, Gracie?"

"I can't believe it!" She seems genuinely giddy. "The Castle Hill Inn! What a dream!"

We're wending down the hotel driveway now. And if I've learned one thing in my travels, it's the longer the driveway, the more exclusive the property.

That said, compared to all the grand mansions we've just seen, the main building here looks more like a quirky guesthouse, with its jutting porches, higgledy-piggledy levels and bell-shaped turret. It's made of wood, not marble, and painted an unassuming beige. But then you discover the *pièce de résistance*—it stands upon its own forty-acre peninsula. Complete with dinky lighthouse.

Plus there's the cut-above welcome: Personal. Charming. Privileged. Everything will be taken care of while we enjoy a glass of champagne and that exceptional vantage point . . .

Ravenna brightens for a second as we approach the outdoor bar, until she realizes a) she has been relegated to sparkling cider and b) U.S. cider translates as apple juice and is thus nonalcoholic. What a swizz.

Glasses in hand, we roam beyond the deck, down to the white Adirondack chairs spaced around the slope of lawn that leads, via a tumble of rocks, to the glimmering sea.

Ravenna chooses to sit apart from us, hoodie yanked low over her face, headphones emitting a tinny blare of defiance.

I pretend she's listening to Frank Sinatra, wooing her reluctant spirit with the laid-back, tilted-trilby vocals of "Summer Wind." I have that song on loop in my mind as I look out across the bay to the bridge we so recently drove in on. A white sailing boat is sliding by, attaching to my heartstrings as it crosses the golden path laid out by the peach-on-fire sun.

"I'll say one thing for the super-rich, they sure know how to pick a holiday spot."

Speaking of which, I can't believe we've never covered Newport on Va-Va-Vacation! Especially with the *Downton* connection.

Apparently The Elms even offers a "Servant Life" tour. I must talk to Krista about this: I think there's a definite market for a more genteel experience. Especially one with such pretty skies.

"I don't know the last time I saw a sunset . . ." Pamela whispers in a trance.

The sky responds by amping up its gold backlighting. The clouds are unusually long and streaky, with random flourishes like the expressions of a modern dance troupe. Blue becomes indigo, orange rages to red, the gold brightens to a glare.

"Best show in town," Gracie raves.

"A toast," Pamela leans forward and raises her glass. "To new beginnings in New England."

"And to old friends," Gracie adds.

"To Georgie," I smile. Even though I've never met him, I love the sound of him.

We take a sip and then give a rueful look in Ravenna's direction.

"Do you think she's going to be like this the whole time?" Pamela frets.

"She is a willful child," Gracie notes. "She'll certainly try to maintain the disdain as long as is humanly possible."

"Well, you never know," I say, already feeling the effects of the champagne. "Travel has a way of transforming people, even when they are at their most resistant."

Gracie's lips purse. "Let's just hope it's for the better."

Even though it's getting a little chilly, the ever-changing colors of the sunset hold us in position. I don't want this moment to end. Ravenna, on the other hand, has already headed off to unpack. I should join her; I do have to change for dinner. And I will. Just five minutes more of this burnished glory . . .

Trotting down the path to our beach house in the now dim, powdery light, I decide upon my white linen sundress, the navy cardi with the big anchor buttons and a sheeny red lip. At the very least I shall coordinate with the other wharfies.

"Knock, knock." I turn the key in the latch but no sooner am I through the door, I find myself stalling. "Oh my!"

Not because I've caught Ravenna in a compromising position (she's nowhere to be seen), but because I am in the presence of such tasteful, grown-up design.

The floors are a honeyed hardwood, the walls whitewashed, the loft-style ceiling painted the most serene hyacinth blue. The four-poster is hefty and masculine, sans canopy, but with duvet and pillows puffed to cloud status. There's a stained mahogany armoire, a coffee table and a large brown leather sofa, all of a reassuringly classic persuasion.

I bet Ravenna wants to get out her spray can and graffiti the entire place, including the sea view that now draws me forward.

Oohhh, a fireplace. My hand reaches to touch the textured slate chimney breast. Nothing makes me swoon like a fireplace. And this one is directly opposite the bed. What could be toastier?

There's even a little kitchenette with state-of-the-art coffee-making facilities, further fueling the fantasy that I have just arrived at my new apartment.

"Yes, I took a place by the sea," I shall tell people. "Everyone needs a little time away from the city."

I ease open the patio door and step onto the deck, taking a moment to listen to the waves' rolling breath and the respondent drag of the shingle. It's so peaceful here. So soothing. Right up until the point at which Ravenna emerges from the bathroom in a billow of fragrant steam.

"Oh, you're here."

"Mm-hmm," I say as I make a beeline for my suitcase, foraging for my canvas wedges. Got one. I'll have quite the peg-leg walk if I can't find the other. I reach deeper within the folds of fabric until my fingertips meet with woven rope.

"So you're not speaking to me now?" Ravenna snips as I pass her en route to the bathroom.

"I didn't think you were speaking to anyone," I say without looking back.

I've been here a million times before. The more you pander, the more they pout. Best let them come to you.

"It's all right for you, you want to be here," she calls after me.

I stick my head around the door. "Why don't you just decide that this is what you want too?"

"Like it's that easy."

"Says the princess from her four-poster," I tut. "Take a look around you, Ravenna. There are worst places to be."

"It's not the place, exactly, it's the company."

"Oh. Thanks for that."

"I don't mean you. In particular."

I frown back at her. "You know, I never met anyone who didn't like their granny before. Mothers yes, but—"

"She started it."

"What's that supposed to mean?"

"She doesn't like me." She tugs at her robe. "She doesn't want me here."

"Maybe if you tried showing an interest in the things that mean so much to her . . ."

"Like old buildings?"

"You know, honestly, it's hokum that you're planning a career in interior design if you're not interested in seeing these miraculous time capsules. Not pictures, not artifacts in museums, but a first-hand experience of how people *lived*—"

"How the elite lived."

"The elite are your future clients," I remind her. "Poor folk don't hire interior decorators. Not unless they're getting a freebie on a TV show."

She shrugs. "It's not my taste."

"It's not about you. Are you going to listen to your clients' needs and wants, or are you just going to give them signature Ravenna every time?"

"If they choose me they'll be choosing my style."

"Do you even know what that is?"

She looks affronted. "I don't have to explain myself to you."

"No, you don't." I really should be getting ready. I return to the bathroom and set my toilet bag on the glossy white sink. Right . . .

"I just don't see how it's relevant."

I know I should just let it go, step into the shower and sluice off my irritation—from multiple directions given all the jet op-tions. But I can't let it lie yet.

I walk back to the nearest corner of the bed.

"I suppose you like Kelly Wearstler?"

Ravenna concedes a nod. "She's cool."

I thought she'd like her—she's basically the supermodel of the interior design world, with a host of celebrity hotels and clients to her credit. I actually love her esthetic. She did the Bergdorf Goodman restaurant in New York in these sublime hues of duck-egg blue and olive. If I'm going there for afternoon tea, I book way in advance so I can cozy up in one of the French canopy chairs—they make me feel as if I'm on a secret assignation.

"What about her?" Ravenna is impatient.

"I was just thinking maybe you'd like to have your own book or two one day, just like her."

"I wouldn't mind."

"Do you know that the author of the first ever interior design book designed the bedrooms down the road at The Breakers?"

She looks mildly curious. "Who was that?"

"Ogden Codman Junior."

"Who?"

"He was an architect from Boston." And then I casually add: "He co-wrote the book with Edith Wharton. Have you heard of her?"

She nods. "We did *Age of Innocence* at school."

"Well, she summered here in Newport, from when she was a tot."

I wait for the "coo" of wonder that this is, in a sense, where it all began, but all I get is a "So?"

My jaw clenches. I'm done.

Chapter 14

❧

And so to the wharf. It's an interesting mix of tourists and locals, restaurants and boutiques, upmarket charm and ye olde pirate hideaway—there's even a tavern called the Black Pearl. Though what Captain Jack Sparrow would make of all the yachtie types in their belted shorts and pastel polo shirts, I don't know.

"Mum, look!"

For a second Ravenna forgets to be sullen and shut-down, so dazzled is she by an entire window filled with outsize cupcakes sparkling blush and lavender.

"Are they real?"

We all peer closer looking for clues amid the glitter, only to realize we are looking into a fancy beauty shop.

"Bath bombs," I conclude. "You know those things that fizz and go crazy when you add them to water?"

"Ohhhh!" Pamela and Gracie nod understanding.

"Can we go inside?" Ravenna asks.

"After dinner."

"Won't it be closed?"

"All the shops here stay open late," Gracie assures her.

We follow some poshly boisterous spirits to the Clarke Cooke House (which has a reputation for hosting the swankiest of the sailing crowd) and opt for the waterfront dining option, both for its scenic aspect and its name: The Candy Store.

As with the beauty shop, there are no *actual* sugary confections at large, just plenty of candy-colored director's chairs in gobstopper pink, lemon-sherbet yellow and flying-saucer turquoise, set around white-clothed tables.

We are positioned near the "missing wall" overlooking the harbor and beside the bar—a grand, wood-paneled affair with a low ceiling fan and mirrored backdrop. Silver champagne buckets glisten on the countertop, chilly with condensation. Cashmere sweaters drape over shoulders. Everyone has good hair. Pamela dubs it Sloanes-by-the-Sea, but without the snobbery.

While studying the booze selection for inspiration, I see a couple perched on bar stools displaying intense "someone's getting lucky tonight" body language and feel a tug of longing for that heady state of first-date flirtation when you're feeling giddily tipsy and entranced, bodies cleaving toward one another, heavy with anticipation of the spinning surrender to come . . .

"Is there a local cocktail you could recommend?" I rasp. I may need a couple.

"Dark and Stormy," Gracie points to the menu. "Dark rum and ginger beer."

"Is that what you're having?"

"Actually, I'm going to try the Newport Water."

Which sounds all very pure and abstaining until you read that it is, in fact, a mix of Veuve Clicquot Yellow Label champagne, Grand Marnier and St-Germain (a sophisticated elderflower liqueur).

"Ooh, I like the sound of that!" enthuses Pamela.

"Ravenna?"

"I'll just have a glass of seawater, perhaps with a dash of leaked engine fuel?"

I can't help but have a little chuckle.

At least she can't complain about the food.

"This is the best swordfish I've ever eaten," I announce. Aside from the fact that it is cooked to juicy perfection, it comes served with minuscule baubles of couscous and a spoonful of aubergine caponata. "Just delicious."

"Same goes double for the clam chowder," Gracie raves. "Taste it." She offers me a spoon.

"Oh." I wince. "I don't know about clams."

"Have you ever had them?"

"Not on purpose." I look around me. "I don't know if I should say this out loud in New England, but I'm not really much of a seafood person."

"Just taste it." She is determined.

Slimy, salty, chewy and inducing of the gag reflex.

That is what I was expecting.

Instead my taste buds are met with a light but hearty, creamy but fresh delight.

"What's that herb?" I ask.

"Dill."

"And these little white cubes?"

"Potato."

"Oh, it's so yummy!"

I can't even taste the clam.

"I knew you'd like it." Gracie is smug.

"Do you think they used to serve it at the mansions, you know, back in the day?"

"Well, it's actually rather interesting about the food." Gracie dabs her mouth with her napkin. "French cuisine was held in the highest regard, so it was all French chefs presenting their food *à la française*, which was basically an extremely lavish buffet display. But then fashions changed and the Vanderbilts led the way by serving *à la russe*."

"Russe?" I frown.

"Russian style."

"Gosh, whatever is that?" I ask, imagining a chain of Cossacks circling the table shouting "Hah!" as each domed plate cover is removed.

"Well, it's actually what we are used to today: being served one course at a time."

"Oh."

"The significant difference being they had eight courses."

"What?" I splutter, secretly envious.

"They began with oysters, then soup, then fish, meat and two vegetables, the entrée, some kind of alcoholic sorbet before the roast—"

"A roast on top of meat and two veg?"

She nods. "Then a salad and dessert. Never mind the wines and coffees and the cognacs . . ."

"That's bonkers."

"But!" She pauses for emphasis. "All of this was served at such a pace that you were lucky to get a bite. No sooner was the last plate set down than they began to remove the rest and serve the next course."

"You're joking!"

Gracie shakes her head. "One young girl was advised by her father to keep a finger on the plate while she was eating, lest it be whipped away."

I'm reeling. "So you could sit down to a never-ending banquet and leave the table hungry?"

"As was frequently the case," Gracie confirms. "They even

went so far as to say that the greatest pleasure you got from the food was watching it all come and go."

"Talk about a feast for the eyes," I quip.

"Bet the servants enjoyed the leftovers," Ravenna smirks.

"They probably ate better than their employers and assorted royals."

I turn to Pamela, surprised that she hasn't voiced a response, and find her looking distracted. Again.

"Everything all right?" I check with her as our plates are cleared away. (With every last morsel scraped from them.)

She looks undecided, then leans forward. "I think I should probably tell you . . . No," she corrects herself, "I *want* to tell you. Before you read about it . . ." She waits for the waitress to finish up and then begins anew: "My husband and I—"

"Ex-husband," snips Ravenna.

"Ex?" I query.

"Not yet." She grimaces. "But yes, we're getting a divorce."

"Can I go to the shops now?" Ravenna gets to her feet. "You can call me when you're done."

"Yes, yes." Pamela waves off her daughter.

Now I feel guilty for being so mean to her. Her parents are splitting up. She's playing up. Not that it's any excuse but . . .

I turn back to Pamela. "I'm really sorry to hear that."

"No, no. It's—"

"Long overdue," Gracie cuts in. "Long, *long*—"

"All right, Mum!" Pamela tenses.

I bite my lip.

"It's one of the reasons I was so eager to get away. And get Ravenna away."

I nod.

"I have a feeling that Brian might not behave in the most dignified manner."

"That's an understatement," Gracie mutters. "The man is the antithesis of dignity—a mean-spirited, parasitic—"

"Mum, please."

"You don't agree?" she challenges.

"Wholeheartedly, but I'm trying to maintain a neutrality for Ravenna's sake."

"Ravenna's not here."

"Well, I don't want to get into the habit of bad-mouthing him."

"That's commendable," I opine.

"It's also part of the problem," Gracie counters.

"What's that supposed to mean?" Pamela huffs.

"You never said out loud all the awful, humiliating—"

"Um!" I scrape back my chair. "I think I might go and check on Ravenna."

"No," Pamela reaches for my arm. "Don't leave on our account. We can contain our bickering."

"But you shouldn't have to."

"I don't want to argue," Pamela reasons.

"Again. Part of the problem."

Pamela closes her eyes, desperate to shut it all out.

Only now does Gracie see that she's gone too far.

She gets to her feet. "I think I'm going to go and see if I can get Ravenna to eat one of those exploding cupcakes."

I wait until she's out of earshot and then scoot my chair closer. "Pamela—"

"I'm so embarrassed!" She covers her face with her hands.

"There's no need to be," I soothe, lightly touching her forearm. "Not now, and regardless of what happens on this trip."

Her face remains covered.

"We're in this together," I tell her. "We've got a cake sisterhood going here: that's a pretty strong bond."

She peeks out at me. "I just feel such a wreck at the moment. I'm all over the place."

"It's perfectly understandable. I think it's so brave of you to undertake a trip like this with so much going on in your personal life."

"I thought it would be a good distraction, and the publishers were adamant about it being now or never—"

"That's why we're going to make it work," I assert. "And I really think it will. I know you've had some glimmers of joy already—with Charlie at the Waldorf, that slice of Mystic Pizza, tonight's champagne sunset . . ."

"I have," she acknowledges. "I just feel like I'm being attacked from every angle."

"You have to tune them out. We can use some mini-marshmallows as earplugs if it comes to it."

She snuffles a smile then reaches for my hand. "Thank you for being so nice."

I give a little "no problem" shrug.

She reaches for the menu. "Shall we order some dessert?"

"I thought you'd never ask," I reply. "And I think you should try one of these Dark and Stormy cocktails. For research."

"Research?"

"I was thinking how great a rum and ginger cupcake would be, especially for the sailors . . ."

Now she really brightens. "You're on!"

Later, back at the beach house, I try broaching the subject with Ravenna.

"I'm sorry to hear about your parents' divorce," I say as I light the fire, hoping to create a comforting vibe.

She doesn't even look up from her phone.

"If you want to talk about it—"

"Why would I want to talk about it with you?"

She has a point.

"No reason," I concede. "Other than I'm here." And then I shake my head. "You're right. I just wanted to say I was sorry."

"Thank you," she snarks. "That makes it all better."

Chapter 15

Next morning I wake up way ahead of my alarm. Ordinarily I might re-squish my pillow and settle back down, but the second I recall our private cove I'm out of bed.

I open the patio door with the stealth of a cat burglar, take a quick look back at Ravenna—no movement. Crossing the fibrous deck, I creak down the steps and transfer onto the cold, wet sand. The sensation thrills the soles of my bare feet, luring me to the edge of the discreetly lapping water.

I have to say, paddling at this hour feels slightly illicit—possibly because I am still in my pajamas. I look back at the other beach houses to see if any curtains are drawn or lights on. And that's when I notice a figure on the rocks.

"Gracie! What are you doing up?" I gasp as I take in her form, elegantly draped in a silver silk robe, as if she is waiting to be painted by some world-renowned artist with a wiry beard.

"I wanted to make the most of every moment here," she sighs.

"Oh, me too!"

Together we take in the straggles of seaweed on the shore, the slanting layers of the low-lying rocks and the translucent blue of the early morning sky.

"Are you a walker, Laurie?"

"Well," I take a moment to decide. "I am an honorary New Yorker, so I suppose I'd have to say yes."

She beckons me closer. "I know Pamela won't want to come and Ravenna will sleep through breakfast . . ."

"What did you have in mind?" I'm curious.

"Cliff Walk."

"Is that as perilous as it sounds?"

"Yes and no."

"Yes and no?" I wasn't expecting that answer.

"Are there opportunities to plunge to your death, yes. Will that be our fate? No."

"How can you be sure?"

"Because we'll stick to the path."

"Okay . . ." I say. Sounds simple enough.

I manage to get into my jeans, sweatshirt and purple Converse without prompting so much as a stir in Ravenna. As I head out to the car, I scrape my sleep-mussed hair into a Pebbles ponytail. All I need now is a baseball hat. I look so ridiculously sports bar next to Gracie's neutral-hued Dame Judi drapery. Not that she bats an eye. I suppose she's seen worse on Ravenna.

Gracie takes an alternative route to Ocean Drive now, weaving us inland past ever more mansions, but also some ragged fields and farm shacks.

"Gracie?"

"Yes?"

"Did I just see a llama?"

"Yes, dear. They've got all sorts here. That's Hammersmith Farm, childhood home of Jackie O. It's where she and JFK had their wedding reception. Obviously before she became an O."

We pass Fort Adams and a new perspective on the marina, then cruise up Memorial Boulevard—the broadest artery of the city.

"Now. There are several access points to Cliff Walk," Gracie informs me as we crest the hill. "But begin at the beginning, I say."

"Oh wow!" I gasp as we're greeted by the wide-open sprawl of a beach.

"Easton's Beach." She smiles at its sandy curve.

I'm surprised to see so many surfers bobbing astride their boards, especially when the waters seem so placid.

"You'll be even more surprised when you see them up close," Gracie gets a twinkle in her eye.

"What do you mean?" I look back at their lithe, licorice-clad bodies.

It's only when a couple of guys come over to load up their car that I see their salty tufts of hair are silver-gray.

"Are they all that age?" I whisper.

"From what I remember from my last visit, yes!"

"I can't believe it. They look so limber and healthy!" And handsome too, I think to myself. "There must be something in the water here."

"Yes," Gracie titters. "Senior citizens!"

The path ahead of us is spilling over with fragrant honeysuckle, delicate pink dog roses and sprays of miniature daisies. Less picturesque are the "CAUTION" signs showing a figure pitching headfirst into the abyss.

Welcome to Cliff Walk.

It's actually not that risky. Though there are undeniably opportunities for you to come a cropper, there is no pressing need to do so. The path is broad and stable and, after a certain point, even offers handrails.

"You know how yesterday we drove past the front gates of the mansions?" Gracie takes my arm. "Now we're going to walk along the back of them."

"Really?" I'm intrigued. "Will we get a glimpse of any?"

"Oh yes," she confirms. "You'll see."

That's if I can prize my eyes away from the shimmering ocean— it's as if Mr. Swarovski himself cast a million crystals across the water's surface, leaving me blinking in bedazzlement. We have a better vantage point of the beach from up here and the little town beyond, complete with English-village-style church spire.

"Morning!"

"Morning!"

We exchange greetings with fellow early risers, including a joyful array of lolloping dogs.

I can't imagine this being my regular morning jaunt. Would you ever become blasé, I wonder, or would you start every day chanting, "I'm the luckiest person in the world!"

"Quite breathtaking, isn't it?" Gracie notices my awe.

"I love how curvy it is; you never know what's around the next . . ." I come to a halt. There's a mansion right there in front of us, completely accessible, not even a "Keep Off the Grass" sign. "Don't the owners mind people ambling around their back lawn?"

"This is actually one of the university buildings now."

"You can study here?" I practically pass out with longing.

Gracie chuckles. "I thought you'd like it."

"Less so that!" I point ahead to a modern block monstrosity.

"We have to count ourselves lucky that the fancy building is still standing. They tried to demolish a lot of the treasures to build apartments."

"Nooo!" I'm scandalized.

"Don't worry, nothing can touch the jewel in Newport's crown." Gracie leads me on and then, with a grand flourish, presents a vast burgundy-roofed villa with all manner of ornate archways, colonnades and balustrades—not to mention acres and acres of methodically mown lawn.

"This is The Breakers," she announces. "Built by Cornelius Vanderbilt II in 1893. For twelve million dollars."

"In today's money?"

"About three hundred and fifty million."

"Wow," I gawp, stepping up to the wire fencing, hooking my fingers in the wire so I can peer a little closer. "Is it really as lavish as they say?"

"Way beyond lavish. Beyond Gatsby even. There's one room that has these silver wall panels and the preservationists couldn't understand why they never tarnished, until they discovered they were coated in platinum."

"Talk about one-upmanship!" I chuckle. "I can't wait to see inside!"

"But we're going to start with Marble House?"

"Yes, I wanted to save the glitziest till last, in a vain attempt to blow Ravenna's mind."

Gracie rolls her eyes. "You'd think with her interest in interior design . . ."

"You'd think."

"Shall we take a wee break by The Breakers?"

We head to a bench on the stepped lookout point and sit for a while in companionable silence. When Gracie speaks again, her tone has softened.

"I didn't mean to upset Pamela last night."

I glance her way.

"I try to bite my tongue but every now and again . . ."

"I understand."

"Years of frustration."

"Mmm-hmm."

"Anyway, I'm glad you were there," she pats my hand, "you know, to offer her some support. It's a very trying time, and things could get trickier before this trip is through."

Trickier? "In what way?" I ask.

Gracie looks as if she's about to tell me something. Something specific and significant. But instead she withdraws her hand and favors ambiguity: "You know, as a mother, you always want the best for your child. It's hard when you see them making choices that take them in the opposite direction."

"I know," I tell her as I tuck the wind-ruffled strands of hair behind my ear. "Not that I'm a mother, but I had one just like that."

"Really?"

I nod but don't go into further detail.

"It's not easy, is it?" She sighs. "Georgie used to tell me not to interfere—that it was Pamela's life and she had to make her own mistakes. But even he said, just before he passed on, that he didn't like leaving her as she was. He had hoped things would have changed for her by then. He didn't want to say good-bye when she was still so unhappy."

"So things have been bad for a while?"

"Not that she ever complains. I don't think she even feels entitled to."

"I've made my bed?"

"Exactly." Her eyes meet mine. "Did you ever try to intervene, with your mother and—?"

"My sister." I complete the sentence. "Oh yes. All the time. But ultimately I think I was just a second source of stress for her."

"So you wish you'd done things differently?"

"I don't know what I could have done, short of hiring the Albanian gang from *Taken* to snatch my sister."

Gracie raises a brow.

"It's this film with Liam Neeson."

"I know the film," she replies. "I'm just wondering if that gang really is for hire."

I chuckle. "It seems simple, doesn't it?—this person is ruining the other person's life so we must separate them. But it's a hard bond to break, mother–child. Harder even than husband–wife."

Gracie nods.

"And it seems they must make the choice themselves or they will fight it all the more."

"Pamela won't hear a bad word said about Ravenna," Gracie concurs. "Even when she is evil incarnate."

I sigh. "Mothers seem to have an infinite capacity to withstand hurt from their children. All they see is their pain and I think they feel responsible for it, as if it is their fault that the child in question is feeling so bad and acting so selfishly—and thus the very least they can do is take it."

"But is that any way to live?"

"No, of course not. But you know what they say—if you keep doing what you're doing, you're going to keep getting what you're getting."

"That's just it," Gracie turns toward me. "I don't know how much longer I'm going to be around, and if it's not me interfering, helping to break the pattern, then who? I can't stand the thought of this going on and on ad infinitum." She lowers her voice as a couple pause beside us to take in the view. "I thought this trip might at least give Pamela the chance to start thinking in a different way, to see that she has other options, but I wasn't counting on Ravenna being a part of it."

"That is unfortunate."

"To say the least. It makes things very complicated. Very complicated indeed . . ."

I study Gracie's troubled face. "Is there something I should know?"

She looks back at me. Uncertain. Conflicted. "You seem like a nice girl, I don't want to burden you."

"Well, if it's something that is going to affect our itinerary . . ."

She grimaces. "It's just . . ."

"Yes?"

"I've been meddling," she whispers.

"In what way?"

"I can't say exactly, not yet." She pauses. "I don't know if Pamela has any inkling, I have to imagine it's crossed her mind, but, well, I just want you to be prepared."

"For what?"

"For anything."

I wait for her to expand on this dramatic vagueness, but instead she gets to her feet and brisks, "Anyway, no point in worrying now."

"You realize I'll be doing nothing but worrying unless you tell me?" I scuttle after her.

"It'll probably come to nothing," she wafts her hand. "And it's certainly of no concern today."

"Well, that's good to know." At least one day out of the next week should be smooth sailing.

Gracie stops suddenly. "Unless—should I call it off? This thing—"

"This thing you can't tell me anything about?"

I wonder how she expects me to answer when I have so little information. Of course I know her intentions are good. And I know things need to change for Pamela and Ravenna. However much that may inconvenience me.

I take a breath. "I think you should do everything in your power to make a difference."

"Really?" she looks encouraged.

"I regret every day not doing more to protect my mother. An Albanian gang would be too good for my sister. I should have done the deed myself."

Gracie reaches over and touches my face. "Then you'll stick with us, no matter what?"

"No matter what," I confirm.

Chapter 16

❧

As predicted, Ravenna skips breakfast. Well, when your stomach is that concave, I'm guessing you've got to be pretty selective about which days you choose to eat.

In a bid to redress the balance, I partake of a double portion. And then it falls to me to chivvy her up.

"You need to be dressed in five minutes," I tell her as I re-enter the beach house.

"I am dressed!" she protests.

"Cut-off denim shorts with pockets hanging lower than the fraying hem do not a mansion tour outfit make," I tut under my breath.

"Do you know that the women who summered here in Newport's heyday used to change up to seven times a day?"

She looks back at me. "Is that a hint?"

"They had a breakfast outfit, another for lunch, tea, dinner—and of course tennis and swimming have their particulars. Even walking required an oversized feather bonnet. And that's all before we get into the dozens of one-of-a-kind ball gowns commissioned for each season," I rattle on.

"So you think I should change?"

"Well," I grimace. "We may not be dining with the Astors, but I think a level of respect would be nice."

"Such as?" she huffs impatiently.

"Do you have any dresses?"

She holds up two options.

"Any dresses not made out of T-shirt material bearing offensive language?"

The only F-word on this trip should be frosting.

We end up with a compromise—my white broderie anglaise skirt worn as a strapless dress with a studded belt and clompy black boots.

I'd do anything to drag a comb through the straggles of her half-up, half-down hair, but I don't want to push my luck.

I myself opt for a tea dress, which instantly meets with Gracie's approval.

"My mother had a frock with just the same print," she says as she inspects the apricot chintz. "Is this vintage?"

"Vintage style," I tell her. "I was spoiled for choice in my twenties, but now I can only fit into the beaded cardis—I can't believe how teeny-tiny the waists were back then."

"Well, I'll tell you something about that," Gracie motions for us to get into the car. "This fashion curator once explained to me that the reason historical displays of clothes are dominated by petite sizes is that those were the garments that tended to survive intact, whereas the larger sizes were easier to alter to accommodate new trends, and then typically passed on to someone a little more slender. So it's not just that everyone back then was a Skinny Minnie, like madam here." She gives Ravenna a pinch.

I expect her granddaughter to twist away in a sulk, but she seems more than content to be called skinny.

Weaving back along Ocean Drive, Gracie and I again marvel at the view while Pamela seems as switched off as Ravenna.

"Everything all right?" I try to be discreet with my inquiry.

"Yes, yes, I'm just going over this afternoon's recipes in my mind."

Something tells me she's had a nasty missive from her husband this morning, or perhaps his lawyer. What a grim state of affairs. At least my breakups didn't involve any costly paperwork. Perhaps there is an upside to having thoroughly insubstantial relationships after all.

"Here we are!" Gracie announces our return to Marble House.

As we step into the lobby, we find ourselves swamped by a swirling honeypot of streaky caramel marble—Alva Vanderbilt said that an interior of pure white (to match the exterior) would have too closely resembled a mausoleum, whereas this warmer hue "catches the sunlight by day and electric sparkles by night." I rather like the idea of "electric sparkles." I suppose electricity was still considered something of a magical phenomenon back in 1892.

"Now that is some chandelier!" Pamela tilts her head back to take in the gold-trimmed glass box that bears more than a passing resemblance to Cinderella's carriage. "I wouldn't want to be standing here if that came loose."

"But what a way to go!" I sigh. "Flattened by a Vanderbilt light fixture."

Gracie beckons us into the Gold Salon, accented with mythological figures and bulbous cherubs, its walls coated in 22-karat gold.

"A gilded room for a gilded age!"

Just as our eyes are adjusting to the Vegas-Versace glitz, she directs us into a small medieval church, with sofas.

"This, believe it or not, was their family room."

Every window is stained glass, every surface piled with dusty, fusty religious tomes; all that's missing is a pulpit. Alva's daughter Consuelo declared it melancholy and depressing.

"It *is* melancholy and depressing," Ravenna confirms.

"This is where her husband-to-be proposed."

"What kind of fool would pick a room like this?"

"An English fool," I reply. "Remember me telling you about the *Downton* connection? Consuelo was the Cora of the hour. And the man proposing was the Duke of Marlborough."

"As in Blenheim Palace?"

"As in Blenheim Palace."

"Consuelo described the proposal setting as 'propitious to sacrifice.'"

"So she wasn't thrilled about the marriage?"

"Not at all. She was in love with someone else, but Alva said she would have no qualms about shooting the rival if Consuelo tried running away with him."

I see Gracie telepathically conveying to Pamela that she would be more than happy to do away with Eon, should she personally not have the stomach for the job.

"My life became that of a prisoner with my mother and governess as my wardens," Consuelo concluded in her memoir.

This motif is heavily reinforced upstairs in the nineteen-year-old's bedroom. Aside from the fact that she was not allowed a single personal item (everything, right down to her vanity set, was hand-picked and positioned by her mother), her bed is like some kind of regal cell. I have never seen chunkier posts on a four-poster, hefty as tree trunks and carved with leafy flourishes, like Renaissance-style totem poles. Between each hang dark claret curtains—ready to be drawn and thus completely enclose Consuelo.

"God, I don't know why her mother didn't just have done with it and chain her up!"

"Well, it's funny you should say that, but she had to wear this awful contraption for her posture—a steel rod up her back that was strapped at her waist, shoulders and forehead."

"What?"

"Suddenly your mum doesn't seem such an ogre, does she?"

Ravenna gives a little snort.

I don't know if it was the result of the contraption, but Consuelo had an extraordinarily long, swan-like neck, and was considered one of Newport's great beauties. I can see it in her face, but the neck? You don't often hear men saying, "Cor, check out the neck on that!" Although you might if you'd seen Consuelo at the time: judging from her portrait, the Kayan tribeswomen of Burma have got nothing on her.

"Not how you'd decorate a teenager's room?" I ask Ravenna.

She doesn't give me much in the way of a reply, just a look of general disgust. There's certainly none of the fresh aquas and cobalt blues that might typify a coastal view room today. Not that you can see much of the view since the windows are so heavily shrouded with fabric. I wonder how many times Consuelo drew back the netting and wished herself free?

"The most ironic thing," Gracie follows my gaze down to the Chinese Tea House at the end of the lawn, "is that Alva later held women's suffrage rallies down there—she was a huge campaigner for women's rights."

"But she just didn't want her daughter to have any?"

"Well, it's funny: she thought that the most empowering thing she could do for her daughter was to elevate her to duchess status, so she could be a person of influence and make her own choices."

"Strange way to go about it."

"Listen to this quote." Ravenna appears to be rather taken with Consuelo's highbrow put-downs: "'There was in my mother's love of me something of the creative spirit of an artist—it was her wish to produce me as a finished specimen framed in a perfect setting.'"

Ravenna fixes her mother with a "sound familiar?" stare and then strops off.

Pamela sighs. "Doesn't every mother dress up their daughter in pretty things when they are little? She says I treated her like a doll. I didn't, did I, Mum?"

"She used to love all that pink froth, as well you know. She's only embarrassed in retrospect, because it doesn't fit with her new image," Gracie bristles, adding, "You just happen to have a lot more photographic evidence because you were featured in so many magazines."

"She says I shouldn't have had her in the pictures with me, that I was exploiting her."

"Yes, because it's positively criminal to want a professional portrait of yourself and your child. Shall we move on to Alva's bedroom?"

Yes please.

We steel ourselves for something even more dark and austere, but instead we're greeted by a shimmering vision in lilac silk, festooned, flounced and ruched within an inch of its life. The carved ivory bed is set on a platform with such elaborate drapery at its head that the only appropriate nightcap would be a tiara. Facing the bed is a desk of purple marble with a writing set, though with that view, the only thing you could effectively pen is a Barbara Cartland novel.

"Wow!"

"I love this," Gracie beams.

"What do you think?" I ask Ravenna.

"It's a bit matchy-matchy."

To say the least. The chairs, the chaise, the footstools are all the same lilac hue.

Quite spectacular, nonetheless. It's just a shame you can't take photos; I'd love to send this to Krista, make out it's my hotel room.

"Who's the woman on the ceiling?"

Ravenna is referring to a soft-focus beauty in a toga reclining amid the clouds.

"Athena," Gracie replies. "Goddess of wisdom and war."

"Aren't those two things mutually exclusive?" I ask.

She smiles. "Apparently the painting was removed from a Venetian palazzo, shipped to Newport and glued above the bed so Alva could feel inspired every morning as she awoke."

"Hmm," Pamela pulls a face. "The first picture I see every morning is me at my fattest taped to the fridge, so I reach for the Special K instead of the bacon."

"So you're focusing on a visual of what you *don't* want to be," I observe.

"Not very aspirational, when you put it like that," she admits.

"Move toward your dreams, not away from your problems." I quote one of the postcards I have pinned above my desk.

Ravenna rolls her eyes and moves on to the next room.

I look back at Athena and wonder whose image I might glue to my ceiling when I get home? Oprah probably. And Pink, because she's one of those "live out loud" people. And she always seems to be laughing. I want to laugh more.

"Well, would you believe it?"

"What's that?" I look back at Pamela, now getting into her guidebook.

"After all that badgering of her daughter to marry a man she didn't love, Alva was the first woman in Newport to get a divorce."

"Really?"

"Yes! She said she wanted to set an example and give other women the courage—to be like a female knight rescuing other women."

"I wonder how her daughter felt about that?"

"Well she got a divorce too! Admittedly after twenty-eight years of dutiful marriage. Oh gosh."

"What?"

Pamela gives Gracie a queasy look. "Even after Consuelo divorced him, the duke still received a payment of two and a half million dollars, every year until he died!"

Gracie squeezes her daughter's hand. "Whatever it costs, it will be worth every penny to be free of that man."

I know they're talking about Brian now.

"He wants the house," I hear her whisper.

"I thought he would. Let him have it; it's only filled with memories of him anyway. Better to have a fresh start."

"I'm too old for a fresh start," Pamela's voice wobbles.

"Nonsense, it'll do you good. You're just tired now, that's all. Good things are coming, I just know it."

She puts her arm around her daughter and guides her onward. Mothers. Always thinking they know what's best for their children. Some a tad more proactively than others.

Chapter 17

∽

And so to the foodie side of things, the reason we're here.

We hurry through the Salon Russe dining room because a) Gracie already told us about "service *à la russe*" last night, and b) the walls are the color of uncooked meat.

They call it "rose marble" but it really does look like a mix of bloodied and browning steak.

"How very unpalatable," Pamela shudders as we scurry on to the kitchens.

"This is where you'd be, Mum," Ravenna smirks as we descend the staircase. "Down in the servants' quarters."

"I wouldn't mind a bit," Pamela enthuses as we step into a spacious kitchen flooded with sunlight from two sets of French windows. "Look at this place! It's just beautiful!"

Even I have to admit, this is a very good-looking setup. There's a row of black cast-iron ovens along one wall, a huge wooden preparation table in the middle and, hung above it, I count twenty-six gleaming copper pots and pans.

"Now that's a lot of cookware." I step closer. "I love how the lids have long handles too—doesn't that make sense, so you don't get scalded with steam when you check on the contents."

"I can't believe they're letting us cook here this afternoon!" Pamela looks brimming over with wonder as she takes in all the mansion-sized details from yesteryear—the hatbox-size cake tins, the sink you could take a bath in, and what looks like a two-person rolling pin.

"Is this for real?" Ravenna, meanwhile, is in the scullery, pointing to an off-white tea set with hand-painted blue lettering spelling out the words *Votes for Women*.

I peer more closely at the china. It really is a very striking design. Funny to think they were into slogans and branding back in 1909, when Alva first kicked off her women's suffrage campaign.

"It seems unfathomable that there was ever a time when women *didn't* get to vote," I note.

"Well, even the president at the time said that 'sensible and responsible women' don't *want* to vote!"

"Are you serious?" I scoff. "Attitudes like that make me fume!"

"It was the same way for Alva," Gracie chuckles at my flush of injustice. "Even as a child she was chasing down equality—riding her horse bareback, punching boys in Sunday school. She said, 'The life of a boy with its excitement and adventure had my entire devotion.'"

She points to the relevant section in the guidebook. Apparently Alva wasn't considered ladylike enough to play with the other Newport daughters, and the boys taunted her saying she couldn't keep up with them because she was "just a girl." This ignited such a rage in her that she determined to show them exactly what she was capable of.

"I was a law unto myself," Alva said. "What more could one desire?"

Wow. I love that! Funny how my opinion of her has altered during the course of the tour—initially I dismissed her as an overbearing control freak, but then I hear this and I'm full of admiration for her feisty, pioneering spirit.

"And, for the record," Gracie concludes, "Consuelo did ultimately marry for love (to a French aviator) so I guess all's well that ends well."

That is good to know. I wonder if mother and daughter made up in later life? Something tells me Pamela is wondering the same.

"If these walls could talk, eh?" She smiles at me.

We pause for a moment, as if we might hear an echo from the past if we listen closely enough, but instead we hear Eminem's "The Monster."

"It's Eon," Ravenna scrambles for her phone. "I'll catch you up at the tea house!"

"Here we go again!" Pamela winces.

"She's always particularly spiteful to her mother after she's spoken to that idiot boy," Gracie explains.

"Really?"

Pamela concedes a nod before turning away.

"I think he eggs her on," Gracie opines.

"But why?" I want to know.

She shrugs. "All part of his controlling games, I suppose."

"Will you look at these dinky china cups!" Pamela clearly wants to change the subject. "You'd need twenty to make up a Grande at Starbucks!"

I'm noticing something of a pattern here. Gracie brings things to a boil then Pamela whips the pot from the stove before anything bubbles over. I wonder if it's necessary for Gracie to try and trigger a change in Pamela's life—she could be on the verge of cracking up of her own accord. I mean, how much peacekeeping can one person perform? She's been doing it with her husband for years, then her daughter, all the while trying to get her mother to pipe down.

Still, if ever you were going to rock the boat, Newport is the place to do it.

After perusing the cabinets of hand-painted china and elegantly fanciful teapots, including one silver genie's lamp specifically designed for hot chocolate, it's a massive comedown when we cross the back lawn to the Chinese Tea House and discover paper plates and polystyrene cups.

"Dear me!" Gracie tuts. "You'd think they could at least offer a basic mug."

"So disappointing." I share her dismay as I take in the help-yourself tea bags and hot-water dispensers.

"Let me see what I can do."

"Mum, no!" Pamela implores. "Leave it."

But Gracie has already latched on to that bone.

She has a point. This is such a one-of-a-kind setting: a Chinese pagoda with dusty jade roofing, red columns and a black lacquered base, set in the grounds of a Versailles-inspired mansion overlooking the Atlantic Ocean.

It's worthy of a ten-tiered cake stand, but instead everything is prepackaged and heaped in a basket.

"Does a cookie *ever* look appealing when it's coated in cling-film?" I query.

"At least the crisps are fairly local," Pamela says, holding up a bag of Cape Cod Sea Salt & Vinegar.

I shake my head. Never mind the hungry poor at the Seaman's Institute, the privileged classes have gone horribly awry here.

"Can you imagine if you took this over as a concession, how amazing the afternoon teas would be?"

"Oh, I'd have a field day!" Pamela's imagination is immediately sparked. "I'd source as many recipes from the original time period, and maybe go a bit contrary—Coffee Cake for a tea room?" she ponders. "And I rather like the idea of something bright but simple like jam tarts. And lemon curd ones. Maybe add in something with a Chinese flair to reflect the surroundings?"

"You could do fortune cookies but have quotes from Consuelo!" I laugh. "Perhaps throw in an Election Day cake—you know, to represent the votes."

Pamela chuckles. "And the centerpiece would be a mansion-sized Marble Cake!"

"Is it difficult," I ask, "to get that swirly effect?"

"Not really, you just split the cake mixture, add cocoa powder to one half and then spoon it into the pan in alternate dollops."

"That's it?"

"Well, then you take a skewer and whirl it around a couple of times."

"That's so cool!"

"You can actually do any color combination you like. And any number of colors."

"So you could do a cake to match every marbled room here?"

"You could indeed."

"I'm back!" Gracie clinks through the doorway carrying three sets of cups and saucers.

"Please tell me you didn't take these out of the cabinets," Pamela blanches as she sees the "Votes for Women" design.

Gracie rolls her eyes. "They sell them at the gift shop."

"Really?" I brighten.

"And you bought them just so we didn't have to drink out of a paper cup?"

"Oh please," she tuts at her daughter. "How many times are we going to get the chance to have tea together in the grounds of a Newport mansion?"

"They will make for a better photo," I admit.

"And they make a lovely keepsake."

"Oh they do!" I coo.

Gracie hands me my set. I couldn't be happier and quickly decant my steaming beverage. (Has to be green tea in a Chinese Tea Room.)

"Why don't we get a picture of all three of us together?" Gracie suggests.

We position ourselves on the pagoda steps, surrounded by the Chinese dragons and curly maned lions and do two poses—one ladylike with little fingers cocked, then another raising our cups with a rallying cry.

At which point Ravenna, who has tracked us down, decides to make a sharp left and pretend she doesn't know us. Suits us fine.

"What a position!" Pamela sighs as she strays to the edge of the terrace and gazes out at the mansion-studded coastline. "Is this the Cliff Walk you were talking about?" she asks as she spies the pathway below.

Gracie and I didn't make it this far, so I'm eager to take a look as well. It's certainly dicier here—a jumble of big gray rocks to navigate—but oh that view when you look back across the glinting water, all the way to Easton's Beach.

As Pamela follows the flutterings of a white butterfly, you can almost see the tension leaving her body. Gracie and I keep quiet, willing her to absorb the abundance of well-being.

"This place makes you feel so dignified somehow," she says as she tilts her face to the sun. "Almost as if nothing bad could find you here!"

"Ready to go?" Ravenna appears on cue.

Gracie and I exchange a look, "*Almost.*"

Chapter 18

And so it's back down to earth at the supermarket. Well I say that . . . This being Newport, even the Stop & Shop has a certain kudos, positioned but a lob away from the International Tennis Hall of Fame.

All the greats have squeaked sneakers on these courts—Billie Jean King, Steffi Graf, Pete Sampras and, my personal fave, John McEnroe.

"You used to be so into tennis when you were a little girl," Pamela gazes wistfully at Ravenna, no doubt imagining her in little pink pom-pom socks. "Remember when I took you to the finals at Wimbledon and you had your heart set on getting Goran Ivanišević's autograph—"

"Are you deliberately trying to embarrass me?" Ravenna cuts in.

"Some would call it reminiscing," Gracie observes.

"And really, there's nothing embarrassing about fancying Goran Ivanišević," I note.

"Oh my god! Will you all stop?"

"Ravenna," I caution.

She glares back at me. Then at her mum. "Just once I'd like *you* to be the one dying of mortification."

Before I can say, "You don't think she feels that every time you open your mouth?" she has stomped ahead of us into the shop.

Pamela shakes her head. "It seems like everything I say is a trigger . . ."

It's not *what* you say, I want to tell her, it's just *you*. But I don't think that will help.

"So, exactly how many Marble Cakes are we planning to make?" Now it's my turn to gloss over the awkwardness and act as if everything is tickety-boo.

We load up on extra flour, eggs, butter and sugar, adding in vanilla extract and baking powder.

"Do you know the rest of the Ivanišević story?" I ask Gracie as Pamela weighs up her cocoa powder choices.

"I think she just had a massive red-faced tantrum when he chose the winner's trophy over her."

"Oh right," I say, all too easily imagining Ravenna blaming her mother for his lack of indulgence. "Good to know that was just a passing phase."

Pamela returns to us. "Laurie, could you grab me some cases for the Dark and Stormy cupcakes while I get the ginger? Nothing too flowery."

"Will do!" I find some gold ones I think are perfect—symbolic of pirate treasure. These are going to be so yummy! "Anything else?"

"I think that's everything."

Ravenna is already at the other side of the till, having made a few purchases herself, though it's doubtful they are a) from the food aisle or b) going to make any contribution to teatime at the Seaman's Church Institute.

(Though I'm certainly proved wrong about the latter.)

.   .   .

After a quick bowl of clam chowder at the Black Pearl's deck café (where we also purloin our dark rum), it's back to Marble House.

Unloading all the Stop & Shop bags from the car, we decide to leave our own safely locked within.

"Aside from the hygiene issues, they'll only get all covered in flour and grease," Pamela explains as she dumps her embroidered slouchy bag.

Ravenna looks most distressed at the prospect. Just when you think she didn't have it in her to care, she's certainly very protective of her bag. Anyone would think she had paid for it with her own money.

"I just need to get my phone," she says, turning away to burrow within.

I think I hear a clinking of glass but say nothing—if she's acquired a couple of Bailey's miniatures to take the edge off, so be it.

"Let's ditch the plastic bags and packaging pronto," Pamela instructs us as soon as we get into the kitchen. "We want to look as authentic as possible as the tour groups come through."

It's good to see her taking charge. She gets a further boost when several of the English tourists recognize her and ask for an autograph, which in turn ignites the curiosity of the Americans, giving her the opportunity to explain about her upcoming book.

"Wish we could taste your baking," they salivate.

"We'll be at the Seaman's Church Institute at three P.M.," I tell them. "If you'd like to make a donation, I'm sure we could come to an arrangement . . ."

"Laurie! We need some more cupcake cases laid out."

We each have our task to perform, mine being equal to my skill level. Pamela and Gracie focus on the measurements and getting the right combinations in each bowl, while Ravenna has actually offered to do the beating and stirring and is doing so with surprising vigor for one with such spindly arms.

"Good outlet for her anger," Gracie notes as Ravenna batters the wooden spoon in circles while pacing the room.

"Oooh, Pamela, what are you up to there?" I ask as she drains the syrup from a tin of pineapple rings.

"Well, you know the motif of the Newport Preservation Society is the pineapple, which is also the symbol for hospitality?"

"Yes."

"I thought I'd do some individual Pineapple Upside-Down Cakes!"

"Oh my god. I know it seems like I say this every day, but Pineapple Upside-Down Cake is one of my favorites!"

I love the way the base takes on a caramelized texture but is still so juicy from the fruit.

"Do you know why pineapples are the symbol of hospitality?" Gracie asks as she measures out the last of the sugar.

"Do tell!"

"When a captain returned from a long voyage, his household would stick a pineapple on the front gatepost to let everyone know he was home and open to receiving visitors."

"Well whattayaknow?"

This is fun. Working together as a team. Chatting as we go. At one point Pamela decides she wants to go one better than paper plates for the presentation, and she sends me to the gift shop to source some china. I come back with some brightly colored "Chelsea" bird designs copied from an original set found at The Elms. I also present Pamela with a local cookbook featuring such enticing gems as Brandy Black Bottom Pie.

We flick through it as we sit outside, waiting for our cakes to bake.

"There's something not quite right about that smell," Pamela frowns at one point, sniffing the air.

"Well, those ovens are ancient," Ravenna opines.

"It's not the ovens."

We convince her there's nothing to worry about, but when the cakes are removed she insists on doing a thorough taste test.

"Really, Mum, there's no need." Ravenna tries to hustle her on but Pamela stands firm.

She takes her first bite. Her face instantly sours.

"What is it?"

"I don't know," she shakes her head. "There's something very wrong here. Mum—you try . . ."

Gracie steps in. "Oh no," she spits her mouthful into the bin. "That's not good."

My mind jumps to all those expectant tummies at the wharf. We can't let them down.

"All set?" It's Avery, the woman who so kindly made the arrangements for us to cook here, needing us to move on.

I look back at Pamela, now frantic, tearing through batch after batch, dismissing them as inedible. "I don't know what it is." She's starting to cry now. "It's the same awful sourness with them all. What did I do wrong?"

"Why don't you go and have a cup of tea?"

I usher the Lambert-Leighs outside and tell them I'll clear up and don't worry, I'll think of a solution.

I can't help but feel this is my fault. Perhaps there's something toxic in these old pans. Some metal base that has long since been outlawed—

"Oh damnit!" I just leaned too far over the giant bin and my mobile has fallen in, along with a heap of sticky pineapple gloop. Great, now I have to reach into all the gunk. Spiky, slimy eggshells, drippy milk cartons and multiple tiny bottles—what are these? I'm fairly certain we didn't use any food coloring. I pull one out.

Tabasco. Pepper sauce. I sniff the opening and recoil at its spicy vinegary waft—the exact tang that has tainted all the cakes.

And then I think of Ravenna chinking as she took what she needed from her handbag, the eagerness with which she joined in the baking process, how she paced as she held the mixing bowls.

That little—

"Nearly done?"

"Yes, yes." I turn to Avery, wiping off my hands. "I'm sorry there's such a lot of waste. It seems we had a little saboteur among us."

She looks concerned. "Anything I can assist you with?"

"Well, it would be great if you could recommend a cake shop near the wharf."

I take her suggestion and vow to deal with Ravenna later—if I expose her now, Pamela will just be even more upset and there will be a lot of tears and drama and the Seaman's Institute teatime will be ruined. I have to set aside my urge to dangle her over the cliff edge and handle the most pressing aspect first.

But then, as I reach into the boot to retrieve my bag, I see Ravenna's precious Mulberry handbag. And that's when I get an idea . . .

Chapter 19

∞⚬∞

The Newport Sweet Shoppe is every bit as wonderful as Avery promised. Before I even get to the cupcakes, I've loaded up with iced biscuits in the shapes of lighthouses, lobsters, yachts and starfish, loving how appropriate they'll be for the sailors, if not exactly typical of an English tea.

I must say the cupcakes look exceptional: tray upon tray of precision-decorated options. Salted Caramel and 22 Carrot particularly catch my eye, while the woman in front of me can't decide between the Key Lime and Raspberry Lemonade flavors.

"Are you all set?" The shop owner invites me to go ahead while her first customer continues to ponder.

"One of everything?" the indecisive woman jokes.

"Actually, I need *all* of everything."

"Excuse me?"

"I need to buy all your cupcakes. Except whichever one you're having," I turn to the indecisive woman.

"Well, if they're that good, I'm going to get both."

While the cupcakes are being packaged, I learn that the owner's name is Amanda Bryan. She and her husband Patrick have been professional cupcake-makers for four years (both are from a restaurant/hospitality background), but she's been baking since she was a child. She even runs bake parties for children at their homes.

"But they need to be older children," she explains. "The little ones just want to lick the spatula."

I ask her what she thinks it is about cupcakes that has made them such a massive trend.

"I think it's because they make people happy," she says simply. "They're small, not as big a commitment as a whole cake, and you can treat yourself for not a lot of money."

Depending on how many you need, of course . . . I explain to her why we require such a bumper batch, and reference our own Dark and Stormy recipe. Although she can't match that, she does have a dozen Chocolate Guinness cupcakes, which I readily snap up.

"And if you've got five minutes I can finish up our Newport Harbor ones. I think you'll particularly like those . . ."

Once again the Seaman's Church Institute gets little more than a swift drop-off, but they are utterly forgiving of the lack of promised Marble Cake when they see the new bounty, especially the Newport Harbor design, which turns out to be a swirl of blue frosting for waves, a little cluster of candy pebbles for the shoreline and a dark chocolate sail as the centerpiece.

"These are perfect!" Deedra coos.

"Yes they are," I sigh with relief.

The others are waiting for me in the car park when I return. Pamela still looks bereft, Gracie is attempting to console her, and Ravenna just wants to be reunited with her handbag.

"Where is it?" She scrabbles around in the boot.

"Oh, I got you this replacement," I say, dangling a cheap mac-ramé affair I picked up at CVS.

"Wh-what do you mean a replacement?" she blanches.

"Well, a hundred or so cupcakes don't come cheap at shop prices. I had to trade something . . ."

I think she might faint. "You traded my Alexa for cupcakes?"

"Mmmhmm. I thought it would help you understand the con-sequences of your actions."

"What actions?" she snaps, feigning innocence.

I hold up the receipt for the bottles of Tabasco that I found in her purse. She tries to snatch it from me.

"Oh no you don't." I whip it away. And then I study her face. "Why would you do such a thing, Ravenna? I mean, seriously, to be that mean-spirited."

Her scowl develops. "You heard her, humiliating me about that time at Wimbledon—"

"Oh please. That's just a mum being a mum. And this wasn't just about getting back at her—what about all the other people you affected?"

Her jaw juts. "I need my bag—"

"What's the big deal? I'm sure your mother will buy you an-other one."

"She didn't buy it." Her eyes are welling up now. "Eon did."

Oh. I hadn't counted on having quite this impact. She looks distraught.

"I have to get it back or he'll—"

"Laurie! Ravenna!" It's Gracie calling to us in a state of agi-tated glee.

Ravenna turns away as Gracie bustles over to our side.

"It's ready! The bus is ready right now! Can we go?"

"Of course," I tell Gracie. "We're all set here, aren't we, Ravenna?"

Ravenna turns back to me. I know she wants to have a banshee-like tantrum and flail out at us, but somehow she swallows it all in and gets into the car without a word.

I might tell her the truth about her bag later today but, for now, she needs to do some penance.

Chapter 20

⁂

When I think of all the London busses I have boarded without blinking an eye—far too preoccupied with finding a seat or getting out of the rain or hurrying to my next appointment . . .

Out of its usual context, away from Oxford Street's giant department stores and burly black cabs, this double-decker looks huge. And red! *So* red. And glossy. And iconic. I run my hand over the engine bonnet—goodness, these things are solid.

"Classic Routemaster 1956," Gracie puffs with pride. "Feel free to step on board!"

The downstairs interior has the authentic itchy-fuzzy seat coverings, but the driver's cab has been opened out so Gracie can interact with us along the way, as opposed to being sealed off in her own cube. Seatbelts have been added in the passenger area, and apparently there are a few more tweaks upstairs.

"Pamela, why don't you lead the way?"

I hear a squeal and clatter before I'm halfway up the curved staircase.

"What is it?" I call ahead.

"Oh Mum! I can't believe it!"

As my gopher head pops up, I see the entire upstairs level has been kitted out with a chintzy-fresh, Cath Kidston-style kitchen—there's a baby-pink oven and fridge, an immaculate white preparation area lined with mixers and bowls and assorted lacy cake stands.

"Everything is secured so it won't slide around as we take a tight corner," Gracie explains. "And I got those cake tins you were talking about the other day." She points to a vintage set in pale-blue enamel, not so very dissimilar to the cream ones at Marble House.

"Oh I love them! I love it all!" Pamela reaches to embrace her mother.

"Happy birthday, love."

"It's your birthday?" I startle.

"Next week," Pamela replies, now stroking the stack of rose-print tea towels. "I just can't believe it!"

I watch as she opens each drawer, holds up each spatula and pastry brush, turns each aluminum baking tray and then pauses beside a framed picture of the three Lambert-Leigh women a good fifteen years ago. Ravenna is up on Pamela's hip, pointing to the candles on the cake Gracie is holding up.

"My forty-fifth birthday," Pamela remembers. "You piped all those tiny roses yourself, didn't you, Mum?"

"I did. One for every year that I wished the best for you."

Pamela gives her a rueful look, as if to say, "I have no idea how things got so bad."

I feel a little awkward, intruding on such a personal moment, and pretend to be intently studying the side of the box of Typhoo.

"One more surprise." Gracie leads us back off the bus and gets us to look up at the destination panel.

The largest lettering spells out NEW ENGLAND. The states are listed in smaller type. But Gracie is most excited about the numbering.

240.

"D'you get it?"

We frown, looking at each other for clues. I was always on the 19 or the 390 in London.

"It's not Golders Green, is it?"

"As a matter of fact it is, but you're thinking too literally. Say it out loud."

"Two hundred and forty."

"Like the Americans do."

I have to think for a moment. "Two-forty."

"Again."

"Two-forty."

"A little slower."

"Two-for . . ." Suddenly the penny drops. "Two for tea!"

Pamela and I laugh. "That's brilliant!"

"Ready to go for a spin?"

The engine chugs to life.

Ravenna, who hasn't said a word throughout the inspection, tucks herself directly into the back row, whereas Pamela and I sit as close to the front as possible, admiring Gracie's dexterity with the giant horizontal steering wheel.

"It's like coming home," she beams as we set off.

This really is incredible—who gets to drive around New England in a double-decker bus with a celebrity chef and on-board cake-making facilities? Heaven or what?

Gracie's living the dream too—blaring out Cliff Richard's "Summer Holiday" and waving to all the fascinated faces we pass on the way to Ocean Drive. When we get there, the local trolley tour bus draws level and the driver calls across:

"Should I be worried about the competition?"

"Nooo!" she chuckles. "We'll be gone by morning!"

"That's a shame!" he says, giving her a flirty wink. "I like your style!"

"I like everything about this place," Gracie sighs as we continue on. "I really do."

"Here comes our photography spot." I point ahead.

Ravenna grudgingly dislodges herself as we disembark and line up on the grassy bank by the water's edge, preparing to snap an image worthy of Gracie's Christmas cards.

"What she really wants is a picture to put on Georgie's grave," Pamela gives us an extra motivation to make a timely click. "Show him she's still got it."

As if anyone could doubt that.

I mean, look at her now—hugging the curves of the road in a vehicle that's twice the size of my apartment, leaning out of the window giving us a joyful woo-hoo!

"She's going pretty fast!" I express concern as I begin to snap.

"She knows what she's doing."

"Tell me that seagull isn't thinking of crossing the road," I fret, eyeing the puffed-chest fella making plodding progress from the rocks to the tarmac. "Can she see him?"

"Mum! Watch out!" Pamela tries to alert her with flailing arms.

She just gives a bigger wave back.

"*Mum!*"

"*Gracie!*"

"*Granny!*" even Ravenna gasps out loud as the bus swerves to avoid the strutting bird, rucks up onto the bank, grabs at the grass and halts just millimeters before plunging into the sea.

The three of us hurtle toward the bus.

"Oh my god! Mum! *Mum?* Are you all right?" Pamela claws her way onto the bus.

Gracie's head is down on the steering wheel.

"She's bleeding!" Pamela shrieks. "She's bleeding!"

It seems to be coming from her jaw. I fumble for my phone, dialing 911 with a trembling hand.

As I hurriedly give our details, Gracie tilts back in her seat, looking dazed, hand going to her face. She tries to speak but winces in agony.

"I think she might have cracked her jaw, it doesn't look right."

I run and grab the stack of rose-print tea towels and use them to stem the flow of blood, which seems to be getting everywhere now.

I try telling myself it's just food coloring, but still my stomach churns.

I can't believe this happy-go-lucky moment has taken such a horrible turn. Did someone up there misunderstand when Gracie said she wanted to immortalize her drive along this stretch of coast?

"The ambulance is here," Ravenna alerts us.

We step out of the way to give the paramedics full access. As they undo the seatbelt and ease her out, she grabs at her ribs. Looks like she might have cracked one of those too—that is a darn big steering wheel and she did brake with quite some force. No airbags here.

We're all stunned to silence as she is strapped to the stretcher. This is real. Gracie is hurt.

I want to go with them to the hospital, but Pamela asks me to stay with the bus.

So what happens now? I want to believe it's just a nasty bump, but I fear the worst. She certainly won't be up to driving anytime soon. And even if she could, and as feisty as she is, would she even want to after this?

I sigh as I think of our original plans—quick spin on the bus, tour of The Breakers, then dinner at the oldest bar in America. Gracie had already decided she was having the local scallops.

I look back at the red behemoth—one minute the promise of unlimited fun, now our ruin.

When she said I should prepare for anything, she wasn't kidding.

And then I well up thinking of her lovely face, all bashed and bleeding. I can't even go there in terms of this being life-threatening. It could so easily have been, but it's not, is it? She was still conscious. She just couldn't speak. She's going to be okay. Not straightaway, but she will be fine, she has to be. I drag my fingers across the front grille and then check my phone. And then check it again.

"Let me know the diagnosis as soon as you can," I text Pamela.

I know Krista won't be available for another few hours, so I call the garage and explain our predicament.

The worst part is having to convince every passing tourist that we are not a new landmark attraction.

But of course that's not the worst part at all. The worst part is that Gracie is in hospital, in all kinds of shock and pain, with her dream in peril.

Chapter 21

Once the bus has been returned to the garage, barely an hour after we collected it, I get a lift to the hospital.

"How is she?" I hurry to Pamela's side.

"They've stitched up her jaw," she replies, looking queasy. "We're just waiting for her X-ray results, for her ribs."

I nod. "And how is she in herself?"

"They've given her something to help her sleep so she's a bit out of it. Obviously she can't speak anyway because her face is all bandaged up." Pamela's brow crumples.

I put my arm around her.

"It really is best you go home and get some rest," the doctor advises. "We'll take good care of her and you can come back in the morning when she's feeling brighter."

"I can't leave her!" Pamela protests. "I need to be here."

But Ravenna is starting to shiver, her bony bare arms showing goose bumps.

"I don't mind staying but can we at least go back to the hotel and get some warmer clothes?"

Pamela sighs, conflicted. "I suppose we could get a few of her things too. In case she has to be here a while."

"Good idea," I confirm. "I'll wait here."

"You don't have to do that."

"I want to."

"Okay, thank you. We won't be long."

"That's fine. I'm not going anywhere."

None of us are.

The second Pamela and Ravenna are out of sight, the doctor returns.

"Ms. Davis?"

"Yes?"

"She would like a word with you."

"Gracie?"

He nods.

"With me? I thought she was sleeping?"

"Not yet. She's resisting the medication—issuing commands to us via pen and paper."

I feel my face light up. She's still here! Feisty Gracie is in the house!

Gingerly I push open the door. She is expecting me—eagerly beckoning me to her side, keen to communicate before she goes under.

She taps at her notepad, having already prepared her first instruction: *You MUST continue on this trip!*

Now she is pointing to her handbag, which I duly hand to her. I watch her rummage inside, pull out a small address book with a Monet print on the cover and then reach for her pen.

Charles Porter.

She taps the paper.

I say his name out loud to assure her I can read the words.

She mimes jiggling a steering wheel.

"Driving? He's a driver?"

She nods vigorously.

"Is he in England?"

She shakes her head and writes *Boston*. And then begins copying out his phone number.

"Boston . . ." I remind myself of the distance via the map function on my phone. "That's actually not too far from here. Not even two hours. So who is he?"

Silence.

"Gracie?" I look up and find her head lolling to the left, sound asleep. I give her a little jiggle. "Gracie?"

Nothing.

My shoulders slump. What now? Am I supposed to call him tonight? Is it really possible this man would drop everything and come to our rescue? Would he have any idea of what he's letting himself in for? Would we?

"Gracie?" I try her again—if she could give me one last burst . . .

"She really needs to sleep now." A nurse pops her head around the door.

"Yes, yes. Of course." I retract my hand, feeling guilty for trying to stir her.

Then, as I reach for the piece of paper, I notice that Gracie has added a message beneath the phone number.

My stomach flips as I read these three little words:

He's the one.

Chapter 22

⁕

I decide not to mention this exchange to Pamela when she returns to the hospital, sans Ravenna.

Well, there's no guarantee that the mysterious Mr. Porter will agree to the assignment and, besides, I suspect he could be a key factor in Gracie's meddling.

"You don't think she had the accident on purpose?" Krista gasps when I finally reach her.

"I wouldn't put anything past her, but I don't think even she can control the wanderings of the local seagulls."

"True," Krista concedes. "So what are you waiting for?"

I look back at the phone number in my hand. "You think I should call him?"

"Of course! Unless you're planning on driving the bus yourself."

"I'm not sure Pamela is going to want to leave her."

"I don't think Gracie's going to give her any choice. Besides, you said she loves Newport. She'll be perfectly happy staying put."

"By herself?"

"She's not exactly a shrinking violet, is she? And she knows her way around, if she gets back on her feet. Plus she can catch up with you guys the second she is able. You'll never be that far away."

"I suppose not." I step out of the way of a trundling hospital trolley.

"Look. We know by now this is the nature of travel—unpredictable. You have to be flexible and accept that things don't always go according to plan."

"I know," I sigh. "But this isn't just a missed connection."

"But it could be, if you don't make that call."

"What do you mean?"

"Gracie was emphatic about contacting this fella, right?"

"Yes," I confirm.

"Maybe Pamela needs to meet him. Or maybe you do?"

"What would it have to do with me?" Now I'm feeling even more uneasy.

"I'm just saying. Everything happens for a reason."

I'm quiet for a moment and then I mumble, "I don't want to go without her."

"Oh Laurie!"

"She's so much fun! I mean, I like Pamela but she's not in the most cheery place, and as for Ravenna . . ." My mouth twists in disgust.

"This is work," Krista reminds me. "You're on a mission. You can hang out with Gracie again once she's well, but until then you have a job to do."

I can't help but smile. This isn't like Krista, being so business-minded.

"Tough love?"

"Selfish love," she clarifies. "We've got a date in Vermont, re-member?"

She's right: there really is so much to look forward to.

"Okay, I'm going to call him now."

"Good girl," Krista cheers. "Call me afterward, let me know how it goes."

I decide I need a slug of Dark and Stormy. We're just a mile from the wharf so I tell Pamela I'm going to get us a couple of chowders. She nods fretfully. I do feel sorry for her. This is all she needs. When it rains it sure does pour.

On the way there my imagination starts to whirr. Bus driver. Boston. Friend of Gracie's. Could he be some old colleague of Georgie's? Suddenly I'm picturing tattooed forearms, a cor-blimey accent and a smoker's cough that causes him to hack out of the window, possibly incurring $2,000 fines all over New England. But Charles is hardly the most geezer-ish name. He sounds more like a gentrified chauffeur. All brass buttons, polished boots and a peaked cap. Or do I just have mansion fever?

There's only one way to find out.

Drink in one hand, phone in the other, I begin to dial . . .

His number rings. And rings. It hadn't occurred to me that he might not answer. Oh!

"Good evening!"

"Er, good evening. Is that Charles Porter?"

"It is."

He sounds in good spirits. And American. I wasn't sure if he was going to be an expat.

"Hello. My name is Laurie Davis, I'm calling on behalf of Gracie Lambert-Leigh."

"Is everything all right?" Immediate concern.

"Well. Yes and no. She's going to be fine, but at this moment she's at the hospital here in Newport."

I hear him gasp.

"She took a bit of a clunk to the jaw in the double-decker."

"Oh Gracie!" He sounds wretched.

"I know, it's awful." I hesitate. "Um. She gave me your number. I realize this is a long shot, but we're looking for someone to drive the bus."

"When do you want me there?"

Wow.

"Well, according to the original schedule, we were due to leave at ten A.M. tomorrow but—"

"I'll be there at nine."

I can't quite believe my ears. "Really?"

"I'll start getting my things together now."

"O-okay." I falter. "Do you know what this trip is about?"

"Cakes, right?"

I give a little laugh. "Yes, cakes." I start to explain a little more but he politely cuts me off.

"I'd better get on—I have a few calls to make; I wasn't expecting to hear from Gracie for another couple of days."

Interesting . . .

"Just text me the address and I'll be there."

"Thank you so much," I marvel. "You're a total lifesaver."

"Well, there's not much I won't do for cake!"

A man after my own heart.

I dial Krista before I've even had a chance to process the conversation.

"He said yes!" I tell her. "He's going to be here tomorrow morning."

"Just like that?"

"Just like that. Dropping everything to come to our aid."

"He's definitely in on The Meddle," Krista decides.

"I think you're right—it seems he was expecting to hear from Gracie anyway, possibly when we got to Boston."

"What does Pamela say about all this?"

"I haven't told her yet; you were my first call. Wait, I'm just getting a text from her now . . ."

I hold out the phone to read it.

"She's decided to go back to the hotel to get a few hours' sleep. That's good," I decide. "She needs the rest. And the chance to have the room to herself."

"Speaking of which—what are you going to do about the sleeping arrangements now you have a man in your midst?"

"Oh." My stomach sinks. "I hadn't thought of that."

"You three girls might have to bunk in together for the first night. Provincetown is going to be chock-a-block."

"As a matter of fact, all four of us were supposed to be in one room there."

"*Cozy!*"

"I found this really unusual suite . . ."

"Does it have a balcony?"

"Yes?"

"Well, let's just hope he's the outdoorsy type and he can sleep out there!"

"Oh Krista!"

"Come on, this isn't the end of the world—you're the Queen of Logistics. You can sort this in your sleep."

"I might have to," I say, looking at my watch.

"Don't lose your enthusiasm. Everything is working out, you've got a driver, and tomorrow you're going to Cape Cod!"

"I know, it's just . . ." I look around me at the lights reflecting on the inky waters, the still gleam of the sleeping boats, and I feel a strange pang of attachment. "I'm going to miss Newport."

I sense Krista smiling. "Don't tell me Manhattan has a rival!"

"Well, of course you can't compare the two, but it's just so lovely here—the coast, the marina, the mansions, even the name of the university: Salve Regina . . ."

"*Mater misericordiae!*" Krista sings.

"Why is that ringing a bell?" I frown.

"Evita. 'Oh What a Circus'?"

"Oh yes!" I laugh.

"You never did tell me how Ricky Martin was as Che . . ."

And so we go off on that tangent, talking about Broadway shows and pop star crushes until everything starts to feel normal again.

Friends. They're the best.

I put off going back to the room as late as I can, hoping that Ravenna will be asleep, but instead she is sitting up in bed changing channels in an angry ADD way, punishing the button on the remote for the sins of the world.

"Do you mind muting that or wearing your headphones?" I say absently. "We've got an early start tomorrow."

"What are you talking about? We're not going anywhere; we're going to be stuck in yachtie hell until Granny's fit to drive."

"Actually, we've got another driver coming in. Charles Porter."

I watch her face for any trace of recognition but there is none.

"So we're just leaving Granny here?"

"It was her idea," I reply. "Of course, if you want to stay on—"

"No, NO!" She gives me a sideways look. "So where are we going tomorrow?"

"I don't think you'll be able to stand the excitement," I tell her, imagining her knee-deep in a cranberry bog. "Why don't you just wait and see?"

"Whatever," she humphs. "This whole thing is lame."

I feel my annoyance flare. I do hope I don't reach over and muffle her in the night with a pillow—you know, involuntarily, in my sleep.

"I think I'm going to sleep out on the deck tonight," I announce.

"Do what you like!"

I take her at her word and make myself a cozy nest under the stars. I doubt I'll last until morning, but for now it's better than being in the presence of a moany spoiled teenager.

I breathe in the night air, and breathe out my exasperations. I wonder a little more about Charles. I couldn't really tell his age from the phone call, but he certainly sounded like a grown-up. Like a real man.

"Don't worry, I've got it covered."

Such a reassuring attitude. It's good to know there are still people like that in the world.

As the minutes pass I realize that I am no longer tied to any concerns; out here in the black of night, I feel suspended in time and space.

Which is real, I wonder: all the flurry and scurry and practicalities of life; or these magical moments that feel weightless, connected to the starlight and the swishing of the ocean?

And so my eyes close.

Chapter 23

⁓⁓⁓

So here we are, sitting in the bay window of the main building's sunny dining room, enjoying the bay view, eating breakfast with Charles. That's me and Ravenna. And yes, she ate. A whole egg on a whole piece of toast. I suppose she had to crack sooner or later.

Charles is a class act with a stylish sweep of silver hair, playful blue eyes and an abundance of old-school charm. (Appropriate, since he's a recently retired English teacher.) He even has a folded handkerchief in his blazer pocket. But his jeans are casual and his shoes endearingly worn. He's pleasingly confident about driving the bus and says he's happy to do anything for Gracie, she's always been so very kind to him.

We're just about to get into how the pair of them met—he's at least twenty years her junior—when I realize Pamela has entered the room and is just standing, staring.

She knows him. And something about him has stopped her in her tracks.

I excuse myself from the table and hurry to her side.

"Where did he come from?" she rasps, gripping my arm.

"Boston."

"No. No, I mean, how did he get here? *Why* is he here?"

She looks utterly dazed.

"He's our new driver. Your mum gave me his number last night."

"And he dropped everything to come here?" Her chest heaves.

"It seems that way. He didn't make a big deal out of it. He seemed to be expecting a visit . . ."

At which point he looks up and catches her eye.

She gulps nervously and then strides across the room, hand extended, "Hello, I'm Pamela. I hear you're a friend of my mother's?"

He hesitates, as if to say, "If that's how you want to play it."

"Charles." He shakes her hand. "Pleased to meet you. Though we have met before . . ."

"Oh yes," she flusters. "About ten years ago, wasn't it? Some kind of antiques fair with my mother? It's coming back to me now."

His shoulders lower, possibly with disappointment.

"It's really very kind of you to step in like this."

"Anything for old friends," he holds her gaze.

"And cake!" I jest.

"And cake," he smiles.

"Well, I suppose we should get going," Pamela chivvies us.

"You don't want any breakfast?" He turns back to the spread.

"No, I'm fine."

"Well, that's a first," Ravenna scoffs.

Charles looks so visibly affronted by Ravenna's rudeness that she quickly reaches for a muffin and says, "Why don't you take this for later?"

Hmmm. Perhaps a bit of testosterone is just what the doctor ordered.

Which reminds me.

"First stop the hospital?"

"Actually, I've already been this morning," Pamela explains. "Mum was emphatic that we just get going but I left her with my iPad so we can Skype when she's well enough, and in the meantime she said she'll e-mail us every day. And vice versa."

"So we're off?" I query.

There isn't exactly a rush for the door. Everyone seems a little more nervous today. For an assortment of reasons . . .

Chapter 24

∽⟊∾

Welcome to Massachusetts.

We're not even half an hour down the road when we transition into our next state.

Funny how a single sign can make you feel so separated from all that went before. If I turn back I can still see Rhode Island, but already it's in our past, geographically at least.

"Massachusetts."

As I hear Charles say the state name out loud, I can't help but think of the Bee Gees. Not a bad thing in and of itself, but then that makes me recall the radio DJ who made a silly pun about "massive chew sets." Why, when my brain lets so much go, would I remember that? I suppose there are some things you just can't un-hear. And some things you can't un-feel, I think, as I watch the stolen glances between Pamela and Charles. There is undeniably some deep connection there. I look forward to Gracie feeling better so I can learn more . . .

As we continue down another corridor of trees, I wonder out loud how different the drive would be in the autumn.

"It's incredible," Charles confirms. "I always say that the fall leaves are to New England what neon is to Vegas—a total marvel to the eye."

"Really?"

He nods enthusiastically. "The blaze of the red maples stops you in your tracks; the color is so intense and . . . *unexpected*. And the pure yellow leaves, when the sunlight is behind them, they just glow." He smiles. "It's like a beautifully arranged bouquet that runs for miles and miles."

I'm smiling too now. He has a rather poetic way about him— even now he's pointing out how the roadside trees have taken on a more feathery, fanlike foliage, as in a Busby Berkeley musical, with an endless parade of showgirls peeling back as we progress.

"Wareham!" I spot a sign to our destination.

This is where we will learn more about one of Massachusetts' biggest exports and Pamela's favorite superfood ingredient— cranberries.

"A.D. Makepeace is the world's largest cranberry grower and supplier for Ocean Spray." I flip to my notes. "Gosh, they've been around since the 1800s!"

"Riveting," yawns Ravenna.

"Not a fan of cranberries?" I snark.

"Not unless they're in a cocktail."

"We'll have a Cape Cod tonight," Charles suggests. "Vodka, cranberry, slice of lime."

"Ravenna's not old enough to drink," I remind him.

"I am in the UK."

"Shame you're not back there then."

"Isn't it just?"

"All right you two," he tuts as we head down a narrow road completely shrouded with trees.

We're deep in the countryside now, yet the bus is coping

admirably with the change in terrain. Charles decides we should give her a name. I suggest Georgie but Pamela doesn't look convinced.

"What about Red?" she brightens. "That's what Dad would call all the busses—'I'm going out with Red today, I'll be home at six!'"

Instant hit.

"Come on, Red!" we cheer as she bumps out of the forest and into a clearing.

Now, when you think of strawberry-picking, you picture low green bushes in which you'll have to forage for the fruit. It's a completely different story with cranberries. They grow in bogs, for one thing, and when the berries float to the top you are confronted with acres and acres of waterlogged pink! I can hardly believe my eyes.

"So when those guys in the Ocean Spray ads are standing there in their waders, it's real?" I gawp. "I always thought it was just a jokey thing, like they were thigh-deep in cranberry juice."

Charles laughs. "No, that's really part of the process."

Our guide joins us to expand further: "Cranberries grow on low-lying vines in the wetlands. Once they are ripe, we flood the bogs with water, a device loosens them from the vine and they bob to the surface where we can corral them."

Ravenna doesn't even feign interest. Her head is down, focused on texting as she paces restlessly around the banks.

"Cranberries were first discovered by the Native Americans, who used them as a fabric dye and healing agent as well as a food."

Fascinating. I look back at Ravenna. Is she paying any attention to where she's going?

"They were also used by colonial sailors as a means of warding off scurvy."

"Is that so?" I nod at the guide then return my gaze to Ravenna. If she's not careful she's going to walk straight into the—

"*Waaahhaaghh!*"

In she goes with an ungainly splosh, so disoriented by the sudden switch from dry land to bog that she lurches forward and goes under, all bar the hand holding her phone, which remains sticking up like a periscope.

God, I wish I had that on video.

As she scrabbles back upright, I get the feeling she doesn't know what to freak out about the most: her hair, her clothes, her dignity!

Pamela charges to her side to help pull her out.

"Don't touch me!" she screeches, spattering her with water.

"But darling . . ."

Ravenna turns away, yanking angrily at her sodden clothes as she attempts to scale the bank solo, but the path is too slippery.

"Take my hand," Charles offers.

For him she relents, accepting the assistance of his steel-strong arm. But no sooner does she have a firm stance than I see her gearing up to launch an attack on Pamela, who has returned to the side of the guide, trying to cover her embarrassment by asking him about the benefit of cranberries on one's urinary tract.

"Oh this should be good," I taunt.

"What do you mean?" Ravenna snaps at me.

"I'm just looking forward to seeing how you're going to make this your mum's fault, like everything else."

"If it wasn't for her, I wouldn't even be here," she spits.

"That's true on many levels," I admit. "But is she really responsible for you not looking where you are walking? Or should she put you back in one of those toddler harnesses with a lead?"

"How dare you speak to me like that!" she gasps.

"Oh I dare. I thought you knew that by now."

"Laurie!" Charles stops me in my tracks, giving me a similar virtual smack to the one Ravenna received at breakfast. "Do you have any suggestions for how we can help Ravenna get a little more comfortable?"

"Yes, of course," I reply, embarrassed that I lost my professional cool. Again. "She can drop her wet clothes in the sink upstairs on the bus, and there's a couple of beach towels I laid out for Provincetown."

"Thank you."

Once Ravenna is out of earshot, he says, "That was a little baiting."

"You don't think she deserves to be challenged?" I protest.

"Unfortunately I do. I'm sorry to see she's ended up this way." He looks genuinely regretful.

"Well. I can't stand by and watch her disrespect her mother in the way she does. I feel very strongly about that."

"So I see," he nods. "So do I."

"Look at this!" Pamela trills over to us. "*Make It Better with Cranberries!*"

For a moment I think she's found a cranberry cure for our situation, but it's actually a cookbook. The unique thing is that all the recipes are local contest winners and the profits benefit the Cranberry Education Foundation. So you can eat as much Cranberry Delight Cake as you like and know you're contributing to a good cause.

"I think I might try out a couple of these recipes on the way to Provincetown!"

Bless her, burying all the pain and shame in her cooking. You'd think it would sour the taste, but amazingly it doesn't. Then again, if you knew just how much chocolate goes into a Magic Bog Bar . . .

Chapter 25

ᔕᔕᔕ

And so we enter Cape Cod. This piece of land has been compared to the flexed arm of a bodybuilder. At the shoulder there is Sandwich (we'll be stopping there on the way back). If you wanted to take the ferry to legendary Martha's Vineyard you would leave from the armpit, also known as Falmouth. Dennis forms the bicep. Chatham the elbow. Eastham and Wellfleet make up the forearm, and we're heading for the clenched fist at the very tip of the cape—Provincetown.

As we drive I'm aware that we have the Atlantic coast to the right and the bay to our left, but there is zero visual reinforcement. Still the green corridor. At one point it narrows to a single line of traffic in either direction.

"I bet this gets bumper-to-bumper during the weekends."

"You have no idea," Charles grimaces.

When I comment on how immaculate the whole area is, Charles tells me you can be fined up to $10,000 for littering. Now that's an effective deterrent. Personally if I see someone dropping litter on the streets of New York, I always pick up the discarded cigarette packet or chewing gum wrapper and chase after the offender chirping, "Excuse me, I think you dropped this!" Krista says it's a wonder I'm still here.

Around Eastham we pass the poshest motels I have ever seen, including one whose main building is a mock colonial mansion. Less Norman Bates, more Bill Gates.

"Look! There's a shop for you—The Kitchen Lady," I nudge Pamela.

It makes a change from all the greenery to have things to point at. I take in every shop and food shack along the way and then, some time after passing Moby Dick's seafood restaurant, I notice the trees switch exclusively to pines of the low, bushy variety.

"We're getting close now." Charles sits up a little straighter in his seat. "Can you smell that sea air?"

On cue, the scenery opens out into a wilderness of sand dunes to our right, while hundreds of white beach houses line the left. The dunes themselves are quite mesmerizing—sprigged with green bushes and wispy grasses, a low band of clouds mirroring their gently sloping forms. I want to flip off my shoes, run up and then scoot down, creating a powder-soft cascade. Apparently I'm not the only one—as we slow I can see sets of deep footprints in the banks and the resulting sand-slide seeping onto the road. We are somewhere special, I can feel it.

"So Laurie, I'm guessing you have Plymouth Rock on the itinerary?"

"We do indeed, we'll be there this time tomorrow."

It seemed an essential stop—where the English first touched U.S. soil. I've even been looking into what cakes they brought with them.

"See that skinny tower over there?" Charles points over yonder. "That's the Pilgrim Monument; it was actually here in Province-town that the *Mayflower* first met land."

"Nooo!"

"I know. Very little-known fact. Often overlooked because, though they poked around for a few weeks, they didn't actually settle here."

"Can't think why," Pamela frowns as she offers round some Cranberry Squares (basically cranberry-studded sponge). "It's darling here."

And it gets a whole lot more darling as we progress into town: pretty wooden houses surrounded by white picket fences and lovingly tended flower gardens, it's definitely more cozy-cottagey than Newport—quaint in the nicest possible sense of the word.

And then we turn onto Commercial Street.

Here we both stick out like a sore thumb (because we're in a big red bus on a dinky pedestrian street), but also fit right in—because in Provincetown, anything goes!

Multicolored flags flap and flutter as far as the eye can see; flamboyantly dressed men, several in mile-high wigs and studded stilettos, whistle and blow kisses at us; the air is filled with excited chatter and *bubbles*—pumping out from the West End Salon—adding an ethereal quality to the bustling party vibe.

"Is there some kind of festival on?" Pamela asks.

"It's like this all summer," Charles replies.

"It seems very gay," Ravenna eyes the multitude of same-sex couples.

"In both the old and new senses of the word," Charles agrees. "It's a very happy, inclusive place. Everyone is welcome."

I smile as I look around me. It's like experiencing what the world would be like if heterosexuals were in the minority. With the significant difference that no one is cursing or judging us.

As we continue past a "caffeine bar" and a series of rather swish galleries, I reach into my suitcase—I have a pair of glitter-encrusted ballet pumps that I never quite have the occasion to wear, but seem apt for today. I might even slick on my neon-pink lip gloss.

"Left here, Charles!" I direct him down Franklin Street, taking us closer to the waterfront.

Unsure that we'll make it up the hill to the hotel car park, I suggest we pull in at the side of the street and snug into the hedgerow, as the road is rather narrow.

"Great spot," Pamela notes as she takes in the beach across the way.

I nod. "And better yet, we won't need the bus again until we leave; everything is walking distance from here."

"Fantastic."

"Where to now?" Charles is ready to play bellboy with the luggage.

I backtrack a few paces.

"This is us!" I point upward—up the winding redbrick pathway bordered with potted flowers of bright yellow, cerise and purple, up to the terrace with the white wicker loungers and the big gray building that rather resembles a dovecote (albeit a deluxe one, with hexagonal turrets and wraparound balconies). This is the Land's End Inn.

I smile at the heavy wooden sign. It feels like a storybook concoction to me, but then I know what awaits us inside.

"Come on!"

Eager to witness everyone's reaction, I lead the way, but Charles and Pamela hang back as we reach the summit, saying they are happy to sit in the garden and enjoy the sunshine while Ravenna de-bogs herself.

I won't argue with that; they clearly need some time alone.

On checking in, we learn that the Schoolman Suite is accessed through a pair of closet doors beside reception. As the owner guides Ravenna on her way, she gives me a quick look back as if to say, "If I never see you again . . ."

And then I have the place to myself.

I feel giddy—there is so much beauty and artistry and originality at every turn that I can barely stand it. It's like stepping through the looking glass into the private home of some world-traveling artifact-collector from the 1930s.

The focal point of the lounge is a vast picture window looking out over the shimmering sea and framing a sculpture of a woman, back arched and hair flowing all the way to her feet. A circular ottoman bears a carved tray that I picture set with petite Cristallerie La Rochère glasses of absinthe.

At the other end of the room is a fireplace so magnificently rugged it makes me want to come back in my next life as a tiger rug, splayed before its fragrant embers.

I sink into the velvety sofa in the middle of the room and attempt to take it all in. I don't think there is one plain surface in the place. The ceilings are beamed and lofted, the walls wainscoted, wood-paneled or wallpapered. The accent tables are laden with decorative vases, ornamental boxes and treasures from the Orient. Even the lamps come beaded, tasseled or Tiffany-ed with multicolored stained glass.

Art nouveau mingles with art deco, brocade with brass, Phileas Fogg with Fu Manchu. Yet for all the antiques and ancient tomes, there's nothing musty-fusty about it. It just feels deeply luxurious and exotic.

"What do you think of this place?" I ask when Ravenna returns, damp of hair and clean of jean.

I know there's curiosity: I can see it in her eyes. Any would-be interior designer would have a catalog of comments and questions. All she gives me is, "Not really my taste." And then breaks into a spasmodic pat-down.

"Forgot your phone?"

She nods.

"I'll meet you outside."

I sigh as I pass a Metropolis-inspired bronze bust. If I can't get her with this place, there's no hope.

I'm about to round the corner to Pamela and Charles when I hear him tell her, "You look better than ever."

"How can you say that?" she scolds. "I've put on so much weight!"

"I like the new curves. You wear them well."

I can see she looks dubious.

"I mean it, Pamela," he says, reaching for her hand. "My eyes adore you."

My heart flips on her behalf. He sounds so sexy. Could he be moving in for a kiss? I can hardly bring myself to look!

"*Ready!*"

Darn Ravenna! She would choose that moment to appear.

The two of them startle apart. But as Pamela turns away I see that she's trying to hide a secret smile. She's flattered. At the very least. Interesting. I think there's a good chance that her eyes adore him too.

Chapter 26

⁓⁓⁓

The stroll back into town continues the picturesque theme. We pass houses painted lilac and sea foam and sky blue, a cluster of artists capturing the ocean view on canvas, and all manner of boutiques and eateries, ranging from tacky to cravat-worthy.

We're having so much fun window-shopping and people-watching we almost forget our assignment.

"What is it today?" Ravenna asks, looking slightly wary as we coincidentally stall beside a sex shop.

"Well, obviously you can't write a book about American cakes without featuring cupcakes."

Even Charles concedes they have become something of a phenomenon.

"And obviously they come in every imaginable flavor and decoration. However. There is one chap here in Provincetown who has gone the other way," I say, slightly regretting my phrasing. "Scott Cunningham only makes one flavor of cupcake in one color, every day of the year."

"Really? That's bold."

"I thought so. In fact, that simplicity and confidence actually inspired a musical to be written about him."

"It didn't!"

"Well, that and some legal hoo-ha about street-vending licenses and the fact that he's extremely good-looking."

"What was the musical called?" Ravenna wants to know.

"*Cupcake.*"

Pamela bursts out laughing, "Oh Laurie! This is too fabulous!"

"I know!"

"Are we actually going to get to meet this chap?"

"We are!" I cheer. "Follow me!"

ScottCakes is positioned downstairs in a corner unit on the edge of a cute bricked courtyard. In a world of precision branding, his signs stand out for their homespun cardboard-and-marker-pen nature, rather like something you might expect to find on a child's lemonade stand. Before we can even get inside, everyone has guessed the singular color of his cupcakes from the paintwork, and the fact that you can see right down into his dinky establishment from the street.

"Pink!" Pamela exclaims.

"Could it really be anything else in this town?" Charles smiles as we make our way down the steps.

Scott is there to greet us, looking even lovelier than his pictures (and his reputation, for that matter). He reminds me of a fair John Barrowman and has such a gleaming complexion that you'd think he'd come fresh from a facial. Apparently he always wears pink T-shirts—be it tie-dye or logo, a favorite being LEGALIZE GAY CUPCAKES. Today he's sporting a baby-pink polo shirt.

He welcomes us into the kitchen area, directly behind the counter displaying his wares, and offers each of us a stool to perch on as he completes our handcrafted cupcakes.

"I call this the Scottswirl," he says as he smooshes the pink frosting around the top of the sponge. "Boop!" he exclaims as he lifts the center to a peak. "Here we go!"

The "real buttercream" frosting has a slightly melted, oozy look to it, rather like strawberry mousse. All of us save Ravenna take a bite.

"Mmmm, heavenly!"

Scott only shares the precise recipe with Pamela. For the rest of us it is reduced to: "Some sugar, real butter and a whole lot of love."

"So tell me Scott," Pamela points to the framed newspaper clippings dotted around the pink walls, "how did all this begin?"

He gives a peppy smile, as if this is his favorite subject in the world. "About five years ago I was an actor living in New York, set to come here to perform in a play for a few weeks. When I got here I knew I didn't want to leave. But what am I going to do? I'm certainly not going to be doing bad commercials to make a living here, so I said to the universe, 'Give me my big success!' Just like that, out loud! And what came to my mind—boom!—was an image of the cupcakes I used to make with the kids when I was a nanny in Tribeca—they were always pink—and the name came too: ScottCakes!"

In the beginning he would only come out at night—a street vendor catering to crowds looking for a sweet pick-me-up after the bars closed.

"There I was, a forty-year-old man, dressed in pink like a fourteen-year-old girl, selling handmade cupcakes at one A.M.!"

And it worked like a charm. Then came the issue with the license and a whole legal battle (which he won) that inspired the musical. (Cue some Benny Hill-esque chases with the local police!)

They changed the name of Provincetown to Summertown and Scott became Tom, but he was there on opening night in Boston, along with 200 mini cupcakes, and even had a little cameo on stage.

"Excuse me a moment!" Scott hops up to attend to some customers.

"Quick!" Pamela huddles up. "I need to think of something new to make—I don't want to offend anyone with the fairy cakes!"

I can't help but chuckle.

"Something with the same ingredients . . ."

Ravenna adopts a huffy look. "Isn't it obvious?"

"What?" her mum blinks at her.

"Butterfly cakes."

Pamela gasps. "That's perfect! You're brilliant!"

I can tell she wants to hug her, but she knows better than to risk physical contact. It is a good call, though. Fairy cakes are, after all, just small cupcakes with flat icing instead of a twister of frosting, whereas butterfly cakes require a little more finessing— cutting a central circle from the top of each cake and slicing them in half to make the wings, which you then press into the butter-cream filling.

"I like to sift over a little icing sugar to finish."

As Pamela moves through the process, I make sure I get a snap of her using Scott's giant pink mixer, as well as the man himself showcasing his shop's gluten-free option—i.e., a shot of frosting.

There's a lot of laughter along the way—particularly as we recall the silver ball-bearings that used to be so popular as cake decora-tions. (We learn that they are actually banned in California due to assorted lawsuits.) Even when we've returned the stainless-steel work surface to a pristine state, we're reluctant to leave.

"There is a magical quality here, for sure," Scott agrees.

"I think you should be upgraded from The Cupcake Man to The Cupcake Angel," I decide as we bid farewell.

"You know this little area is known as Angel's Landing?" He points out of the window.

"I didn't know that!" I say, getting a little chill. (I can so see him with silver wings and a tinsel halo!)

Pamela seems equally enchanted. "This place makes me want to be gay in my next life."

Charles raises a brow.

"Well, they just seem to keep the exuberance of youth going a lot longer."

Nobody is ready to return to the hotel yet, so we continue our perusal of Commercial Street and its eye-popping sights, like this life-size black bear sporting a feather boa, propped on the porch of the Purple Feather Café & Treatery.

As we step up for a closer look, Ravenna makes a casual exit: "Just popping back to one of the shops. I'll catch you up in a minute."

Pamela looks fretful as she sees her daughter disappear into the pedestrian flow.

"Do you want me to hang back and keep an eye?" I offer.

"Would you?"

"No problem."

I start weaving back down the street, trying to catch a glimpse of her, wondering which shop she has stepped into. Not this "clam-shell" jewelers or Monty's Emporium, though he does have a rather fabulous line of Mermen ornaments—*Splash* from the waist down, Village People from the waist up.

"Gotcha!" I mutter, as I spy her level with ScottCakes. "Oops!" I duck into an art-gallery doorway as she turns back, as if checking to see if she's being followed. When I dip my head out again, she's gone. "Darnit."

I take a few paces forward, glancing down into Scott's as I do so. And there she is. Purchasing and then inhaling one of his cupcakes. My jaw drops. She eats!

Apparently this place really brings out the depraved hedonist in a person, because she's now ordering a second. And then posing for a photo with Scott, giggling with him. Must be the sugar rush. I have to say she looks amazingly pretty when she's smiling.

Oh jeez, here she comes now!

I turn to hide myself and collide with a seven-foot drag queen in voluminous Cleopatra robes.

"You on the run, hun?"

"I just need to—"

"Hide?" she says, opening up the wingspan of her dress and inviting me in. I have no choice but to burrow into her fake boobs as her arms close around me.

I don't know how she can wear so much man-made fiber in this heat and still look so ridiculously glamorous. Just as I'm thinking her spiky neck collar is going to make a permanent indentation in my forehead, she releases me.

"All clear! It was the Kristen Stewart kid you were avoiding, right?"

I nod.

"She's gone back down the street."

For a minute I stand transfixed by her face. The artistry of her teal eye makeup, the expert shading enhancing her cheekbones, the glitter pressed carefully onto her lips.

She in turn is studying the matching sparkles on my shoes. "Very Dorothy," she notes. "You know what color shoes the Pope wears?"

"I want to say red?"

She nods. "And when he clicks his heels together he says, 'There's no place like Rome!'"

I burst out laughing. "That's a good one."

"Here!" she hands me a flyer. "Tea Dance today at the Boat-slip."

"Really?" My face brightens. "That is actually perfect!"

"I know. I'm your fairy godmother."

And in a swirl of gold lamé, she's gone.

Chapter 27

❧

My first thought regarding the Tea Dance is what a terrible shame it is that Gracie can't be with us to enjoy the tinkling piano, potted palms and silver sugar tongs. In reality there are none of these. No wafts of Darjeeling, no ladies in modest frocks, no gentlemen offering to take you for a spin around the dance floor. Well, actually, that's not true. There are a few of those. A few hundred. Shirtless. Sweating. Arms aloft, pounding and throbbing along to the music. Several of them are only wearing tight swimming trunks, giving a whole new meaning to "One lump or two?"

"Ah," I stall. "This may not be quite what we had in mind."

"You've brought us to a big open-air gay rave," Ravenna smirks.

"Yes," I confirm. "Yes I have."

"Hey!" One chap with an elaborately tattooed right arm comes up to Pamela. "Are you with this guy?" He motions to Charles.

"Um. Well. Not exactly," she falters.

"Great, you wanna dance?" he turns to Charles.

Ravenna looks even more tickled by this.

All I can do is look on helplessly.

"Sure," he surprises all of us. "Why not?"

"What?" Ravenna hoots.

We stand amazed as he merges with the seething bodies before us. He's actually quite a mover, instantly in time with the beat.

"This is weird, he looks kind of cool," Ravenna is in awe.

"He always was a good dancer," murmurs Pamela.

"How would you know?" Ravenna frowns. "I thought you met him at an antiques fair?"

"I think this young man is trying to get your attention," Pamela redirects her daughter's attention.

"Oh no, no," Ravenna backs away from the extended hand. "Not me. I don't really dance."

"Oh please," the young man wheedles. "I only ever get to dance with dudes. Just once I'd like to dance with a pretty girl!"

This gets her. It doesn't hurt that he's really good-looking—full six-pack on display, T-shirt tucked into his Diesel jeans pocket, blond hair whisked up into a Tintin peak.

"Just one dance?"

Ravenna tries to resist but he's gone to full puppy-dog pleading.

"One song, that's it," she relents.

"Whatever you say, baby girl," he says, kissing her hand and leading her off.

I look at Pamela. "I don't know what to say."

Fortunately she starts to laugh. "This could be exactly what we need."

"D-do you want to dance?" I feel a little awkward asking her.

"I think I might need a drink first."

"Me too. Let's find the bar . . ."

An hour later, Charles is now up on some tabletop, shaking what his mama gave him, yet still managing to look emphatically heterosexual, which of course makes him the beau of the ball.

"This is so hilarious!" Ravenna whoops and whistles along with the rest of his admirers. I'm guessing she's taken a few sips of her young escort's drinks, but I'm hardly in a position to judge. Pamela suggested we needed to cut to the chase with some shots and now I'm feeling wonderfully blurry and absorbed into the scene.

When Donna Summer's "Last Dance" comes on, we're all just one heaving, pulsing, sing-a-long mass.

"Cleo!" I wave to the Cleopatra drag queen.

She blows me a kiss back and in my mind the entire place fills with glitter.

There's something really fun about being sweaty and disheveled when everyone you are with is in the same state of disarray. Hungry now, but not inclined to go back to the hotel to change, we buy a batch of lobster rolls from one of the walk-up windows near the beach and have a picnic on the sand.

"I don't know the last time I danced like that," Pamela marvels as she licks the mayonnaise from her fingertips.

"I've never danced like that!" Charles laughs.

"So you say," I tease.

"Do you have a partner, Charles?" Ravenna wants to know.

"A partner?" he chuckles. "No, not currently."

"Have you ever been married?"

"Once, a long time ago."

"But no girlfriend now?"

"Ravenna!" Pamela scolds her. "That's a lot of personal questions."

"I don't mind," he says. "The thing is, Ravenna, once you've experienced true love, it's hard to settle for anything less."

"Well I think you should consider putting yourself out there again. You'd obviously have your pick."

"Of gay men at least!" I try to make light of the situation.

"Oh, look at that!" Pamela points to a man paddling past in a bright yellow canoe, with two small dogs in pink life jackets balanced on the front.

I reach for the camera and then scan the rest of the vista—restaurant terraces buzzing with happy chatter; little rowing boats strewn along the shore; dogs frolicking and no one making a fuss; guys walking hand in hand, laughing.

"I don't mean to sound prejudiced in any way, but the world would be a very dull place without gay people," I slur slightly. "They've got the whole *joie de vivre* thing down."

"They really have," Pamela confirms.

We sit for a moment, happy to be part of their rainbow world, looking out across the glassy-smooth water and wiggling our toes deeper into the sand.

And then Charles asks, "Who's game for trying the Portuguese kale soup?"

"I just want another lobster roll," Pamela responds.

"I'll try it," Ravenna offers, quickly adding, "Kale is a superfood."

Sounds to me as if she thinks it will cancel out those cupcakes. And maybe here it will . . .

As we head back to the hotel, Pamela and I fall into a natural meander, pausing to peer into assorted girlie gardens while Ravenna and Charles stride ahead.

I watch them walking, perfectly in sync. No skulking from her now.

"He really does seem to bring out the best in her," I observe.

"He's her father."

"*What?*" I blurt, tripping over the uneven paving.

Pamela nods. "You're the first person I've ever told. Other than my mother, of course—hence the setup."

I can't believe this! My brain tries to catch up.

"Were you expecting to see him on this trip?" I ask.

"I thought perhaps in Boston . . ." She trails off. "I didn't expect him to be driving the bus!"

"No," I mumble. "But you're glad to see him?"

"I am." She gazes fondly at the back of his head.

"So you didn't meet ten years ago?"

"Twenty-one."

"I see . . ."

"I was on a break from Brian, coming up to my fortieth birthday, despairing that he was ever going to propose. Mum said it would do him good to miss me. She was never a fan, didn't care for his 'tone.' Anyway, she and Dad were going to visit some long-lost relatives in Boston, she invited me to join them. So I did."

"And that's where you met?"

"My mother was parading every eligible man before me, I think in the hope that I wouldn't go back to Brian. Charles wasn't one of them—technically he was still married at the time, just about to start divorce proceedings—but he's the one who caught my eye."

"He is a good-looking fella."

"It was more than that," she sighs. "He had a gentleness to him and a humility, the polar opposite to Brian. At first I thought it was just that—the contrast—but then I realized it was the first time I felt understood by a man. When he looked at me I felt like he was really paying attention, that he wanted to *know* me. All of me. And it felt so wonderful, to have someone on my side, someone caring, who I didn't have to guard against. I felt myself blossoming in his presence, as silly as that sounds." She looks away.

"It doesn't sound silly, it sounds ideal. I think we all wish for someone who brings out the best in us." I feel a yearning for this right now. "It must have been hard to leave him, at the end of the trip."

She nods. "It was unthinkable. At first. But then you're home, back to reality. And there was Brian, waiting with a proposal. Of course my first instinct was to say no—how could I possibly settle now that my heart knew what it was to soar?—but then I realized I was pregnant, so choosing Brian seemed like the more responsible, if deceitful, thing to do. I mean, we were already living together—good or bad, he was the known quantity, whereas Charles was essentially a too-good-to-be-true holiday fling. He lived in a different country, he was tied to his school there. I'd just signed up for another series of *Teatime with Pamela* in the UK. He already had one child and a soon-to-be ex-wife. It was just too complicated."

"Gosh." The paths we choose. I wonder how many times she has wished she could rewind to that day and make a different choice. "Did Brian ever suspect Ravenna wasn't his?"

"He'd make comments from time to time. She doesn't resemble him in any way physically, but then in her teens she seemed to develop his mean spirit. And he was quite proud of that."

"What about Ravenna?"

"She has no idea. The plan was to tell her on her eighteenth birthday, but I've been putting it off." She looks so sad now. "Sometimes I can hardly bear to think of what I did."

I take her arm, afraid she might cry.

"And Charles?" I ask as we continue on. "He never met her before today?"

She shakes her head. "He's been waiting a long time for this moment."

"Wow."

"I know. He wants to tell her tomorrow in Boston—on home turf, I suppose. I just don't want to rush into anything."

"Oh I wouldn't worry about that," I want to tell her. "She can't despise you any more than she already does."

But of course I keep quiet.

"I've thought about him every day," Pamela says, looking ahead at her love. "Always missing him. Missing the hope he brought into my life but somehow not feeling deserving of it." She shakes her head. "All my issues, standing between him and his daughter. I can't believe I've held him at a distance all this time."

I turn to face her. "I know what it is to regret, Pamela. But now is the time to look forward. You have a chance to make things right."

"I can never make it right—"

"Don't give up," I implore, gripping her hands. "You have to believe things can get better."

I mean it: she *has* to, because then I can believe it too.

Chapter 28

And so to the Schoolman Suite. The color scheme appears to be a celebration of New England foliage—emerald-green paintwork, orangey-gold wallpaper, red accent walls. And then along come the trademark traveler's treasures: a tarnished Moroccan lantern strung overhead, a rich Persian rug beneath our feet and a pair of bow-legged coffee tables that look as though they've been lifted from the back of an elephant in Siam.

Pamela and Ravenna are sharing the king-size bed at the top of the wrought-iron staircase. Their loft area has a particularly beautiful window in the shape of a fan. Of course it's dark now, but that's going to be quite something to wake up to.

"Sleep well," I say as I leave them to it.

My bedroom is off the living room, through a pair of sliding doors. The walls are of scalloped wood, similar to some of the houses we saw today. It has dusty pink accents, fringed lamps and a floral bedhead that I am more than ready to be propped against. But I feel I should offer it to Charles one more time before I succumb—I personally only lasted an hour on the deck in Newport.

"Honestly, I'd be perfectly happy sleeping on one of the sofas," I insist as I lean out into the cool air.

Instead of replying, he beckons me over. "I hear Pamela told you?"

Ah. He wants to talk. "She did," I confirm. "Congratulations?"

"I know this isn't what you signed up for, a lot of family drama on this trip."

"Actually I sort of did. I promised Gracie I'd stick it out, come what may."

He smiles. "She's a force of nature, that one."

"Yes she is."

I'm about to turn back inside when he asks, "Are you close with your father?"

"No," I say simply. "I never really knew him."

"Well, I can certainly relate to what he's missed out on."

I'm not quite sure what to say in reply. "I think Ravenna is very lucky to have a dad like you, however belatedly. And you two have got plenty of time ahead of you."

"If she accepts me."

"I don't think it's you she's going to have the problem with."

Charles heaves a sigh. "She carries a lot of resentment toward her mother, doesn't she?"

"She does. But I think there's hope."

His eyes meet mine. "Thank you for saying that."

I feel tears welling as a voice within murmurs, "I wish I had a dad like you." I take a steadying breath. "Anyway, I should get to bed, early start tomorrow."

"Of course."

"Last chance to swap." I hesitate.

"Honestly, I'm fine. I love camping. And this is more like, what's the new term?"

"Glamping?" I smile.

"That's it."

"Good night."
"Good night Laurie."

Despite all the thoughts swirling in my head, I fall asleep as soon as my head touches the pillow. But within a few hours I'm awake again, parched from our Tea Dance boozing. I desperately need a slug of water and remember there are glasses in the bathroom. Of course at home I can feel my way around in the dark but here I fear that would involve knocking down a series of irreplaceable heirlooms. Using the light from my phone I beam a pathway, but when I push open the mirrored door, I see that someone has beaten me to it.

There on the floor is Ravenna, lit by the jewel-hued moonlight and chugging with silent tears.

"What is it?" I hurry to her side. "What's the matter?"

She shakes her head, turning her face away from me.

Oh my god—has she found out? Did she overhear something?

"Ravenna . . ." For once my approach is gentle.

"I don't want to talk about it!" she protests.

I bite my lip. "Is it really so awful?"

She nods her head vigorously. "But you wouldn't understand."

I sigh and then settle onto the dusky grape carpet beside her. "Try me."

She looks back at me, wary but desperate.

"Go on," I encourage.

"*I put on two pounds.*"

Is she serious?

"That's why you're so upset?" I gawp.

She nods.

"Nobody will even notice!"

"Eon will."

"I assure you he won't. He might even like it."

She scoffs. "He *wouldn't* like it. And he *would* know."

"How can you be so sure?"

She wipes her tears with the heels of her hands. And then she looks me right in the eye. "He weighed me before I left."

This stops me in my tracks.

"He *weighed* you?"

"He was worried that spending so much time around my mother would involve a lot of eating. And he was right. You've no idea what I've gorged on today," her voice trembles. "It's totally gross."

My jaw is still slack. "He actually got you to stand on the scales?"

"Yes."

"And that didn't ring any alarm bells with you?"

"What do you mean?" Her pink eyes peer into me.

"It didn't strike you as a little creepy? A little controlling?"

"He just wants the best for me."

"And that 'best' comes at a particular weight?"

She sighs impatiently. "There's not an exact number. He just doesn't want me to end up like my mother."

"Meaning?"

"He doesn't want a fat girlfriend."

"He said that?" I feel physically sick.

"Yes."

"He said those words?"

"What's the big deal? He's just being honest. I respect that."

I lean back on the wooden siding of the bath, taking a moment to compose myself. "You know, I had a boyfriend say that to me once. It's such an ugly sentiment, but he said it so casually, like he was just giving me a friendly tip-off. When in fact it was, of course, a threat."

"It's different with Eon. He says he doesn't want me to change because he loves me just as I am," she pouts.

I give a little snort. "You can justify his comment all you like, but tell me, how does it make you *feel* when he says that kind of thing?"

She concedes a shrug. "Well. It's not exactly reassuring."

"It's not meant to be. It's designed to keep you on your toes—to keep you feeling vulnerable, on edge." I look at her. "Is that how you feel?"

"Well, I do sometimes wonder if I'm wearing the right thing or whether he likes my hair a certain way . . . But doesn't every woman want to look nice for her man?"

"Of course, but she shouldn't be afraid that his feelings for her would be altered by how she looks on a particular day."

"I think it's different for Eon because he has such a heightened sense of style," Ravenna explains. "He's just started working in the fashion industry."

"Oh jeez."

"What's wrong with that?"

"Nothing, in and of itself. It's just a fantastic excuse for him to run his mouth on how you look every day."

"The thing is, he's so perfect. I hate to feel like I'm letting him down."

Wow. What a brilliant trick he has performed, convincing her that he is perfect and that she is the one with all the flaws.

We sit for a moment in silence.

"So what happened with your boyfriend?" Ravenna asks. "How did you respond, you know, when he said he didn't want a fat girlfriend?"

"I said, 'And I don't want a misogynist boyfriend.'"

"Really?"

"But I didn't break up with him. Not straightaway. It took a few more weeks, but I knew in that moment that it was done. Because, as much as he didn't want a fat girlfriend, I knew I could never be with someone who would say such a thing to someone he supposedly loved."

"So you don't think it's love?" She sounds nervous now.

"It's not. It's a whole mess of other things. But it's definitely not love."

"What's going on in here?" Pamela is at the door, eyes all scrunchy as they try to adjust.

"Oh! Just some girls' talk—we didn't want to wake you so we sneaked in here." I get to my feet, blocking Ravenna from her view. "Everything all right with you?"

"Yes, yes, I just need a wee."

I reach behind me and help Ravenna to her feet. "All yours. See you in the morning."

"Mmmf," she mumbles.

As the door closes, I look back at Ravenna.

"To be continued?"

She nods.

Chapter 29

∾∾∾

When I returned to bed, I dreamed of my sister Jess. But it wasn't the druggy Jess tormenting me. It was worse. It was the lovely version of her. The one I'd all but forgotten about, the one I now barely acknowledge ever existed.

In order to write off a family member, you have to stay keenly focused on all the ways they've done you wrong, all their character flaws, all the reasons why there is no redemption to be had. It doesn't do to remember how proud you felt watching them in the school play, or their contagious giggle, especially when you are dreaming and can't guard your heart against the feelings that go along with those memories.

While I was sleeping, I went back to our childhood playtimes. We were a good team then: I would make the practical arrangements, select the toys and the snacks; she would bring the imagination that turned a bed sheet slung between two chairs into an African safari tent or the rug beside the front door into a magic carpet ride.

With her talent for transporting us to all manner of exotic

lands, you would have thought she would have been the one who had favored a career in travel, but instead she decided to follow in our father's footsteps selling life insurance. (It was one of the few things we knew for sure about him—his job.) Now she was using her imagination to conjure up never-ending scenarios in which you die unexpectedly, leaving your family in abject poverty. Even though she earned a decent salary and I was always offering her great bargains, she rarely went on holiday. The first time she asked me to help her plan a trip was to Goa. I should have known that something was up. In my experience, most people want to visit India when they are looking for an inner shift—they want a new perspective or just to feel something very different to the norm. Jess wanted to leave the very next week, but it was monsoon season so I told her to hold off for a couple of months, and it was during that period that she chose to poison off all her potential for greater happiness with the drugs. And that's all I have to think about to make the good feelings about her go away.

Emerging from my room, I am relieved to discover that Charles and Pamela are already up and out, so I make a beeline for the deck, relishing having it to myself.

There's not a wave as far as the eye can see, just glimmering ripples spotted with bobbing boats, canoes and inflatable loungers. At least that's the view toward the pier. Over in the direction of the dunes, it's clear, unadorned periwinkle blue.

I take an elongated breath—I love this combination: a light ruffling breeze with an underlying burn from the sun. I close my eyes and let my vision glow to red as strands of hair lift and swish across my face. As I stand there, I feel my heart rate slowing, my breathing easing. I might believe I could meditate in such a moment. Or maybe this is as good as meditation. It's funny, inner peace is nothing I've ever particularly aspired to. I always wanted to be a woman of action. But now I can see how blissful inaction can be.

Even the Adirondack chairs seem to offer fantastic back support. As I take a seat I rest my head back and wonder how long I could stay here, were it not for my obligations. At what point would I have had my fill? I'm always rushing on to the next thing, ricocheting around a schedule—what if I just stayed here? Forever. A quick check of my watch tells me I'm going to have to go for quality over quantity, so I attempt to let this feeling seep into my bones and create a memory from it so I can always come back here in my mind. As Krista says, "Travel broadens the mind, but the mind can always travel." Now I've been here, and felt this bliss, I have an open invitation to return, wherever I am.

I think that's why, in my mind at least, it's sometimes worth paying over the odds for a room, because you're buying more than a bed for the night, you're buying an experience, investing in your ability to be amazed by the world, which to me is the most rejuvenating sensation of all. It's so easy to feel tired and jaded by the humdrum, but you can get through all that if you know that a beautiful feeling is coming your way. I think it's terribly important to remind yourself of how you really want to live your life. If we keep a treasure box of what we love in our minds, we can try to make choices that keep us moving in that direction.

I remember writing a "Holiday Blues" page for Va-Va-Vacation!, dedicated to those people who slump horribly after they return from their two weeks in Greece, or wherever. One of the secrets is to ask yourself: what is it that you love so much about being there and how can you have more of that in your life? Of course, some things are a quicker fix than others: you can easily have more tzatziki, but you can't buy two weeks of sunshine from Sainsbury's. You might consider a second job—even one day a week for six months could buy you a second holiday. I mean, what would you be doing with your time anyway? If you're spending most of the time watching TV, wishing you had someone else's life, it might be worth considering. I know one of our readers got a Saturday job in a Greek taverna and ended up making friends with the owners and staying at their family home in Skiathos for free.

There are lots of possibilities out there for people of limited means, if you are willing to get a little creative and go that extra mile for what you love.

"Where is everyone?"

By utter contrast, here is Ravenna.

"Gone for a stroll," I tell her. "They left a note."

Ravenna steps up to the edge of the deck. "Is that them there?"

I lean forward, squinting. "Yes, looks like it." I feel a mild flush of anxiety, hoping they won't stop and kiss right in front of us. Their body language certainly looks inclined in that direction. "Shall we go down to breakfast?"

Ravenna gives me a look.

"Coffee?" I rephrase my invitation.

We creak down the stairs, exit through the closet doors and behold the continental spread. A big jade buddha watches over the teas, an art deco maiden the cereals. I fill my bowl with fresh strawberries and pineapple, pluck a berry muffin spilling over from its casing and stir honey into my camomile and lemon tea. Life is good.

Taking our seats on the veranda, I notice Ravenna is the only one hunched over her phone. Everyone else is reading newspapers or books. So much more relaxing. It makes me nostalgic for the time before portable technology. Out of respect for my surroundings, I keep mine in my bag.

"Do you know I don't think I had my first coffee until I was in my late twenties? I hear schoolgirls today saying they need their caffeine fix, when the most I'd get was a Robinson's Barley Water."

Ravenna looks back at me. "You talk a lot."

"Well, there's just so much to say, isn't there?"

She shrugs and returns to her phone.

"You prefer texting to talking?"

Her thumbs halt. I feel as if she's about to say something potent when Pamela and Charles clomp up the steps.

"Morning all!"

"Morning!" I chirrup back. "Ready for some breakfast?"

"Actually, Charles took me to the Portuguese bakery and I had my first malasada."

"Malasada?" I attempt to repeat.

"It looks like a big doughnut that's been run over," Pamela begins, "but when you bite into it you find the texture is more like an airy ciabatta that's been deep-fried and coated in sugar."

"That sounds strangely good."

"Oh, it is—I love that sensation when you release the grease."

"Gross," Ravenna recoils.

"There's quite the Portuguese tradition here," Charles says as he pulls up a chair. "Their festival is one of the biggest events of the summer—there's parades, dancing, the Blessing of the Fleet . . ."

I notice Ravenna listens when he speaks. Looking between them, I search for a family resemblance. It's hard to tell with her mess of hair and giant sunglasses, but perhaps there's something in the chin area?

"What do you think, Laurie?"

"Sorry, what was that?"

"Do we have time for one quick detour as we head out?" Charles wants to know. "Just ten minutes?"

He says he'd like to give us a closer look at the dunes—you can even drive along the beach there.

I grimace. "I'm not sure Red is cut out for off-roading."

He chuckles and explains that we'll just pull over at the side of the road and then cut through on foot.

I'm very glad we do. It's a fascinating sight—great swooping dunes of palest blond sand, whiskery with grasses, burrowing down to the occasional dark-green oasis.

Charles points to a grayish shack on the horizon, one of a dozen or so spaced out along the coast.

"Looks like the ultimate writer's retreat," I joke.

"You're right! Some of the greats have stayed here: Eugene O'Neill, Tennessee Williams—Jack Kerouac even conceived part of *On the Road* here."

"What?" Now that's a trip!

"Do you know E. E. Cummings?"

"I'm not sure," I reply.

"He wrote the most beautiful poem called 'I carry your heart with me . . .'"

Charles looks like a movie star as he quotes it to us, the wind ruffling his hair, making him look all the more romantically rugged against the backdrop of shifting sands.

I can't help thinking, "If he was twenty years younger . . ."

"Today, if you're a writer or an artist, you can apply for a residency at a couple of the shacks. There's no electricity, no running water; they just drop you off in a dune buggy with your supplies and come back a week or so later to pick you up."

"I don't know if I'd like that," I shiver. "Wouldn't it get a bit spooky at night?"

"It's actually all right. At least it fitted my mood at the time."

"You stayed in one?" Ravenna is impressed.

"It was a long time ago. I thought I was going to write the Great American Novel but it just turned into a great outpouring of my broken heart."

My eyes flit to Pamela. She does look a tad guilty.

"Can we read it?" Ravenna asks. "Is it published?"

"I never finished it."

"Still waiting for the happy ending?" I find myself asking.

He looks wistful. "I think in a way I was always waiting for her to come back to me."

"And now she's here," I want to say. In fact, now they're both here—the two missing women in his life.

As he answers Ravenna's questions about the décor of the shacks—"I'm picturing lanterns and bunk beds and itchy blankets!"—I step back and oh-so-discreetly take some candid snaps of the three of them. Perhaps this full-circle moment will make a nice memento for him. Or a sadly poignant one, depending on how things go with today's revelation.

Chapter 30

∽∽∽

On our way to Sandwich, I get an e-mail from Gracie asking if I can set her up with a "bachelorette pad" in Newport. She's well enough to leave hospital, but not up to traveling, so she just needs a nice spot to recuperate.

I know just the place. The Cliffside Inn is just a few steps from Cliff Walk, strolling distance from town; there's a gourmet breakfast every morning and social tea in the afternoon, so plenty of opportunity to mingle with the other guests. Plus they have a garden suite available that avoids any of the staircase-wheezing of the main building, and it has a separate lounge area so she'll be able to entertain, as I know she'll be making friends in no time. (Apparently her facial bruising is quite a conversation-starter.)

"Do you think we should divert back there and get her settled in?" Pamela asks.

I look back at the e-mail. "If Pamela suggests coming back for any reason, please dissuade her. It is imperative she keeps moving forward with Charles."

"I think what she needs most is peace and quiet," I reply. "If we go back she'll be less inclined to sleep and get the rest she needs."

"You're right," Pamela nods. "She's not a fan of being fussed over, anyway."

Fortunately our arrival in Sandwich distracts Pamela from any further fretting on the subject.

"Do you think you have to pass some kind of test to live here?" I wonder as I take in the Bree Van de Kamp perfection of it all. "You know, proven skills in lawn-trimming and picnic-basket-arranging and all-round wholesomeness?"

There's even a father teaching his son fishing in the sunlit river beside the old mill.

Sandwich is the oldest town in Cape Cod, first settled in 1637 and named after Sandwich in Kent. Neither one has anything to do with sliced bread—the name comes from the Old English meaning "trading center on sand." Rather more dramatic is the U.S. town's motto: *Post tot naufragia portus*, which translates as "After so many shipwrecks, a haven."

It is that. And the Dunbar Tea Room is a haven within a haven. A former carriage house with a cozy fireplace, it made the cover of *The Great Tea Rooms of America*. Since we're still full of breakfast, it's just a quick snoop and a photo opportunity beside their cake buffet.

"Nice piping," I hear Ravenna mutter.

Pamela is impressed by the range of teas on offer (I catch her discreetly pointing out the "Courtship" tea to Charles) and the promise of a real Plowman's Lunch.

"Well, whatever you order, you know it will be filling." Charles looks around for a response. "Get it? Sandwich. Filling."

Half an hour later, we arrive at Plymouth Rock.

"Is that it?" Ravenna is unimpressed with the lump of pale-gray stone caged in a mini Acropolis at the water's edge.

It's definitely one of those landmarks that you arrive at and then say, "Now what?"

Fortunately I have something particular in mind.

The Plimoth Plantation is a reminder of America's Think Big mentality. Instead of a few artifacts in a museum, they have taken 130 acres of prime coastal land and rewound the clock so you can really understand how the people lived, and ate, back in 1627 (seven years after the arrival of the *Mayflower*).

Once you get beyond the visitor center, there is no trace of modern life. The road slopes down and you find yourself surrounded by grassy fields and grazing cattle, sandy roads and a series of small thatched, timber-framed homes. Costumed role-players invite you to step inside and see the earth floors and ash-heaped hearth with its blackened pans and metal pail currently boiling water. There's a heavy wooden table set with pewter plates and hand-glazed pitchers and, over in the corner, an early design for a canopy bed.

Pamela asks one reenactor, bulky in her excessive yardage of Pilgrim fabric, what kind of cakes they might have prepared in those days. She answers "mostly spice cakes and Shrewsbury cakes" and then leads us down the main drag to an alfresco communal oven where the daily bread was baked.

"No TV, no mobile phones, no liquid eyeliner, can you imagine?" I nudge Ravenna.

"I don't even want to," Ravenna shudders. "Can we move on?"

It turns out that we are touring out of sequence because, after a forage through the forest, we discover the Wampanoag homesite—home to the *original* settlers.

After seeing so many Westerns as a child, it's almost unnerving to walk among these moccasin-clad Native People with their beaded wristbands and feathered dream-catchers. These are not lookalikes cast in a role, but actual descendants of Native tribes creating a living history exhibit. I feel part-intruder, part-voyeur as I watch a woman hoick her baby into a papoose while another tends to the campfire, but they are unfazed and welcoming. With the possible exception of a bored-looking teen, slumped atop a log, looking as though she'd rather be at the mall with her friends.

"Shall we go into the longhouse?"

It is here we discover one of the most beautiful women I have ever seen, sitting amid the raccoon furs and raffia weavings, rhythmically stirring something porridge-y. She looks like the fantasy of Pocahontas: long black hair braided to one side; sheeny, caramel skin set against the buttery suede of her fringed dress. She tells us that the bowl she is holding, similar to a hollowed-out coconut, is what they would use to portion their meals—it replicates the size of the stomach so you would only eat enough to fill that. And then when you were hungry you would eat again. Which sounds so much more reasonable than our stomach-stretching three-course meals.

I ask if they have any kind of teatime tradition and she says no—if the children were craving something sweet, they would give them berries. Ravenna is utterly rapt. For the first time she joins in with the questions—does Wampanoag have an English translation? Did she make her earrings herself? We're just learning about how the more elderly members of the family would sleep closest to the fires at the center of the longhouse, when I catch sight of Pamela beckoning me outside—she wants me to give her agent an update on the phone, which feels so inappropriate in this setting that I all but clamber into a blueberry bush so as not to ruin the vibe for my fellow visitors.

When I stumble out again, I find Ravenna pacing impatiently.

"This is absolutely outrageous," she spits. "I just can't believe it!"

"Believe what?"

"Do you realize that these people had no disease and no obesity before the bastard English came along with their smallpox and diphtheria and sugar and *ruined* them? They welcomed these strangers off the boat, shared their skills for harnessing nature's bounty and in return they enslaved them, took their land, wiped out half of them. I mean, for god's sake, Laurie!" She looks wild-eyed at me. "How can this be?"

I sigh, defeated. "It's not right, is it?"

"Well. I know we can't go back in time, but surely there must be something we can do?" She looks so earnest, like she wants a solution *right now*.

I don't know what to say, other than it makes me feel thoroughly ashamed to be English. But I am sufficiently impressed by Ravenna's first unselfish request to get my thinking cap on as we head back to the bus.

"There is one thing," I venture as we pass the Craft Center. "If you are going to move into interior design, you could think about incorporating some of their handicrafts when you get a commission. Perhaps they'll even become your signature look; that way you're helping improve their economy, bringing their work to a new audience and keeping the conversation going about them . . ."

"That's actually a good idea. Except for one thing."

"What's that?"

She sighs.

I wait.

Finally she speaks: "I don't know if that's what I really want to do. You know, as a career."

Ah.

"Indian Pudding?" Pamela appears before us, this time offering a dollop of brown gloop from the café. "This is the closest thing to a native dessert, made from cornmeal, milk and molasses."

I take a spoonful—it's actually tasty and textured, with a spice that makes my tongue tingle. "Nutmeg?"

"And a bit of cinnamon and ginger," Pamela confirms.

"I was thinking of trading bread pudding, what do you think?"

"I'd say that would be spot on," I smile, though my gaze has strayed back to Ravenna, busily chewing at her thumbnail.

She does have my sympathy. It's no picnic when you don't know what you want to do with your life. And it makes it all the more easy to be swayed by people like Eon. As they say, "If you don't stand for something, you'll fall for anything."

Chapter 31

๑๛๑

We have one more stop before Boston—a ten-minute diversion to Quincy, home of the very first Dunkin' Donuts shop in 1950.

"We diverted for this?"

I know that's what everyone is thinking, because I'm thinking it myself. What can I say? Not every stop on our itinerary is a winner. I suppose I expected the whole town to be in a time warp, which in some ways it is, just not in a cute pink neon/red Chevy kind of way.

"Shall we just hop out for a quick pic?" The signage has got to be worth a snap.

A few years ago, this particular branch went through a retro-fication, returning to the original "handwriting" typeface and adding a sit-up counter. Mind you, the enduring pink and orange color scheme is pretty kitschy wherever you go.

"Well?"

No one seems keen to leave the bus.

"They do a Boston Cream Donut—it might get us in the mood for tomorrow's pie?"

"I suppose I could do with a wee." Ravenna hauls herself up.

Our uneasiness increases as we enter. Let's just say the clientele is less than chic. But what did I expect? We're not in some Parisien macaroon store. It's then I spy the couple holding hands in the corner. Eighty if they're a day. They look equally affronted by the lack of grooming in the assembled youths. I can tell they still starch and iron and take the time to comb their hair just so.

"Do you think they had their first date here?" Charles whispers to me.

I smile back. "I think that's the only possible explanation for them being here—nostalgia."

"Rather sweet, isn't it?"

"It really is," I say as I look back at them, clinging on for dear life across the Formica tabletop. "At least they have each other."

"Here you go!" Pamela hands me my Boston Cream Donut.

I take a distracted bite. And then my senses kick in. "Oh my!" She smiles at my reaction.

"I rather like it!" I like the splurge of mild custard, the not-exactly-chocolate-as-we-Brits-know-it topping, and the doughnut aspect, which is more akin to a synthetic soft white roll than its deep-fried cousin.

"Not overly sweet, is it?" Pamela notes.

I shake my head as I take another bite.

"Shame we're not here in October." Charles looks the picture of regret.

"Why's that?"

"For Halloween they do a Boston Scream Donut!"

We all laugh. Except Ravenna, obviously. She's on her phone again.

"He doesn't seem to make her very happy, this boyfriend of hers," Charles notes as he watches her pacing outside the window.

"No," Pamela and I agree.

"Perhaps it's time she moves on?" he suggests.

"It's definitely time for us to move on," I say, as a series of low-slung jeans bundle in.

So much for a quick getaway.

"What's that noise?" Ravenna joins us at the front of the bus. "Can you hear it? That clunking-dragging sound?"

"We hear it," Charles replies. "I don't know what it is but I know it's not good."

"Are we going to make it to Boston?" I can't think of anything worse than getting stuck here.

"We've just got about ten miles to go, but I'm thinking we should go straight to the garage and get it looked at." He catches my eye. "If that's not going to mess with the schedule too much, Laurie?"

"It's fine," I tell him. "We don't have set appointments until tomorrow morning. Do you have a particular garage in mind?"

"I do. The best mechanic in the business is in Cambridge, just across the bridge from Boston. It would be hell to park in the city, so we might be better off leaving the bus there until we head on to Maine."

So that becomes our plan.

I'm surprised by how daunting it feels, entering the grimy hustlings and honkings of a big city after the gently twittering countryside. I'm glad we've got a native Bostonian on board. Charles makes an excellent tour guide, pointing out assorted landmarks on our way. My Top Three are:

1. Newton—this is actually just a road sign to a town twenty minutes away, but it's where Fig Newtons got their name. No need to actually visit—I've learned my lesson there: just good to know.

2. Fenway Park—home to the Boston Red Sox and a significant

backdrop in Ben Affleck's gritty bank-robber movie, *The Town*. Which is really good. I love Ben Affleck.

3. Harvard University—be still my beating heart! It's literally two blocks from where we pull in to the cavernous mechanic's workshop.

No sooner have we disembarked than Pamela is guiding me over to the garage entrance for "a quick word."

"Everything all right?" She seems a little flustered.

"Yes. Um. I know you've supplied a list of places to visit today . . ."

"Just suggestions, really. Nothing set in stone."

"I know. And I do want to visit them. Especially those cupcake places on Newton Street—"

"Newbury," I correct her.

"Right. Got Fig Newtons on the brain now."

"But?"

"Charles feels we really shouldn't keep Ravenna in the dark any longer."

"Time for the big reveal?"

She sighs. "It's not the setting I would have chosen, too much going on, but he just feels that the longer we withhold the truth, the more betrayed she's going to feel."

"So you need some time, just the three of you?"

I can barely control my excitement—*Free at last, free at last!*

"Would you mind?" She looks concerned.

"Not at all," I say, a picture of stoicism.

"We could reconvene in the hotel lobby, say at six thirty P.M.?"

"Sounds perfect. In fact, I'll probably hang around here for a while, so why don't I bring all the cases across with me in a taxi? That way you guys can head off straightaway?"

"Really? Oh Laurie, you're such a gem!" She throws her arms around me.

"Just doing my job!"

"Well, you're doing an excellent one, thank you!" she pips before returning to the bus to gather her necessaries.

I can't believe it—four whole hours with no one to chivvy or cajole. I can do exactly as I please!

"What's going on?" Ravenna skulks over, looking suspicious.

"Nothing. I just said you guys should go on and I'll sort out the luggage and stuff." I tilt my head at her. "Glad to be back in civilization?"

"I suppose."

I want to say something to prepare her for the news she is about to receive. Some form of subtle heads-up to cushion the blow. It doesn't matter how disconnected she claims to be, this is going to cause her whole world to tilt and shift. There will be a lot of confusion, a lot of questions, a lot of brain-swirl. Even though the upshot is that she gets a great new dad, the shock isn't something I'd wish on anyone. Not even Ravenna.

"Why are you looking at me like that?"

"Like what?"

"I don't know. All weird."

"Ravenna!" Her mother calls to her. "Are you ready to go?"

She looks back at me. "Why do I feel you're up to something?"

"I'm not!" I protest.

"Well, what are *you* doing now?"

"I'm just going to look around the university campus," I say, nudging her on her way. "Just be open to having a good afternoon. Text me if you like . . ."

She turns back with a sneer. "Are you getting separation anxiety or something?"

"*Ravenna!*"

"Coming!" she huffs.

As they exit, Charles waves back at me. "Bye Laurie!"

"Good luck!" I call after them.

All three turn back.

What did I just say?

"You know, finding the perfect cupcake!" I chirrup.

Oh god. What an idiot.

I don't like being privy to secrets. Something always seems to slip out. At least by 6:30 P.M. it should all be out in the open. Not that I think for a minute this is going to be a breeze. I should probably check to see if any extra rooms have opened up at the hotel—there's a good chance Ravenna will need some private pillow-pummeling time. I know if it were me I'd need to be lying down to try and process it all—basically replaying my entire life from my first memory, scanning for clues or hints that this new truth was on its way.

Anyway! This really is not my business and I don't want my precious few hours of free time to be consumed by fretting over their family drama. My only concern right now is ditching the rather drab Pilgrim neutrals I dressed in this morning and switching to something more preppy—a sweater slung around my shoulders at the very least.

I rummage through my suitcase, which is sadly devoid of petite blazers and cable-knit V-necks. I'll have to settle for my studded lemon shirt-dress, with the collar upturned, of course. I must have something navy I can wear with it. Aha! This canvas belt. Now if I just had an armful of intellectual books—I'm not sure a stack of greasy cookery books is going to cut it.

I clatter down the stairs with renewed vigor—I'm going to Harvard! And then I come to a halt beside the driver's seat. There's still no sign of the mechanic, though Charles insisted he'd be here any minute. I look around. All is still and quiet. When am I going to get another chance like this? I hop into position and grab the enormous steering wheel. I don't know how Gracie maneuvered this great thing, I really don't! I jiggle the gear stick and start making growly-chuggy engine noises like a five-year-old boy, bouncing in the seat and calling, "All aboard!" as I pull up beside my imaginary bus stop.

"Fares please!" I do my best cockney accent. Actually, that would probably be the conductor. Either way I hear myself calling out, "That'll be tuppence ha'penny. Ding, ding! Next stop Piccadilly Circus!"

"Now that's a deal!"

I'm startled by a grinning face. My embarrassment is intensified by the fact that the man in question is so darn attractive—in just one glance, I register his Hugh Jackman quality (rugged mixed with a good-natured twinkle), tousled brown hair that probably never goes the same way twice and a light-up-your-life smile. I can't even speak.

"You must be Laurie," he climbs aboard, extending his hand to me.

I look down, expecting it to be blackened with axle grease, but it's quite clean.

"Are you the mechanic?"

"I am."

"Did you just get here?" I'm a little concerned about my recent outfit change upstairs, although I like to think that being on the top level I was out of view.

"About ten minutes ago. I've had a quick look at the engine. It's simple enough to fix, but I won't be able to get the part until tomorrow morning."

I nod, trying to get my brain back on track. "That's fine, we don't leave until the afternoon."

"Great," he replies. "So what are your plans for the day?"

"Um," I pause. I have no idea if this is touristy or nerdy, but I say it anyway. "I want to go to Harvard!"

"Really?" He looks intrigued.

"Mostly so I can say, 'I went to Harvard.'"

He grins.

"I hear they do really good tours."

"They do," he says, consulting his watch. "But I think you just missed the last one."

"Oh no." My face falls.

"That's okay. I can take you around if you like?"

I hesitate.

"I've heard their spiel enough times. Plus I can give you the inside scoop!"

My head tilts like a curious dog. "Do you know someone who went there?"

"Yes," he confirms. "Me!"

"You went to Harvard?" I gawp.

He nods. "Class of '96."

"And now you're a mechanic?"

He chuckles. "Not by profession. It's just something I do on the side. My grandfather used to work at this garage. He taught me everything there is to know about cars and engines."

"Really?"

"He said it was especially important since I was going to get a poncy education. Didn't want me to be the kind of man who could write a twenty-thousand-word dissertation on Mayan culture but couldn't tie his own shoelace."

I chuckle delightedly. "He sounds a good man."

"The best. He died three years ago but I'm named after him so . . ."

"He lives on?" I suggest.

"I hope so."

I feel an empathetic pang. I can tell he misses him.

"What was his name?" I ask.

"Harvey."

I smile to myself. Adorable. Suits his grandson well.

"Ready?" he says, offering me a hand down from the driver's seat.

I nod, more than ready for a dream come true.

Chapter 32

ᴄᴦᴦᴩ

As we round the corner, I can't help but flinch.

"Are you okay?" Harvey looks concerned.

"This is Harvard Square?" There must be some mistake.

"Not what you were expecting?"

"Not at all."

I was picturing shiny-haired youths whirring by on bicycles, coattails fluttering in the breeze, highbrow chatter smattered with quotations from Thoreau, Sartre and Zuckerberg, maybe a few horsey laughs and a playful ping of a bow tie. What I get is grunge, and plenty of it. Slap-bang next to the Harvard subway, at the precise point where Harvey tells me the official tour begins, there is a menacing mess of skanky guys with matted hair, strung-out expressions and dogs on strings, hassling passersby for money. I step out of the way of some babbling looney-tune and nearly collide with an elderly gentleman who doesn't appear to have bathed since the university was established in 1636.

"I don't want to be politically incorrect," I begin, "but why are these *particular* people congregating here?"

"Two reasons," Harvey says matter-of-factly. "A steady flow of tourists to beg from, and a major homeless shelter two minutes' walk from here—the Harvard Square Homeless Shelter to be precise."

"Gosh," I can't help but snort. "Talk about a dramatic juxtaposition."

"A lot of the students volunteer there."

"That must be quite a shock to their systems."

I imagine some toff trying to explain cutlery etiquette to a wild-haired man with crumbs in his bird's-nest beard.

"It's not as privileged a group as you might expect." Harvey challenges my presumption.

"No?"

"About seventy percent of the students are here on financial aid. I couldn't have afforded the tuition any other way." He places a protective hand on my back. "Come on, let's get you on the campus."

We hurry across the road, away from the grime and onto the hallowed grounds.

Now this is more like it. No sooner do we pass through the entrance arch than I find myself in the vast grassy courtyard of my imaginings. Historic redbrick buildings surround us, some with rather more recent history.

"See this corner room up here?" He points upward. "That was Matt Damon's dorm."

"No!"

"Of course he dropped out, but all first-year students are obliged to reside here on the campus."

"Even if you're Natalie Portman?"

"Even if you're Natalie Portman. Or Natalie Hershlag as she was known when she was here."

"I can't believe it. Everyone must have been staring at her twenty-four/seven." I know I would have been. "Any other celebs?"

"Tons. Michelle Obama. Barack someone or other. Oh, and girls seem to get a kick out of knowing that Stockard Channing went here."

"Rizzo went to Harvard?" I hoot. "Oh, that's brilliant." I make a mental note to tell Krista.

"You know the crazy thing? It's only in the last twenty years that women have got the same certificate as the men."

"What, before that they got a girl's version of a Harvard degree?"

"Exactly."

I'm sure Alva Vanderbilt would have had a thing or two to say about that.

"Now there's actually more women getting degrees than men."

"That's excellent," I cheer.

"For you," he smirks, stepping into the shade of one of the elms. "Where did you study?"

"I didn't," I confess. "I think that's why I have this weird fascination for university life. I'm always wondering what I missed out on."

"It is a very particular experience," he concedes, hand instinctively going to his liver.

"It's not just the partying, I love the idea of all that *reading*."

"Yeah, it's a bummer that books aren't accessible in the real world."

I give him a playful swat.

"No libraries. No bookshops. No Amazon," he taunts as he backs away from me.

"You know what I mean," I huff, instinctively following him.

"Actually, I've got a couple of good Harvard book stories for you if you want to hear them?"

"I'm all ears!"

He directs me to a modest stone building. "This is the site of the old library. The night before it burned down, one student was so engrossed in the book he was reading that he decided to sneak it out, which was utterly forbidden—"

"Do you know what it was?" I interrupt. "Which book?"

"*The Christian Warfare Against the Devil, World, and Flesh* by John Downame."

"My point exactly—I'm fairly certain Barnes and Noble don't stock *that*. Go on."

He twinkles back at me and then continues. "Well. He had every intention of returning it the next morning, but of course only burning embers greeted him. Now he was conflicted—he was in possession of the only remaining book in the entire collection, but by unscrupulous means."

"What did he do?"

"He went to the president and confessed."

"Good for him! And what did the president do?"

"Expelled him."

"He didn't!"

"He did." Harvey chuckles.

I shake my head. "That's harsh."

"Rules is rules."

I look back at the building. "So is this the new library?"

"Oh no. That's over here." He offers me his arm. I like the feel of his linen shirtsleeve on his forearm. He has a very manly physique for an intellectual. Takes after his granddad, no doubt.

"This," he says, motioning to a vast beaux-arts beauty, a mere twelve columns to the front portico, "is The Widener. Named for Harry Elkins Widener. Another bibliophile graduate."

"Stunning," I murmur in reverence.

"Off he goes to Europe on a book-buying voyage, and he happens upon a copy of Bacon's *Essays*—as in Francis Bacon—circa 1598."

Talk about an ancient tome.

"So eager is he to get back, that he takes the first Atlantic crossing he can get passage on." Harvey pauses, looking expectantly at me.

"What?"

"The year is 1912."

I think for a moment. "Not the *Titanic*?"

"Yes! He's traveling first class so he gets a spot on one of the lifeboats, but he loses it when he goes back to the cabin to get the book—"

"Oh, he didn't!"

"He did. And consequently he drowned."

"Do all your stories have such downbeat endings?"

"I'm not done with this one yet," he grins, inviting me to splay a little beneath a nearby tree. "His mother is keen to honor him and so she approaches the president of Harvard and says she wants to build a library in his honor, sweetening the deal with a multimillion-dollar donation. Eager to please, Harvard says they'll demolish the current building and start afresh. Well, this worried her—what if they did that to the Widener Library a few years down the line, when a mother with a greater sob story comes a-calling? So she made certain conditions to her donation: firstly, not a brick could be altered. So as the collection expanded—and there's fifty-seven miles of bookshelves in there—they had to go underground. Four stories."

"What?" I look back over at the building now, viewing it as something Bruce Wayne might have devised.

"There must always be fresh flowers in the office and, on account of the way her son died, every Harvardian must be able to swim in order to graduate."

My eyebrows rise. "You had to swim for your degree?"

"Well, actually they had to stop that when the various disability laws came in."

"Amazing. You just don't get stories like these at your local polytechnic."

"Don't sound so hard done by—your people have got Oxford and Cambridge!"

"I know! My *people* do. I don't." My eyes narrow. "What's it like, *really*? To be a part of something so legendary?"

He leans back against the tree trunk and ponders. "Well, you certainly feel a sense of honor and responsibility in a way, to do your best. I mean, you're walking in the footsteps of presidents here. But at the end of the day, a class is a class."

"This is just a classier class of class."

"Who says you're not smart?" He beams at me.

"I didn't say I wasn't smart, I'm just not *educated*." I watch as a group of Bright Young Things jolly across the quad and wonder if I might get some glasses when I get back to New York. "I'd like to be inside one of these brains for just ten minutes. To know what it's like to be *that* clever."

Harvey sits forward. "You know, these aren't all straight-A kids."

I frown. "Surely, to get in—"

"Grades are one aspect. But a third of the assessment is what you do that's different—they want to know in what *other* ways you excel."

He gives me some examples from his year—one guy had volunteered with Habitat for Humanity in El Salvador; another organized a sponsored cycle around Peru to raise money for the Cystic Fibrosis Foundation; someone invented a system to keep zoo animals more mentally stimulated and, rather bizarrely, there was a flying trapeze artist named Montana who, after graduating, became the first woman to dive off the perilous cliffs in Acapulco.

Visionaries. Questers. Daredevils. Men and women of action.

"I love that!" I marvel. "Bonus points for having a souped-up zest for life. So what was yours?"

He looks shy for the first time. "It wasn't such a big deal. No exotic locations or daredevil feats."

"Is it a secret?"

"No," he smiles. "It concerns old people, so I didn't win any of the sexy points."

I find that hard to believe.

He takes a breath. "I compiled the autobiographies of sixteen octogenarians."

My head tilts. He's going to have to go into more detail.

"It was actually my grandfather's idea. He had all these friends who didn't have any family and were destined to become Nursing Home Zombies, his words, and he said they would die in there and no one would know all their incredible stories. Even if no one ever read them, he felt there should be a record. And so we started this project—This Is My Life. I teamed up with some English majors and we started interviewing his friends. And then their friends." He plucks a blade of grass. "It was remarkable how lively they became when they were reminiscing, their childhood memories were so keen, and it was fascinating to hear of love lives, the choices they made, their regrets, their triumphs. It seemed to be a very satisfying process for them, reviewing all the events that had led them to this day, reflecting on their life, making peace with it and now feeling that they had some kind of legacy, that they wouldn't be forgotten."

My eyes are a little damp.

"We put together all their photographs, labeled and dated, and even did a present-day portrait—for the women we got their hair and nails done, for the gents, we arranged a proper hot-towel shave and trimmed their ears!"

I chuckle in delight.

"The project is still running now, and of course these days we can create e-books so their stories will always be accessible."

"That's wonderful."

"Plus we do a bit of advocacy in these homes—if anyone is having any issues, we make sure that everything is taken care of in a prompt manner."

"Something tells me you don't take no for an answer."

He gets a playful look in his eye. "They call me The Heavy."

If I found him attractive before, I am now heart-heavingly smitten.

My whole life, it seemed as though the dating choices were Man A who drinks too much or Man B who considers video games a participation sport. I couldn't even really list the redeeming qualities of the men I dated—I just fixed on them after some passing physical attraction. They paid me some attention and that was that. Sold to the lady with low self-esteem! Did I ever once take the time to consider their admirable qualities or review their acts of valor? I did not. It was enough that they had a good head of hair. Just the idea of dating someone inspirational or altruistic is Blowing My Mind.

"I need a minute!"

I lie flat out on the grass and stare up at the sky, imagining what life might have been like had I teamed up with someone like that. What it might have triggered in me. Could I too have done something vigorous and life-enhancing?

And then I think of Pink's dad's words: *Be what you want to attract* . . . and I jolt upright.

Harvey laughs. "Talk about wishing you could step inside someone's brain for ten minutes! It looks very busy in there."

"I was just wondering what my contribution might have been— what I would have chosen to do to make my mark."

He shuffles around to face me, the sunlight filtering through the trees, casting patterns on his shoulders. "Let's see—I'm guessing you've traveled a fair bit?"

"I've traveled a lot," I tell him, explaining a little more about my job. "But I never left a place better for my being there."

"Are you sure?" His voice softens.

I look back at him. Something weird just happened to my insides.

"I mean, you've inspired people to take journeys off the beaten path; you've brought money to local families; maybe made a certain worker feel special or take extra pride in his job."

Goodness, it's like listening to Sherlock.

"Maybe you smiled at someone—and you have a lovely sunny smile—and they passed it on and made someone else's day better."

I blink back at him. "You've got a good imagination."

"None of us knows what our legacy will be—who we touch and impact without even realizing."

I wonder if he knows, if he can tell the impact he is having on me right now.

I hear some distant clock chiming.

"So." He claps his hands together. "I hear you ladies like cake?"

"Yes," I sigh, feeling more trivial than ever. "That, in essence, is my major."

"In essence?" He conjures his best egghead look. "Now would that be almond essence or perhaps rose?"

I want to fall on top of him and roll playfully in the grass until he ends up on top of me, panting down, gradually lowering his face to mine in my very first campus kiss.

"Laurie?"

"Yes, sorry, you were saying?"

He jumps to his feet and then reaches back to pull me up. "I've just thought of the perfect place to take you for afternoon tea."

Well that's it then. My life is complete.

Chapter 33

❧

If Alice in Wonderland and Cyndi Lauper opened a restaurant, it would look like this.

Eye-jazzlingly lurid paintwork of thick purple gloss slams up against leprechaun green and hot pink. Zebra-print banquettes, giant diamond-patterned flooring and sprayed-gold chairs. One piece of wall art looks like Klimt, another like Scottish tartan.

I can't quite believe my eyes. "What *is* this place?"

"UpStairs on the Square," Harvey says, way too matter-of-factly for such a fantasyland. "Have you heard of the Hasty Pudding Club?"

"Maybe," I mumble, still trying to adjust to the assault of color.

"It's the oldest college social club in America, founded 1770. Notorious hangout for Harvard types. This was the restaurant upstairs from that club, open to all. Quite the scene."

"I bet."

"People used to say it was like stepping into the third installment of *Brideshead Revisited*!"

I chuckle delightedly and then turn to face him, "Did you hang out here?"

"Inasmuch as I used to work here."

I catch my breath. "Did you make cakes?" *Please tell me you made cakes, please, please, please . . .*

He laughs. "I was just a waiter."

I don't know if my face falls but he quickly adds, "I could probably get hold of the recipe for the Zebra Cake if you like?"

"Zebra Cake?" In this setting I wouldn't be surprised if it was served by a stripy pantomime horse.

"It's basically a big wedge of chocolate cake with multiple layers of *dulce de leche* buttercream."

"So, not sickly at all," I confirm.

"You know, when I used to work here, there was this young girl who always wore her best party dresses and she would eat candied violets and sleep under the bar."

"A real girl?"

"Yes," he laughs. "She was the owner's daughter. Is the owner's daughter, all grown-up now. She wrote a book about her life within these walls." He looks around, seemingly searching for a familiar face.

"Hey Dom, do you have a copy of Charlotte's book?"

The raven-haired waiter ducks behinds the counter, waves one in the air and then scoots to our table, serving cloth over his arm, presenting it with full panache.

While Harvey explains my particular interest, I admire the cover—a young girl peeking over the top of a pink-clothed table, reaching for a lone slice of cake (a woman after my own heart). The backdrop is a creamy mint and the red lettering (which wouldn't be out of place in the window of a French café) reads: *CHARLOTTE AU CHOCOLAT—Memories of a Restaurant Girlhood* by Charlotte Silver.

"This looks wonderful!"

Dom leans in. "I'll let you keep it if I can borrow this man's brawn for ten minutes."

I raise a brow.

"We need to shift a dresser upstairs and the youngsters just aren't cutting it."

"Do you mind?" Harvey asks me.

"Of course not—I couldn't be happier sitting here."

"Ah yes," he smirks. "Finally you have your hands on one of those elusive books!"

I watch him and Dom exit and then take a breath, my heart so high in my chest it feels as if it's nudging at my chin.

Look at me—reading a book in a Harvard hangout by a girl who used to hang out here! Well, more than hang out, I discover as I flick through the pages, this was her true home: "It was as if the lights were always on at the Pudding and off everywhere else."

I must say the author does have a lovely turn of phrase. Even the chapters have such evocative titles: The Lavender Blonde, Cabana Boys, Anything Can Absorb Champagne . . .

"Your tea, madam." A waitress sets down a cake stand, quite the opposite of what I was expecting. I envisaged some Mad Hatter affair, but instead I see three tiers of plain stainless steel topped with a Captain Hook loop. Curiouser still, the cup and saucer wouldn't look out of place at Lady M, they are so simple and white.

Well, I suppose they'd hate anything to clash with the décor.

"Would you like me to take you through your treats?"

"Oh, yes please!"

Savory-wise, the waitress references Gruyère quiche and salmon on pumpernickel, then come the scones and lemon tarts with blueberries and the signature chocolate-dipped pecan turtles.

Obviously I have to take a photo. Or ten. I feel a little guilty that I'm enjoying such a treat when Pamela is probably in the midst of a maelstrom of abuse about now. I picture Ravenna pelting her with an armory of cupcakes and curses—torn between the fact that she actually likes and respects Charles, and wanting to punish her mother for deceiving her for the past twenty years. Of course, sugary tea is meant to be good for a shock, and I did recommend the Boston Tea Party attraction, but then again I don't want any one of them going overboard with the tea chests . . .

"Gosh, I wish your brain had subtitles!" Harvey slides back into the booth beside me. "You look troubled."

"I am. It's the hellish decision of which bauble of yumminess to enjoy first." I decide to spare him the family saga.

"Hmmm. May I recommend the rather understated almond cookie?"

"You may!"

Between sugar surges, Harvey asks me if my mother baked.

I tell him she was more of a Mr. Kipling aficionado.

He looks confused.

"What you would call store-bought." I speak American to him. "They came in little wrappers."

"Like Twinkies?"

"No, no!" I recoil in horror. "These actually had an expiry date. And they were good. Still are. You can get little Country Slices and French Fancies. And individual Bakewell Tarts. Oh! I've got to write that down. That would be the perfect trade for Maria's Linzertorte."

"Me with the Harvard degree and I can't understand a word you're saying."

"It's just the girl equivalent of car parts." I grin. "Gosh. That was incredibly sexist of me."

"Incredibly," he says, his voice turning low and flirtatious. "So if I said carburetor . . . ?"

"I'd say cannoli."

"Manifold."

"Mille-feuille."

"Muffler."

"Muffin."

"Cylinder head."

"Banana bread."

"Let's call the whole thing off!" he sings.

We burst out laughing.

I'm having the best time!

Our conversation hops all over the place, from the songs we can listen to twenty times in a row to the awful clothes we used to wear as teenagers. And then my phone jangles. It's just a nudge for me to watch the time. I don't want to be late for Pamela.

"Do you know the Omni Parker House Hotel?" I ask Harvey.

"Of course. Everyone knows the Parker House."

"How long would it take to get there from here?"

"'Bout twenty minutes."

I nod. "I've got to take the suitcases over and get everyone checked in."

"No problem. I'll drive you."

"Really?"

"Of course. I'd be happy to." He holds my gaze.

I look back into his eyes. They really are blue. But not in a glittery prism way, more of a classic Paul Newman hue.

"I've got one more for you."

I can just about manage a nod.

His lips part to form the word "Chassis."

This throws me for two reasons. One is that "chassis" in America often refers to a woman's bottom, and thus gives me a mild sexual thrill. Secondly my brain is short-circuiting because all I want to do is kiss him—melt onto his mouth like icing on a lemon drizzle cake. I know it would feel so good, unleashing the longing and surrendering to that spinning-out sensation. Like Alice falling down the rabbit hole.

"Did I get you?" he inquires.

"Actually," I prepare my bluff, "I was thinking of Chiffon Cake with crème de cassis."

"No wonder you looked so dreamy—that sounds really good."

"Doesn't it?" I say, biting my bottom lip. "Oop!" I lean back as the waitress plants the bill between us. Her *mot du jour* being "chaste."

As Harvey gallantly pays, I take a last sip of now-cold tea and think quietly to myself: And in answer to your question, "*Yeah, you got me . . .*"

Chapter 34

つつつ

The Omni Parker House Hotel is where the Boston Cream Pie originated. And Parker Rolls (soft dinner rolls). And scrod. This last one sounds delicious, doesn't it?

It's actually a chef's term to cover assorted types of young whitefish—could be cod, could be haddock—when they weren't certain what was going to be the freshest catch of the day. Scrod. It doesn't matter how many times you say it, it still sounds like a total appetite killer to me.

"Checking in?" The bellman looks rather surprised by the volume of luggage when I tell him that we're just here for one night.

Up the stairs we go and into the lobby. Classic wood-paneled grandeur with a somewhat gaudy-flourish-y carpet design. We pass an extravagant floral centerpiece set beneath a vast chandelier and lift doors seemingly made from intricately engraved gold shields.

"I suppose it'll do."

Harvey smiles.

"Good evening," I say as I approach reception. "I'm checking in three people for two rooms, reservation under the name of Davis. Laurie Davis."

Harvey mutters something I miss.

"What was that?"

"You sound very professional."

I'm about to reply when I notice an older lady struggling next to me. She's having trouble balancing her walking stick while trying to hoick her handbag up onto the reception desk to pull out her purse.

"May I help you?" I offer.

"I don't have enough hands!" she tuts.

"It's quite a lot to contend with at times, isn't it? Here," I take her arm but now she's gripping onto me, which still only leaves one hand free for her handbag. And it has a zipped top.

"Mind if I hold you steady?" Harvey inquires, stepping behind her and gently placing a hand on each of her shoulders.

Her wobbling abruptly ceases. She looks surprised by her new-found sure-footedness and then chuckles, "I feel twenty years younger!"

With both hands free she is now able to negotiate her wares. As she signs in, her bony-crinkly hands start to move to the music filtering through the lobby—"Unforgettable . . ."

"You like this song?" I smile.

"Oh, it's my favorite!"

I look to Harvey. He leans close to her ear. "Would you care to dance?"

"Oh, I . . ." She stops herself, takes a breath and then nods.

In one seamless move he places a secure, supportive arm around her frame and then lifts his free hand to her shoulder height. She raises her hand and places it in his. As they oh-so-slowly and carefully sway, her milky-blue eyes never leave his. She is looking up at him with such attentive wonder, I feel my own eyes glossing.

To be held so assuredly, to feel your body move in such harmony with another. To share such beautiful lyrics. To *live them* in that moment.

When the song ends he doesn't dip or unbalance her, merely raises her hand to his lips and gives a little bow.

"Thank you!" she whispers with a little gulp.

"My pleasure," he says, most sincerely.

I feel a sudden rush of love—love for her, love for him, love for Nat King Cole, love for *everything*.

"Do you need any help to your room?"

"Oh no, dear, they know me here. Here's Barney now."

"Well hello, Mrs. Jenkins!" A cheery bellman greets her. "I guess it's that time of year again."

"It is." She nods. "Another year, a little slower."

"I've told you, we can always pop you on one of the luggage trolleys, get you around a little quicker."

She tinkles a laugh. "Now you know I must try and retain a little dignity."

And off they go.

I turn back to Harvey. "That was so lovely of you!"

He lifts his sleeve to his nose. "I think I smell of lily of the valley now."

I lean in for a sniff, wishing I could stay there, nestled in his personal space. But the receptionist has other ideas:

"Your room keys, Ms. Davis."

"Oh! Thank you!" I take the cards and then slump a little with the awareness that our time together is drawing to a close.

"Well," I take a breath, "thank you for a wonderful afternoon."

His head tilts. "Do you have any plans for tonight?"

My heart gives a little Bambi leap. "Not necessarily . . . It all depends on how things went for the others today."

He nods, in a strangely knowing way.

"They should be here any minute, if you'd like to wait with me?"

We take a seat in the expansive lounge area, on one of the outsize sofas that would be great to cuddle up on and watch TV. Or, in this case, one's fellow guests.

"You get all sorts in here, don't you?" I note as a full-tilt businesswoman all but hurdles a three-toddler family.

"It's quite the hub in town. In fact, if we were sitting here a hundred and fifty years ago, we might have seen Charles Dickens strolling through."

"Really?"

"He used to live here."

"Here in the hotel?"

Harvey nods. "For two years. He was part of the Saturday Club, with the likes of Ralph Waldo Emerson and Henry Wadsworth Longfellow."

He pauses to allow my swoon and then adds, "This is where Dickens gave his first recitation of *A Christmas Carol*."

My heart heaves. "Oh to have been in that audience."

"Well, you say that, but there's a dark element," he leans close. "One of the regular members of the Saturday Club was John Wilkes Booth—the man who assassinated Abraham Lincoln."

"Laurie!" I hear Pamela's voice call to me.

Here we go.

I compose myself before I turn toward her, not quite sure what will greet me. But nothing could have prepared me for this.

Charles, Pamela and Ravenna are all wearing matching skull-and-crossbones T-shirts, only instead of the skull there's a cupcake.

"W-wh . . . ?" I can't even form the word.

They grin back at me like fools.

"We had the best day," Ravenna is first to speak. "Mum got all excited because there was this cupcake shop that has this huge window display saying zero calories, zero carbs and we get inside and it's a T-shirt shop!"

"Johnny's Cupcakes," Charles chips in.

"They have the T-shirts all set out in baking trays in glass display units just like a real bakery!"

"And baseball hats in the fridges."

"And there was this giant antique mixing bowl."

Their chatter converges.

"It was rad!" Ravenna concludes. "Then we went to this huge Anthropologie store," she holds up her bags. "I got four dresses! Mum liked all the homeware, of course. Show Laurie what you got!"

Pamela dutifully takes out a yellow daisy/navy anchor motif apron and an individual cupcake stand with a carved wooden pedestal.

"They had so many lovely things!"

"I liked it because they had a sofa area for weary males," Charles chips in.

"And because they played John Lennon," Ravenna beams at him.

I can't believe my eyes. They are all so lit up. So happy. Can it really have gone that well?

"Hey!" Charles notices Harvey, keeping a low profile on the sofa. "How did you get on, son?"

"Great," he says, looking right at me as he gets to his feet.

"With the bus?" Charles clarifies.

"Easy fix. You'll be good to go tomorrow."

"That's a relief."

Ravenna harrumphs. "I was kind of hoping we might have longer here."

"She's a Boston gal all right!" Charles says, pulling her into his side.

As the introductions are being made, I'm wondering, did Charles mean son like "fruit of my loins," or was that just an example of cross-generational palliness?

"I'm ready for dinner now if you are?" Ravenna prompts, obviously impatient to get back into the fray.

"Oh gosh! I'd have to soak my feet first!" Her mother looks weary.

But Ravenna isn't looking at her mother. She's looking at Harvey. In. That. Way.

"Perhaps you could take her, Harvey?" Charles exacerbates the situation. "She's spent the whole day with old people."

"He's old too!" I want to say. Too old for her, at least.

"Um . . ." His eyes flick to me.

I look away. It's not my place to disrupt the plans. I'm just the help.

"Harvey?" Charles nudges him.

"Of course, I'd be happy to. Laurie, would you care to join us?"

Oh, he's so lovely!

"Actually, I'll need to keep Laurie with me," Pamela intervenes. "I want to go over the next stage of the itinerary with her."

My heart sinks.

"In fact, there's one quick thing I need to check right now . . ." She pulls me around the corner, ducking behind a potted palm.

"Yes?" I say, trying to keep the testiness out of my voice.

"I couldn't do it!" she bleats. "We had such an amazing day, I couldn't risk spoiling it by drudging up the past. It was like being a family!"

"But without her actually knowing that you are one?"

Pamela grimaces. "Don't be cross! I don't know the last time I saw Ravenna laughing." She peers back around the corner. "And now she's got the chance to spend the evening getting to know her brother."

"Her brother?"

"Well, half-brother."

"So Harvey is Charles's son?"

"Yes, isn't he a dreamboat?"

"Yes, he is," I confirm. "I think Ravenna thinks so too."

"What? Oh don't be silly!"

I hold her a little further out. "Do you see the way she's looking at him?"

"Well," she falters. "No, she has a boyfriend. She wouldn't—"

"She may be thinking about leaving said boyfriend. She may be on the lookout for someone new!"

"It's fine," Pamela bustles. "Harvey won't encourage her. He knows the situation, even if Ravenna doesn't."

I try to tell her that he doesn't have to encourage her, that he has to just *be,* but she won't have it. She's far too attached to the fantasy that everything is going to sort itself out and no one is going to get hurt.

I plan to grab a few minutes with Harvey while everyone else heads upstairs, but Ravenna decides to play best mates with me, linking arms and saying she wants me to help pick out an outfit for tonight. For her date. She doesn't say those last three words but I can see them hanging in the air.

"Nice to meet you," I give Harvey a frustrated little wave as I'm tugged toward the lifts.

"I'll see you tomorrow, with the bus?"

"Oh yes!" I brighten. There's still hope!

It doesn't help, when you're feeling ousted, to have the ouster parade before you in a series of dress styles you could never carry off yourself.

Behold the slinky shift with the bohemian detailing that hits mid-thigh. I've always wondered what it must be like to have those giraffe legs with no actual flesh on them. Now the polka-dot mini-dress with the ruched bust area and the cutout above the waist. Just the area I'd love to expose. Then comes the midnight-blue lace-layer dress with the teeniest of cap sleeves. Very Alexa Chung. Only similar physiques need apply.

"You can stop there," I tell her. "That's the one."

"Really?"

"You could go anywhere in that."

"Not too girlie?"

"Well, I know you're not wearing it with stilettos and pearls."

"No!" she grins. "I'll rock it up a bit."

As she's trying assorted options she ponders, "Do you think Harvey could be as nice as his dad?"

Okay. She knows that much, that he's not just the bus me-chanic. That's something.

"I think there's a good chance of that, yes."

Ravenna smiles. "Who wouldn't be nice with a dad like that?"

"Well . . ." God, what can I say?

"Charles was telling us all about him today. I thought he sounded pretty cool. Wouldn't it be funny if . . ." She stops suddenly.

"What?"

"Oh nothing."

If she's waiting for me to say "if you ended up dating the son of the man your mum is seeing," it's not going to happen.

"What shall I do with my hair?" She moves closer to the mir-ror. "Up or down?"

Thankfully there's a knock at the door.

"Is it him?" she gasps. "Have I taken too long?"

It is in fact the maid, wanting to perform the turn-down service.

"Help yourself," I welcome her in, tucking myself into the arm-chair beside the TV to give her room to maneuver around the bed.

As I watch Ravenna touching up her cat's-eye flicks, I have a pang of sisterly sympathy for her. This happy high she's experiencing is like a sugar rush—it's not going to last. When I think of the amount of times I've got all dressed up only to come home in tears . . . If someone had tried to talk me out of my optimism, would I have listened? I can't believe her mother is setting her up for an even bigger fall.

"Okay, I'm all ready!" Ravenna reaches for the macramé bag, and in one move destroys her chic.

"Oh, that won't do." I get to my feet.

"What?"

"The bag ruins it. Let me see what I've got."

I drag my suitcase to the corner. It's in here somewhere . . . "Ta-daaa!" I pull out her Mulberry.

Before she can speak, the maid gasps. "Is that an Alexa? I see it in the magazines!"

"Isn't it cute?" Ravenna smirks at her.

"Ohhh!" She clicks her fingers in awe.

"Do you want it?"

"Excuse me, madam?"

Am I hearing this right? This surely can't be happening.

"It's got bad associations for me. I'd like you to have it."

Ravenna takes the bag from me, then tries to present it to the maid, who backs away as if it's on fire.

"No, no, I couldn't!"

"Yes you can!"

"Noooo! They check us when we leave. They'll say I stole it."

"No they won't. Laurie will make sure of that, won't you?"

I nod. "Of course."

This wasn't quite the plan. The bag was supposed to be a gesture, reminding her she has someone on her side.

Her eyes narrow at me. "I can't believe you had it all along."

I shrug.

"So who paid for the cupcakes in Newport?"

"I did."

She nods. I wonder if she might thank me but no.

"Okay, I'm leaving. Don't wait up."

I say I won't but I know I will.

As soon as everything is settled with the maid's two-thousand-dollar tip, I reach for the phone.

"Hi Pamela, it's Laurie." As I speak I press at the headache forming on my brow-bone. "Did you want me to come to you to go through the itinerary or—"

"Oh no! No need," she cuts in. "I was just saying that to get you off the hook. I'm sure you'd rather just relax tonight."

I can't believe it!

"The evening is yours to do as you please."

Is it really?

I bid her good night, put down the phone and then press my face into the pillow and scream.

Chapter 35

I never usually have a problem with being alone in a big city. I've done it so many times. But it's a little different when you are part of a group and everyone pairs up and heads off in different directions. Without you.

I wonder where Harvey has taken Ravenna? I would have guessed Newbury Street, but she's already covered that today. I toy with the idea of staying in—renting a movie, ordering room service. But I know I'll just end up clock-watching and wondering what everyone else is doing. No. I'm heading out. Maybe I'll find myself a nice piece of scrod . . .

Saturday night is not the night to be dining alone in a crowded restaurant where every place setting is at a premium. So I head to Quincy Market, famous for being America's first open market and home to a barrage of food options: Bangkok Express, Ueno Sushi, El Paso Enchiladas, Pizzeria Regina; every nation is accounted for. Local might be a good choice—I could have clam chowder. Or oysters. Or pull up a seat at the Cheers bar where nobody knows my name. But no. I order a hefty, oozy chunk of moussaka from Steve's Greek Cuisine and then can't find anywhere to sit to eat it. Darnit! Why didn't I just get a hot dog?

It's a warm night so I keep my food wrapped and retrace my steps, passing the hotel and the Freedom Trail and crossing over to Boston Common, the local equivalent of Central Park.

A concert is being set up in the first dell. It looks as if it could get loud so I keep walking, past the carousel and the unsavory-looking individuals gathered by the Soldiers and Sailors Monument, settling in a family-friendly area beside a lake with giant swan boats. I find myself smiling as I watch them gliding beneath the weeping willows. I'd like to try that with Harvey. Actually, I think I'd like to do just about anything with him! He's got that way about him that makes you really engage with your surroundings. He knows so many interesting things. And he's so playful—

My phone rings. I virtually send it flying into the water in my eagerness to answer it.

"Krista!"

"Gosh. You sound pleased to hear from me!"

"I thought you were Cirque du Soleil-ing tonight?"

"I am, we got here early. I just wanted to see how you're getting on. What's the scoop?"

Where to begin?

I bring her up to speed, at speed, including a rapturous account of my time with Harvey.

"Should I worry that the most romantic encounter I've had with a man involves watching him dancing with another woman?"

"Not at all!" she tuts. "I would have felt exactly the same way. He sounds so masterful-yet-cute!"

"He is! And his *mind* . . ."

"You fancy his mind?" Her voice lowers.

"I really do!"

"Now we're in trouble!" Krista laughs.

"The thing is, I'm being ridiculous really. It's not like he's a real possibility . . ."

"Why ever not?"

"Well, let's be frank. He is rather out of my league."

"You know, I don't even think that's a thing anymore."

"What do you mean?"

"Well, ever since I got together with Jacques, I've realized you can't say someone is out of your league because you don't know what they are looking for. You might presume certain things based on their looks or their status, but in actual fact you could be the very thing that is missing from their life."

I smile. "I suppose you're right. All the same, I probably should try not to get too carried away. I don't want to set myself up for another fall."

"Oh, fiddlesticks to that! Why shouldn't you enjoy this stage, no matter where it leads? At least he's an improvement on your usual taste—I mean, with Charles as a father, he practically comes with a Certificate of Excellence!"

"I know!" I laugh. "Oh, I wish I could trade places with Ravenna right now!"

"Do you feel at all weird about him being out with her?"

I pause. "I did have this moment when I first saw her go all googly-eyed at the sight of him and I thought, 'Oh no, he has this effect on everyone, I'm just another sucker!' but, you know, honestly, the weirdest part of all is how nice she's being. She's like a different person!"

"Huh," Krista muses. "And you think Charles is the key?"

"I don't know how else to explain it! I think he must be having an impact on her on some deep genetic level."

"She feels safe with him, cared for . . ." Krista continues the theory.

"He's got this way with her."

"Brings out the best?"

"Like you wouldn't believe."

Krista is quiet for a moment and then says, "Can you imagine if our dads came back into our lives at this age?"

"It's pretty unfathomable, isn't it?" I reply. "I think I'd be even more mad if he was as nice as Charles—all those years missing out on a positive male role model!"

"Yeah, at least our dads are duds to the end."

"Consistent," I laugh.

"Oh! Music's starting! Gotta go!"

"All right, enjoy the show and say *Bonjour* to Sebastien for me!"

"Will do! Bye!"

Sebastien is Jacques' half-brother and one of the featured acrobats with Cirque du Soleil. I am utterly in awe of his talent. All the miracles his honed, toned body can perform.

I look down at my foil tin, dripping with red oil and minced beef debris, and drop it into the bin.

Where to now?

I decide to have a mooch down Newbury Street, buzzing with young people having fun. The boutiques are open late but for once I don't feel like shopping. Instead I find myself drawn down the quieter side streets, feeling as though I'm stumbling onto the set of *The Age of Innocence*. I stop to take in the iconic elegance of the brownstones, picturing Harvey coming down the steps to greet me in a wing collar and jaunty felt hat, maybe even carrying a cane. And then I feel oddly sad because, whatever Krista says, I know I'm reaching for the moon with him.

Yes, he did ask to see me tonight and it would have flowed so effortlessly from our afternoon together, but now what? To see each other again would require advance planning and travel and way too much thinking on my part. I run my hand along the black gloss railings and sigh. I despair of myself at these times—turning a perfectly lovely encounter into a source of anxiety. I think it might have something to do with getting a taste of something I've convinced myself I don't want anymore. It just brings up all this *wanting* in me. Well. No more on this topic tonight. I have to move on . . .

I walk and walk some more. It's dark now and not a little chilly. Perhaps it's time to head back? Tired and throbbing of feet, I attempt to hail a taxi, but each one I spy is occupied. I take out my phone to find out exactly where I am and discover the battery has died. Oh great. There's no one around here to approach for directions and all the shops I pass are shuttered closed; I must have crossed over into some kind of business district. I'm getting a teeny bit spooked now, but try to act nonchalant while lengthening my stride. I just can't believe I didn't pack a map as backup. Or my phone charger. Or a cardi.

It really doesn't do for the travel expert to get lost. I wonder for a moment if I might cry. I've been waiting for an opportunity to do so. To just let go and let it all out. I feel it welling up inside of me now. If I think of how much fun everyone else is having while I'm wandering the streets like a stray dog, I think I could push myself over the edge . . .

But then I see a glimmer of hope in the distance: chocolate-brown lettering and a cupcake motif.

"Sweet"—the sign cuts to the chase.

As I draw closer I see a haven of tufted pink banquettes and white marble tabletops. My pace quickens. I open the door and, once inside, heave a sigh of relief. All is well with the world. Nothing bad can happen to you when you are surrounded by cupcakes. And these are pristine with plump rounded frosting and innovative flavors like Honey Blackberry (filled with blackberry jam and New England's Carlisle honey) and Peach Cobbler (laced with cinnamon sugar and topped with streusel crumbs). Oh, this one is so Krista: Pina Colada—pineapple filling and coconut-cream icing, with its own paper umbrella! There's even cupcakes for her dogs—or should I say *pupcakes!*

"May I help you?"

"Could I just have one of the Boston Cream Pie cupcakes, please?" Well. When in Rome . . .

"For here or to go?"

"Well, that depends," I begin. "I don't suppose you could direct me to the Omni Parker House Hotel from here?"

The server grimaces. "It's tricky," he says, coming out from behind the counter and leading me to the door.

I brace myself for a sequence of "left at the statue of Benjamin Franklin, third turning on the right after City Hall, if you get to Bunker Hill you've gone too far," when he says, "It's there!"

"What?" I squint up the street. "Oh my god!" I laugh. "The cupcakes led me home!"

The question now is: will there be anyone to come home to?

Chapter 36

≈≈≈

The answer is no.

I get into my pajamas, make a cup of hotel room tea (which always tastes weird), grab my cupcake and *Charlotte au Chocolat* book and climb into bed.

For the most part I am cozy and absorbed, reading about the charmingly eccentric characters that worked Upstairs at the Pudding. Not least Charlotte's mother, eternally sporting giant sunglasses, moving in a haze of Joy perfume and Coco Pink kisses. The description of her shoe collection seals the deal: "Jeweled satin evening boots . . . stacked Lucite slippers, heels with feathers, heels with ribbons lacing ballerina-style up the ankles."

She would even cook in them: "Her heels dug into the cutout holes of the rubber mats behind the stoves as she swept through the grease and flames and grunting men."

I am so there!

But every now and again, my eye strays to Ravenna's empty bed and I get a "She's still not back!" jolt of anxiety.

What if the truth accidentally slipped out? How would she react?

I just hope she's not traipsing the streets alone like I was. Not that Harvey would let anything bad happen to her, I'm sure of that.

It can only have been a matter of minutes after I give in and switch off the light that the door creaks open.

"Laurie? Are you awake?"

"Mmmmf." I decide to play groggy in case she starts telling me a bunch of things I don't want to hear and thus can pretend to have fallen back to sleep.

"I had such a brilliant time!" she trills. "He took me to an old prison!"

"He what?" This statement rouses me a little too much.

"A hotel that's an old prison. We went to the restaurant there, it's called Clink!" she giggles. "I've even got pictures in one of the cells."

She perches on the end of my bed and shows me her jailbird poses.

Oddly my mind goes back to Consuelo Vanderbilt, but Ravenna is clearly a far more willing prisoner.

"Do you know that in the 1930s the mayor of Boston was incarcerated there and he actually got reelected *while he was still behind bars*?" Ravenna hoots. "And Frank Abagnale Junior, you know, the con artist from *Catch Me If You Can*? He was there in the Sixties. Harvey knows all the most interesting stuff!"

If Krista were here she'd say I'd met my tour-guide match in Harvey. And listening to Ravenna quote him I almost feel like I am reliving the evening with them. I can even picture his expressions and get a warm feeling hearing that he ordered the chocolate fondue for dessert. When she says, "I think he's got a sweet tooth!" I think, "I *know* he has a sweet tooth." As if I have prior claim just because we shared afternoon tea. I can't help it! She's reminding me of his loveliness and how much fun he is to be with.

"He's just such fun to be with," Ravenna echoes, making me feel a teeny bit foolish.

It's then I remember my mum telling me that you don't want a man with obvious appeal or everyone will be after him. I'm sure every woman who meets Harvey is instantly smitten—what's not to love? Maybe he's just universally charming? I mean, even his own flesh and blood seems to have a crush.

Of course Pamela could be right, Ravenna could be admiring him in a purely platonic way. Lots of people hum while they're taking off their makeup. I turn away from the bathroom light and settle back down into bed, reminding myself that this is not my concern. But as I lie there I finally put a title to the song she's humming—"I Could Have Danced All Night . . ."

Chapter 37

The next morning, as Pamela emerges from the lift, I finally see the family resemblance between her and Ravenna: both have identical walking-on-air love glazes.

"I take it you had a nice evening with Charles?"

"Oh, it was heaven," she swoons, hand to heart. "He took me to his place, cooked me dinner—"

"He can cook?"

"Actually no, but the wine was wonderful!" She giggles. "We sat out on his little terrace and just talked and talked . . ." She drifts off for a second's reverie and then asks, "What about you?"

"I really just walked and walked."

"Oh, like the explorer you are!"

I give an obliging smile.

"And Ravenna? How did she seem after her time with Harvey?"

I take a truth breath. "In a word? Smitten."

"Oh isn't it lovely that they're getting along so well?"

"Um—"

"I think everything is just going to work out perfectly. Is she coming to the demonstration?"

"Actually, she was just about to Skype Eon when I left."

"See? Everything is still on with those two, I knew it."

"Pamela—"

Before I can grab her by the shoulders and shake her out of her blissfully delusional state, hotel manager John Murtha steps up to greet us.

"I don't know if you've had much time to look around the lobby, but there are a couple of things I would like to point out before we go down to the kitchens . . ."

"Absolutely," Pamela follows his lead, away from me and my words of caution.

I heave a sigh. Well, I suppose nothing can really worsen in the next hour or so. Perhaps I'll do a Pamela and postpone all nagging concerns and concentrate on the cake.

Not only is Boston Cream Pie the official state dessert of Massachusetts, Mr. Murtha shows us a framed proclamation from the mayor declaring October 23rd Boston Cream Pie Day, each and every year! The Parker House has its own day, too, on account of being the longest continually operated hotel in America. Though, interestingly, the Parker Restaurant opened on this site long before the hotel.

"So food really does come first here!"

Down in the kitchens we are introduced to Tuoi, the resident Boston Cream Pie expert—she's been making them fresh here every day for the past fourteen years.

"Imagine that!" I whisper to Pamela. "The same cake every day for over a decade!"

Originally from Vietnam, the petite yet perky Ms. Tran is apparently a big hit with dignitaries visiting from her homeland and often helps with translations. She's certainly following an esteemed tradition, since Vietnam's former prime minister and president Ho Chi Minh used to work here as a pastry chef. And if you think that's crazy, Malcolm X was a busboy in the hotel restaurant.

"That's also where JFK proposed to Jackie," the manager tells us. "Table Forty, under the window."

"Oh," I laugh. "Apparently we're doing things backward—we just came from where they were married!"

"Newport?"

"Yes," I reply.

"Beautiful there."

Pamela and I share a look, our thoughts going to Gracie. There's a good chance that we should be able to Skype with her today, fingers crossed.

So. The Boston Cream Pie was created on this very spot in 1856 by a French chef named Sanzian. The description is a little misleading, since it is actually a cake, but the sponge layers (two of them) were made in shallow pie tins.

We watch with amazement as Tuoi takes a long, razor-sharp knife and trims away the millimeter of golden crust from the surface, revealing the palest, most delicate sponge within.

"To make it extra light," Mr. Murtha explains. "It's also nice and moist on account of the rum."

I flash back to the Dark and Stormy cupcakes for a second, wondering if Ravenna might one day fess up and apologize for the Tabasco fiasco. Mind you, that confession seems pretty small in the grand scheme of things today.

"Now the custard."

Tuoi heaps cool dollops on the base layer and smoothes it out like a plasterer. The final layer rests gently on top.

"Chocolate ganache." She reaches for the silky mix of melted chocolate and heavy cream.

Apparently chocolate was considered a delicacy back in the 1800s and people weren't used to having it on a regular basis (can you imagine?), but no doubt it helped this cake quickly become a signature item.

"Originally the ganache was simply poured over the cake," John explains. "There wasn't much artistry to it, and in fact that look is coming back in. However, Tuoi is going to show you our distinctive style."

This is where it becomes a Generation Game challenge. I can only imagine the mess I would get into trying to apply the perfect chocolate gloss without drippage, let alone create the spider's-web effect on top.

She takes a small cone and pipes a white chocolate spiral from the center out—no wobbles or splurges, just a perfectly fine continuous line.

"Wow."

Then she takes a knife and pares across the surface, again from the center out, as though creating demarcations for the slices. It conjures the most exquisite pattern.

"Now that's an expert hand," we applaud her.

The last touch are the shaved almonds coating the outer edge of the cake. These are an addition to the original recipe, just to make it extra special.

Mr. Murtha tells us that they also make scaled-down individual Boston Cream Pies. "Pastry chefs today want to be on trend and decorate the plate—after all, people eat with their eyes first."

So very true. I'm already visually devouring the BCP.

"Ready?" Pamela invites me to take a forkful at the same time as she does. "Mmmm." We savor the soft, subtle flavor.

Despite its dark chocolate cloak, it really is supremely light. One might even go so far as to say "Babycakes light."

"It's the kind of cake you could have two slices of and still get up and move around after eating," is my official word.

"So I'm guessing this is your most popular dessert at the hotel?" Pamela inquires.

"We even offer it on the breakfast menu!" John laughs. "And of course people come in and have a slice for afternoon tea."

Pamela takes that as her cue to set up her wares, apologizing that she cannot invite Tuoi onto the bus as planned. Then again, there's a lot more room to maneuver here.

"I think in my next house I'm going to get a bigger kitchen," she decides.

Interesting! Sounds as if she's now willing to let the house go to Brian and start anew. Possibly not a million miles from where we're standing today . . .

"My first thought for our trade was a Custard Slice because a) there's the custard connection, b) it's equally light and c) the top layer actually has a very similar design to the Boston Cream Pie, but with the colors in reverse. However, when I looked into it, I found it's really defined as a mille-feuille of French origin, so I decided to go with an egg custard tart." She shows them an image from one of her earlier cookbooks—little nubbly pastry case with a slightly sunken yellow filling and a smudgy dusting of brown on the top. "Now these aren't the prettiest things to look at but they do have a unique texture and taste and I quite like the irony that they resemble little pies!"

I love watching Pamela work. She really comes into her own in the kitchen. All the hesitations and introspections of the day go out of the window and she is fully engaged. And, like Tuoi, she is ridiculously fast and dextrous.

"Do you know they even had these at the coronation banquet for Henry IV?" she notes as she brings the cream to a gentle simmer on the stove. The pastry case is already baking and she's working on the filling with the eggs and sugar and vanilla. "Now it's terribly important that the nutmeg is fresh," she continues. "And freshly grated. Which shouldn't be a problem seeing as you're practically neighbors with the Nutmeg State!"

I must say I am a fan of an egg custard tart. I like the crumbly density of shortcrust pastry and the sleek slipperiness of the custard. You do need a cuppa with it, though, as the pastry can be a teensy bit clogging.

Pamela agrees, insisting on brewing up for everyone so they can have the full experience.

"Though really I do prefer these tarts cold as opposed to fresh from the oven."

Sadly we don't have time to chill, already it's time to move on. A certain mechanic awaits . . .

Chapter 38

ᕮᕮᕮ

"Perfect timing!" Charles walks into the lobby just as we reach the top of the stairs.

He leans in to kiss Pamela on the cheek, which responds with a flush, and then he gives me a warm smile. "So, Harvey called . . ."

Now my cheeks are flushing. Dammit.

"And he needs another hour or so on the bus."

"That's fine," I fluster.

"I thought I'd take you girls to the Boston Tea Party—it's on the list, right Laurie?"

I nod vigorously.

It is, after all, the most famous tea-related activity in America.

"I'll just go and see if Ravenna's ready to go."

Ravenna is more than ready. Washed, dressed, packed, she's even got my suitcase in position by the door.

"How did it go with Eon?" I ask, checking the wardrobes and under the bed for anything left behind.

"Oh. You know . . ." She squirms a little so I don't push the topic.

"Right. I think we're all set," I reach for my case. "We've got a little diversion before we go to the garage—"

"Why, what's the matter?" She looks concerned.

"Nothing. Harvey just needs more time so we're going to stop off at the Boston Tea Party attraction on the way."

I see her disappointment. "Okay. But we won't be there long, will we?"

"Just an hour, I think."

She nods. "That's all right."

Well, as long as you're happy, Ravenna . . .

As eager as she is to see Harvey again, I almost feel like I'd rather not. At least not with an audience—just the thought of trying to curtail any stray beams of adoration is stressing me out. And I don't want him to think I'm being dismissive if I avert my gaze, as I almost certainly will. Gawd. Will I ever grow out of my teenage-girl mentality when it comes to men? I find any/all romance-related emotions so disruptive. I take a breath and tell myself to disengage—let go of any attachment to the outcome. Stay in the present moment.

Well, I say that. We're actually being invited to go back to 1773.

The Boston Tea Party Ships & Museum is one of those interactive affairs with costumed reenactors. (Love the knee-britches, brass-buttoned waistcoats and tricorn hats!) We are given alter-ego name tags and invited to heckle and rally in the mock courtroom as we protest against the taxation on tea by the British Government (Boo! Hiss!). But the best part is boarding the ship and throwing chests of tea into Boston Harbor. Of course they're attached to a rope and get hauled back in again, zero tea leaves swirling in the water. Just as well, because we have to get Pamela to do this multiple times to get the right shot.

"Let's try and do one where it's just you and the old ship and then one that also has the Boston skyline in the background, for a bit of contrast," I suggest.

As I back away to get the right angle, I realize Charles is on the phone to his son and suddenly find it hard to hold the camera steady.

"Okay!" He beckons us on. "Time for a quick stop at Abigail's Tea Room, then Harvey should be done."

"Fat Rascal!"

"Excuse me?" Charles startles.

"It's a cake!" Ravenna giggles, pointing to the display.

Basically a chunky-fruity-nutty-zesty scone, originally from Yorkshire.

"It seems to have a face," Pamela peers closer.

The girl in the frilly bonnet serving behind the counter confirms that they use glacé cherries for the eyes and thinly sliced almonds for the teeth. A few are set askew, rather giving the look of the village idiot.

"How peculiar!" she giggles. "Do you think I might I have a quick word with your pastry chef?"

While the girl goes to check, we look around us—Newport's mansion tea rooms could certainly learn a thing or two from here: ye olde recipes, real china teapots with historically significant designs and all the staff in period costume—a positive bustle of aprons and shawls and frilly cuffs.

"Would you like to come through to the kitchen?"

While Pamela trots on her way, Ravenna decides to return to the gift shop, leaving me with Charles.

"Listen, I want to thank you again for being so understanding and accommodating of the situation between me and Pamela," he says as we settle into a table overlooking the water.

"Oh, of course," I give a light shrug. "I'm happy to see her happy."

"She said you raised a concern about Ravenna and Harvey?"

I want to die. "Nooo. I don't mean to interfere. I was just concerned that any, um, *attraction* on her part might further complicate things . . ." I look around to check that Ravenna hasn't returned.

He nods. "We're going to tell her today. When we get to Maine. Much fewer distractions there."

"Whatever you think is best," I find myself backing down. "No rush."

God, how embarrassing. I feel even more self-conscious when we arrive at the garage. Now I definitely can't look at Harvey. I don't want anyone thinking I'm stirring things up because I like him and want to keep him for myself. Even though I'm aware that he's looking in my direction, I busy myself, pretending to be checking that everything is in order, all the cases are present and correct, etc., etc.

But then at one point my head does jerk up. And this is when Ravenna says:

"Why don't you come with us?"

I look around for Pamela and Charles but he's busy introducing her to one of the mechanics that used to work with his father.

"That would be okay, wouldn't it Laurie?"

"Um . . ." Oh god, oh god!

"It does sound fun," he says, looking directly at me. "I wouldn't be able to leave right now, I've got a business dinner tonight, but maybe tomorrow? Where are you headed to after Maine?"

"Um. Er . . ." I am so thrown I have to check the itinerary that five minutes ago I knew by heart. "New Hampshire," I say, trying to will Pamela and Charles to come back and intervene. "We're staying at the Mount Washington Hotel."

"I've always wanted to go there," Harvey enthuses.

"That's settled then!" Ravenna looks pleased as punch.

"Isn't that a terribly long drive from here?" I fret.

"Well, it is the way you're going but, direct from here, it'll just take me a couple of hours."

"That's nothing!" Ravenna confirms. "Hey Mum! Guess what?" she skips over and tells them the Good News.

Now Pamela and Charles are looking back at me with "What have you done?" eyes.

How did this happen on my watch?

"I haven't messed up your plans, have I?" Harvey looks concerned.

"No, no. It's a really big hotel, with a separate inn and a motel, so there'll be no problem getting you a room—"

"But?"

I lean in and whisper. "I'm just very aware that everyone knows *the situation* except for Ravenna."

He sighs. "I know. I was so tempted to tell her last night. There were so many opportunities. But I thought it wouldn't be right, you know, coming from a relative stranger . . ."

I raise a brow. "That's actually a very apt term!"

He smiles broadly. "I missed you last night."

My stomach flips. Suddenly I'm so glad that I'll get to see him tomorrow. Anything beyond that would be just Too Darn Long.

Chapter 39

೧೧೧

I keep my head down during the good-byes and then opt for a seat at the back of the bus, pretending to be thoroughly absorbed with amending the itinerary, which is partly true. By the time we cross into New Hampshire, it seems as if everyone is vaguely pleased to hear from me again.

"So come on Laurie, tell us a bit about where we are and why we're here."

"Well, Charles," I say, feeling as though we're doing a local TV segment. "We've come to lovely Portsmouth, New Hampshire, to taste a local treat called the Popover."

"The Popover, you say?"

"Yes, Charles, it's actually akin to a British Yorkshire Pudding, but instead of being served with roast beef and gravy, it comes with butter and maple syrup."

"What?" Ravenna splutters. "This country is weird."

"Don't knock it till you try it!" Pamela suggests.

"And where, pray tell, will we be tasting this rather unusual teatime treat?"

"Why, at none other than Popovers on the Square!" I say, leading us through this most English of towns, complete with market square, ye olde street lamps, and the occasional cyclist with a dring-dring bell.

The redbrick café with its black and gold frontage is rather more American in scale, with a capacious, tasteful interior, fully accommodating of mothers with prams. We gawp at the gaudy display of sugar-centric goodies and I give a ta-daaa flourish as I spot the Popover. But next to all the piped cream, drizzled caramel and fondant roses it looks rather drab—as if a taupe-coated care-taker had wandered on stage during a showgirl routine.

"Even the carrots on the carrot cake have little faces etched in them," Ravenna notes.

"Well, the Popover dates back to the 1870s, which was a rather plainer time." I try to defend its lack of pizzazz.

"I suppose we have to try it . . ."

We take our samples out onto the front terrace for a good peer and prod. Our assessment is that the batter is lighter, the texture crispier and the color darker than your average Yorkshire pud.

"And it rises up and over, as opposed to sinking in the middle."

"And it's dry inside," I note as I prize mine open. "No sogginess."

"More of a Yorkshire puff than a pud."

"Yes, mine has a hollow interior, as if it's been crossed with a choux pastry."

"Could you trade them a profiterole recipe?" I suggest.

"Technically that's French."

"What's a slightly puffy, not-terribly-attractive English cake?"

There's a silence while we all think. Ravenna comes up with an Eccles cake, which pleases me greatly, but then we get dis-tracted by a bleeping sound.

"It's Gracie!" I locate its source. "She's coming through on Skype!"

"She can speak again?" Ravenna looks faintly disappointed.

"Mum!" Pamela yelps as her face appears on screen. "How are you? You look so much better out of the bandages."

"I've got the movement back in my jaw"—she jigs it and then yelps in pain.

"Mum!"

"Only joking! I'm fine! What about you?"

Pamela explains that we're briefly passing through coastal New Hampshire but will be returning to spend more time inland tomorrow.

"I've been following your progress on the map. Looks like you're bang on schedule."

"We are," Pamela shoots me an appreciative glance. "I'm just sorry you can't be with us. Are you terribly bored?"

"Oh, how could I ever be bored here? Today I had a lovely tour of The Elms and discovered my new favorite cocktail—the White Lady. Apparently the former owner used to get everyone squiffy on it while they were playing mah-jong in the conservatory—"

"Wait!" Pamela cuts in. "Who's that in the background?"

"Oh, that's Gerald," she breezes. "My new friend."

"Is he staying with you?" Pamela peers more closely at the screen.

"Are you really in a position to judge?" Gracie peers back at her. Charles slides his arm from around Pamela's shoulder.

"Don't be silly, Charles! Cuddle up! You know this is what I've wanted to see."

"Granny!" Ravenna hoots. "Did you matchmake this whole thing?"

"Just a little. You know I want to see you all happy."

"We are," Ravenna confirms. "Thank you!"

Gracie does a double take at her granddaughter. "So you know? You're pleased?"

"Mum!" Ravenna howls, leaping to her feet as Pamela sends a brown river of tea into her daughter's lap. "What the—"

"Oh I'm so sorry, darling. Quick, let me mop you up in the ladies'!"

Gracie waits for them to scuttle out of earshot and then sighs, "I might have known it was too good to be true. I take it Pamela is still waiting for 'the perfect moment'?"

"Something like that," I whisper, as Charles goes to fetch some napkins to clean up the table. "She doesn't want to spoil Ravenna's good mood."

"If walking on eggshells was an Olympic sport . . ." Gracie tuts.

"I have tried to encourage her."

"Oh, I know what a thankless task that is."

"Anyway, I think tonight could be the night. I'll give you an update first thing in the morning."

Gracie gets a funny look on her face.

"What?" I ask her.

"Can the others hear me?"

I step out on to the sidewalk, pretending to be showing her the square.

"What is it?"

"Gerald is taking me surfing tomorrow morning."

"What? You've only been out of hospital five minutes!"

"Oh, I'm fine! I'm not going to miss out on a chance like this over a few bruises."

"Gracie, you amaze me!"

"I think the hardest thing is going to be getting into the wet suit," she grimaces. "Gerald says we should have a run-through tonight."

I raise a brow.

"Well, why not, eh?"

I smile back at her.

"Why not indeed!"

Chapter 40

∽∾∽

Within minutes of leaving Portsmouth, we cross another state line.

"Welcome to Maine!" I cheer. "Home to two hundred and thirty miles of rugged coastline, top-notch lobsters and the infamous Whoopie Pie."

"And Stephen King."

"What?"

"He lives here," confirms Charles. "Most of his books are set in Maine."

"I didn't know that!" I say, shuddering as I flash to the infamous sledgehammer scene in *Misery*.

"And *The Shawshank Redemption* was set here. And *Murder She Wrote*."

"Do you have any more cheery information?"

Charles thinks for a moment and then offers, "Maine is the only state in the U.S. with a one-syllable name."

"Is that true?" I'm quite impressed by this.

"And it produces ninety-nine percent of the blueberries in the U.S."

"I've got a lovely blueberry muffin recipe here somewhere." Pamela reaches for her recipe file. And then we all fall quiet. Each lost in our own thoughts.

I notice there's a lot of yawning as we proceed. And yawns being contagious, it seems as if at least two sets of jaws are being extended at any given moment.

"I wonder . . ."

I take out the map and consult it.

To reach our scheduled destination of Camden, we'd have to be on the road for at least another three hours, allowing for one "bathroom break," which always seem to take half an hour, what with the diversion off the freeway, stretching of legs and mulling over the wares at the local gas station.

I sigh. I was really set on the Hartstone Inn, not least because the husband is a chef. If you saw the images of the breakfasts on the website, you'd want to go there too. Caramelized French toast with cumin-dusted bacon. Need I say more?

"Oop! Sorry!" Charles swerves dangerously. "I think I just dropped off for a second."

"Right! That settles it! I think we should find somewhere closer to spend the night. We're not too far from Portland, which seems a decent-size town."

"City," Charles corrects me. "Maine's largest."

"Well, then, that should work!"

"Wait a minute," Ravenna reaches for my arm. "Does this mean we're going to miss out on the outlet shopping?"

I can't believe it. She's actually studied the itinerary.

"No, no," I assure her. "We can still do that tomorrow; that's where our baking appointment is."

"*We're makin' whoopee!*" growls Pamela.

"Are you going to sing that every time?" Ravenna rolls her eyes.

"You know, Harvey was up this way last summer," Charles muses. "He might be able to recommend somewhere . . ."

"Actually, he was talking about Maine last night," Ravenna perks up. "Shall we call him?"

Before she can offer to do the deed, Charles has tapped his phone and plugged in his earphones.

"Hey son! Yeah, good, she's running great. Listen, we're looking for suggestions of where to stay in Maine, somewhere in the Portland area . . . Yup. Uh-huh. Oh, that's right, you went there with Molly. Really? That good? Okay." He hands me the phone. "He's going to text the number of the hotel."

Just knowing he's about to send a message makes my hand tremble. I stare expectantly at the screen, resisting the temptation to text him first. As in, "Who's Molly?"

An ex, presumably? Everyone has exes. Nothing wrong with that. Provided she is an ex. I shudder again, remembering the minefield that is a new relationship. Not that this is a new relationship. It's just wishful thinking. *And breathe* . . .

"Here we go!" I announce as the number comes through. "Inn by the Sea, that sounds nice."

I press dial and then hold the phone to my ear, hyperaware that all eyes are upon me.

"Hello, yes, I was wondering if you had a couple of rooms available for tonight? Bit short notice, I know . . ."

I cross my fingers.

"We'd be happy to accommodate you," the receptionist smiles into the phone. "Allow me to review your options."

It seems we could each have our own room if we wanted. Which would leave certain possibilities open for certain parties . . .

"Just a second!" I touch mute. "Pamela, how many rooms?"

"Um," she falters, face pinkening.

"Two," Ravenna cuts in.

"Two?" I query.

"Grown-ups in one. You and me in the other. I'm not sleeping by myself after the Stephen King comment. I don't think anyone should."

I blink back at her. Did she just condone her parents sharing a room?

Charles and Pamela exchange a look.

"Unless you two are planning on a long courtship?" Ravenna teases.

"I think twenty years is long enough!" Charles winks.

"I thought you said you met ten years ago?"

Pamela looks stricken.

"Well," Charles clears his throat. "It seems like twenty."

Chapter 41

∽∾∽

The Inn by the Sea is one of those places that makes you feel instantly soothed and in safe hands.

Set on Cape Elizabeth amid five acres of certified wildlife habitat, this is where "luxury comes naturally." As we check in, my attention repeatedly returns to the floor-to-ceiling windows, showcasing the serene sprawl to the shoreline. It may be clouding over now but it's still the perfect antidote to the bustle of Boston. I know everyone is going to get a good night's sleep here.

Well. Perhaps some of us still have more catching up to do than others.

Charles and Pamela's room is amazing—more akin to an architect's apartment: on the left as you walk in is a bijou version of your basic dream kitchen, with white paneling and granite breakfast bar; ahead is a lounge area—groovy stripy carpet, tweedy-beige high-backed sofa and a texturally tantalizing armchair of woven seagrass; patio doors lead to a wooden deck, which in turn overlooks the swimming pool. Turn back inside, head upstairs and you find a vast expanse of bed with fresh flowers on the bedside table and an oversized bathroom of honeyed marble with a shower area that could easily accommodate a trawler-full of lobster fisherman.

"You'd be crazy to leave all this," Ravenna decides as she leans over the upstairs balcony. "Why don't you just get cozy and order room service?"

The look on Pamela's face says, "Who are you and what have you done with my daughter?" but she doesn't argue.

Charles, by contrast, steels himself for the task in hand: "Actually, Ravenna, perhaps you would care to join us? There's something we wanted to talk to you about . . ."

She pulls a face. "Can it wait till tomorrow?"

"Well . . ." Charles looks at Pamela.

Pamela looks at me.

I can't believe I'm the deciding vote! Oh gosh, I suppose it can't do any harm leaving it a few more hours. Just as long as they tell her before we next see Harvey. I give Pamela the nod of approval.

"Tomorrow's fine," Charles confirms, leaning in to give Ravenna a peck on the side of her head. "You have a good night."

She looks delighted by his affection and then turns to me, "Shall we see if we can get a table by the fire?"

Ravenna is referring to the fireplace in the lounge bar—a cozy nook with seafaring art on the walls and a mantel illuminated with tea-light candles and a glass storm lantern. The windows are starting to spatter with rain, so we're all the more grateful to nab the pink linen sofa beside the fire, even if our cheeks start to flush a matching hue before we're halfway through the list of entrées.

"Got to be the herb-grilled Kettle Cove lobster for me!" I set the menu down.

Ravenna looks uncertain—perhaps it was too much to hope that she would eat two nights running.

"Did you know that lobster has fifty percent fewer calories than an equal amount of chicken breast, and only a fraction of the fat?"

"Is that true?"

I nod. "To quote lobsterfrommaine.com: 'If you swam every day in the cool, crystal waters off the coast of Maine, you'd be healthy too.'"

She chuckles and then looks back at the menu. "Do you see how they've named their local suppliers—Fern Hill Farm goat cheese, Backyard Farm tomatoes—that's rather nice, isn't it?"

"It is," I confirm.

I can't believe this new side to her—to think all this sweetness was hiding under that cloak of resentment! I wonder what she's thinking right now? She looks so twinkly and content . . .

"You know, this is where Harvey sat with Molly." She hugs a cushion to her chest. "Apparently she couldn't believe her luck. Chowed down under the table and then fell asleep in front of the fire."

I raise an eyebrow.

"I love French bulldogs, don't you?"

A surprised smile spreads across my face. "Absolutely love them," I concur.

"They have a doggy menu here. Molly had meat "roaff" and a K-9 ice cream!"

I experience a moment of concern. Is this why she wanted to come to the bar rather than the restaurant—to sit where he sat, then relive every moment of their evening together? Don't make me regret postponing her chat with Charles and Pamela . . .

I'm relieved when she starts talking about the dogs she grew up with—"Pixie was the first. She used to follow me everywhere. When she'd sleep she'd always nuzzle in and lay a paw across me, like she was cuddling me!"

There she is—there's Babycakes! For the first time I can see them as the same person.

"Then there was Billy and Bonanza . . ."

Our talk of dogs evolves to include the entire animal kingdom—from teacup piglets to giant pandas, and now North American cottontails.

The bunny element was introduced by the waiter, explaining how the hotel has been involved in a habitat restoration project.

"I think it's wonderful when hotels are environmentally conscious," the formerly jaded Ravenna enthuses.

"They're big on that here," he confirms. "Even the key cards are recycled and compostable!"

"Goodness," she gasps, and then laughs, "Quite literally!"

Ravenna is being so easygoing, so amenable, that I find myself sliding my muddled blueberry martini over to her.

She blinks back at me. "Really?"

"You've earned it."

"Rewarding me with alcohol, eh?"

"Oh, don't put it like that!" I tut and then tilt my head. "Now you come to mention it, it's the same thing when you're a child, isn't it? You get sweets for being a good girl. They're the treat, the reward. And then you grow up and they become the naughty element."

Speaking of which . . . Our waiter is back.

"Can I tempt you ladies with some dessert?"

"You choose," Ravenna diverts the menu to me.

"Hmmm," I deliberate. "Sea Glass is the name of the hotel restaurant?"

"Yes, ma'am."

"Well then, I guess we should have the Sea Glass Peanut Butter Buster Parfait with the fudge sauce. You know, something light."

He grins back at me. "Excellent choice."

"And another blueberry martini please."

Ravenna inhales happily. And then she drifts off. Gradually her expression changes and she stares deeper and deeper into the fire.

I'm just wondering if I should give her a little pinch when she says: "You know, this is the longest I've been away from Eon."

I wait for her to continue.

"It was weird at first. I felt all disorientated and unsettled but now . . ." She narrows her eyes at me. "Don't say I told you so!"

"I won't."

She sits back in her chair, sighing, "I feel so much better about myself when he's not around."

I press my lips together. Not a word.

"I told him in Boston that I wouldn't have any reception in Maine. And it's like I can breathe again."

I smile. "I know just what you mean."

"I can have my own thoughts and I'm not constantly worried or feeling like I'm doing something wrong."

I nod.

"I don't want to go back to him." Her voice quavers. "Not now that I know I can feel this way."

I reach for her hand. "You don't have to," I tell her quietly.

"But—"

"Don't worry about it now. Don't let any thoughts of him spoil the enjoyment of where you are. He can't get to you here. No one knows where we are, except us four, and Harvey. We've dropped off the itinerary altogether!"

She smiles back at me. "I like the sound of that." And then she twists around, waves at a passing Labrador and asserts, "And I like it here."

"Me too."

"Harvey has good taste."

I give a subtle nod. And then change the subject. To his father.

"So, you actually approve of your mum and Charles getting together?"

She shrugs. "I read online today that my dad had been seeing his secretary for the past seven years."

"Oh gosh." I falter. "That can't have been nice, to hear about it like that."

She shrugs. "He's an arse."

I'm confused. "But—"

"He's always been an arse. They should have split up years ago."

I can't believe what I'm hearing. "I thought you were in his corner."

"Only to piss Mum off."

I lean back and study her. "When did it all begin?" I ask. "Hating your mum?"

She takes another sip of martini and then starts picking at the silver studs on the chair arm.

"We don't have to talk about it, if you don't want to."

"No, I don't mind. She's not so bad really. I mean, I've been thinking, you know, about what you said . . ."

"Which bit?"

"Well. Thinking about if she was dead, for one thing. How I'd feel then."

"And how would you feel?"

"I'd hate myself for the rest of my life."

Her eyes look a little glossy now.

"You know, I've just heard one thing for a really long time— about how she exploited me and tries to control me and doesn't want me to have my own identity."

"Is this some kind of voice in your head?"

"It's Eon's voice. *All the time.*"

"Why would he say those things?"

She sighs. "Probably because it's what I wanted to hear when we first met. I was really angry with her. About something. I don't even remember what now. Maybe a piercing or a party . . . Either way, he was on my side. He was always on my side, it seemed."

"Against her?"

She nods.

"It was like he was the only one who could see what I could see."

"So he fanned the flames."

She squirms, rubbing her brow. "I feel bad now. Some of the things I said . . ."

"To her or to him?"

"Both."

"Well. The good news is that your mum will forgive in a second. In fact, she's already forgiven you everything—past, present and future. That's just how she is."

"She's too soft with me."

"You're too precious to her."

Ravenna crumbles, hair falling forward, eyes spilling over. "I've been such a cow!"

"I know," I say as I gently rub her back.

She laughs through her tears.

"Well, I do know. I've seen it with my own eyes."

She peers back at me. "Do you hate me?"

"No," I say sincerely. "I mean, at the moment, quite the opposite."

"Really?" she gulps, wiping her nose with the napkin.

"I admire you. For being able to see things with new eyes. For being honest about your mistakes."

"I have to make it up to her," she insists.

"All you have to do is be nice. And forgive her."

"Forgive her for what?"

Now that's the million-dollar question.

"Well. For spoiling you. Because you're right. She did. And perhaps for trying to protect you from things . . ."

"What kind of things?"

Careful, Laurie! This isn't your secret to tell.

"Just life," I shrug. "And hurt. And people on public transport."

She laughs.

"And for bringing you here against your wishes."

"Oh, she's so forgiven for that. I'm having a really good time now."

"Really?"

"You know I am!" she grins.

"So that just leaves the future." I get a twisty sense of foreboding as I say the words.

"Is that really part of the deal—I have to forgive her for everything she does in the future too?"

"Well, it's a lot to ask, but if you could—that would be really something."

"I'm going to try."

I smile proudly. "Loganberry nightcap?"

"Don't mind if I do!"

Chapter 42

⁓⁓⁓

The next morning Ravenna is up before me.

"I felt a little muzzy-headed so I went down the beach," she tells me as she hunts through her case for something respectable to wear. "It's pretty wild down there. Not a soul around." She gets up and shows me her shots of the deserted coastline. "I went to post these picture on Facebook but then I thought he'd see. And I want to keep it for myself a while longer!"

"You know, I think there's going to be very little chance of a signal today—weaving through the White Mountains, the elevation has got to be six thousand feet . . ."

Her face brightens. "You reckon I've got one more day?"

"At least," I confirm.

Her pep continues all the way to the breakfast room—she walks straight up to our assigned table, gives Charles a peck on the cheek, chirrups, "Morning Mum!" and leans in for a skinny-armed hug.

It's fleeting but it's there, and to Pamela's credit she doesn't fall to the floor and start praising the sweet baby Jesus. She just stares at the breakfast menu, taking in absolutely nothing.

"The crab cake and avocado Benedict looks good," I nudge her, discreetly pointing to a neighboring table.

"Everything looks good," she says, still in a daze. "Everything."

"So Ms. Organizer Extraordinaire," Charles addresses me. "What do we have on the schedule today?"

"Well, it was a toss-up between the Barns and Quilts Tour and a Dry-Stone Wall Building Workshop . . ."

"So Maine!" He smirks contentedly.

"In actual fact we are going to begin with a bit of outlet shopping."

Ravenna raises her juice skyward.

"But! Before you despair, you should know that there's a very manly component—as in the L.L.Bean flagship store."

L.L.Bean is the U.S. equivalent of Millets, providing all the kit you need for camping/kayaking/hunting/fishing/geocaching, etc. One unique aspect to this store is that it's open twenty-four hours a day. (And has been since 1951!) Because you just never know when you're going to need a pocket-size water purifier or a critter-proof backpack.

The other notable aspect is the giant tan and brown hiking boot beside the main entrance, standing sixteen feet high.

"Excuse me, would you mind taking our picture?" I hand my camera to a stout gentleman as we assemble around it.

We smile, each of us kicking a leg in the air. And then break into a spontaneous rendition of "These Boots Are Made for Walking . . ."

Gosh! I puff as I press my heart back inside my body—this is starting to feel like a family.

. . .

Main Street Freeport has to be the nicest outlet setup of all time—instead of a low-rise lineup of identikit shops, each store is housed in its own—well—house. Each more historic-looking and picturesque than the last. Even McDonald's is disguised within colonial clapboard. Despite the Coach outlet calling Ravenna's name, she decides to join us first inside L.L.Bean. Just out of curiosity. If she starts showing an interest in the "RV chic" drawstring shorts and chambray skirts, then I really will start to worry. But I think it's legitimate that we city girls are so transfixed by the softness of the fleeces that we each get one (hers in plum, mine a dark teal) with the aim of being extra cozy in the mountains tonight.

My stomach flips at the thought of seeing Harvey later. Definite nerves. Though I think my greatest concern is that we won't get any time alone. Sadly the odds of us being given a suite and encouraged to get room service are slim.

"Where's Mum?" Ravenna asks Charles, when we locate him in the winter sports section.

"Looking at the cookery books, where else?"

"They have a cookery book section?" Ravenna is amazed.

"What, like cooking by campfire?" I laugh.

Within minutes I'm holding a book called *Campfire Cookery.*

Ravenna squints at the cover image. "What's that supposed to be?"

"That's a s'more."

"A s'more?"

"As in the singular of s'mores—the great American campfire tradition. You toast marshmallows on a stick and then squidge them between two graham crackers—that's a sweet crispy biscuit—with a layer of chocolate."

"Wow."

"Because when you take your children out to the wilderness you really want to get them hopped up on sugar before they go to bed," Charles tuts behind us.

"Sounds like you're speaking from experience?"

"My son has a very sweet tooth."

"Yes he does," Ravenna and I confirm in unison. Which is rather embarrassing.

"So did you go camping often, when he was a boy?"

"Harvey was always more of a reading-with-his-flashlight-after-dark type than into whittling spears out of sticks. I'm surprised he turned out to be so good with engines."

I can't help but smile at the image of him in his sleeping bag, poring over some childhood tome. Like *War and Peace*.

"So the tent would glow orange into the wee small hours?" I ask.

"A beacon for all the local bears."

"Did you ever see one?" Ravenna gawps. "A bear?"

"Oh yes. The first time that happened was the last time Harvey's mother came with us."

This is the first time Charles has mentioned his ex-wife. I realize we don't know anything about her. I'd like to ask what she was like, but Ravenna has a more pressing concern: "Sh-she wasn't eaten by the bear?"

Charles laughs. "No."

And then he asks, almost shyly, "Do you think you'd ever want to try it, Ravenna?"

She thinks for a minute. "A week ago I would've said 'not in a million years,' but now . . ."

He smiles. "Maybe one day I'll take you."

"Could we have s'mores?" Her eyes brighten like those of a six-year-old.

"Until you couldn't take any s'more!" he chuckles.

I edge away, leaving them to it. It feels a little close to the mark: a glimpse of the childhood Ravenna might have experienced, if Pamela had chosen Charles.

My fingers trace along the bookshelves, hooking out the ones that catch my eye, until I bump up against the woman herself, perusing *Notes from a Maine Kitchen*, with *The Wild Blueberry Book* tucked under her arm.

"It all sounds so fresh and delicious I can't stand it!" she reels as she turns the pages. "What have you got there?"

I hold up *A Moose and a Lobster Walk into a Bar* and *Cabinology—A Handbook to Your Private Hideaway*.

Until today, my fantasy property was a Carrie-esque walk-in wardrobe, but now I can't help thinking how cozy it would be to have a log cabin or perhaps a converted lighthouse to retreat to every now and again. Especially if I had someone like Harvey to retreat with . . .

"Do you think I could get away with antler chandeliers in a Little Italy apartment the size of a garden shed?"

Charles takes the books from me and sets them back on the shelf.

"I think it's time for us to move on."

Chapter 43

❦

So what exactly is a Whoopie Pie? Does it in any way resemble a whoopee cushion? Yes—if whoopee cushions were made of sponge and you squished a pair of them together with a sticky marshmallowy filling. The shape is certainly similar—round, tapering off at the edges.

"It's sort of like the sweet version of a burger," Ravenna decides. "Only flatter."

In all my research for the ultimate Whoopie Pie-maker, Amy Bouchard's Wicked Whoopies had the greatest claim to fame—"As featured on the Oprah Winfrey show."

(Quite a boon for business, as you can imagine—her company, Isamax Snacks, now make over 10,000 Whoopie Pies *a day!*)

We've opted to trade Battenburg because a) it's got one of the stranger names and b) it looks like something a child might have invented—pink and yellow squares indeed!

All the baking will take place aboard Red, but I hang back, keen to nose around Amy's brightly painted café-shop, brimming over with baskets of goodies, each a-rustle with sprigs of cellophane. When I hear the company motto, I have to call Krista.

"Did you know there are at least ten smiles in each Wicked Whoopie Pie?" I ask her.

She chuckles and says she's ready to place her order—she just needs a rundown of the flavor options.

"You really wanna know?"

"Hit me."

I take a deep breath and begin, "Peanut Butter, Strawberry, Raspberries and Cream—"

"I want that one!"

"I've only just begun! Chocolate Chip, Mocha, Red Velvet, Maple—"

"I might like that!"

"Mint—"

"I might like that too."

"Vanilla Bean, Banana Cream," I continue to progress along the baskets. "Gingerbread—"

"That's the one. For sure."

"Orange Creamsicle, Lip Lick'n Lemon and Black Forest."

"I want the Black Forest!"

"I know. I've already got it for you."

"Oh, I love having a friend who knows me so well! I take it you got the Banana Cream?"

"Of course." I grin and then peer out of the window. "I can't believe I'm going to see you tomorrow! It feels like longer because there's still a whole state between us."

"And a potential love affair," Krista teases. "Are you excited about seeing Harvey again?"

We get the chance to chat awhile, until I notice that Pamela is beckoning me outside and down the street.

"So," she begins in a confidential tone. "Last night Charles was telling me that the Mount Washington Hotel is where the International Monetary Fund and the World Bank set the gold standard, back in 1944."

"Makes a change from whispering sweet nothings, I suppose."

Pamela gives me a look. "The point being, I think I've come up with the ideal match for that particular venue."

"Oh yes?"

"Pound cake!"

I give a little chuckle. "That's a good one!"

"It's such an easy recipe—pound of sugar, pound of flour, pound of eggs, pound of butter." She recites the basic ingredients and then gives me a particular look. "So easy that anyone could make it."

I take a step back. "You're not suggesting I do?"

"Yes I am. And here's why: remember you highlighted the spa at the Mount Washington because they invite guests into their herb garden to pick their own rosemary or candytuft or whatever to infuse their treatment? And you thought I might want to work that into my recipe?"

"Yes."

"Well, Charles pointed out that that might be a really good way to get Ravenna into a relaxed, receptive state. I mean, no one ever has a hissy fit in a spa."

There's always a first time, I think to myself.

"We looked into a mother-daughter room where we can get a massage and then a wrap, and they leave you alone for at least half an hour, so I'm thinking, lying there, candlelight, soothing music playing . . ."

Ideal place to drop the bomb.

"That's not a bad idea," I concede. "Most likely she'll be covered in mud or some scrub so she wouldn't be able to just run off."

"Exactly," she concurs. "So will you do it? Make the pound cake?"

I take a breath. Do I really have a choice? "Okay," I tell her. "Provided we stop off and get some extra supplies in case I mess it up."

"You won't mess it up," she assures me. "If you apply the same care that you apply to making travel arrangements . . ."

I give an uncertain smile, hoping I can live up to her confidence in me. "Are you ready to go now?"

She claps her hands together. "One quick layer of marzipan and we're outta here!"

Chapter 44

∾

For the first hour and a half of our journey, we remain in Maine. Despite passing towns with a European flavor—Lisbon, Poland, Paris—the inland countryside looks all very English. But then we cross into New Hampshire, right at the border of the White Mountain National Forest, and suddenly I'm getting visions of all-American holidays spent hiking and biking, rafting and rollercoasting, all with pressed shorts, side-partings and freckle-faced children named Chip and Cindy.

Personally I rather like the idea of touring the covered bridges and chugging along on the Conway Scenic Railroad, but we only have time for a quick pit stop at McKaella's Sweet Shop. Pamela wants to trade a slice of Battenburg for McKaella's legendary rainbow layer cake, which totally trumps us in the color spectrum—from the base up it's pink sponge then tangerine, sunshine yellow, green, blue and lavender at the top, with layers of cream-cheese buttercream in between.

"It really is beautiful!" Pamela admires the smudgy pastel effect.

"As if a brush with multicolored stripes has been swept around the cake."

"This has certainly been our most colorful day," I decide. "It's just a shame they don't make . . ." I stop suddenly.

"Don't make what?" asks Ravenna, as she holds up an Eat Cake First T-shirt to her mum.

"Nothing," I zip my lips.

"Are you ready?" Charles sticks his head round the door. "We don't want to be late for tea!"

"I'll catch you up in a minute," I say as I usher the others back onto the bus.

"What are you up to?" Pamela wants to know.

"You'll see tonight."

"Is my pound cake about to get a makeover?"

"It depends if McKaella has what I need. And that's all I'm saying for now."

Back on board with my secret stash, I experience a sudden surge of fun and freedom—this has to be the most epically scenic stretch of road so far. I feel like a swooping, gliding bird as my eyes take in the undulations of prosperous green splaying out in every direction. Hard to believe that some of the coldest temperatures and strongest winds in the whole of the United States have been recorded here (gusts can reach up to 230 mph), for today it is pure perfection. Pure being the word—can you imagine how fresh the air is here? I inflate my lungs and marvel at the brightest blue sky.

"Isn't this glorious?"

Everyone is in good spirits, their eyes a little wider and brighter.

"You know Bill Bryson hiked around here for *A Walk in the Woods*?" Charles informs us.

"I love Bill Bryson," I coo. "Totally cracks me up."

"Me too," Pamela concurs.

"He used to live in New Hampshire," Charles adds. "In the same town as Jodi Picoult. And less than two hours from Dan Brown."

"Wow. Imagine if they'd started a book club!"

When Pamela laments her mum missing out on all this beauty, we decide to Skype her, giving her the full panorama.

"Oh, I feel as if I'm on the bus with you," she laughs. "Show me where you are heading."

Ravenna holds the iPad up to the front window and then gasps, "What's that?"

There, set against the most majestic of mountain ranges, and looking like its own gleaming white kingdom, is the legendary Mount Washington Resort.

We give a collective "oooooh" of wonder. Can this really be our home for the night?

We keep Gracie with us as we begin curving up the main driveway. Off on the left is the Bretton Arms Inn—that's where I'll be staying tonight. For the first time since we set off, I have my own room. I try not to dwell on my suspicion that Ravenna specifically requested separate quarters so she could entertain Harvey after hours. It's actually a good thing that she has some space for her own thoughts tonight. And if she needs to talk, she is welcome to come and visit me. Unless of course *I* am entertaining Harvey . . .

Up we go, ever closer to the magnificent main building—now we can see the wings extending out, the different levels accented by the signature red roofing and the circular entrance porch that makes you want to swirl in a ball gown. What can I say? Some places just swell your heart—you can feel your chest expanding, just to let in more wonder. Ravenna reaches for my hand and gives it a squeeze.

"Happy?"

She nods. "I feel like a different person."

I can't help but think that within a few hours she will literally have a new identity.

"Oh, I wish you could join us for tea," Pamela sighs at her mother's image.

"Don't worry," Gracie trills. "I'm meeting the gang for cocktails."

"Cocktails? At this hour?"

"Well, at our age you don't want to risk waiting for five P.M. to roll around!"

"Oh, Mum!"

Gracie gives us a cheeky wave before signing off, "Enjoy the fairy tale!"

Most "grande dame" hotels I've experienced (including this trip's Waldorf Astoria and Omni Parker House) have rather dark, wood-paneled lobbies. The Mount Washington is flooded with light. The walls are a lemony buttercream and the endless white columns add an airiness that puts you in mind of a health-enhancing promenade. Even the rugs have a fresh look—every flower, herb or tree depicted in the soft weave is indigenous to the area. I could probably do without the mounted moose's head center stage, but I like the story behind the mural of a woman looking down on us from a white balcony—the owner's wife, Carolyn Stickney, used to watch guests arrive from behind a net curtain, possibly so she could check out what the competition was wearing! I'm just relieved that Ravenna has taken a more girlie turn with her outfit today, even if she still looks as if she has used her mother's whisk to style her hair.

"Now the Princess Room where we're having tea is so-named

because Carolyn became one—eight years after her husband's death, she married a French prince."

For a room with a pink arced ceiling garlanded with gold, it's surprisingly cozy. Even the candelabra are more suggestive of candlelight. Snug beside the fireplace sits a pair of my favorite French canopy chairs, only this time in a rich red with ebony trim. But one particular detail causes my stomach to flip. For there, nestled amidst the bite-size scones, tangy lemon curd and sterling silver tea strainers, is Harvey.

"You're early!" Pamela startles.

"I hope that's all right? My meeting was over in minutes and I thought you'd probably be here for tea," he smiles as he greets each of us.

As I await my peck on the cheek, I can't help but notice he's gone a bit Clooney-suave with his slim suit trousers and tailored shirt. Even though Ravenna nabs the seat closest to him, it seems comfortingly significant to me that our outfits complement each other—his dark navy picking out the Wedgewood-inspired print of my dress. I rather like the idea that a stranger walking into the room might identify us as a pair. (You know you're smitten when . . .)

"Your Kir Royales." The waiter sets a dark-pink flute of bubbly before each of us.

"Cheers!"

As we raise our glasses, I notice Ravenna's cassis-splashed liquid has a subtly different hue, and suspect Charles has discreetly substituted her champagne for fizzy apple juice, keeping her this side of legal while also feeling included. Because he's just *that* good.

"So the meeting went well?" he asks Harvey as he makes his selection from the wooden chest of teas.

"Quite the opposite," Harvey grimaces. "They've officially

pulled out now." He turns to the rest of us. "The sponsor for a project I've been working on."

"What kind of project?" Pamela wants to know. As do I.

"It's something we do every July—get some urban kids out on the water, teach them to sail. It sounds pretty basic but it's been life-changing for some of them—newfound focus, sense of teamwork; just being outdoors is a major plus."

"Anything but sitting in a darkened room playing video games," Charles mutters.

"This is the first year we were taking them to Newport, which is a pretty big deal in the sailing community, but the hotel that was going to accommodate us has opted out, so now we've got to find somewhere new for them to stay," he heaves a sigh as he adds, "at the height of the season."

"So now you're struggling with availability *and* price?" I empathize.

"Exactly. I was on the phone the whole way here and all I'm getting is 'fully booked.' I really don't know how we're going to turn this around."

"Can't you help, Laurie?" Ravenna looks expectantly at me before turning back to Harvey: "It's what she does."

"I did wonder about asking your advice but . . ." He looks awkward. "We don't have a budget per se; everyone involved is volunteering their time."

"That's not a problem," I'm quick to assure him. "I'd be happy to help if I can. I mean, what are we talking about here? How many kids? What age? Can they be divided into groups or do they need to be kept together? How many supervisors? Can they be trusted not to wreck the rooms? Is it one group for the month or do they change every week?"

"See!" Ravenna claps her hands together. "See how good she is!"

"Well . . ." I reach for my teacup, tilting it up to cover my face.

"Have you ever been sailing?" Harvey asks me.

"Does the Staten Island Ferry count?"

He chuckles. "Not really. Anyway, we don't have to get into this now—I can e-mail you later with all the details, if it's not too much trouble? I know you're up to your eyeballs with this job."

"We've just got tonight and Vermont and then we're pretty much done, right Laurie?"

I nod. "I can take a look while you're having dinner."

"You're not joining us?" He looks disappointed.

"No. I have the feeling I'm going to be full of reject Pound Cake."

Plus, of course, it's only right that the four of them should enjoy a proper family dinner. Provided everything goes according to plan at the spa. And it has to. I think Pamela knows it's crunch-time.

"Okay, we both have our challenges now," I give her a bolstering hug as she prepares to head on her way. "Just be clear and honest and be prepared to answer a million questions."

She nods. "And you make sure you preheat that oven and grease the tins."

Suddenly my challenge doesn't seem quite so daunting.

Then again, I hadn't counted on having a second pair of hands in the mixing bowl . . .

Chapter 45

We agreed to park Red beside the Bretton Arms and use the shuttle to and from the main building, not least to spare the valet parker the trauma of wrangling seven tons of London Transport's finest. (You should have seen his face when we first pulled up!) I don't know which is more intimidating to me—being left in charge of the bus, or being alone in Red's kitchen.

Ah cooking, how you intimidate me. Suddenly I'm all fingers and thumbs. Even this shortest of recipes takes on the gravity of Tolstoy. I'm getting a twisty, out-of-my-depth feeling, and all I've done so far is set out the ingredients.

"Knock, knock! Laurie, are you up there?"

Harvey! My heart flusters and I instantly get the shakes. "Yes, yes! Come on up!"

"I wanted to see if you'd like a hand." He smiles willingly.

"I thought you were going to play golf with your dad?" Not the most welcoming response.

"Well, I convinced him that he'd really rather take a nap so I could do what I'd rather be doing—"

"Cracking eggs? Mixing gloop?"

"Just can't get enough of it!"

"All right." I take a breath. "But let's be clear. I don't have a clue what I'm doing here, so I need you to cross-check my every move."

"That won't be a problem," he says with mock lasciviousness.

My heart is properly palpitating now. How on earth am I supposed to concentrate in such close quarters?

"Right. First things first—we need to sieve the flour and salt."

I begin tapping the sieve as Harvey goes to pour the flour through, only instead of a gradual sprinkling it comes out in a big dump, creating a great genie-like puff in the air. Which then gently layers onto his shirt. I go to flick it away with the tea towel, but I've picked the only damp one and now I've made a white paste across his navy sheen.

Oh jeez.

"It's my fault, I should have changed before I got here—I only packed one smart outfit."

"We can rinse it off under the tap," I beckon him to the sink. "It'll dry in no time with all this oven heat."

He tries to maneuver under the water flow, but can't get close enough. "Perhaps it's best if I just take it off. Do you have anything . . . ?"

I hold up one of Pamela's flouncier aprons.

"Not exactly the most masculine design," I note, "but it will do the trick."

He gives a hapless shrug. "In for a penny, in for a pound cake!"

I chuckle at his wit. "You're quite au fait with English sayings, aren't you?"

"I had a Brit in my class," he says as he unbuttons his shirt and reveals a broad chest with a tantalizing whisk of hair—the ultimate in come-lay-upon-me burliness.

"What about your trousers?" I push my luck.

"You want me to take them off too?" He looks most amused.

"Well. It is a risky situation for them," I say, holding up my white-dusted hands.

"This is not how I saw my afternoon going," he says as he reaches for the zip. "Well, not exactly anyway."

As he turns to set them off to the side I get to admire his boxers. Banana Republic, I'm guessing. His legs are nice too. Strong thighs. I reckon he could pick me up and carry me without them buckling at all. And what a nice change that would be.

"Laurie?"

"Yes?"

"Something's bleeping."

"Oh, it's just the oven reaching the desired temperature," I say, wrenching my attention back to the job in hand. "Right! We need to cream the butter and the sugar with the handheld mixer set to high, until light and fluffy."

Let the shrill whirring begin.

"Next add the vanilla extract," I continue to read.

"How much?" Harvey queries.

"One teaspoon. Then the eggs."

This is when all hell breaks loose. There's nine of them. We were supposed to add them gradually and reduce the mixer speed to low, but we don't do either, and the fact that I've opted for way too shallow a bowl means that in a matter of seconds we look as if we've been ambushed by a paint-baller.

"Noooo!"

In my desperation to cut off the power I knock over the bowl, creating a vanilla-scented Vesuvius oozing into a skiddy pool on the floor. As I frantically attempt to push back the countertop drippings, Harvey goes to reach across me to the paper towels, but slips as he does so. I try to grab him from falling flat on his lovely boxers, and end up lunging over him, covering his arms with slimy gunk, my chin jolting into his chest. "Youch!" Some part of me just wants to say to hell with it and writhe on the floor like a pair of cake-mix mud-wrestlers, but a new voice enters the fray:

"Hellooo! Anyone home?"

We freeze.

Out of the corner of my eye I see Charles's head pop up from the stairwell. I watch with horror as he takes in his half-naked son, our compromising position, and the overall mucky devastation.

"Just wanted to check that everything is going okay."

I can't speak.

"Right! Good! See you later!"

"Oh my god!" I mouth to Harvey, waiting for the jolt of his father disembarking. "What will Pamela think?" I squeak.

"Don't worry, he won't tell her."

"How can you be sure?"

He raises a brow. "You don't think my father can keep a secret?"

He's got me there.

"God! He must think I'm so unprofessional!" My hands cover my face.

Harvey smirks. "Nice face mask. Very Mrs. Doubtfire."

"Oh no!" I wail as I catch sight of my reflection.

"Here. Allow me . . ." He reaches for one of the tea towels and gently wipes away the gunk.

It feels oddly soothing. When I think of how I scrub at my face with my Neutrogena wipes, and here he is, big ole mechanic hands, barely glancing my skin.

"What?" He catches me studying him.

I take a breath. "I want to be nosey."

"Okay," he pauses, waiting for me to ask my question.

"How is it possible that someone as lovely as you doesn't have a significant other?"

He looks shy for the first time. "I could ask you the same question."

"Well, you could, but I asked first."

He laughs and then sits back as he answers, "I really just had to take a break. I kept making the same bad choices over and over, so I thought it would be a good idea to step back and try to figure out what I was doing wrong."

Sounds familiar.

"And have you figured it out?" I ask.

"Nope," he deadpans. "Except for one thing: lately my grand-father's advice has been coming back to me—he used to talk about choosing a woman with a strong work ethic."

"Really?"

"He said as pretty as women are, they are not here as decoration—each must find their true purpose. And the harder they work at their purpose, the happier they'll be. And the happier they are, the happier you are."

I smile. "Wise words. You know what my grandfather used to say to me?"

Harvey cocks his head.

"What the hell are you doing with that idiot?"

After a speedy cleanup we go back to square one with the recipe. Things go a lot more smoothly this time—we read one line ahead before making any moves and use Harvey's muscles instead of the electric mixer. Now the loaf tins are safely baking away, we can resume our chat.

"You know, I don't think there was ever a sense in our family of making a conscious choice with relationships," I say as I set down the oven gloves. "They just seemed to happen, and then you dealt with the fallout as best you could."

"It's pretty daunting stuff, isn't it? In terms of how much damage the wrong person can do to your life."

"It really is," I concur.

"I've had a few horrors. My own mother was no peach—when I think of how she treated my dad . . ." He shakes his head.

"There're some crazy women out there," I admit.

"And some crazy guys," he acknowledges. "And then there's us."

Oh, how I love the idea of an "us."

He reaches for one of Pamela's rosebud teacups. "Did you see the painting in the Princess Room of all those guys in suits sitting round sipping tea?"

"No," I say, slightly disappointed that he's changing the subject.

"Apparently it's a Prohibition-era painting and that wasn't tea they were drinking."

"Ohhhh."

He leans closer. "There's this speakeasy burrowed into the lowest level of the hotel . . ."

"Mmm-hmm?" I try to focus.

"It's called The Cave, and it's where all the illegal boozing went on in the Twenties. They had a spyhole down there so they could see when the police were coming up that long driveway for a raid, and when there was an alert they used to empty all their liquor into this one container and then sit there pretending to be sipping tea."

"Ingenious!"

"Well, here's the best part—when the coast was clear, they would line up at the container and scoop out a teacupful of all the mixed whiskies, brandies, rums and gins!"

"Sort of like a Long Island Iced Tea but without the Coke!"

"Exactly!"

"I say all this because I was thinking we could meet there to-night, after dinner. Say around ten?"

"You want me to meet you in a dark cave with a history of corruption and excess to drink hard liquor?"

"I do."

"Sounds like heaven."

When the timer pings, I feel a curious stomach-flip of nerves. Oh, please let the cakes have cooked well.

I reach for a toothpick.

"What are you going to do with that?"

"Etch my initials in the side—you know, like gold bars have markings stamped on them?"

"Really?"

"No!" I chuckle. "Pamela said it's a good way to see if the cake is sufficiently cooked. I stick it in; if it pulls out clean, it's done."

"Ah, the moment of truth!"

I do the deed. "I think that's all right, don't you?"

"It certainly smells done."

"Too done?"

"No, delicious done."

I smile proudly as I turn them out onto the cooling rack. "Right, now for the finishing touch." I reach into my bag and pull out my secret stash from McKaella's Sweet Shop—a can of gold spray paint.

"You're spraying it gold." Harvey doesn't miss a trick.

"Yes," I cheer. "Like a gold bar—for the gold standard that was set here. What do you think?"

"Aren't you worried that might be a teeny bit on the toxic side?"

"It's not like the kind of paint you use on cars," I tut. "It's edible."

"Whatever gave you that idea?"

I shrug. "We were dealing with a lot of colored sponges today, and it got me wondering about metallic cakes."

"Because people love the idea of chewing on metal." Harvey's brow twists.

"Well, you Yanks are always going on about buns of steel!"

He splutters out loud at this one, and then asks if he can have one quick spray.

"Of course."

He turns his back to me. Shakes the clickety can and turns back holding up his index finger.

"What James Bond movie am I?"

I roll my eyes. "*Goldfinger.*"

"I would have done *The Man with the Golden Gun*, but I didn't come armed today."

"How very un-American of you."

He looks serious for a moment. "I shouldn't even joke about it. America's great shame is its gun crime."

"I must say it does seem bonkers to an outsider. So much senseless violence."

He sighs heavily and then asks, "Should we go?"

I nod, the mood sober. Until he turns to pick up his clothes.

"Ah." He hesitates. His hands may be clean but his body is a mess of batter-spatter. "I didn't really think this through . . ."

I have visions of him riding the shuttle bus in his undies and then streaking through the main reception.

"You know, my room is just across the way," I try to sound casual. "If you'd like to take a shower?"

He sighs with relief. "I would. But how am I going to get between here and your room?"

I think for a minute. "We could put a second apron on to cover your back?" I try that, but now he looks as though he's wearing a young girl's pinafore dress.

I bite my lip.

"I know you want to laugh."

"I so do!" I confess. "You know, short of wrapping you in greaseproof paper like a deli sandwich, I have no solution. I think you're just going to have to make a run for it."

He tuts himself. "If my grandfather could see me now . . ."

"At least if you hold a tray of the cakes it will put your look in some context."

He cocks a skeptical brow.

"Come on, everyone's heard of the Naked Chef, the Barefoot Contessa . . . You can be the Bicep'd Baker!"

He pulls a joke strongman pose—gosh, I wish taking a photograph was as simple as blinking your eyes.

"All right," he says. "I shall attempt this with as much dignity as I can muster."

And then promptly falls down the stairs.

"Just kidding!" he calls back to me as I rush to his aid.

I shake my head. "Perhaps it's best if I go first?"

Chapter 46

Scurrying through the lobby, we give a cheery wave to the receptionist, then take the stairs two at a time.

"See, that wasn't so bad," I say as I reach for my room key.

He looks back at the dark carpet. And the white flour footprints we have left behind.

"Don't worry, I'll ask to borrow the Hoover from Housekeeping."

"You like to take care of everything, don't you?"

"Try to."

"These rooms are nice," he says as he surveys the home-from-home décor—a mix of floral and plaids, with one of those sumptuously deep beds that would inevitably elicit a sigh of contentment on contact. And I'm not just saying that because he's standing so temptingly close to it.

The bathroom is particularly lovely, with streaky marble, bright chrome accents and streaming sunlight.

"Do you want to go in first?"

"No, no," I insist. "After you. Let me just grab a towel."

I spread it over the tartan armchair by the window and settle in, relishing the thought of this gorgeous man naked on the other side of the door. I hear the shower turn on and power-jet over him. He's singing "Come Fly with Me." Well, a version of singing. I'm relieved to know he has at least one flaw—it makes me like him all the more.

And then the door opens and from the steamy haze he steps forth.

"Good as new!"

Better, I think to myself. Better than anything I've ever seen. I want to touch him but he's all sheeny-clean and fragrant and I'm still a dusty mess. Nevertheless he stands daringly close, smiling, just smiling, right into me.

"Why don't I wait for you?" he offers. "I can help carry the cakes."

"If you like . . ." I love that he wants to linger.

"I'll sort the Hoover, then wait downstairs while you're getting ready. Give you a bit of space."

For the first minute after the door closes behind him, I just stand in wonder. That is so considerate. The former men in my life would have switched on the TV then repeatedly asked what was taking so long as I flustered to find something to wear under their disapproving gaze.

Today I calmly opt for my strawberry-red Forties-style dress to color-match the roofing of the hotel. Like you do. Then I decide to speed up my hairstyling by scooping it into a bun on the top of my head, pinning a tiny scarlet velvet ribbon at its base.

"Wow!" Harvey scrambles to his feet as I appear before him. "When did the team of hairstylists arrive?" He peers more closely at my bun. "Did you really do that by yourself?"

"I used a hair doughnut, it's really easy!"

"A hair doughnut?" he hoots. "Gosh, you really take this cake stuff seriously!"

"Which reminds me," I laugh, "I never did tell the others about the man who invented the doughnut hole!"

His eyes narrow. "You're just messing with me now, aren't you?"

"No!" I laugh as we step aboard the shuttle. "We were supposed to visit Rockport in Maine, but we never got that far."

"Okay," he turns to face me. "You have the duration of this shuttle ride to bring the story to life."

"You don't want to hear it!"

"Yes I do," he replies. "I like listening to you."

The feeling is *so* mutual.

"Let me take you back to New England in 1847," I begin with my grandest intonation. "Elizabeth Gregory, mother of ship's captain Hansen Gregory, would often make deep-fried dough treats for her son and his crew, filling the center with hazelnuts or walnuts and thus call them dough*nuts*."

"But what about the hole?"

"Well, that came about during a terrible storm at sea. Hansen suddenly needed both hands free to steer so he jammed his doughnut onto one of the wooden spokes, thus creating the first hole."

Harvey looks unblinkingly at me.

"Of course, there is another theory that says the dough was rarely cooked properly in the middle so that's why they poked it out."

"My money's on that," Harvey opines.

"You know the funniest thing?" I add, as we pull up outside the main hotel. "Hansen Gregory was buried at Quincy—home to the very first Dunkin' Donuts. Coincidence? You decide!"

We're just about to step through the entrance when my phone rings—Krista! I explain that I just need to check that everything is on schedule for our meet-up tomorrow.

"No problem, take your time. I'll rustle up some drinks and meet you on the veranda."

"Perfect!" I grin. "Hello? Is that the loveliest friend any girl could wish for?"

"Someone's in good spirits!"

"Yes I am! Everything is going peachily. Well, except for a new accommodation challenge which I'll e-mail you about later. Anyway! Is everything cool with you? Are you driving?"

"I am! I've just found out about this dog-themed chapel at St. Johnsbury—I thought I'd take Mitten for a quick nose!"

"Sounds absolutely barking."

"Funny . . . So listen," I notice a change in her voice, "I've got something to tell you."

Why does my stomach drop at her tone?

"It's Jessica. She called."

That's why.

"I don't want to hear it."

"I know. But I feel duty-bound to tell you."

"Why?" I challenge. "Has something happened?"

"No. Well, nothing bad."

"Okay, then I don't want to know."

Krista sighs. "She's coming over to America and she really wants to meet up with you."

"Well I don't want to meet up with her." I step away from the doors. "Look. I know you want me to face this thing, Krista, but honestly, I think it would make matters worse."

"Okay, okay," Krista backs down. "I'm just saying."

I huff. "You know I don't mean to be rude to you."

"And you know I don't mean to be a killjoy. It's just . . ."

"What?"

"You've been talking a lot about forgiveness lately, with Ravenna anyway, and I thought some of it might have rubbed off."

Oh, that's a low blow.

"I've got to go."

"Okay," she chirps. "See you tomorrow."

I sigh. Now I feel like a horrible person.

The veranda at the Mount Washington resort is beyond compare. Stretching for nearly a thousand feet, the broad expanse of white-washed wood is lined with elegant Grecian pillars interspersed with hanging baskets spilling pretty pink petunias. Beguiling enough in its own right, but then you layer in the spectacular view: the gracious curve of the lawn, the turquoise pool, the wedding terrace and, in the distance, the Presidential mountain range. So much to marvel at, and yet, try as I might to conjure my brightest smile, Harvey instantly senses something is awry.

"Not bad news I hope?"

"No, no," I say as I settle into the white rocker beside him. "She was just letting me know that my sister is trying to get in touch."

"Are you guys *out* of touch?"

"Very much so."

He cocks a brow. "So who's not forgiving who?"

I don't react well to this. Does he think this is a case of one sister having borrowed the other's dress and spilling red wine on it?

"Some things are just unforgivable," I clip.

"Yes," he nods. "I used to think that."

I wait for him to expand on his comment but instead he hands me my drink—another elegant flute of champagne. We chink. We sip. We look at the view. I can't let it lie.

"My friend seems to think I'm being a hypocrite, having spent the week preaching forgiveness to Ravenna."

"Regarding her mother?"

"Yes. But their situation is different. Pamela didn't have any bad intentions. She was trying to make the best choice for herself and her child. Admittedly she's been a bit of a slowpoke in terms of bringing Ravenna up to speed—"

"So the intention is key?"

"I think so, yes."

"And with your sister . . . ?"

"Well, I'm not saying she intended for my mother to die, but she was certainly fully aware of how destructive her behavior was."

Harvey looks shaken. "I-I'm sorry, I didn't know."

I shrug and look away.

"What happened?" he asks gently.

I hesitate. I never talk about the details. But the words start to form of their own accord.

"They were arguing again. Jess wanted money. Again. For once my mother said no to her. My sister flew into a rage, stormed out of the house, my mother followed. She was so upset she didn't check the street and a car . . ."

His hand reaches for me.

"It's okay. No need to continue."

"She didn't even look back," my voice wobbles. "Jessica. She just kept running."

He sighs.

"I had to hear about it from one of the neighbors."

"Oh Laurie."

As he expresses his sympathies, his words feel like a gentle stroking of my hair.

"So when you think of your mother now . . ." he ventures.

"I'm just so sad. Like my heart is broken. I can't bear to think of how distressed she was in her last moments. I hate that there's nothing I can do to make it better."

He nods. "And when you think of your sister?"

"I'm just so angry." My eyes flare as I look up at him.

"Understandably." He holds my gaze.

I get the feeling he wants to say something more.

"What is it?"

He sighs. "Well, you know the problem with holding on to the anger is that you're the one who suffers the most."

"I know," I huff. "It's like holding on to a burning coal with the intention of throwing it at the other person, but you're the one who gets burned." I quote my pal Buddha. "I do get it. In theory."

"Sooner or later you have to put it into practice or it will be the ruin of you. And I wouldn't want to see that."

His eyes are so kind. I can tell his concern is genuine.

"Do you want me to help you try and break this down?" he offers.

"Right now?"

"Right here, right now, with this beautiful view to motivate us."

I feel uneasy.

"It's just a conversation."

I take another sip of fizz. If there is anything he can say that can ease the pain, I suppose it has to be worth a try. "Okay," I say in my tiniest voice.

"So. First question: have you ever done anything you're not proud of?"

"Yes, of course."

"A few things you regret, a few things you're a little ashamed of?"

I nod.

"Where you could, did you try and make amends?"

"Yes."

"You seem annoyed with your sister for trying to do the same."

"It's too late with her," I explain. "Too much damage has been done."

"What if it had been you who caused the accident?"

I feel instantly sick.

"How would you feel?"

"I would never forgive myself," I reply. "I'd be haunted every day."

He lets me sit with this feeling for a while. Which I don't really appreciate. It's just too awful to comprehend. The burden would be unbearable. The same burden that Jessica carries . . .

"Let's talk about the drugs for a minute. You're not buying that the addiction is something beyond her control—you see it as a personal weakness."

"I know it sounds harsh, but yes I do."

"Is there any aspect of your life where you've felt you don't have complete control? Any actions you have taken that weren't really in your best interests?"

He's got me there. When I think of all the appalling, degrading choices I have made regarding men. If anyone really knew what I had tolerated without speaking up and defending myself—well, I don't suppose they'd have a very high opinion of me. They would wonder what on earth was holding me in such a toxic place. Why I didn't just walk away and leave the relationship. Oh my goodness— was that my addiction? I just happened to get the less visible, more socially acceptable version?

I look up at Harvey.

"Different weaknesses have different taboos," he observes. "We're none of us so very different from the other."

I let my head fall back in the chair, glad I'm sitting down.

"Ultimately I think it comes down to this question: What do you want to honor? The crime, as in the awful thing that happened that day, because that's what you're holding on to the tightest, or do you want to honor your mother's memory? All her wonderful qualities."

My heart aches as I answer. "I want to honor her."

"The thing is, she's still here in you, isn't she? Half of you is made up of her DNA."

I nod.

"And half of your sister. She lives on in your sister too. Do you really want to turn your back on her? Is that what your mother would want?"

"Not at all," my face crumples. "She'd want me to take care of her. But I just can't seem to find those feelings for her anymore; all the trust has gone. I don't even think of her as my sister now."

"I know the drugs can do that. They can create a whole new persona with no redeeming qualities. But what if Jessica is still in there? What if your little sister is trying to come back to you?"

My eyes instantly well up—little Jess! My little Jess, the one I used to protect so fiercely. Perhaps too much. Perhaps I didn't let her fight enough of her own battles, so that when temptation came a-knocking she didn't know how to say no.

Harvey reaches for my hand. "There are no guarantees with this. Much as we wish things could go back to the way they were before, they will never be quite the same. But she is your mother's daughter. And she needs you."

My eyes bulge with tears.

"Let me grab you a tissue."

I try to hold my face steady so the tears don't spill over. This pain feels different. It goes even deeper. Jess lost her mum too. Now we're all we have left of her, on this planet at least.

I look out across the mountain range and feel that she's everywhere, her love reaching as far and wide as I can see.

"Oh Mum!"

"Laurie? Are you all right?" It's Pamela and Charles approaching with matching looks of concern.

I blink away my tears, sniff all the emotion back in as I get to my feet.

That's when I see someone who faintly resembles Ravenna.

. . .

Her hair has been blown dry into sheeny, voluminous waves. She's wearing a long-sleeved, high-necked black chiffon dress with cream lace panels, managing to look both sexy and demure.

"What do you think?" she twirls before me. "It's the other dress I got at Anthropologie—bit *Downton Abbey*, isn't it?"

"It's stunning—you're stunning!" I reach for her hands. But her attention has already wavered. She looks beyond me. "Have you seen Harvey?"

"Yes, he's just—"

"I'm right here," he says, discreetly palming the tissue.

I give him a little smile to know that I'm all right. And I am. It's hard not to be buoyed up with so much happy energy surrounding me. I can feel it in every photo we pose for—the easy way arms are wrapped around the person next to us, the closeness of the huddle. It's like a group hug every time we reconfigure.

And then the attention turns to the cakes.

Harvey keeps quiet about the part he played, and Charles, as predicted, is equally discreet.

"I can honestly say I've never seen anything quite like it before." Pamela takes in the golden gleam. "You're one-of-a-kind, Laurie."

"I'm going to take that as a compliment. Do you want a taste?"

"Oh no, I trust you."

"Is that code for 'I don't want to get an upset stomach before dinner?'"

"Nooo," she laughs. "I can tell they are perfect."

While the others get embroiled in a conversation about what this place must be like in the snow (Krista would be interested to learn that they do dogsledding here), I lean in to Pamela and whisper, "Did you tell her?"

"I did, but—"

"You did?" I gasp. "Oh, that's wonderful! She's obviously taken it brilliantly."

"Mum, are you coming?"

Time for dinner.

As I watch them walking off, arms linked, I feel all the more churned up. Perhaps it is possible. If Ravenna can do it, and look so radiant on it, perhaps I can too.

I'm just getting up to leave when Harvey comes dashing back.

"Did you forget something?" I look around our chairs.

"Yes," he says as he scoops me into his arms. "This."

And then he kisses me. It's full force yet dreamily tender, all pent-up passion and compassion, desire and yumminess. I feel I might faint from the rush.

"Mmm," he smiles into my eyes, clasping me closer, intensifying the yearning. I think he's about to lean in for more, but instead he gives me a kiss on my nose, making me giggle.

"Speakeasy at ten?"

"I'll be there!"

Chapter 47

I forgo the shuttle bus on my way down the hill—I want to savor this sensation of soaring and zinging, and revel in this reviving air. He kissed me! The most wonderful man I've ever met just kissed me! In this moment I feel utterly invincible and my heart feels *huge*. Suddenly I can't wait to solve his accommodation issue, show him what I can achieve when I set my mind to it. But, first things first. I need to apologize to Krista.

"No you don't," she counters. "After I put down the phone I was thinking about the ways you've been like a mother to me—how you're always interested in the minutiae of my day, always have my best interests at heart, are always cheering me on. You know I never had that with my own family, and if I lost you—"

"You won't lose me. I'll always be here for you."

"I know," she sighs. "I'm just saying, I understand. And I won't mention Jessica again."

"Well," I can't help but smile. "Here's the thing—I may have had a mini-breakthrough. Just enough for me to consider seeing her."

"What?" she gasps. "I-I can't believe it!"

"Neither can I."

"You know I'll be there with you for the whole thing, if you want?"

"Thank you. I suppose it's time. And if it doesn't go well, then I'm no worse off."

"I think it's very brave of you."

"Well. If my two favorite people think I'm being a stubborn ass—"

"*Two* favorite?"

I smile. "I really hope Harvey comes to Vermont tomorrow so you can meet him, and tell me if he's really as lovely as he seems to my eyes."

And my heart, I want to add.

For the next hour, Krista and I get busy with the Newport situation, checking availability and finding that even the basic $60 motels have jacked their prices way up and only have the odd room available.

"I don't like the idea of having them dotted around town," I tut. "I need a block booking. And a big pile of cash."

"What about some kind of fund-raising event?" Krista suggests. "Old English cakes come to New England? I'm sure you could get a bit of media coverage for that—maybe even the local TV station?"

"Mmm, Pamela is a bit camera-averse at the moment."

"Well, she was at the start of the trip, but wouldn't you say she's feeling a bit brighter and more confident these days?"

"I would," I concede. "Perhaps we could even take over the Chinese Tea Room at Marble House—she got really excited about the prospect of baking there."

"Or maybe have an event on one of the boats—High Tea on the High Seas?"

"I love that!"

We rattle back and forth until Krista's hunger gets the better of her. "I need to go and find a burger joint."

"You do that. I'm going to put in a call to our secret weapon."

Gracie.

She may be several White Ladies down but she's still sharp as a tack.

"Leave it with me," she says. "I think I might have an idea."

When I look at the clock again, I'm surprised to see it's already time for me to leave for the speakeasy. I'm certainly in stealth-mode as I enter the hotel, praying I don't cross anyone's path as I make my way there. But, just as I turn down a never-ending corridor, I see Pamela and Charles heading directly for me. There's not a stairwell or lift to duck into, so I have to brazen it out.

"Well, good evening to you—I trust you had a lovely dinner?"

"We did," Pamela smiles, but Charles looks fretful.

"I'll see you back at the room," he excuses himself.

Pamela sighs as she gazes after him. "He's losing patience with me."

"How so?"

"He thinks you're right about Ravenna's attraction to Harvey. He says it's going to make things even harder when we tell her."

My jaw drops. "I thought you told her at the spa?"

"I did tell her, in painstaking, loving detail. But when I finished I realized she'd slept through the whole thing."

"What?" I despair.

"I guess she was a little too relaxed. And then she got a blow-dry and her makeup done, so there wasn't a spare moment."

"So what's the plan now?"

"Everyone has just gone back to their rooms to get a sweater, then we're reconvening on the veranda."

"Everyone?"

"Well, we're going to call Harvey after we've had the conversation. Depending on how it goes."

I nod.

"I'm so nervous!" Pamela confesses.

I take her hand. "Look, aside from the Harvey aspect, I think she's going to be really pleased."

"Do you?"

"Yes. She obviously adores Charles and she's happy to see the two of you together. Maybe there will be some confusion or embarrassment regarding Harvey, but if you give her time to come to terms with it all . . ."

Pamela nods. "I'd better not keep everyone waiting."

"No. On you go."

For a moment I just stand there. I can't believe she still hasn't done the deed! It was all too good to be true. As if Ravenna would have reacted so breezily. I don't know what happened at dinner to make Charles so concerned, but I suppose I can ask the object of her affection myself.

I'm on the patio level now, looking for the entrance to the speakeasy. Aha! Here we are: through the brick arch and down a narrow tunnel that does indeed resemble a cave. I'm feeling my way along the rough-hewn rocks when a body barrels into me. It's only as I stumble back and turn toward the light that I realize the body belongs to Ravenna.

"Wait!" I call after her. "What's going on?"

"Did you know?" she turns on me.

"Know what?"

"Did you know that Harvey is my half-brother? Did you know Charles is my . . ." Her voice cracks. "Did you?"

I go to speak but nothing comes out.

"You knew!" she spits. "You knew and you let me . . ."

"Ravenna," I step toward her, but she slashes at my out-stretched arms, hurtling away into the night.

Oh god.

I feel a presence behind me—it's Harvey, hanging back in the archway looking ashen.

"What happened?"

He shakes his head. "It's not good."

"Tell me."

He slumps back against the wall, rubs his face and then begins, "I was at the bar waiting for you and this person comes up behind me and places their hands over my eyes . . ." He looks at me. "I thought it was you so I reached back and I can't even remember what I said but when I turned around she kissed me. Just out of nowhere! I mean, I knew she'd had too much champagne at dinner, but I didn't see that coming."

I close my eyes. My worst fear has come to pass.

"She wouldn't back down," Harvey continues. "I kept trying to get her to chill, to just take a moment, but she was so insistent—"

"So you told her?"

"I didn't even mean to. It just blurted out of me. I think it was the shock." He hangs his head.

I sigh with frustration at how inevitable this was. I saw this coming a mile off. I should have done more to stop it.

"I don't think I should be the one to go after her."

"No," I agree. "I'll call Pamela. It's time they talked."

"Honestly, I don't think she's going to be in the mood. You should have seen her face." His brow rucks. "What have I done?"

"This isn't your fault," I insist. "Everyone knows she should have been told sooner."

"I think I'd better go and find Dad."

"You do that."

He hesitates. "I'm sorry. I messed up our night."

I shake my head. "Don't worry about it. Another time. Go now."

He nods and sprints on his way.

I take a few moments to consider the wreckage and then find myself instinctively dialing Krista, forcing me to get logistical.

"So, most likely scenario is that she will lock herself in her room. I don't know if she has enough money for a taxi but, even if she did, I don't think she'd know where to go. We're kind of in the middle of nowhere here and it's pitch-black out there."

"That poor girl."

"I know," I sigh. "If only her mother had been paying a little more attention at the spa."

"I don't know," Krista tuts. "For whatever reason, she didn't really want to tell her. She's put it off for twenty years, after all."

"Is it the shame, do you think? Or what?"

"I don't think Pamela's good with confrontation. Some people will do anything to avoid it. Plus, I think she's afraid of her own daughter."

"I think you could be right. And I don't think this is going to help ease that—she looked like a wild woman."

Krista sighs. "I wonder . . ."

"Wonder what?"

"I'm still in St. Johnsbury, which is less than an hour from you. Would you trust me to handle this?"

"What do you mean?"

"I don't think Ravenna is going to want to be around any of you tonight. Will you give me permission to step in?"

"You sound like the cleanup crew in *Pulp Fiction*."

"If that's how you want to view it."

"I don't know how Pamela would react . . ."

"I don't think Pamela's going to be in a fit state for anything, she'll just be wailing and wracked with guilt."

"Sounds about right."

"And Charles needs to take care of her. So. Time is a-ticking. You decide—is it a yes or no?"

I take a breath. I trust Krista. She's never once let me down. I don't know how to fix this myself, but she seems to have a plan.

"Go for it," I tell her.

"Okay. I'm on it. Just text me her room number. I'll update you when I can."

I send the text with trembling fingers and then walk up to the bar. "Could I please have a teacup of your hardest liquor?"

"Certainly, madam."

"Thank you."

Now I just have to sit back and wait.

Chapter 48

The first call I get is from Charles, letting me know that he's put Pamela to bed with a sleeping pill since she was threatening to camp outside Ravenna's door until she let her in—sometime around the twelfth of never. He says he thinks it's better to give Ravenna some breathing space. He's written her a note, slid it under her door and it's up to her to make the next move. No more drama. Everyone needs to stay in their own room and get some rest so we can reconvene with clear heads in the morning. I don't know if that last comment was directed at me and Harvey, but romance is the last thing on my mind now. Well, maybe not the last, but not the most pressing.

I go to my window and look out into the night, wondering what Ravenna is doing with all that rage right now. You hear such awful things about young people these days. I hope Charles is right to give her space. Part of me would want to break her door down. Which is why I gave Krista the go-ahead. God, I wish she'd call.

I wonder if anyone has contacted Gracie? Probably not. No need to worry her at a distance when there's nothing she can do.

I pace. I lie on the bed and stare at the ceiling. I pace some more. I flick through the TV channels just to keep myself awake.

Three excruciating hours later, my phone rings.

"Krista?"

"I've got her. She's safe. We're at the Trapp Family Lodge."

"Oh my god!" I feel a huge flood of relief. "How did you do it?"

"Well, you said she had a soft spot for dogs, and no one can resist Mitten."

"You got him pawing at her door?" I know this trick from when I stayed with Krista and Jacques in Quebec.

"Yup. And then basically I offered to get her away from you lot and she jumped at the chance."

I cringe. "So what now?"

"Just come here tomorrow as planned."

"Well, we weren't due to arrive until mid-afternoon, should we—"

"No. Don't rush here. She needs as much time to herself as possible."

"So, later?"

"No. No more switcheroos. Keep to the schedule. And bring Harvey. Unless she faces that embarrassment now, she's never going to be able to have a normal relationship with him."

"Is she okay? I mean, in herself?"

"No. But she will be."

"Oh Krista!"

"Gotta go! I don't want her knowing I've contacted you."

"Okay!" I close the phone and hug it to my chest. Thank god she's all right. Or—at the very least—in good hands. Now I just have to explain to the drama-averse Charles that my best friend has kidnapped his daughter.

Chapter 49

What a difference a day makes.

Yesterday, as we approached Mount Washington, everyone was bright-eyed and bushy-tailed. Today, as we wend on our way, there's a heaviness in the air. The Road Trip has become a Guilt Trip, with at least three out of four of us feeling partially responsible for Ravenna's anguish. Of course, Pamela feels *wholly* responsible, and has returned to the ragged, exhausted state she first arrived in.

"Perhaps you'd like to ride with Harvey?" Charles suggests, possibly wanting to give his beloved the freedom to complete her meltdown in private.

I am pleased to be with Harvey but it's not the cheeriest atmosphere.

"I can't imagine how fried her brain must be right now," Harvey sighs as we meander through the greenery. "Can you imagine the shock?"

"I know. My biggest concern is that it might push her back into the arms of Eon."

"Eon?!"

"The name says it all really. He's not good for her. Not at all. But he's an obvious person for her to call because he's always so eager to bad-mouth Pamela."

"That's not cool."

"No," I sigh, genuinely concerned.

"Don't worry," he reaches for my hand. "We won't let anything bad happen to her."

I smile. "Is that your brotherly protection kicking in?"

"I think it is!" he grins and then adds: "Maybe you could drop Krista a line? See if she can keep an eye on that situation?"

"I certainly can."

I take out my phone but, before I can tap the first word, the ringer jangles.

"Gracie!"

The one member of the group who is still in a state of blissful ignorance regarding last night's farrago.

She's so bursting with good news that I decide not to rain on her parade straightaway.

"Is young Harvey around?"

"Young Harvey is right here, let me put you on speakerphone."

"It's a long time since I was called young," Harvey smiles.

"Well, everything's relative," Gracie replies. "Right! I think I've solved your accommodation issue."

Harvey looks at me with wonder—can this be true?

"Last night, when you called, Laurie, Gerald and the gang were talking about the things they most miss in life, and nine out of ten of them said, 'Having the grandchildren to stay.' They miss that youthful energy, the surprising things they'd say, the new slang! Of course, some of them never did have any grandkids, and said they didn't even know any teenagers." She takes a breath. "So I said I might be able to help with that . . ."

"What exactly do you have in mind?"

"Well. Shirley said she's got five guest bedrooms that can take two or three girls apiece. Eli lives next door and he said he could match that for the boys. Faye says her favorite thing is making a giant stack of pancakes in the morning—since her husband died, she's stopped doing it, but she would love to get going again, so she's offered to provide breakfast. Of course, now everyone wants to pitch in in some way. And you know I've got the transport covered with the bus. I can't wait to get back behind the wheel."

"Are you serious?" I gasp.

"You know very well I am."

"Yes I do," I puff.

"The kids will flip out at the bus—new Facebook profile pics all round!"

I laugh. "It might just upstage the yachts."

"I can live with that!" Harvey grins. "Gracie, you are a marvel. Is there anything I can do to help?"

"Well, if you're anything like as good-looking as your father—"

"Gracie!"

"I'm just teasing. But a little bit of flirtation wouldn't go amiss. I get the feeling that Faye just wants to hear she's pretty one more time."

"As a matter of fact, Harvey does have a way with the older ladies," I say, remembering the lovely woman at the Parker House Hotel in Boston.

"You my pimp now?"

"Do you have a problem with that?" I ask.

"In this context, no."

"I think we have a deal, Gracie!"

"Great. We can firm up all the details and dates later. So, where are you now?"

I tell her we're about half an hour from the Trapp Family Lodge in Vermont.

"Dare I ask whether any revelations have been made?"

My jaw juts to the side. What is the best way to phrase this?

"Ravenna does know—" I begin.

"Hallelujah!"

"Unfortunately she didn't find out in the best possible way. She's actually already at the lodge with my friend Krista. Not exactly in the best mood."

"You mean she didn't hear it from Pamela?"

"No. They haven't actually had a chance to talk since she found out."

"That daughter of mine," Gracie despairs. "She brings these things on herself. She's always been like this, always putting things off, waiting until tomorrow . . ."

Harvey looks a little uncomfortable.

"I know. It's not ideal. But what's done is done. Now we just need to try and make everything better."

Gracie sighs. "Well, raindrops on roses, whiskers on kittens and all that."

"Indeed. We'll keep you updated."

Harvey and I spend the rest of the journey trying to name all the songs in *The Sound of Music*.

It's crazy to think it's based on a true story—a nun and a baron fleeing the Nazis with a gaggle of singing children in tow. Perhaps crazier to think that Ravenna is taking the role of Captain—one whistle blow and here we all come running.

"This is the road," Harvey says as we turn off the main highway onto a rather more uneven, tree-crowded strip.

Pamela and Charles are following behind us, no doubt hearing the scrapings of a few branches on their rooftop.

I'm finding it hard to picture anything more than a tree house nestled in these environs when suddenly the lodge comes into view. Apparently the von Trapps fell in love with Vermont because it reminded them of their native Austria, both in its scenery and climate. In turn they've certainly added their own home-from-home flourishes: the main building is like a giant ski chalet—the windows have jutting triangular hoods, there are stencil-like cut-outs in the brown wooden balconies, and an abundance of window boxes brimming with bright orangey-red flowers.

If I could yodel I would.

"It looks so wholesome," Harvey notes.

He's right. I can't think of a more inappropriate setting for a family drama. Mind you, I suppose the von Trapps had their fair share. At least we don't have any Nazis to deal with.

We follow Krista's instructions of getting a coffee and congregating on the terrace.

(She stayed up all night talking to Ravenna, letting her vent and release as much as she possibly could. I think it helped that Krista represented a fairly neutral stranger, as I once did.)

"So how does Krista advise that we play this?" Pamela is eager to begin.

I can't help but smile—she makes her sound like a crisis negotiator, which in a way she is.

"Well, I would have thought Ravenna should see you first, but Krista wants Harvey to kick things off."

"What?"

"She has to deal with the surface humiliation before the core betrayal. I think she wants to pick off the easiest ones first."

"Are you part of this?" Pamela asks.

"I'm third in line apparently. After Charles."

"And I see her last?" Pamela is aghast.

"You are the deepest pain. All of this stems from you. If you see what I mean, not wishing to—"

Pamela throws up her hands. "Oh, what do I know? I've done everything wrong so far."

Charles pulls her in for a hug. "Don't go down that road. You have to set a positive example."

"Here's Krista now!" I jump to my feet, ready to introduce her, having to slightly tone down our usual squealing pogo-fest.

As she assures them that Ravenna is still this side of sanity, we stand shoulder to shoulder, pressing into each other, communicating all manner of age-old friend messages from "I'm so glad you're here!" to "Have you checked out Harvey? Isn't he gorgeous?" and the obvious "I can't wait to have a proper catch-up later."

Krista explains that we'll take our turns visiting Ravenna and she'll act as mediator if necessary—there's a little balcony she can wait out on while the conversation is taking place.

"So how exactly do you recommend I approach this?" Harvey wants to know.

"My guess is that she's not even going to be able to look at you," Krista replies. "So that's your challenge, to make light of it and get some eye contact."

He nods. "Okay. Let's do this."

I feel a little uncomfortable sitting with Charles and Pamela, so I excuse myself, saying I'm just going to find the loo. I dawdle as I do so, having a little nose around the property. It's a sprawling affair with assorted alcoves and cabinets filled with Austrian memorabilia, and stairwells featuring vintage *Sound of Music* posters in every possible language—*La Famiglia Trapp! Sonrisas Y Lágrimas! Meine Lieder, Meine Träume!* Several have Julie Andrews's drab

pinafore reimagined in flouncy cerise with a baby-pink undershirt—
Hollywood's version of a nun's modest dress.

I look at my watch. I probably should be heading back.

"Anyone need a top-up of coffee?" I ask as I approach the table.
"Or perhaps a nice camomile tea?" I switch, realizing everyone is
sufficiently twitchy as it is.

Within two minutes of me sitting down, Harvey appears.

"How did it go?"

"Not too bad," he says as he pulls up a chair. "At first she just
focused on the dog. I think he is a great comfort to her."

I nod.

"I told her a few of my embarrassing drunk stories to break
the ice and then I basically said it's not as weird as it seems, it was
just a misinterpretation of our instant bond. We got on really well,
we'll continue to get on well and I want to take her sailing."

I smile. "Really?"

"Well, I figured there's lots of hot yachtie guys to distract her
from this Eon character . . . Can't hurt?"

"No, that's a good plan," we confirm.

"Okay, Dad, you're up."

He seems uncharacteristically distant.

"Are you okay?"

He nods. "I just can't bear to think of her in pain."

"So tell her—tell her that exact thing."

Charles nods, takes a bolstering breath and heads on his way.
He is gone awhile. A long while. Then again, they do have twenty
years of catching up to do.

In some ways it is in Pamela's interest that Charles is going
first. Ravenna knows how besotted he is with her mother, so the
pair of them sitting there slagging her off for keeping them in the
dark so long is not an option. But they will certainly be able to
share that regret. All the missed years. I try to imagine how I

would feel if I were Charles—all the significant birthdays, all those kiddy squeezes, falling asleep on your chest, waking up on Christmas morning, crayon cards to Daddy . . . It's a lot to accept. I can't help imagining how much nicer Ravenna might have turned out if he'd been there during her upbringing instead of Brian. All those years of tension and negative brainwashing. Oh dear, now I'm getting mad with Pamela! Hopefully they can focus on making up for lost time rather than lamenting the past. Which isn't to say there won't be a few tears . . .

When Charles finally reappears, his eyes are indeed red and watery.

Pamela is inspecting the flowers at the edge of the terrace and Harvey has gone to make some Newport/sailing calls, so he comes to me first.

"She let me hug her!" He's so choked he can hardly speak. "I thought I'd lost her so soon after finding her . . ." His voice catches.

"Oh Charles!" Now I'm welling up.

"I don't want her to go back to England."

"University doesn't start until autumn . . ." I trail off. I'd better not go making any promises that aren't mine to keep.

"I hope she can stay on. Ohhh." He clamps on his chest. "These women!" He looks over at Pamela.

"I know. They get under your skin."

He looks shyly at me. "Ravenna said I give her hope that she can be a better person. She said she hasn't felt right for a long time. She wants to be different."

This is incredibly positive. Still I can feel the butterflies swirling at the prospect of my own impending encounter. I'm about to head to the room when I get a message from Krista.

"Ravenna wants to take a break for a couple of hours," I update Pamela. "I think this might be a good time for us to meet the pastry chef?"

"Oh, I couldn't."

I cock my head. "Have you never filmed an episode of *Pam-Cakes* in the midst of a ding-dong with Brian?"

She sighs. "It's what kept me going through it all."

"Well then," I smile, offering her my arm.

We've come too far to fall at the last hurdle.

Chapter 50

∽∾∾

We've seen some pretty fancy kitchens along the way, but Pamela declares this to be her outright favorite. It's easy to see why. The DeliBakery is perched on a lookout point on the edge of a field bordered with sprightly pines leading to the slithers of mountains beyond. Better yet, the windows of the kitchens are so expansively panoramic you feel as if you are part of the view. Today it's all about layers of sun-fueled green. In the winter, pure white; in the spring the meadows are sprigged with flowers. I can only imagine the autumn splendor.

Add to this a pastry chef with a major personality (whatever the American equivalent of Irish charm is, Robert Alger has it) and Pamela is back in the game.

Today certainly has an international flavor. Maria's Linzertorte is, of course, of Austrian heritage, but all the while that Robert is setting out the ingredients for the base—butter, sugar, eggs, cinnamon, flour—he and Pamela are chatting about his time spent at the Shangri-La in Singapore.

"It's a different world in pastry out there," he notes.

"Their embellishments are sublime," Pamela agrees. "So delicate."

"I didn't realize cakes were a big thing out there?" I chip in.

"Oh yes, afternoon tea is bigger there than in England. We used to serve two hundred and fifty a day. Everything was arranged on a big island and you could pick whatever you wanted. It was phenomenal."

He tells us about a wedding cake he made for a 4,000-strong wedding party, including the Prime Minister of China and the Sultan of Brunei.

"The bottom tier was four feet wide!" he remembers.

"What?" I gasp.

"And they had private jets flying in orchids from Hawaii and Africa for the decoration."

I can't even begin to guess at the cost.

"Out there, a pastry chef is like a movie star."

The thing that really gets Pamela chuckling is the fact that he used to make cakes and chocolates using Durian fruit—a notoriously pungent and thorny fruit (looks like a puffer fish). It is actually banned by many of the top hotels in Southeast Asia because the smell is so revoltingly pervasive.

"And you know what? I was selling a one-kilo cake for forty-nine dollars and I couldn't make enough to keep up with the demand!"

He has a roguish twinkle that lets you know he took great pleasure in testing the patience of the general manager over this recipe.

"If you ever come across it, by the way, don't drink alcohol along with it, because the fruit *ferments* . . ."

And so to the comparatively tame Linzertorte.

I was surprised how willing Pamela was to include it in her book. She said we had maple syrup covered in the recipes for

Johnny Cakes and Popovers and, besides, who doesn't love *The Sound of Music?*

Apparently the real Maria was a big fan of sweets in general, but it took the original chef—Marshall Faye—quite some time to get the American Linzertorte recipe to meet with Maria's approval. He used to take a slice up to her apartment to taste and she would say, "It's good, but it isn't quite right." Time after time.

Then one day her youngest son Johannes (who runs the hotel today) mentioned that a lot of currants were grown where Maria grew up, and he suggested mixing a little redcurrant in with the raspberry jam.

"Now that's a Linzertorte!" was Maria's enthusiastic response.

We watch now as Robert spreads the redcurrant jelly/raspberry jam combo over the base and then creates a crisscross lattice effect with the remaining pastry.

"Yum," we say as we taste a slice of one he prepared earlier. It's sweet but with a subtle tartness. "I like it!"

Robert smiles. "That for me is the best part of my job—seeing the enjoyment on my customers' faces. It's what makes my day better."

"So true," Pamela concurs. And then takes her turn with the similarly almond-y and jammy Bakewell Tart.

When we've finished in the kitchen we find Charles and Harvey testing the Johannes von Trapp lager out on the deck. For a moment I think we might get to relax in the sunshine with them, but my phone bleeps. I am summoned.

Harvey offers to escort me on the short walk back to the main building, to ward off any lonely goatherds.

"Ready to take your turn?" he asks as we pause before the entrance.

"I am," I say. "All I can do is explain that I was desperate to give her a heads-up, but that it wasn't my place to do so."

"I think my dad mentioned that you wanted her told sooner."

"That's good of him." I take a breath. "I don't think she'll be long with me. I'm not a significant person in her life. I was starting to get fond of her but, in reality, I'm the most easily dismissed."

"Hardly," Harvey laughs.

"You know what I mean. She never needs to see me again."

"You know I do, don't you?"

My heart skips a beat.

"You do?"

He takes a step closer. My internal organs do a fandango. He places his hands lightly on my hips. And then he leans down to kiss me.

"I can't believe it." The first time Ravenna says these words her voice is low with shock. The second time it's a shriek. "*I can't believe it!*"

Oh my god. She was right there in the entrance. Now she's taken off running. Up the hill.

"I'll go after her!" Krista appears, ready to break into a sprint, or possibly get Mitten to round her up.

"No," I halt them. "This one's on me."

Chapter 51

"Don't come near me!" Ravenna howls as I catch up with her in the middle of a field.

"I have to talk to you about this!"

"It's not bad enough that you let me make a fool of myself, but then you have to get it on with him! Oh my god!"

Suddenly I realize just how grotesque this must seem. To me, Ravenna was never a reason to hold back because she was his sister. But is that really an excuse? Is this really something I should have been indulging in while I was working? It just seemed like the most marvelously irresistible perk. Until now. Now I'm utterly disgusted with myself.

"I'm so sorry."

"Really?" she scoffs. "How long has this been going on?"

"It was just one moment yesterday, that's—"

"We both kissed him on the same day? Gross! *Gross!*"

I don't know what to say. I just feel so tacky.

Ravenna continues to pace like a wild cat while I descend into a slump of shame.

Finally she stops dead in front of me.

"You know your sister is here."

"What?" I turn cold.

"She's here at the hotel. I wasn't supposed to tell you, but I'm not as big on the secrets and lies as the rest of you."

"H-how is that even possible?"

"She flew in this morning."

I feel my breathing accelerate. My god. This is all happening too fast.

"Takes the wind out of your sails, doesn't it?" Ravenna taunts.

I nod.

"So now it's your turn."

She goes to turn on her heel but the sound of my world crashing stalls her.

"I can't do it!" I cry. "I can't face her."

"You have to. I had to."

"I can't!" I whimper. "I can't feel all that pain again."

My face falls into my hands. Suddenly there is no more holding back the emotion; it has to come out, full force, like a gushing, roaring eruption from the very core of me. And then, somewhere in the midst of the chugging tears and gasps for breath, these words escape me: "*I want my mum back!*"

Then they come again, "*I just want her back.*" And my heart splits open.

"Ravenna!" Pamela is calling to her daughter from the gate.

But she doesn't move.

"You should go." My breath catches as I try to speak. "And I don't blame you for being angry with me. I would despise me in your shoes. I'd hate everybody."

"Ravenna!" Pamela calls again.

"Wait there."

As Ravenna hurries away, I let it all stream out of me, surrendering to the swirling, engulfing pain.

"She's never coming back," a voice in my head taunts me. "You're never going to see your mother again."

My face is dripping faster than I can wipe away the fluids, when suddenly assistance arrives in the form of a pink husky tongue.

"Mitten!" I can't help but laugh at his fervent attempt to clean me up.

And then I realize that Ravenna is standing beside me.

"He did a good job with me last night," she says. "I thought you might want a turn."

Her expression is different now. Her eyes are no longer lasers trying to destroy me; she actually looks concerned.

"This is so backward!" I gasp as I try to calm the pup, my voice still juddering and jerking. "I'm supposed to be comforting you."

"I made you cry."

"It's not you, it's—"

"She's not really here. Your sister. I just said that so you'd know how it feels to get sideswiped."

"What?"

"Krista told me about your situation last night. I think she was using it as an example of a bigger scale of forgiveness."

My hand goes to my chest. "I thought I was going to have a panic attack."

"You kind of did."

I sit back on my heels and shake my head. "I don't think there's any hope for me. I thought I might be ready to face her, but obviously I'm not."

"Not today. But you might be in a week or two."

"I don't know," I sniff. "How am I ever going to look at her and not think of my mother?"

"I wish I could just trade you mine."

"Don't say that! You don't mean it."

She looks back over at Pamela. "No. I probably don't. I'd better go and face her."

I watch the pair of them heading back toward the hotel and then hang my head. I have not handled this whole thing well. What was I thinking with Harvey?

"Laurie?"

Oh god, that's him now.

He's standing at a cautious distance.

"Hi."

"Are you okay?"

I nod, wiping under my eyes as I scramble to my feet. "I think it's best we keep a bit of distance between each other for a while."

"We haven't done anything wrong, you know that?"

I sigh. "Well, I don't know. I was supposed to be working, not . . . Anyway. I can't bear to hurt Ravenna any more than I already have, so . . ."

He nods. "I was thinking, I should probably go. At least that way she won't be wondering if we're meeting up behind her back."

Though it makes sense, I definitely feel a wrench at the thought of him leaving.

"I'll most likely go on to Newport, firm up the arrangements with Gracie's crew."

"Good idea." I can't even look at him.

"I hate to leave you like this."

"I'm fine," I force a smile, ignoring my urge to run to him and burrow into his chest. "I have Krista. And Mitten here."

"He does look like pretty good company," he smiles.

"He's the best."

"Okay. Well. You take care."

I nod, unable to speak.

Once I'm sure he's out of sight, I experience another flow of tears. My heart hurts so badly right now.

I think of all the people who have stood in this field, spinning around with their arms flung wide, whereas I just want to lie down until snowfall.

I may well have done that very thing, had Krista not sent me a text to say that she's nearly done and to meet me in our room.

Suddenly I feel like I have a home to go to.

Mitten pulls me all the way there, ever eager to race ahead, even when there is no sled to pull.

The room we're sharing has a rustic Austrian design—pine beams and bedheads and a large booth embedded in the bay window, complete with a table I can set for dinner. I go ahead and order a pair of Wiener Schnitzels and Apfelstrudels so Krista will have some sustenance as soon as she gets in.

Here she is now.

As I open the door, she pretends to be wheezing her last breath, dragging herself in on her hands and knees.

"Helluva day?" I chuckle.

"I don't know how therapists do it! I'm wrung out!"

"How was it going with Ravenna and Pamela?"

Krista pulls a face, flipping onto her back and letting Mitten tread on her splayed-out hair. "It's messy, as you would expect. I think they're going to be at it for most of the night. I just had to leave them to it."

"Absolutely, you've done more than your fair share."

"Do I smell food?"

"And wine," I confirm.

"Praise be!" She jumps back to her feet. And then stops as she comes level with my face. "You've been crying!"

I nod. "The noisiest kind."

"Oh honey!" She pulls me into a hug. "I'm here now. You can tell me all about it."

"Like you haven't dealt with enough today already."

"Oh nonsense. I've always got time for you."

And so we hole up in our booth, chatting and sipping Riesling until it's time for Mitten's last wee of the day.

It's so tranquil in the moonlight. So still. All I can hear is the sound of Mitten snuffling at the shrubbery.

"You're going to get culture shock when you go back to New York," Krista notes.

My heart feels a little heavy at the prospect. I don't feel ready for this journey to be over.

"I'm just sorry you didn't get to meet Harvey properly."

"Oh, I saw enough of him to know he's the real deal."

I look up at her. "He is, isn't he?"

"Hey, don't give up on that working out, you said he wants to see you again."

"I know, but it feels a bit unseemly, all things considered. I mean, it's not like we could have a relationship without Pamela and Charles knowing, which of course in turn means Ravenna."

"Listen, she knows you're way overdue for a good man. She may give you her blessing yet."

"My lovely optimist!" I say, linking arms with my best friend as we stroll onward.

"She said it herself," Krista shrugs, "she wants to be a better person."

I nod, not entirely convinced it would stretch that far.

"I meant to ask you, did Eon come up while you were together?"

"He did," Krista shudders. "But I managed to hold her off calling him, playing on the fact that she'd so recently been propelling herself at another man. Of course he's flipping out that he hasn't spoken to her, and posting all kinds of pictures of himself with super-skinny models on Facebook . . ."

"Classy."

"He's such an idiot. I know she doesn't want to go back to him, she's just in a bit of turmoil at the moment."

"I really hope she doesn't."

Krista stifles a yawn, which in turn triggers one in me, and then Mitten gives the most comically exaggerated jaw stretch confirming, quite categorically, that it's time for bed.

"Tomorrow is a new day," I say as we head back.

Chapter 52

When I first wake up, it seems as if all is well. The sky is a soaring blue, I'm here with Krista and Mitten, we have tickets to the von Trapp History Tour and breakfast is an extensive buffet.

"Best meal of the day!" Krista cheers as we begin lifting assorted metal lids, wafting at the resulting steam and peering within. "I seriously think I could live off breakfast foods for the rest of my life—I mean, you've got your bacon and sausages and eggs and pancakes and waffles and oatmeal and cereal and yogurts and fruits and bagels and pastries and muffins—"

"And no salad or vegetables."

"Well, there's mushrooms and tomatoes. I love a cooked tomato."

I'm slightly on edge, expecting the others to walk in at any moment, but so far we're safe, tucked in a far nook by the window overlooking those benevolent mountains.

"Plus look at the breakfast drinks—coffee, tea, champagne for your Bucks Fizz or Mimosa, every kind of fruit juice and maybe some kind of smoothie—"

"Okay, I'm convinced!" I laugh. "But I think that's quite enough coffee for you." I move her cup to the far side of the table.

She expels a long sigh. "That was good."

I too set down my napkin, trying to sound casual as I say, "I wonder how everyone is doing today?"

"Mmm, I wonder. Do you think all this will affect their plans to fly back to London tomorrow?"

"Good point. I don't know."

"I can't see Gracie wanting to go back at all."

"I agree," I sigh. "She's found a new home. A new life."

I can't help but feel a pang of envy.

Krista checks her watch. "Come on, it's time for our tour."

We congregate in a barnlike building on the grounds, at least forty guests eager to learn the behind-the-scenes secrets of the story that inspired *The Sound of Music*.

"This is so perfect!" Krista enthuses as she takes out her notebook. "You know we're running a Salzburg guide to tie-in with the fiftieth anniversary next year? This should give us some nice tidbits!"

I have to say the insider insights are a welcome distraction. The one that surprises me the most is that it was Maria, with her austere convent upbringing, who was the strict one, not the Captain! But the biggest gasp from the group comes when we learn that Maria signed away the film rights to her autobiography to a German producer for a modest sum, who then sold them on to Broadway and Hollywood. The von Trapps never got a cut of the blockbuster's profits. Krista and I are just speculating how many millions they missed out on, when two latecomers join the group: Pamela and Ravenna.

"Oh no!" I hiss at Krista, burying my head. "I think we should go. I don't want them to feel uncomfortable."

"It's fine," Krista dismisses my concern. "If they are uncomfortable they can leave. We were here first."

"Since when did you get so assertive?" I blink back at her.

"It's dealing with the dogs all day—on the sled you have to let them know who's boss."

"But that's just it, I'm not the boss here."

"*Sssssh!*"

Great, now we've peeved the people next to us. Perhaps if I just act as if I haven't noticed them?

It doesn't help that the guide is now leading us to the family burial plot, even if it is an exceptionally pretty, peaceful, flower-entwined area of the garden. As the voices become a distant mumble, I think of standing beside Mum's headstone, setting her favorite Gerbera daisies in the vase, and for the first time ever I wish that Jessica was standing beside me. And then my eyes stray to Pamela and Ravenna. Standing together, even after all they've been through. I don't know if it's because I got my meltdown out of my system yesterday, but suddenly I feel a little braver, a little more hopeful . . . Could I see Jess? Could I forgive her? Could we be close again?

"Laurie? Are you coming?" Krista chivvies me along, back into the hotel. Here we're invited to watch a short documentary with Maria von Trapp. Gray hair braided atop her head, she is utterly disarming in her honesty, confessing that when the Captain proposed to her in real life, she burst into tears and ran all the way back to the convent!

"Not quite the reaction he was going for," Krista chuckles. And then I feel her nails digging into my arm. "Oh my gosh—look at the von Trapp we got!"

At the end of every tour, an authentic member of the von Trapp family appears to answer questions and sign autographs. We get

Sam von Trapp, Maria's grandson, who just happens to be a former ski instructor and Ralph Lauren model.

"I'm going to see if he'll do an interview for our 'Man of the World' page."

"Good idea!" I'm just about to join Krista in the queue when Pamela approaches.

Here we go.

"I just wanted to talk to you about the schedule for the end of the trip."

I'm quick to react. "Yes, of course. There's no problem with me finding my own way home. Krista can drop me at the nearest train station and I'll just head on back to New York and tie up all the ends from there."

"Oh no, that's not what I meant," she reaches for my hand. "We still need you for the fund-raiser in Newport."

"The fund-raiser?"

"Yes, we're going ahead with your idea for the High Tea on the High Seas. Harvey is there making the arrangements now."

"About Harvey," I gulp awkwardly. "I feel I should apologize to you for being so horribly unprofessional—"

"Oh please," she cuts me off. "As if we haven't all gone a little astray on this trip. I mean, compared to my mother and me, you've been positively chaste."

I give a little snuffle. "Thank you, for being so understanding."

"Not at all. So, what I was going to say was, I really want to get back to Mum as soon as possible, and Charles says if we leave now we can get to Newport for happy hour. I know this isn't quite what we had on the schedule—"

"That's fine," I assure her. "I happen to be very familiar with the accommodation situation in Newport, so I can make those arrangements right now."

"Great," she chirps. "We can all go and pack and see you back at the bus in an hour?"

"I can do that, if you're sure Ravenna won't mind me being on board."

"It's a big bus, it'll be fine. I'm just sorry to cut short your time with Krista."

She's got me there. For a moment I wonder about asking Krista to come with us—we could do with an extra pair of hands, and the fund-raiser was her idea, after all—but she and Jacques have a big event at the farm this weekend, so she needs to get back.

"We'll see each other very soon anyway," she says, "what with Jessica's visit on the cards."

"Yes," I reply. Though I experience a queasy dip at the prospect, Krista's presence is reassuring. Even if I do fall apart, I have someone to hold on to, someone who will get me through. "It's going to be okay, isn't it?"

"It really is. I'll make sure of that. And as far as this place goes," Krista gives a fond look back at the lodge, "maybe we'll come back here again in the autumn or when it's all fireside-cozy with snow."

"That would be lovely," I sigh.

It's always a wrench leaving Krista, always a bit stomach-churningly sentimental. "You're the best," I say as we share our final hug good-bye. "I couldn't have got through any of this without you."

"We're a good team," she confirms. "Now go and savor every last moment of this trip. Fill your lungs with sea air!"

She always knows the right thing to say—suddenly I can't wait to get back to Newport . . .

Chapter 53

~~~

The drive takes us just over six hours with Ravenna and Pamela sleeping most of the way, clearly spent after all the emotional upheaval.

I keep a low profile, but chat awhile with Charles when I notice he's getting drowsy at the wheel.

"So, seeing as we weren't in the same vehicle when we crossed into Vermont, I never did get to hear about the native writers here."

Charles smiles. "Let me see. Vermont . . ."

He mentions a few Nobel and Pulitzer prizewinners and then knocks it out of the park with, "Rudyard Kipling wrote *The Jungle Book* here. He lived in Vermont for four years after he married an American woman and his first child was born here."

"Please tell me he named him Mowgli!"

"Actually it was a girl, and her name was Josephine!"

The conversation moves on to Krista, with Charles asking how he might thank her for all her support; then he says how sorry he is to hear about my situation with my mother and sister.

"If there's any way I can be there for you as you have been here for us, please let me know."

I sigh. That's so kind.

Before too long we're back in Newport. My heart smiles with relief.

We've seen some beautiful places along the way, but there's something extra-special about this one. Even the accommodation genie was working overtime, supplying us with a cancelation at the Cliffside Inn so I am able to place Pamela, Charles and Ravenna in the cottage suite next to Gracie. They seem very happy to be reunited. Even Ravenna hugs her granny and Gracie doesn't roll her eyes as she clasps her to her chest. I actually think I see a little tear escape from her eye. It's been a long time coming.

"I'll see you around noon tomorrow," I say as I excuse myself. The outsider once more.

I'm staying just fifteen minutes' walk away at The Attwater. It's absolutely perfect for our Va-Va-Vacation! readers. Bright and hip *à la* Jonathan Adler, you even get the use of an iPad for the duration of your stay. I picked up a pizza on the way here, and now I'm sitting out on the communal deck by myself, pulling apart the slices and trying not to think about Harvey and how much I loved to be in his presence. I suppose I could wander into town if I wanted, have a final Dark and Stormy, but something in me doesn't want to move. So I stay out here until night falls, trying to stave off the notion that the trip is finally over. I just wish things hadn't quite ended this way.

I awake to a beautiful bright morning. The perfect day for a sail. As I inhale the sunshine, hope radiates through my queasier emotions.

For the first hour of the day I sip herbal tea in the hotel café.

Soothed by the white and mint-green décor, I try to get centered and remember what it feels like to sit quietly and studiously by myself. It's been chaotically sociable this past week. It's a good thing I have this time to adjust and remember what my normal life is like, without them.

Next to me are the parents of a gurgling baby. I smile as they interact with this pudgy-fingered, wobbling delight, faces lit up with glee. And then I'm surprised to find my eyes welling with tears. It just hits me now and again, that I don't have anyone to call my own. I think I'm a little more stirred up than normal because of how it felt to be with Harvey. Just to have someone look at me that way—with such enchantment, as if our hearts were really resonating. It felt good to register in that way. Of course I know I always matter to Krista. But she has her own life now. I can't build anything new with her. But that's okay. I'm sure I'll be fine once I'm back in Manhattan. It's just every now and again this great wanting wells up inside of me and I can't help but wonder what it would feel like to really belong with someone.

Feeling the need for fortification, I return to the breakfast bar for coffee and the comfort of a fresh-from-the-oven cinnamon-apple scone with juicy chunks of real apple. It's so good that I'm tempted to ask the on-site baker to rustle up a batch for our fund-raising tea. But I haven't been invited to contribute to that menu. I so wanted to be involved in the final bakerama, but instead Pamela has asked me to spend the morning sorting through the photos from the trip, captioning the best and forwarding them to her agent. Apparently the publisher wants to see whether they can incorporate some scrapbook-style montages. And yes, I probably have better skills in this area.

I take out my laptop, slot in the memory card and watch the slideshow of the past week play out before my eyes:

New York. There's Charlie Romano! I smile at his familiar

face. The vast kitchen at the Waldorf Astoria; Pamela inspecting the beetroot puree for the Red Velvet Cake. I think that was the most sophisticated taste sensation of the trip, though I wince recalling the bitterness of that pure chocolate. Of course there are no pictures of Ravenna at Tiffany's, but I recall that episode all too well. And the hair-raising drive out of the city and into Connecticut. Mystic Pizza. Warren and the Nutmeg Spice Cupcakes. The glorious approach to Rhode Island over the bridge. All those boats in Newport Harbor. The mansions. Votes for Women teacups at the Chinese Tea House. The awful moment when Gracie crashed the bus. It's quite bizarre seeing the pictures of the minutes before—ironically we have some great ones if she still wants an option for her Christmas cards.

Here we are at the cranberry bog, now with Charles. Then Provincetown. I can't help but chuckle at these ones. I didn't realize Pamela had taken so many of Charles on the podium at the Tea Dance. And there's such a nice sunset one on the beach with us all eating lobster rolls. Oh, and the Land's End Inn! My favorite sleepover. And the first time Ravenna confided in me.

And so it progresses. Plimoth Plantation. The retrofied Dunkin' Donuts at Quincy. Boston. I'm privy now to the moment they bought their matching Johnny Cupcakes T-shirts—while I was waltzing around Harvard with Harvey. I think of our Alice in Wonderland–like tea at UpStairs on the Square and see they got their afternoon cake-fix at the Georgetown Cupcake, with a close-up of the Bubblegum Pink Vanilla option. Then there's Tuoi, demonstrating the spider-web effect on the Boston Cream Pie. And Pamela and I trying our first bite.

Though I have to edit myself out of the collection for the agent, I'm happy to have so many personal memories to treasure.

Popovers in New Hampshire. Then Maine. I loved that dinner I had beside the hearth with Ravenna. I wish I had a picture of that.

Whoopie Pies galore. Oh, and then that gorgeous drive through the White Mountains, weaving up to the Mount Washington Hotel. Look how happy everyone is in the veranda collection—Ravenna glammed up and radiant, Pamela and Charles comfortable now with being photographed entwined, Harvey and I having just shared a slapstick afternoon baking gold-bar-style Pound Cake. The champagne toast before the glass shattered.

I sigh, leaning back on the banquette. For a moment I just stare up at the rather unusual green-glass chandelier above me, following the looping curves of its arms. I remember joking with Pamela about the Vanderbilt chandelier crashing down on us. How I wish I could rewind to that day at Marble House and that things had played out differently.

Timing is indeed everything.

I look back at my laptop. The next picture is of the Trapp Family Lodge. Then Maria's Linzertorte. And that beautiful view from the kitchens. From these pictures you wouldn't have an inkling of all the emotional wrangling that was going on behind the scenes. And that's exactly how it should be for the agent. Only a few people will ever know what really went on during this past week or so.

Chapter 54

⁓⁓⁓

When I arrive at the Cliffside Inn, Gracie is busy loading up the boot of Charles's car with covered trays.

I take a peek. "Wow—that's a lot of cupcakes."

"This is nothing," she clucks, "most of the goodies have already gone over to the wharf on the bus. I just was finishing the frosting on these."

"You guys have been busy!"

"Pamela and Ravenna were up all night."

I nod at the significance of this, not just of them working side by side, but also how motivated Ravenna must have been to redeem herself for the last bout of baking here.

"Okay, all we need now is the grand prize and we're good to go."

I raise a brow. "Grand prize?"

"It was Charles's idea—he said we should come up with something special to auction off. They've stored it for us in the kitchen of the main house."

We cross the layered lawn and head up the steps of the lovely

cream and sage Victorian mansion, distinctive wrought-iron fili-
gree adding a lacelike trim to the rooftop.

I peer into the parlor room while Gracie is chatting to owner
Nancy and see that teatime involves a selection of one-off vintage
teacups and an ornate silver urn to dispense the custom-blend
Harney & Sons tea. Very nice.

"Laurie, come and look!"

Gracie beckons me into the kitchen and reveals a huge tableau
of a cake. Or should I say cakes, for there are seven individual
sections making up all the states in New England, plus New York,
and each is shaped accordingly—Rhode Island is a teeny slither,
Maine a great slab, Massachusetts the most fiddly, complete with
Cape Cod extension.

"She was thinking of making the individual cakes from the recipes
we sourced on location, but it got tricky with the Popovers and Johnny
Cakes, so she went with different-flavored sponges and buttercreams—
rums and maple syrup, nutmeg and cranberry; you get the idea."

"Amazing," I coo, admiring the different colors and textures
she has created for each top layer. "I don't know if I've ever seen
Pamela do such intricate work."

"She didn't. This is all Ravenna."

"What?" I gape.

"Start to finish. She did the whole thing."

"How is this possible?"

"Oh, she always had the gift, ever since she was a little girl.
It's just been a long time since she's used it."

"I'm stunned!"

"You and me both."

We're lucky to find parking at the wharf—the place is heaving.

"Can you believe the response?" Gracie surveys the crowd.

"All these people are here for the tea?"

She nods.

"They'll never fit on one boat."

"We've got five going out now—Harvey spoke to some of the locals and they've been great. You can go on the rumrunner with him and Ravenna."

"Oh no-no," I recoil. "I don't think that's a good idea."

"You have to, or you'll mess up the schedule."

My eyes narrow at her. "Squeezing in one last meddle?"

She gives an innocent shrug. "I'm just saying it's all arranged."

I sigh. "Do they have life jackets on board?"

"She won't throw you over."

"What makes you so sure?"

"You're bigger than her, you can stand your ground."

Great.

"Laurie!" It's Pamela waving over to me. I eagerly scoot to her side.

"Everything looks phenomenal!" I cheer, taking in all the cake-laden boats. "What a success!"

"I know!" she pips. "I just did an interview with the local radio station—they're going to do a piece on my book when it comes out and then syndicate it!"

"Fantastic!"

She beams at me. "You've been an absolute star, Laurie. Truly."

"Well, it's been my pleasure. I just feel bad—"

"Don't feel bad." Charles steps up behind me. "If you're going to be part of this family, you have to accept that we're none of us perfect."

I could cry, right here and now! He said family!

A low whistle sounds.

"It's time to set sail."

Before I know it, I become part of the surge toward the rumrunner.

It's a low, long boat of golden wood, open at the front, canopied at the back. I feel a dip of nerves as I spy Ravenna and then Harvey. They are both turned away from me, facing out to sea, so I scurry starboard and busy myself with arranging the cakes and greeting our guests. At least *they* are pleased to see me, if only for my "genuine English accent."

And then I hear someone addressing me as "first mate."

I turn and see Harvey.

I feel too self-conscious to reply, but it is the best feeling ever to connect with his eyes. That's all I needed.

"Ravenna!" I startle as she appears in front of him. "I hope you don't mind me being on the same boat as you, it wasn't my suggestion."

"I know. It was mine."

"What?"

"I need to talk to you," she pulls me off to one side.

I'm not sure if I'm ready for what she has to say, so I start babbling about the brilliance of her prize cake—the design, the execution, hopefully the flavor. "You're giving your mum a run for her money!"

Ravenna pulls a face. "I think I've had enough to do with her money, don't you? Time to make some of my own."

My eyes instantly well up with pride. "Really?"

"Well, I have got an idea about running Traveling Tea Shop tours, but that's not what I wanted to talk to you about." She takes a breath. "I've been thinking about your sister . . ."

Oh gawd.

"What if you meet up with her and it's a complete and utter nightmare, even worse than you thought."

I blink back at her.

"I mean, what if that's it between you two? Suddenly you don't have a sister."

Is this supposed to be helping?

"So you'd have room for a new one. And I always wanted one so," she wheedles, "I could be your backup sister. You know, if this one doesn't work out."

I don't know what to say. I did not see this coming.

"Or have I been too much of a nightmare?" Ravenna's brow furrows.

"You been a nightmare? What about me?"

"If I'm going to forgive everyone else, I might as well forgive you too."

I laugh, still a little thrown. And then I realize she's genuinely waiting for an answer. "You know, people can have more than one sister."

Her face lights up. "That's true." And then her face falls. "Oh *no*! I've just realized this isn't going to work."

I knew this was too good to be true. She's reeled me in, now she's going for the stinger.

"Why not?" I dare ask.

"Because then you'd be kind of related to Harvey, and we can't have that."

"Oh no," I fluster. "I won't . . . We haven't . . ."

"Yes you will. With my blessing." She gets to her feet and, in front of all the assembled tea guests calls, "Harvey! Did you hear that? You need to start kissing Laurie again!"

My hands fly to cover my face. She didn't just do that! I can't believe it! I peer out between my fingers and see Harvey saluting her with an "Aye, aye, Captain!"

I reach out and drag her back to a sitting position.

"Are you serious?"

"Yes. I was thinking about this too—we've both made bad

relationship decisions in the past, now we have an opportunity to make good ones: I have to stay away from Eon and you have to spend more time with Harvey."

I feel a little dizzy. "How did your heart get to be so huge?"

She shrugs, sending a happy glance over to Charles on the neighboring boat. "I am my father's daughter."

"And your mother's too," I remind her.

"Yes. And my mother's. And I wouldn't be either right now if it wasn't for you."

"Oh!" I swat away her words. "You would have worked it out without me sticking my oar in."

"No I wouldn't. That day at Tiffany's in New York? No one has ever spoken to me like that. Of course Granny is always muttering stuff under her breath, but no one has ever been that direct. I had every intention of running off, of screwing up the whole trip, but there was just something about the way you spoke to me. That's why I came back—I knew you'd always tell me the truth."

"Oh dear, that didn't go so well."

"At least the truth about my behavior. And how I needed to change. Even with the whole family deception, which I know you were opposed to, you've been the most honest person to me that I've ever known."

Again my eyes sheen. "Thank you."

She opens her arms and we fall into a hug.

"Hey, you'd better cut that out," Harvey teases, now standing before us. "You'll get Marc all jealous."

"Who's Marc?" Jeez! I leave these people alone for one night!

"The hottie-yachtie." Harvey points over to a young chap now taking the helm—total Tommy Hilfiger ad, all tanned and glowing and energized. The polar opposite of Eon.

"You know, he's totally into you but too shy to ask you out," Harvey whispers to his sister.

"Don't be ridiculous!" Ravenna flushes, hand instinctively going to her hair. "I only met him an hour ago."

"Well, I've already vetted him and I approve—"

"Oh, you approve?" she hoots.

"Hey, I'm looking out for you from now on, sis. Okay?"

I see the relief in her eyes—he means it. No more Eon types. *I never have to go through that again.*

"Okay," she nods, then looks back at Marc. "Did he really say he liked me?"

"The guy would fight pirates for you."

She heaves a sigh. "Maybe I'll go and talk to him."

"They look good together," I acknowledge as their slender forms and big smiles mirror each other.

And then Harvey slips an arm around me and I think, we *feel* good together.

He turns to face me. "I like it so much better when we're in the same place."

"Me too," I smile.

"Won't you stay? At least for the summer? It's too hot in New York anyway."

"Yes you do get a nice breeze around these parts," I say as my hair binds around my face.

"You should have brought your hair doughnut!"

I laugh out loud. "Well, I'll know next time."

"Here, let me untangle you."

Oh-so-gently, he eases the strands of hair from my face, smoothing them back into a ponytail, held in place with his hand.

"Are you going to stay like that for the whole trip?"

"Well, actually, I was wondering if you wanted to go for a swim?"

"A swim? As in jump off the boat?"

"Well, we do have a ladder, but jumping is definitely more fun."

"What about the tea guests?"

"They're welcome to join us—everyone was invited to bring swimwear."

"But I'm not exactly dressed for it," I pull at my dress.

"Oh, the fish don't mind, I assure you."

It's a dare. And it feels like the biggest chance of my life. Something deep inside me is saying yes. Do it!

"Okay!"

Harvey gives a little cheer and then he takes my hand and—"Ready?"—together we make the leap.

Down I go into the cool, swirling blue, water rushing and burbling at my ears, tugging and twisting at my dress. As I pull back up to the surface, I feel as if I am wriggling loose of all my former heartaches and disappointments and striving upward to something bright and new.

I gasp for breath, blink the salty water from my eyes and then grin at Harvey.

"This is heaven!" I say, dipping my head back and feeling my heart surge with exuberance. "I love it here! I love being with you!"

"Then have this life with me." He swims closer, just a foot-swish apart now. "Be with me."

I answer with a kiss. And then I keep kissing him. What can I say? This man is yummier than any cake I ever tasted!

EPILOGUE

~~~

My eyes were puffy for a whole week after meeting up with Jessica. The tears started the instant she walked in the room. I did look at her and see my mother, just as I had feared, but that actually gave me a rush of compassion, the likes of which I hadn't experienced in years. I hugged her right there and then, which took both of us by surprise. I think one of the reasons I moved so swiftly toward her was that I could see the drugs were gone. She looked like herself again—instead of some dark being crouching behind her eyes, they were clear and bright and hopeful.

She told me about the rehab program she had been attending and the new man in her life who is all vegan-tofu-yoga-crystals, so now I can despair of her in a whole new (but much healthier) way. We were holding hands so tightly as she spoke, like we were making up for lost time and trying to show each other that there would never be such a chasm between us again.

When she said she was sorry for everything that had happened, I felt such a sense of release. That little word, when heartfelt, can mean so much. Suddenly the burden of grief was no longer exclusively mine. We would bear it together, and blame would be edged out with love and understanding. Just as my mother would have wished.

"You know I tried to find him? Our father?" she said at one point.

"And did you?"

She nodded. "He wasn't even that far away. Just the next town over. But he didn't want to meet up. He said his life had moved on and that I needed to do the same." She shook her head. "When I think of all the years I took out my hurt on you and Mum, the people who were actually there for me . . ." And then she took a breath. "So now I'm in the mode of making amends. And the only way I can think of to make it up to Mum is to make it right with you."

And the funny thing is that in that moment all I felt was grateful. For a while there I had lost my mum *and* my sister. But now I'm back in touch with the one person who knew all my mother's delightful ways as well as me, the one person who knew what it was like to grow up in her care and call her Mum—the person who could trigger a million happy memories. And so that's what we did. We brought her back to life with our conversation.

And now I feel her with me all the more.